One of the double doors was hanging open and a wicked wind was whipping through the foyer causing the unclaimed name tags to blow off their tables.

Still, all in all I think tonight was a success. Tim didn't see me. And we finally got to stand up to Barbie and Amber and that weasel Joanne. Too bad so many people had to see it. Although I do know a few who would like to have seen Barbie put in her place once and for all.

I turned down the main hall looking left and right for signs of Sawyer walking it off. Poster boards advertising various after-school clubs and sports try-outs hung on the walls above the long bank of gray lockers. Nothing down B hall. Nothing down . . . wait a minute. Who was that? Someone was lying down at the end of C hall in front of our old lockers.

I turned to walk down the dark hall towards her.

Why is she just lying there? Why does she have pompoms?

A flash of lightening lit up the hall and I saw her eyes opened and staring vacantly and the room started to spin. The crack of thunder shook the walls and lockers rattled on their hinges. It wasn't Sawyer.

It was Barbie.

And Barbie was dead . . .

Books by Libby Klein

Published by Kensington Publishing Corporation

Class Reunions Are Murder

Libby Klein

KENSINGTON PUBLISHING CORP.

http://www.kensingtonbooks.com

KENSINGTON BOOKS are published by

Kensington Publishing Corp.
119 West 40th Street
New York, NY 10018

All Kensington Titles, Imprints, and Distributed Lines are available at special quantity discounts for bulk purchases for sales promotions, premiums, fund-raising, and educational or institutional use. Special book excerpts or customized printings can also be created to fit specific needs. For details, write or phone the office of the Kensington special sales manager: Kensington Publishing Corp., 119 West 40th Street, New York, NY 10018, attn: Special Sales Department, Phone: 1-800-221-2647.

Kensington and the K logo Reg. U.S. Pat & TM Off.

ISBN-13: 978-1-4967-1303-2
ISBN-10: 1-4967-1303-6
First Kensington Mass Market Edition: February 2018

eISBN-13: 978-1-4967-1304-9
eISBN-10: 1-4967-1304-4
First Kensington Electronic Edition: February 2018

10 9 8 7 6 5 4 3 2

Printed in the United States of America

Acknowledgments

I'd like to thank David who taught me,
Annie who believed in me,
John who took a chance on me,
and all those who worked tirelessly
to fix thousands of commas that were in the wrong places.
And to the classmates at my High School Reunion,
I swear I wrote these chapters before attending.
Any similarities were shocking for me as well.

Chapter 1

I was being bullied by stationery. The note had arrived the day before by courier service—and it had to be a trap. I glared at it on the coffee table wondering if I dare open it. I pulled my knees up to my chest and hugged them to calm my shaky nerves.

The sender wasn't a mystery to me. We had hated each other for years. She was flaunting her wealth as usual. Expensive linen stationery, ebony embossed script addressed to Ms. Poppy McAllister (I hadn't been called that in ages) and a monogrammed *B* in silver filigree in the upper left corner.

I read the return address again:

> Barbie Pomeroy Clark
> Pemberton Estates
> Cherry Hill, New Jersey

I didn't know whether to rip it into tiny pieces or set it on fire. Maybe both. I was older and wiser now and I wouldn't fall for her schemes anymore. After all these years, why Barbie would think I'd care about anything she had to say was beyond me. *She has a lot of nerve, I'll give her that.* I fought back the horrible memory of high school that had piggybacked in with Barbie's engraved audacity. "I don't know what lie she's selling, Fig, but I'm not buying."

Figaro blinked at me with his *Oh, great. Here comes some drama* look.

"Well, of course I believe people can change. Just not *her*."

Figaro jumped down and turned his back to me.

"Really, Fig, cats can be so judgmental sometimes."

All night the envelope had lain there, like the presence of a chainsaw-wielding serial killer in my house. I was tired of obsessing about it. I hadn't had a decent night's sleep in months what with all I'd been through. Of course, my addiction to infomercials might be partly to blame. If it could chop, roast, juice, store stuff, or be ShamWowed, I had it. At least the infomercials swallowed up the silence.

I'd never thought I could miss the sound of John's incessant snoring, like a 747 coming in for a landing, but during those endless nights while I lay on the sofa listening to shouting pitchmen, I knew I'd give anything to hear that sound again. I missed him. I missed the way his glasses sat crooked on the end of his nose and how he smelled like coffee and aftershave. I even missed tripping over his books all over the house. Every room had a narrative history or stuffy memoir lying somewhere. All those arguments over something so trivial and fleeting.

I dug into the couch cushion for the Pepperidge Farm bag I'd lost around three a.m.

Oatmeal cookies for breakfast. That sounds reasonable, I thought, and crammed one in. *You know what these need? Chocolate fudge frosting.* But I didn't think I could handle a grief-and-frosting hangover *and* Barbie. Beautiful, rich, successful, married-to-money Barbie.

So I suffered through plain cookies, flipped the envelope over so I wouldn't have to look at her name again, and changed the channel.

"Today we are making . . . *FISHHHH!"* I giggled. Julia Child had to have been half lit during the taping of most of her shows. Still, she'd been one of my childhood idols along with that other influential kitchen icon—the Swedish Chef from *The Muppet Show*. I spent many a Saturday afternoon watching Julia cook and dreaming of the day I would be a fancy French chef.

The bar was set pretty low growing up in South Jersey in the '80s. Most of my role models worked as waitresses or chambermaids. The main goal was to lie on the beach all summer until your skin was leathery and crocodile-like, and to save up enough tip money to scrape by and survive through the off-season. You weren't popular if you weren't beautiful, and you weren't beautiful without a tan and bikini body.

So much for aspirations and goals.

My "old lady dress" with the cellulite-covering skirt-of-shame that wasn't fooling anyone was the railroad spike in the social coffin. Of course, my red hair and freckles gave me my superpower (which is the ability to burn under a table lamp) so the threat of looking like rock lobster kept me off the beach and in the free air-conditioning of the public library every summer throughout high school.

I drew the fat straw. So while the cool kids worked summer jobs lifeguarding and selling Italian water ice, I roamed the library shelves of Jane Austen and Leo Tolstoy. These were my people. They understood me and they didn't judge. There had to be more to life than parties and popularity. At least that's what I told myself. So my summers were spent in conversation with dead authors. ("Oh Jane, really? Heathcliff said *what*?" "Leo, does every character have to have *three* names? I can't tell who's speaking.")

I had one goal in life. Get out of South Jersey and get as far away as possible. I vowed I would never go back. That's pretty much the only successful thing I'd ever done. And now this high school reunion fiasco had arrived to jeopardize all that.

I looked at the envelope again. It tried to suck me in. A furry nudge on my leg made me look down. Figaro had come back to apologize for his harsh dismissal of my cowardice—or maybe just to curl up next to me on the plush white sofa that had been my bed in recent months. I offered him a lick of my cookie. He sniffed it and politely refused. John would have taken a bite. . . .

"This big house is too empty for just the two of us, Fig, but there is no way I'm giving Georgina the satisfaction of moving out."

The way Figaro's ears pinned against his head at the mention of the Wicked Witch, I could tell he agreed. Georgina was my mother-in-law. Or as Figaro and I called her, domineering overlord. She'd made my life miserable from day one. But then I wasn't exactly what she had been hoping for either. John was her baby and I ruined him.

He was the first genuine friend I made at William & Mary when I ran into him on the quad. Literally barreled into him with all the grace of a water buffalo. It was my freshman year and I was still following the map handed out at orientation. I was so engrossed in trying to find Psych 101 that I didn't see him sitting on the lawn. He was so engrossed in his paperback of *Lord of the Rings*, he never saw me coming.

He wasn't what you would call tall, dark, or handsome.

He was more short and squatty. Your average geek before being a geek was fashionable. Stocky and muscular in a way that reminds you of a bulldog. With blue eyes and dark brown hair that curled at his neck. His dark-rimmed glasses coupled with his plaid shirt and faded blue jeans made him look more suited to the chess club than the football field.

I tripped over him and face-planted right in his lap. I was so mortified I started chattering nonsense like I do when I get nervous. Stuff about how I'm directionally challenged, and I really wanted to be a pastry chef not a psychologist, and I loved the relationship between Frodo and Samwise. When I ran out of steam, John was looking at me with wide eyes, his glasses askew on his nose from the impact of Hurricane Poppy. I realized my hand was still resting on his inner thigh and I promptly removed it. "I'm so sorry."

He straightened his glasses and said, "If you're looking for the psych wing you aren't even close. It's probably because your map is upside down. Come on, I'll take you there. My name's John, by the way."

From that moment on we were fast friends. He was like the big brother I never had. We talked about everything. Books, movies, school, family. He came from a very wealthy family with political ties on Capitol Hill. He was a grad student in his first year of law school and there was a lot of pressure on him to excel. I learned later that his family had been grooming him to run for the Senate one day. They never forgave me for destroying their plans.

John said I was the funniest girl he'd ever met, and before me he didn't know how to relax. We hung out as often as we could. John tutored me in calculus and I made chocolate crepes for him on my dorm hot plate. After a few weeks, I finally convinced him to let me go to a frat party. He didn't want me to be around "the debauchery" but I was insistent that I was a big girl and it was all part of the college experience. I don't think he attended many parties in his own fraternity because the other guys kept slapping him on the back and calling him "The Professor." He wanted to impress his "brothers" and I just didn't have any self-control, plain and simple. So we drank ourselves half blind and the next morning woke up in bed together under a blanket of shame. Things were awkward between us for a couple of weeks, but we finally came to the place where we admitted that we valued our friendship too much to let it be ruined by one mistake. I was never going to tell my fiancé, Tim. John was never going to tell anyone. After all, we weren't even sure anything had happened. Not really.

And then the morning sickness started. Peeing on that stick was the scariest thing I had ever done. I couldn't look at it so John was the first person to know we were having a baby together.

His mother was furious. She demanded that I get an abortion. She said I was trying to trap him and had ruined his career in politics. A career John never actually wanted, by the way. Many years later he told me that I had saved him from a life of misery, but first we had to go through hell from the fallout of our "blessed union."

Georgina was pushing me to deny any connection to John and protect her family from scrutiny in the public eye. She also said it was the only way I was ever going to get any support from them. If I publicly claimed the baby was John's, I would be on my own, a poor white trash single mom on government assistance, and their family would deny any connection to the baby. Nice.

John didn't take this treatment of me well. He told Georgina that if she ever threatened me or said one unkind word to me again, he would personally call the tabloids and ruin the family name. He intended to marry me and if she ever wanted to see her grandchild, she would treat me with respect. A part of me may have fallen in love with John that very day, but I didn't know it until much later.

"Merrrow."

"Oh yeah. I forgot about you for a minute." *I was so lost in my thoughts.* I resumed petting his majesty.

Sir Figaro Newton is my best friend in the world, now that John is . . . gone. I couldn't bring myself to think the real word. *Passed* was the fill-in term.

"Mrrrp?"

Figaro is a black smoke Persian with a cotton candy coat; his fur is white with black tips, giving him a shaded, smoky-gray color. Little children are terrified of him because of his bright orange eyes. They think he looks like a Halloween cat but I think he's beautiful. We probably could have won ribbons in cat shows if he wasn't so ornery and uncooperative. He had a sixth sense and knew when I was sagging into a foul mood. Like now.

He flopped across me, as if he were a pillowcase and someone had just ripped the stuffing out. He either wanted to cheer me up or keep me alive until he grew thumbs and could work the can opener by himself.

Figaro was, in technical terms, "a little loopy-doopy." It could be disconcerting to have a sidekick who'd go completely limp and flop over like he'd just passed out. Sometimes with a stretch and a roll, sometimes with a thud as he hit the floor. It was his feline idea of performance art. He thinks it sends the message that he's not a threat and wants to be friends. Mostly it sends the message that he's crazy and could begin foaming at the mouth any minute. Many a child has run away from his famous death scene screaming, and left him lying there confused.

Just now he was staring at the envelope I was ignoring—then staring back at me. Envelope. Me. Envelope . . .

"Stop that. I know I'm a chicken. *Bwaaak!* There. Happy? We need a distraction, Fig. Sitting here covered in cookie dust and wallowing in self-pity is starting to lose its appeal. You know what goes good with oatmeal cookies? Chocolate milk."

Figaro gave me a droll look.

"Fine, I'll get it myself." *I shouldn't be talking to cats anyway. People will think I've lost my mind.* "Are you listening to me, Figaro?"

Figaro buried his face under one smoky-gray paw. I brushed the crumbs off my Eeyore pajama pants, crumpled up the cookie bag, and headed to the fridge.

Leaving the envelope shouting "Coward!" at my back, I slippered my way into the kitchen and looked around the marble morgue. I hated this kitchen. Georgina had designed every inch of the steel and granite monstrosity to impress. Impress whom, I had no idea. Image was very important to John's mother, and he had promised it was easier to let her have her way. Then she'd leave us alone. Silly man. A kitchen is supposed to be the heart of the home. Well, this one matched that of its designer, cold as a dead fish.

Memories flooded back again. Good ones. John and I did have some fun in here. . . . I loved to cook ("Clearly!" chuckled my reflection in the stainless-steel refrigerator door), and John loved to eat. He invited company over every weekend just to weasel some *boeuf bourguignon* or *coq au vin* out of the deal. He was always willing to help out with the prep work as my *sous-chef.* Mostly he just got in the way, but I enjoyed having him next to me.

Since he'd been gone these six months, I'd lived on Pop-Tarts and cookie dough. What was the point in cooking for one? Now any cooking I did took place in the microwave.

Take that, Georgina. Apparently, a pathetic, silent defiance was all I was capable of.

As I put my hand on the refrigerator door I found myself stared in the face by Georgina's event reminder, or as I called it, "The Summons." Georgina expected me to attend a black-tie charity gala in two weeks in John's honor. My mother-in-law firmly believed in hosting benefits for her cause of the month, as long as the press attended and she got lots of exposure in the news media. You know, "for the charity." Since Georgina was under the impression that she owned me from the moment I said "I do," I was required to be there in black taffeta and pearls, playing the "I'm-here-in-place-of-my-poor-dead-husband" card for extra media credit. Grief is good for donations. I was praying either for a house to fall on Georgina or the Rapture to take place. God's choice.

Really, I'm beyond pathetic. I could just say no.

But I never did.

Depressed *and* disgusted with myself, I got a glass of chocolate milk out of the fridge and added extra chocolate syrup to it. I still had enough dignity to not eat frosting for breakfast. But I did grab a bag of peanut butter cookies from the pantry (peanut butter is protein after all) and scuffed my way back to the living room.

Ousting Figaro from my spot, I changed the channel to the BBC. Nigella was at the open refrigerator, wearing her bathrobe, eating an entire cake with her bare hands. *How long before that's me?*

Figaro fixed me with a penetrating gaze. *That's you since six months ago, Dumpling.*

"I've got to get out of here."

The phone rang. I ignored it, hoping they would go away.

"Call from . . . Montgomery . . . Sawyer."

Audible caller ID is a wonderful invention. So is an answering machine set to screen out friends who have a guilt trip planned. Over the speaker I heard:

"Ohmygosh! Did you get it? Poppy, I know you're there. You never leave the house. Pick up! Pick up! Pick up!"

I was not answering, even for her. I didn't want to talk. I knew what she wanted and there was no way I was going back to New Jersey for a high school reunion. I'd rather have my eyes poked out with fondue forks.

"Poppy!!"

I grabbed the phone. "Yeah, I got it but I'm not opening it because I don't believe for a minute that she means well. There's probably snake venom on the card."

Sawyer Montgomery had been my other best friend—Figaro read my thoughts and cocked one eyebrow—since she and I met halfway through the fifth grade. After my father died, my mother shuffled me off to live with Aunt Ginny, and checked herself into a nervous breakdown. Some sadist decided that my first day of school would be Valentine's Day. I'd gotten one Valentine addressed to "Extra" and a bucket of self-pity. And thanks to my mother's version of a Dorothy Hamill bowl cut, I looked like Moe from the Three Stooges. Everyone thought I was a boy. Sawyer and I became fast friends once I explained that I was indeed a girl and wearing a dress and not a plaid polyester kilt.

"It's gonna be a ton of fun seeing everyone again after all these years."

Sawyer was lighthearted, fun, and perky.

I was not. Especially when sleep-deprived.

"Yeah. I'm gonna be the ton, and everyone else is

gonna have fun with that. Do you know how much I've put on—" I was going to say, "in six months" but went with "since high school?"

"Connie and Kim got notes from Barbie too, almost a month to the day from when the official reunion announcements came out. What do you think it means?"

I heaved a sigh and snatched the envelope off the table and tore into it. My eyes flew across the stationery resting ever so briefly on every other word, afraid that if I took it all in at once I would be choked from overexposure to evil.

"I think it means she wants to pour a bucket of blood on us. Then burn down the gym—and dance on our corpses."

"Maybe she wants to apologize for making our lives miserable for six years."

"Sure. And maybe I'll get a flying unicorn that eats rainbows and farts cupcakes."

Figaro gave me a wide-eyed look that said, *Don't you dare*!

"I was just trying to make my point."

Sawyer sounded confused. "Who are you talking to?"

"No one. Listen, Barbie and Amber made it their mission in high school to bully and embarrass us every chance they got," I went on, defending my position. "We don't hear from them for twenty-five years, and all of a sudden Barbie sends each one of us an exclusive invitation requesting a secret meeting during the reunion. How stupid do you think I am?"

"She says she has something important to tell us, but we all need to be there in person. I think we should at least hear her out. Aren't you at all curious?"

"Of course. Just not enough to be in the same room with that b—"

Sawyer cut me off. "Come on, please. I don't want to

face them alone. If we all stick together we can show Barbie and Amber they can't hurt us anymore. Now quit trying to squeak out of it."

Clearly, Sawyer had an agenda.

"I'm not trying to squeak out of it." Lie number one. "I just haven't had time to sign up yet." Lie number two. "I'm not sure I can break away right now for the trip up there." Lie number three. I put down the chocolate-syrup-laden milk and picked up the remote to switch over to Alton Brown—*Ooh, biscuits.* Really, I was hoping Sawyer would forget about me and I could conveniently forget to show up.

"Mm-hm." Sawyer always had the irritating ability to see right through me. "Your schedule is *that* busy? Sitting on the couch watching Paula Deen in your pajamas while eating Ben & Jerry's out of the carton has you completely booked?"

See? Irritating.

"First of all, I'm not eating ice cream. I'm eating cookies. Secondly, I'm not up for it. I'm exhausted. And I don't think I'm ready to be around all those people right now."

Sawyer launched into a Condoleezza Rice–inspired monologue.

"Now you listen to me, Poppy McAllister Browne. John would not want you glued to the couch and cooking shows. He wanted you to go out and live your life to the fullest and have adventures and meet people and have FUN! You know I can't face those two by myself. After all they did to us, and especially not now since my divorce has been finalized. And Kurt will be there to parade some new sleaze around. We made a pinkie promise in the fifth grade that we'd always be there to back each other up, and I've kept my end of the bargain!"

I was wishing I'd gotten the can of frosting after all. "How long did you practice that speech before calling me?"

"'Bout half an hour. How'd I do?"

"It was pretty good."

"Thank you. I like the part about the pinkie promise the best."

"That was a strong point."

"So . . . are you coming?"

I sighed deeply. Sawyer had always been there for me. How could I abandon her now? Even if it was just a stupid high school reunion. "Fine. I'll RSVP this afternoon."

"Oh, good! I signed you up an hour ago. We're going to have so much fun!"

I hung up the phone and looked at Figaro, who had fallen asleep and was doing a weird face-plant into the couch. I nudged him to make sure he was breathing, at which he croaked out a plaintive mew.

Yes, everyone knew I was a sad pushover. Especially my best friends. Would I ever stop being this way?

Figaro opened one eye. *Only if you ever want a shred of self-worth back . . .*

How did I let this happen? I looked at the note on the coffee table again. I didn't know what was worse: a weekend with Barbie and Amber, the Queens of Mean, or running interference between Sawyer and her lowlife ex-husband, Kurt.

Kurt was a royal piece of work. Sawyer had married him a few years out of college. It was love at first sight— for Sawyer. It was probably love at first sight for Kurt, too. It usually was. As soon as he saw Sawyer across the room at the Ugly Mug where he tended bar, he dumped the bimbo he was with and trotted right over to introduce himself as God's gift to pretty girls everywhere. She fell for him as soon as his cheesy line was cast. Unfortunately,

Kurt fell for lots of other women while he was married to my best friend.

But then, Sawyer was an easy target. She'd never come to grips with how beautiful she was. At five-foot-ten, with chestnut hair and green eyes in a pretty little heart-shaped face floating above all those curves, she could have been a model. *Oh, how I wish I had a body like hers,* I thought, and took a bite of another cookie to console myself.

"I'm going to do something I don't want to do, to stand up for a friend. There, Figaro. That makes me worth something."

Even though he was asleep I knew what he was thinking: *When are you going to learn to stand up for* you?

Again, with the back talk.

"I guess we're having a road trip, Fig. Seeing as how Sawyer isn't letting us out of it. And it's a great reason to finally go visit Aunt Ginny. We're long overdue."

Figaro opened both eyes wide. If looks could eviscerate . . . He despised the cat carrier.

"Don't make me use the kitty tranquilizers. You know they give you a hangover. We're going to have to face her sometime. It's been years."

She's your aunt. Why do we need to face her?

"I need you there for moral support."

Figaro responded by licking his paw, wiping it on his ear, and ignoring me.

Yep. Best friends forever.

Chapter 2

Friday afternoon dawned bright and early and my alarm clock let out a loud *meow*, letting me know that I had overslept and his belly was a quart low.

I lay on the couch and tried to find something physically wrong with myself. Nothing serious enough to set off warning bells, but enough to justify canceling the trip. *Is that my spleen? Maybe I'm sick with a spleen illness and shouldn't travel. No, that seems too rare. What about subdermal hives? Nope, there's Benadryl for that.*

What was wrong with me? Why did I agree to do things I knew I'd regret? *Sure, I'll pet sit your ferrets. Of course I have time to come water your twenty-seven plants every day while you go on a cruise. I would love to go to a class reunion with people I hate so I can be reminded that I didn't amount to anything.*

Was I really going to do this? Leave my obscurity and my cans of frosting, and travel to the last place on earth I ever wanted to see again?

CLASS REUNION.

I sighed. Maybe I could come up with something that

would get Sawyer off my case and me off the hook before it was too late.

Fig and I had a busy day ahead of us. He needed to eat, sleep, eat, and sleep. And I needed to take stock of my wardrobe, cry for twenty minutes about having nothing to wear, then throw random pieces of outdated and too-tight clothing into a suitcase and rush out the door.

Right now I had to deal with Aunt Ginny's voice in my head. *Never leave the house a mess.* Great. My guilty conscience was doing impressions. I shuddered at what was to come when I finally faced the redheaded dynamo.

I ran around the house tidying up for Aunt Ginny, who was apparently my own little Jiminy Cricket. I even made the bed I didn't sleep in. At least I yanked the covers and comforter around while Sir Figaro lay there like a pooh-bah and body-surfed the commotion, generally being a nuisance without lifting a paw to help.

Once that was done, I decided that something as daunting as packing to spend a weekend around people who last saw you twenty-five years younger and sixty pounds lighter shouldn't be attempted without an extra-large shot of courage, so I headed into the kitchen to shotgun a burst of energy.

C'mon, Poppy. What's the best excuse for staying home you can think of . . . ? Ebola? Asian bird flu? Terminal acne?

Figaro followed, darting about my ankles in some cat dance meant to tempt me into opening a can of something stinky.

"Yer killin' me, Smalls. Help me get out of this thing."

Figaro looked up, between lip smacks, at the refrigerator door.

"You're right, we could tell Georgina we're going out of town and won't be here to do all the grunt work for her charity event. She'll pitch a fit big enough that we'll never have to leave again. But then we'd just be stuck here with her."

Figaro gave me a sideways look that said he'd already invested more time in this discussion then he'd wanted, and he went back to choking down his minced fish parts.

I needed some coffee to clear my head.

I love the smell of coffee. Some days I wish I could just strap the coffee bag on and wear it like a doctor's mask. I am straight up addicted to coffee. Well, not really coffee. What I'm addicted to is milk with a little espresso thrown in for color. Anything out of a Mr. Coffee—not so much. John bought me an exquisite Italian espresso machine to celebrate his making partner in the Stevenson, Greene and Gorman law firm. I chose powder pink to piss off my mother-in-law.

I made, and then downed, a double cappuccino, then marched off to face the firing squad in my closet. I haven't worn anything dressier than pajamas or yoga pants in weeks. Who did I have to impress? Jamie Oliver didn't care what I was wearing; he started his career as the Naked Chef. That was a rather disappointing first episode.

I pulled out the plain black dress I had bought just a few months ago. It was my funeral dress. Something in my gut nagged at me that this wasn't a good idea. Wearing the same dress you buried your husband in to a lame-excuse-for-a-party surely carries a bad omen with it.

I could tell Sawyer I was still in mourning and couldn't go out in public!

What are you—a character on Downton Abbey?

Now I had Sawyer's voice in my head. It was getting crowded up there. Fine. That wouldn't work.

I waved the dress in front of me. "What do you think, Fig?" Figaro had curled up inside the open suitcase to make sure the loose cat hair was packed. "It's the nicest thing I have, so it will have to do. The last thing I want to do right now is go shopping."

Figaro yawned in agreement.

I ushered him out of the bag and packed the weekend essentials for the both of us. Then I took a quick shower and dressed in some loose-fitting gray yoga pants and a green William & Mary T-shirt that had been John's, towel-dried my hair, and put it up in an old scrunchie that had lost most of its scrunch. It sagged to the right and most of my hair drooped against my head. I looked like an escaped mental patient.

I heard Aunt Ginny's voice in my head again. *Always strive to look your best. A lady takes pride in her appearance.* I looked in the mirror. Great. I hoped Aunt Ginny didn't organize another fashion intervention for me. Aunt Ginny means well, but she has all the subtlety of a marching band in a cemetery.

As I puttered around doing the necessary chores to secure the house for the weekend, Figaro did his part by being underfoot and in the way until I pulled out the dreaded cat carrier.

Sensing a disturbance in the force, Figaro conveniently vanished into thin air.

Normally, all I had to do was utter the word *treat* and Fig was right there doing figure eights at my feet trying to put the Mesmer on me to give him a little crunchy fishy snack. Now all the shaking of treat cans and whirring of can openers in the world wouldn't bring him out of his hiding spot. I knew he was sitting somewhere, smugly thinking he'd outsmarted me. I finally found him under the bed in the guest room, wedged in the corner, his eyes glowing at me in the dark like a deranged Ewok. "Would you please come out?!"

That was it. I couldn't leave the cat!

You're pathetic. You know that?

My inner-Sawyer was getting impatient.

Okay, no more rummaging for excuses. It was enough effort having to rummage for Figaro.

"I want to get this weekend over with, get Sawyer off my back, and come back to my sofa and my therapist, Little Debbie. It's bad enough we waited till the last minute. We don't want to incur the wrath of Aunt Ginny by showing up in the middle of *Jeopardy!*"

The Ewok just blinked at me.

"Figaro, we're going to miss the ferry." I crammed myself under the bed, huffing and wheezing, and nabbed him around the middle, pulling him out with no small amount of growling and protesting. He didn't like it much either. Once he was in his carrier he settled in and curled up like he'd wanted to be there all along and I was sweating and covered in dust balls.

"You can be a little devil—you know that?" Two faux-innocent orange eyes blinked at me as I dragged my suitcase and the carrier out to my 1992 Toyota Corolla.

I stood there and sulked. I couldn't conjure up a good attitude about going, but I failed to come up with a viable enough excuse to stay home, so I told myself to get it over with and we hit the road.

Relax. It's just a reunion. What could go wrong?

Chapter 3

For the first forty minutes Figaro howled like a yeti. Then he moaned like his life was in danger. Then he hocked up a hairball and settled in for a nap. I found a coffee shop with a drive-through window and ordered a large raspberry mocha—for the caffeine—then spilled half of it in my lap when Figaro let out a death howl because he realized we'd started moving again. For the next two hours I had to drive with third-degree thigh burn, and I swear Figaro smiled at me when I glared at him in the rearview mirror.

When we were safely on the ferry, I decided I needed to get my mind away from the impending face-off with Aunt Ginny and settle my super-caffeinated nerves, so I took the cat carrier and went up on deck for some fresh air. Angry red-glowing eyes peered at me from its dark interior.

I suppose I was looking for an omen as much as escape from my dark foreboding, a sign that despite my misgivings about this trip everything was going to go smoothly and I'd be back home in pork-rind heaven before I knew it.

Figaro was curled up in his crate watching the activity

until the tourist sitting next to us thought it would be fun to feed a french fry to the lone seagull flying beside the boat. Rookie mistake.

I said, "I wouldn't do that if I were you," but it was too late.

South Jersey seagulls, it is not commonly known, belong to the Teamsters Union. They're like pit bulls with wings. Within five seconds, about fifty seagulls were reenacting the telephone booth scene from Alfred Hitchcock's *The Birds*, making the tourist drop her plate of fries and run screaming for the door.

As omens go, this was not a good one.

Figaro was hissing and spitting and swatting at imagined birds in his carrier and I had to use two hands to wrangle it back down to the car. His fur was still standing up when we docked in Cape May and disembarked.

I went into desperate-prayer mode: *Please, God, don't let Aunt Ginny launch right into me about how long it's been since I've been home and how I've let her down. Oh, and P.S., please help me find Spanx to look twenty pounds thinner before the reunion. Amen.*

I crossed the bridge onto the island and into the historic district. Shady streets were lined with colorful Victorian houses built in 1879 by a real estate developer from Philadelphia. There was a building boom going on to restore Old Cape May, as many of the buildings had been destroyed in the Great Fire.

My great-great-grandfather bought our house to use as a summer beach cottage. It's been in my family ever since although it's rumored that a great-uncle almost lost it to Henry Ford in a poker game.

When I pulled up in front of the gingerbread Queen

Anne, I knew right away that something was horribly wrong.

I rubbed my eyes.

The House of Dracula did not vanish. Aunt Ginny's place looked deserted and . . . creepy. The once-grand Victorian glared back in a woeful, "What are *you* looking at?" state of disrepair that I had never seen before. The buttercup yellow paint was peeling, exposing weathered bare wood, some of it gray with mildew from the constant damp air of being one block from the Atlantic Ocean. The gingerbread trim and spindles of the balustrade had faded and become so drab you could no longer make out their vibrant "Easter egg" pink and purple colors. Thick morning glory vines had grown up covering the once quaint wraparound porch. Bare, climbing rose vines were gnarled and twisted out of control making the house look like the backdrop for *Little Shop of Horrors*. Boxwood bushes were overgrown and blocking first-floor windows. What looked like at least two seasons of dead leaves lay in piles around the yard and the grass was so tall there had to be snakes hiding underneath. Pythons, at least.

Figaro—as if sensing doom—flicked and thumped his tail against the carrier, and his eyes darted back and forth as I unbuckled it and removed him from the car. He jumped inside the carrier when the lighthouse weather vane squealed as it swung in the wind. I rested the carrier on my hip to force the lopsided wrought-iron gate open, with much protest from the rusty hinges, then leaned a rock from the yard against it to keep it from slamming back into us.

As I trudged up the uneven walk toward the porch, the front door creaked open. A little old lady with bright orange hair peeked her head out.

"Poppy? Is that you?"

Aunt Ginny is a bit of a free spirit. Her age is estimated at around eighty. No one knows for sure how old she is because she won't tell.

"I mean—it *looks* like you but then it's been *sooo long*."

Oh boy. Here we go.

Figaro rumbled out a cat growl.

Looking at Aunt Ginny was a vision of my future. If I had her emerald green eyes I'd be the spitting image of her at forty-two. Her *I-Love-Lucy*-red hair may have been from a bottle now but most of her life it was homegrown. My blue eyes and broad shoulders come from my German grandmother on my mother's side, but my porcelain skin and freckles come from Aunt Ginny's Scottish heritage.

I clomped up the front steps to give her a hug. "It's nice to see you, Aunt Ginny. I missed you so much!" Then I pulled back to see her better. I didn't know it was possible for someone to shrink this much in just a few short years.

"What happened? You're a hobbit!"

"That's what happens when you don't come home for *twenty years*. People change."

I could almost hear Figaro gloating at me.

"Really? We're going to do this right now?"

She blew me off. "After you get settled in we need to have a talk about something. Something important."

Oh boy. I wasn't even in the door. "What's going on?"

She waved her hand in dismissal. "Not now. Wait till you get your stuff unpacked and rest up a bit."

Oh. My. God. I need to be rested up for it.

Looking around, it was obvious something wasn't right.

The care of the garden had been abandoned and weeds dominated every corner. This would be the perfect hide-out for a Disney villain. On the other hand, if Aunt Ginny was preparing to enter a "Best Halloween House" contest, she'd outdone herself.

The yard had been full of wisteria and roses when I lived here. It was beautiful. Now it looked like the old girl had been abandoned. *Gulp.*

A sense of dread spidered its way up my spine. But once Aunt Ginny made up her mind, I knew only too well, a buffalo stampede couldn't make her change course. I would have to wait until she was ready to talk.

She stepped out onto the porch, looking wiry as ever. If only I'd inherited *those* genes. At this range, she smelled of Bengay, Polident, and Oil of Olay. I hoped it was okay to combine all those without causing nerve damage.

"I see you're still full of spit and vinegar!" she chortled. She scrunched her face up to the cat carrier. "What in the world is *that*?"

"That's Figaro. I told you about him. I even sent you pictures. Don't you remember?"

"I don't know, I'm old. It's hard to say what I remember." She screwed up her face and peered back in the carrier. "It looks like a dust mop."

Aunt Ginny was laying it on thick. "I'll take it, whatever it is, while you get your bags." She snatched the carrier from me and gave it a vigorous shake. "There. That'll either shake whatever it is out of its bad mood or make it *really* angry. No pouters around here."

Dear God, take me now . . .

From inside, Figaro gave a distressed moan and threw me a vengeful look.

I left them to whatever bad mojo they were creating and scampered back out to the car. Now that I'd let myself be dragged here I had to face the truth:

I'd avoided coming home, even though Aunt Ginny had been begging me to visit for years. There were too many bad memories in this old house. I had made a lot of bad choices when I was younger, and had locked the shame away in my heart. I still had visions of my mother driving away when she abandoned me. I took a lot of my hurt out on Grandma and Aunt Ginny, who didn't deserve it. They were so good to me.

I rewarded their generosity by cutting all the hair off Grandma's dolls. When I got older, I was always getting detention for smoking and suspension for cutting school. I still hadn't gotten over the look of disappointment on their faces when they caught me sneaking out with Tim in the middle of the night to do God-knows-what. Okay, *everybody* knew what—especially Grandma and Aunt Ginny. It was all so disgraceful. I especially tried to tamp down the painful memories of Tim and what happened between us, but they were escaping like sewer rats from the now-opened manhole cover of my soul—just as I'd known they would, and I wasn't ready to face them yet. Guilt washed over me as I heaved my suitcase out of the trunk.

"What's this doohickey for?" I heard Aunt Ginny say from the front porch.

I turned to see her messing with the door of the cat carrier.

"Aunt Ginny. I wouldn't—"

With a flip of the latch, Aunt Ginny opened Figaro's carrier, and he took off like a cheetah flying through the Serengeti, launching himself into the dark interior of Aunt Ginny's haunted mansion.

"Whoa! It just shot right out of there."

Aunt Ginny peered innocently inside the carrier, as if Figaro would magically reappear. "Oh, dear. I sure hope it doesn't break anything irreplaceable."

Inside the house something crashed.

I dropped my suitcase, ran back up the sidewalk and inside the house to find him. It's never a good sign when a family visit *begins* with destruction and mayhem.

Bounding up the front porch and into the main foyer, I saw ahead of me the grand staircase that led up to the second level. Dust motes were swirling in the air from the clearly un-vacuumed treads. This seemed a good indication as to which way Figaro had rocketed. Faded portraits of McAllister ancestors lined the walls and a potted spider plant lay like a washed-up dead octopus on the marble floor. I would have to come back for it later.

I was about to rush upstairs but changed course at the sound of thumping on the piano in the front parlor to my left. It sounded suspiciously like a furry little terrorist racing across the keys. My ill-fated piano lessons in here as a child probably didn't sound much better.

Peering into the parlor, a room with wraparound bay windows and crown molding, I saw no sign of His Royal Destructiveness. I'd loved this room as a kid, because it was round and it was the first floor of the three-story tower with the pointy witch's-hat roof. Now it was all graying wallpaper and smelled like mothballs.

The sound of glass breaking in the next room told me he was on the move.

"Figaro!"

I ran through the parlor into the main formal dining room and scanned for smoke-gray fur. We used to eat Thanksgiving and Christmas dinners next to the cozy fireplace at the long mahogany table that now had a bunched-up table runner and two broken candlesticks rolling toward the edge. There was another crash in the distance.

Oblivious to the terror she'd unleashed, Aunt Ginny

hollered from the kitchen, "Come on in here and make yourself at home. Would you like some lemonade?"

"Yes, please!" I hollered back.

I straightened the table and picked up a silver picture frame that was lying on the floor next to the hearth and looked around to see if anything else was clawed, bitten, or otherwise damaged. To the left, the dining room exited to a screened-in porch—a must in South Jersey where the state bird is the mosquito—leading out to the wraparound porch running along the side and front of the house. Through the door I could see the once-lovely white wooden hanging swing on the porch where I used to daydream instead of doing my homework. The swing was now in ruin, hanging lopsided on a rusted chain, a tetanus shot waiting to happen.

At the back of the house I could hear what sounded like a miniature moose galloping over hardwood floors.

"Figaro, *come here!"*

"You want some madeleines with your lemonade?" Aunt Ginny called.

"Sure, that's great! Thanks!" *Whatever. Where is that cat?*

Through the dining room was the kitchen and butler pantry, a sort of walk-in closet for dry goods and canned produce that were put up the summer before. Just off the kitchen was one of my favorite features of the old house, the secret stairs leading to the second and third levels, the third level being the old servants' quarters. Of course, no one in my family had had servants for many years. (Unless you count all the chores I had to do growing up, which I counted.)

"Did you see Figaro come through here?" I asked Aunt Ginny, who was in the kitchen loading up a silver tea tray with a plate of madeleines, a pitcher of lemonade, some floral napkins, a vegetable peeler, a pack of birthday candles, a pair of champagne flutes, a bottle of aspirin, a pint of farmer's market cherry tomatoes, a pack of double-A batteries, a pair of chopsticks, a whistle, and a lottery ticket.

"I think he went that way." She pointed a pair of silver sugar tongs toward the sunroom on my right.

I eyed the tea tray for a moment, then gave a quick look back at Aunt Ginny before I picked up a box of tea bags from the floor and set the trash can upright again.

To the left of the kitchen, in the back of the house, was a great room that had been converted into Grandma Emmy's bedroom and bath a few years ago when she declared that she was "too old to traipse up and down all these blasted stairs anymore!"

I was heading toward the sunroom when I heard several thuds coming from the front of the house. And there, finally, I found Figaro innocently taking a bath in the dark-wood-paneled library next to a pile of books that had mysteriously fallen off the floor-to-ceiling bookcase next to the stone fireplace. His rampage appeared to be over so I put the books back on the shelf, pointed a warning finger at him—which seemed to amuse him—and went out to retrieve the suitcases.

I put our bags next to the grand staircase and set up Figaro's litter box and food and water bowls in the mudroom off the kitchen.

I hadn't really had a chance to get a good look around, what with the mad chase and all, but I now realized there was some sort of dark cloud over the house. Everything was in the right place, but it all seemed a bit dreary—like the life had been drained from it.

Despite my desire to spend a little time with the woman who raised me, the gloom of the house only reinforced my one true goal: Get the reunion over and make tracks home like a kid with a bagful of Halloween candy.

Aunt Ginny exited the kitchen carrying the tray and announced, "Violet lemonade and lavender madeleines. Shall we go into the sunroom?" The room was in the back corner of the house, occupying the other tower room with curved windows, which made it bright and warm and inviting, although today there was quite a curtain of dust dancing in the sun's rays.

"That sounds wonderful!" I took the tray from Aunt Ginny and set it down on the tea table, and we positioned ourselves next to each other in the comfy, overstuffed chairs. "Why so formal?" I teased, gripping a madeleine. I was tempted to down them two at a time, to regain my composure, but refrained. "When I lived here as a teenager, I drank out of the Flintstones glass we got from the gas station."

"Bamm-Bamm is worth more than the crystal now." Aunt Ginny took a flute of lemonade and placed a little flowered napkin on her knee. "And I don't get to entertain much anymore. It's such a shame to see nice things collecting dust on the shelf."

You're telling me. I've heard of dust bunnies, but this room could be under a fog advisory.

I took a long look at Aunt Ginny and thought about how lonely she must be, in this big house all by herself. Maybe that's why it seemed so dreary. It was the pervasive atmosphere of loneliness.

"Why you looking at me so queer?" Aunt Ginny narrowed her eyes at me as she took a bite of a madeleine.

"What? I'm not. I was just thinking that you must be getting tired of taking care of this big house all by yourself." I grinned. "Maybe I should find you a man."

She swallowed and cocked her head to look at me with

raised eyebrows. "What are you, some kind of nut? I need another man like I need a hole in the head. I've had enough of that foolishness in my life." She smoothed an imaginary crease in her apron and looked away from me.

"Have you been keeping yourself busy without Grandma?" I tried to subtly pry a bit to get Aunt Ginny to spill it. Something was amiss here, but I couldn't put my finger on it.

"Sure, you know. This and that. I've got my routine."

She gave me a halfhearted smile but wouldn't meet my eyes. Oh, she was a crafty one. I would have to sneak up on her conversationally—warm her up, then trick her into answering.

"So what's been going on?" I tried again.

"Nothing. I thought you weren't coming up to this shindig. What made you change your mind?"

I let out a little groan and rolled my eyes.

"Ah, Sawyer," Aunt Ginny answered her own question. "I had a feeling she was behind it." Then she sniffed. "I guess coming *home* was not a big draw."

My heart broke for her. "I should have come up a long time ago. I haven't seen you since Georgina's stunt at the reading of John's will. And before that I was so busy taking care of him that I didn't have time for anything else."

Aunt Ginny shook her head. "You got that right. A person could be lying dead in a ditch before they'd get a visit from you. But that mother-in-law of yours is a piece of work. You shouldn't let her push you around like that."

Apparently, that privilege and duty was saved for Aunt Ginny herself.

"I remember my second husband, Virgil, had a mother that made Satan look like Snow White. You need to forget about Georgina and get back on your feet. Take care of yourself for a change."

"I don't have the energy to take on Georgina."

Aunt Ginny nibbled another madeleine while she listened and watched me with those sharp green eyes. "I had some of that depression after my fourth husband, Cecil, ran off with the tramp that pulled the lottery balls out of the air tank on Channel Two. I didn't want to be around nobody." She gave a definitive nod.

Aunt Ginny had masterfully blown through five husbands. When I was little, I overheard my uncle Danny say, "Being married to Virginia is like being strapped to the back of a tiger. You know it will eventually kill you but it's so exciting you just want to be along for the ride." He left over twenty years ago to buy a Baby Ruth at the drugstore and never returned. That's when her sister, my grandma Emmy, moved in. Grandma passed on about three years ago so it's just Aunt Ginny now.

"It's no wonder you look a wreck." Aunt Ginny clucked her tongue at me in sympathy.

"What?" I choked on my lemonade.

"Well, you're a mess with a capital *M*. Just look at you. Face all swollen, bags under your eyes."

I wiped at my T-shirt self-consciously, feeling like a schlub. "I haven't been sleeping well."

"What you need is some companionship. Why don't you stay with me for a few weeks instead of going back to that empty house? You could be my alibi."

Say what now?

"Your thingamiebob is shaking." Aunt Ginny pointed to my iPhone. I picked it up and checked the screen.

"It's a text from Sawyer saying that it's important that I make it to dinner tonight so she can tell me something.

A text is like a note that she typed on her phone and sent it to my phone for me to read."

"I know what texting is," Aunt Ginny said, giving me a severe look. "I don't live under a rock. I have a Droid. I am up on stuff, you know."

"Oh." I stifled a giggle. "I didn't realize you were *up on stuff*. I beg your pardon. What do you need an alibi for?"

And since bad luck stalks me like a weird ex-boyfriend, just when I was finally about to wheedle some info out of Aunt Ginny, a loud crash sounded from the kitchen and a gray blur thundered through the sunroom with his ears pinned back. Figaro skidded to a halt at my feet, then serenely began to lick his paw. *Nothing to see here folks. Move along.*

I prodded him with one foot. "What did you do?"

Figaro looked at me mid-lick like, *Who? Me? I've been here the whole time. But somebody better go check the kitchen before Aunt Ginny does.*

"I'll just go see what Figaro has gotten into." I sighed with one last look to the poster cat for innocence.

As I left the room. Aunt Ginny was leaning down to him and I could hear her say, "Listen, buddy. You and I are gonna be friends, but if you make a mess in my house I'm gonna hang you by your tail from the chandelier. *Got it?*"

Figaro responded with a soulful *mrow*, which I took as agreement to the terms and conditions of surrender.

The kitchen hadn't changed since I was in elementary school. The room was covered with faded wallpaper in country blue with pink flowers. The walls were peppered with grapevine wreaths and wooden plaques of cows and pigs and ducks wearing frilly bows. I searched for signs of Figaro's latest achievement. There on the floor in the corner by the refrigerator was a decorative birdhouse in the shape of a cat face with feathers glued to the hole that was its mouth. A couple wet feathers were lying a few feet away. You didn't have to be Nancy Drew to solve this mystery. I put the offending decoration on the counter, planning to glue it back together later, and spotted a business card from Rosalind Carson of the Department of Youth and Family Services, lying next to the phone. What was that all about?

I walked out of the kitchen in time to see Aunt Ginny wrapping a yellow scarf around her hair Katharine Hepburn–style, preparing to go out.

"Where are you going?"

"You'll be busy catching up with your girlfriends and tonight is my pottery class!"

"Oh. Okay. Well, I guess we'll talk after pottery then. Before you go, I was wondering why you have a business card from a social worker."

Aunt Ginny picked up her purse and keys and put on her Jackie O sunglasses. "Well, that's what I need to talk to you about. She wants to meet with you."

"Meet with me? About what?"

"She thinks I'm crazy and wants to put me in a home. You girls have fun tonight. Don't wait up."

Then she eyed Figaro, made a gesture like she was hanging herself and let her tongue fall out of her mouth.

Figaro's ears flattened against his head.

And with that she was out the door with the scent of White Shoulders wafting in her wake.

Chapter 4

I drove over the bridge into Wildwood and down to Morey's Pier. Passing a few boarded-up shops and game stalls, I would have been tempted to play a water gun horserace if I wasn't short on time and full of anxiety over what new bomb Sawyer wanted to drop on me at dinner.

The aroma of sausage and peppers mingled with whatever deep-fried funnel-cake-battered treats were being made at the moment. I stopped short when I saw a sign for deep-fried peanut butter cups. The little voice inside my head whispered seductively, *Where have you been my whole life?* One small, two-thousand-calorie beauty wouldn't kill me, would it? But someone calling my name snapped me out of it.

"Poppy!"

I turned to see Sawyer, waving her manicured blue nails madly at me from under the MACK'S PIZZA neon sign. I ran over, yes, I said *ran*, a sight sure to traumatize me if it were ever caught on video, with my arms outstretched to give Sawyer a hug. "Hi! Omigosh! I can't believe you're here!"

"I know," I said out of breath. "I can't believe it either."

I held her away from me and took a long look at her. Sawyer was stunning. With her perfect tan she looked gorgeous in a sapphire blue one-shoulder top, white summer capris, and gold gladiator sandals. "You look fantastic, I hate you!" We both giggled, and she hugged me again.

"I have a surprise for you; please don't be ma-ad," Sawyer trilled.

Oh, sweet Jesus, please don't be Barbie and Amber. My blood pressure couldn't take it.

"Here's hoping for Colin Firth in a tuxedo!" I held up my fingers crossed to hide my nerves.

Sawyer giggled and took a step to the right and flung her arms out in a *tada!* move—and there, grinning and waving from the back table, were two of our closest friends from high school, Kim and Connie.

Relieved, I let out my breath. "Oh, thank God."

"I thought we could have a little pre-reunion tonight." She gave me a big superstar grin. "This is going to be awesome."

"Sure. That was sweet of you, Sawyer. Thank you . . ." I said, thinking, *Aaaaaand they're already astonished at how big my thighs are. . . .*

"I'm so glad you don't mind. They were really excited to see you again."

"No, I definitely don't mind. I was nervous you were luring me here to tell me something horrible."

Sawyer's face turned scarlet and she let out a nervous laugh. "What? No. Not *horrible*."

"Wait. What do you mean not *horrible*?" *I think I'm going to be sick.*

Sawyer wouldn't look at me. "Well, I mean, we're all going to tell you together. Later."

She took off for the back of the Pepto-Bismol-colored pizza parlor where she thought there was less chance that

I would make a scene. I tromped behind her with a scowl on my face and nausea rising. I was heading right into an ambush.

I was assaulted by the scents of tomato, oregano, and garlic being propelled around the room by the numerous white ceiling fans. Maybe I could rally enough to force down a slice . . . or three.

Once we joined the other girls at the bright pink booth there were hugs all around and we each commented on how well we all looked and how no one had aged a day since graduation and other delusional fantasies. A waitress came over to take our order—four birch beers and a large white pizza with extra garlic. I wasn't kissing anyone, so what did I care?

As we began to relax and catch up, I took a good look at each one of them thinking how great their hair looked and how mine resembled a lazy bird's nest. They were wearing cute little outfits and had carefully applied makeup. I had a mystery stain on my T-shirt and a zit on my chin. Maybe I'd let myself go a tad. It had been a rough decade, sue me.

I snogged into my birch beer and realized in horror it was Diet Coke. I tried to catch the eye of the waitress, but she had mastered the art of looking around without making eye contact in an *Oh, good, no one needs me, time to sneak a cigarette out back* kind of way. I realized Connie was asking me something about my trip so I smiled and nodded.

Connie was always a bit of a tomboy. She preferred jeans and running shoes to dresses and pumps. She played the tuba in the marching band and was a proud member of the AV club. It didn't take long for the bullies to zero in on Connie as one of their prime victims. They spread ugly rumors about why she didn't shower in the girls' locker room. But Connie was tough. She didn't let them get to her. She fought back.

One day Connie brought chocolate-covered grass-hoppers to school to pass out to all the bullies. And like the city of Troy to the Trojan horse, they took the bait. No one ever said bullies were smart. Now she was married with a family of her own, and in an ironic twist of fate, our resident tomboy had two of the prissiest girly-girls you'd ever meet.

Shaking the sense that something dreadful was yet to be revealed, I focused on her as she brought us up to speed on her life. Then again, any person whose life involved more than flipping channels had my attention.

"I almost didn't make it out of the house." Connie dug through her purse—pulling out assorted barrettes, two magical fairy princess dolls, and one Cinderella sock with a hole in the toe—before finding her cell phone. "I'm sorry, but I need to check for emergency texts from Mike. He was relieved from his shift at the jail late, so I had to drop Sabrina at ballet by six and then the drawbridge coming into Wildwood was up."

Another waitress walked by with a tray of drinks for the next table over.

"Excuse me." I tried to get her attention to bring me my birch beer, but she fled like I was an empty lot on the wrong side of Wildwood. My throat was a desert—was there no mercy here?

"How *are* Mike and the girls?"

"They're good." Connie shifted uneasily. "Sabrina is fifteen now and takes dance and gymnastics twice a week and has cheerleading practice every day after school. Emmilee is seven and collects ponies, Disney Princesses, and refuses to wear anything that doesn't have polka dots.

It can be so . . . tiring." She ran her hand through her pixie-cut, chocolate-brown hair and let out a tired sigh.

I would love to have two children. Instead I have two chins and a cat.

I tried to keep the tone light to put Connie at ease, and suppressed my psychic pain like I was stuffing in a giant cannoli. "Gee. I'm exhausted just thinking about it. I feel like I need to go lie down."

Connie laughed nervously. "They keep me busy, that's for sure. It's all so . . . exhausting, though."

I looked around the table and noticed that none of the girls would make eye contact with me. Something *was* up. I knew it. What were they hiding from me?

"Sabrina made assistant captain of the cheerleaders at Caper High this year." Auntie Kim tried to keep the conversation going as she filled me in on more of her adopted niece's accomplishments. Kim has never given in to "the oppressiveness of conventional marriage." But she and her boyfriend, Rick, and their iguana, Betsy, have been living together happily for fourteen years. No children. Unless you count Betsy. Which, despite her reindeer-antler-wearing presence on their family Christmas card, I didn't. But then that's probably why she indulges Connie's girls every chance she gets.

"Oh, good for her!" Sawyer chimed in just as our pizza arrived.

"Excuse me, ma'am," I said to the waitress, who now reeked of nicotine, "I think you brought me a Diet Coke by mistake."

"You think or you know?" she snapped at me.

"I *know* it's Diet Coke and I *want* a birch beer, please."

"Okay. Then you should have asked for that in the first place." With a shrug, she seized the Diet Coke, muttering about tourists under her breath.

I turned back to Connie. "Is Emmilee going to take dance and gymnastics like her big sister?" I asked, trying to be interested in a subject that cut my heart out with a blunt Swiss army knife.

Connie, who had just feigned exhaustion with "it all," now very energetically launched into a spiel about what her youngest was doing, and I smiled. Truthfully, she was the kind of mom I would like to have had or been.

I grinned at Connie's machine-gun download and tried to stay focused before turning my attention to Kim.

Kim was the counterbalance here, our free-spirited wild child. She'd had a patch of her head shaved over one ear to show off her row of piercings and her right shoulder was tattooed in full color vines with flowers and hummingbirds down to her wrist. A blue streak adorned her otherwise dirty blond curly hair.

The waitress, Dame Smokarella, was over by the pizza ovens talking to her coworkers without a care in the world. I tried to mentally command her to bring me a drink, any drink, heck I'd take the Diet Coke back! She kept right on flirting with the cook, who was all T-shirt and tattoos.

There was a break in the conversation about the kids, then Sawyer leaned in and whispered, "I have a confession to make, girls."

Here it is. This must be the secret they've all been acting so squirrely about. Lord, give me strength.

"I've been cyberstalking Kurt on Facebook, and he's been bragging about coming to our reunion with Tonia Lipinski."

What? If that's the big secret I'm disappointed I wasted so much anxiety on it.

Kim pounded her fist on the Formica tabletop. "What? Tonia Lipinski? That low-class pole-dancing tramp?"

Kim failed Mr. Shellington's third-period Diplomacy class.

Mack's other patrons were starting to stare at us. Some had slices of pizza held midair. A mother of three small boys shot us a wrecking-ball kind of look. Our waitress looked back at our table and I seized the chance to mouth, "Soda, *pleeeeease*."

Connie, the voice of reason, asked, "Do you think he's just going with her so he can be there to see *you*?"

Sawyer calmed down. "Well . . . I don't know. I feel ridiculous assuming he's even thinking about me."

"*Of course* he's thinking about you," Kim said, slapping her hand on the Formica table and sending her greasy paper plate flying. "He knows he lost the best thing he ever had when you kicked his sorry butt out."

One of the boys, who looked to be about four, piped up. "Daddy's butt is sorry too, right, Mommy? You said so. . . ." and the woman gave Kim a pointed look before quickly shoving the boys out to the boardwalk.

"Coming home early from work to find him with the waitress from the Boiler Room on my grandmother's antique quilt was the final straw. I had put up with his stumbling in at two a.m., covered in stripper glitter and cheap beer, late-night phone call hang-ups, and finding a leopard-print thong behind my Snoopy cookie jar. That was the moment I knew Kurt was beyond help and my marriage was over."

I remembered the night well. Sawyer didn't scream or cry. Just walked into the bedroom, locked the door, and called me. While Kurt was pounding on the door trying to explain how "this isn't what it looks like," Sawyer was throwing his things out the bedroom window. The next day she turned the shop over to her assistant, filed for divorce, and drove down to Waterford to stay with John and me for a few days.

I was dying for that birch beer, but darned if that waitress wasn't up front petting the inked tiger on the cook's arm.

I started wishing that tiger would jump off his bicep and bite her right on the . . .

"But I'm not sure how I'll react to being in the same room with Kurt and another woman. I'm so glad I'll have youse guys there for support. Especially you, Poppy."

"What? Oh, of course. That's what friends are for." *That and not judging you for how much raw cookie dough you can eat in one sitting.*

"Enough stalling. Let's talk about this." Kim pulled an embossed envelope out of her bag and laid it on the table. There was a filigree-monogrammed *B* in the corner. "What is she up to?"

We all pulled matching envelopes out and placed them on the table.

"It can't be any good, that's for sure," Connie said.

"Maybe she sent it to everyone," Sawyer added thoughtfully.

"I called some of the girls from marching band and none of them got one," Connie replied.

"I asked Skooter and Bobo at the garage and they didn't get one either." Kim looked at each one of us skeptically.

"Maybe she only sent one to the people they were mean to," I said, then added, "No, that can't be it. Just about everyone would have received one."

"Well, I think she wants to apologize. It was a long time ago and I bet she regrets that she and Amber were so hurtful when we were kids," Sawyer offered.

"I think you're out of your mind is what I think," Kim replied. "If she wanted to apologize she could have done it *in* the note. Not ask us to meet her in person in C wing at nine o'clock during the reunion."

Connie's nose wrinkled. "And why so secretive? She wants to apologize but doesn't want anyone else to know she's doing it? That's weird."

"Well, one thing is for sure," Sawyer added. "I'm not going without you guys."

"Agreed. We stick together and watch each other's backs. If I know Barbie and Amber, it's a plot to humiliate us." I put my envelope back in my purse and the girls followed suit.

There was a long pause while Connie and Kim both looked at Sawyer as if they were waiting for something. I felt a nagging fear begin at the back of my neck.

Kim finally broke the silence.

"So, um, have you ever heard anything from Tim after all these years?"

I felt my breath catch at the mention of Tim's name, and my heart started beating a little faster. I remembered the night I called Tim and told him that I had made a colossal mistake and now I was pregnant. He asked me if I loved the guy. I told him the truth. John was like a brother to me; there were no romantic feelings on either side. It was one drunken blur. At first Tim said we could work it out. He would drop out of cooking school, get his job back as a busboy at Seasons, and help me raise the baby. I realized right there that I loved him too much to let him put more of his life on hold for me. Not to mention how much it would hurt John to not be involved in raising his own child. I couldn't do that to either of them. So I told Tim it was over. I would always love him, but he needed to move on. It pains me to admit that he didn't put up a fight.

"Not a peep. I guess he went his way and I went mine."

"Haven't you even Googled him to see if he got fat or rich or married?" Sawyer asked, surprised. "It's not a big deal. Lots of people do it."

"Well, okay, once." *Once, twice, seventy-five times. What difference does it make?* "But I didn't find anything. There are a lot of Tim Maxwells."

"What do you think you'll do if you run into him at the reunion?" Kim's eyes darted from me to Sawyer and back to me again. Connie leaned forward in her seat like she was afraid she would miss my answer.

Probably pretend I don't speak English and limp away like the gargoyle I've become. "I don't have to worry about that. Tim won't be at the reunion." I wiped my mouth with my napkin. "He graduated the year before us."

The girls sat there with stunned looks on their faces watching me. I thought they were being rather melodramatic about the whole thing. Then I remembered what Sawyer said about Facebook stalking. "Why? Is he coming with someone from our class that I don't know about?"

Connie and Kim looked at Sawyer, waiting for her answer. Sawyer closed her eyes for a minute and took a deep breath, then said, "Well, actually. That's what we wanted to talk to you about."

Is the room spinning? It feels like it's spinning. This is it, isn't it? This is the big announcement.

"We wanted to tell you when we were all together to help you deal with it."

Yep, the room is definitely spinning. "Deal with *what*, exactly?"

Kim pulled her invitation out of her purse. "You really didn't read any of the info on here, did you?"

Okay, now I was starting to feel nauseous. Mack's was about to have a cleanup in booth number four. "Nooo." It came out barely a whisper.

"Tim's restaurant is Maxine's Bistro. It's right here on the invitation. He's catering the event."

My heart was beating like I was trying to run a 5K for the first time since high school, and I was getting a little light-headed. My eyes started to burn and I had to blink away tears. Connie reached across the table to take my hand.

"Oh, Poppy, don't cry. It can't be that bad. Are you afraid he'll say something mean to you?"

"No." I was dumbfounded. How do you explain to someone who looks like Sawyer that your worst nightmare is being seen fat and dumpy by your first love? She had tears running down her cheeks now. Of course, Sawyer cries with all of her emotions.

"I'm so sorry, hon. I shouldn't have assumed you knew."

"He's *only* the caterer," Kim tried to help. "He won't be walking around greeting everyone. I'm sure we can keep him away from you."

"If you're not afraid he'll be rude to you then what is it?" Connie asked again.

"I just . . ." My voice faltered. "I just haven't seen or talked to him in twenty-five years. After the way things ended—the last thing I wanted was for Tim to see me like this."

"Like what?" Sawyer asked, genuinely confused. Sawyer, bless her heart, could only see the best in people.

I was already regretting eating that third piece of pizza. And every piece of pizza I'd had in the last two decades. They all appeared at once in my mind, like a jeering mob. "I don't want him to take one look at me and be relieved that he dodged a bullet."

"Everyone wants their ex to think that they were the one that got away," Kim stated.

"You have nothing to be ashamed of. You've had a great life and a wonderful husband who was madly in love with you. Tim should be jealous that he missed out on all that you had to give." Connie unrolled some toilet paper from her purse.

I'd have to think about that later.

"If he's only interested in looks, he's shallow and doesn't deserve you, and you're the one who dodged the bullet." Kim gave me a fierce look, daring me to disagree.

Everyone nodded, but I wasn't buying it. "I'm just going to have to try to avoid running into him."

"I'll help you," Sawyer put her arm around me, "I'll be your buffer."

"We all will," Connie agreed.

"No one will even notice you when I show up in my lace gloves and bustier," Kim said with a straight face. She leaned back and folded her arms across her chest. "Oh, yeah. You heard me."

We all burst out laughing and even our waitress looked back to see what was going on.

It was late, so Connie had to get home to Mike and the girls. As we stood up to collect our things the waitress walked over to the table and put a birch beer down in front of me.

"Are you freaking kidding me with this?"

Only she didn't hear me, because Mr. Pizza Chef was flexing his pecs, making them dance back and forth.

Sawyer and I waved good-bye to Kim and Connie as they walked down the boardwalk to get to their cars. Then she looked at me and said, "I'm worried about you."

Geez, why so serious all of a sudden?

"What? I'm all right." I hated being pitied. If anyone gets to pity me it's going to be me.

"I want you to get some rest while you're up here, okay?"

"Yes, Mom," I replied, hoping to stop Sawyer from fussing over me. "Speaking of moms, have you spoken to Eileen lately?"

"The last I heard she was in India in search of the Dalai Lama, looking for enlightenment."

I raised one eyebrow in question and Sawyer went on.

"She read *Eat, Pray, Love*, and she figured she already spent a lifetime with the *Eat* and *Love* parts, so she may as well give *Pray* a chance."

"That does sound like Eileen. With all the searching she's done to find higher consciousness, you'd think she would be able to hover on thin air by now."

"Just think of all the money she could save on airfare traveling around from Machu Picchu to Osaka with a wiggle of her nose. She could stop eating food and just absorb minerals from the universe." Sawyer opened her arms wide and waved them about like she was floating.

Sawyer. She had been my rock, my spirit-lifter, my best friend, forever. Bless her heart, she'd come through for me again.

We exploded in a fit of giggles as we walked arm in arm down the boardwalk. Only thirty-six more hours and I would be out of South Jersey and on my way back to a Tim-free zone in Virginia.

Chapter 5

Spending the night in my childhood home was causing painful memories of my childhood to surface. My father died when I was four and my mother checked out mentally, so I was shipped off to live with Aunt Ginny. Growing up as a fat kid in a beach town was enough for me to be an after-school special in the making.

I wanted to go to cooking school in Paris at Le Cordon Bleu, but I would settle for the Culinary Institute of America in New York. Tim and I had enrolled together. We had been dating for three years, a lifetime for a teenager or Hollywood celebrity. He asked me to marry him when I was only fifteen, and I said "yes." He was older than me, but he delayed college so we could go to school together. He was going to enter the Culinary Arts program and I would take the Pastry Arts courses. We would get married, have two kids, a five-star restaurant, and a cat named Snicklefritz—Fritz for short. Our plan was set, or so I thought. The only piece I ended up with was the cat, and I should have been more specific about that one.

Grandma Emmy was adamant that I would never make any money as a chef. She didn't think Tim would either.

This was before the days of the Food Network and *Cake Boss*. So she gave me an ultimatum that she would only pay for college if I went to William & Mary in Williamsburg for a practical major promising success and wealth, i.e. Business Management. Looking back, I think Grandma wanted to make sure I could take care of myself and not rely on a man to provide for me. But flow charts and statistics were not the stuff my dreams were made of. I was devastated. I don't know why it didn't occur to me to apply for scholarships or school loans or even work my way through culinary school. The Jersey Shore success bar of life wasn't just set low, it wasn't even in the game. It was being used for drunken limbo on the beach.

I had to get out of New Jersey. I kissed my twenty-year-old fiancé good-bye and set off for Virginia ready to embark on a long distance committed relationship while I earned my degree so I could make a million dollars and retire at forty and take up pastry as a hobby. (We were overly optimistic during the Reagan administration.)

But life has a way of twisting into shapes you couldn't possibly see forming. A wild party, a peach-schnapps-fueled hookup, and the end of my college career and engagement . . . all in a few short hours. Somehow, I never managed to get my life back on course.

When little girls dream of their wedding day, a shotgun is usually not involved. Mine was a very small, quiet wedding. Most of the guests were people neither John nor I knew. I guess his mother figured it would be a good opportunity to schmooze some of her husband's political contacts. Only my grandparents and Aunt Ginny attended on my side. My mother couldn't handle the shame of a pregnant daughter getting married in the backyard so I had Granddaddy walk me down the patch of yellowed grass that doubled as the aisle. John's aunt made a snide comment about the audacity of my wearing white and said that I wasn't fooling anyone as I passed by. All through the ceremony I kept waiting for Tim to rush in like in the movies and shout, "Call off the wedding!" Saying that I couldn't possibly marry someone else because he loved me so much and we were meant to be together. But it never happened. Just a bunch of strangers milking the open bar and my family watching with pity in their eyes.

My wedding day was an embarrassment and it brings me shame every time I think about it. Everyone knew I was pregnant. My cousin Susan made sure of that. I suspect there were some "early deliveries" six months after a couple of my cousins' weddings, but I didn't ask and they weren't talking. John's mother's cover story was that it was a shame I wasn't able to discipline myself to lose some weight before the ceremony.

On my wedding night, I locked myself in the bathroom and cried. When I slipped out to get into bed, I thought I heard John sniffle in his sleep. I thought he must have been as miserable to be married as I was. It was years later that I learned that he had been crying because he heard me sobbing and it broke his heart. How I wish I could take it all back now.

I dropped out of college, having finished only my freshman year, and got a job bagging groceries at the A&P. John was too close to graduating and I insisted he finish school and get his law degree while I worked to pay the rent for our meager studio apartment. Then, in a few years after our child started kindergarten, I would go back to school to get my degree.

Six weeks after the wedding I woke up in the middle of the night in a cold sweat with terrible cramps. John threw the covers back and I screamed when I saw the growing pool of blood. He called 911 but by the time I got to the hospital it was too late. We had lost our baby. I was losing a lot of blood and the doctor couldn't find the source. Somewhere I lost consciousness. When I came to in the recovery room, John was holding my hand and crying. The doctors had to perform an emergency hysterectomy to save my life. I would never have another baby.

We planned to have the marriage annulled. I couldn't even get out of bed in the morning let alone fill out paperwork. John's family kept their distance mercifully. I'm sure they were relieved, but even they weren't the kind of monsters that would wish this on anyone. Grandma Emmy and Aunt Ginny came down to stay with me for a couple of months to help get me back on my feet. Between their love and John's constant strength I managed to not do something stupid to myself.

John asked me to hold off on the annulment until we both recovered from the loss of our baby. He said we had suffered so much trauma already that we should just stay together as friends to support each other. Falling in love with him was easy.

It didn't happen right away. It sort of snuck up on me. It wasn't the powerful take-your-breath-away kind of high school infatuation that I'd experienced with Tim. It was richer. More mature. More appreciative. I started to notice all the kind things John would do for me. Like how he set out my vitamins so I'd remember to take them. And he'd turn on the electric blanket before I'd go to bed so it would be warm for me.

One night I had to fill in for a cashier who called in sick and when I got home John had warmed up leftover macaroni and cheese for me and videotaped a movie that I had wanted to see but would have missed. I kept staring at him across the little oak table in our apartment dining room as the pieces were falling together for me. He asked me what was wrong and said I was making him nervous. I went over to him and took his hand, I looked him in the eyes and asked, "How long have you been in love with me?"

He gave a nervous little laugh. Then cleared his throat and quietly confessed, "Since you landed on me in the quad."

"Why didn't you tell me?"

"You're in love with Tim."

I realized that John had always wanted what was best for me even when it hurt him. How could I not help but fall in love with him? I saw a man who had his heart on his sleeve and I had unknowingly stomped all over it again and again. My heart filled with so much love for him I thought it would burst. "You have stayed by my side and loved me through the darkest hours of my life, and I have fallen completely in love with you, Mr. Browne. It would please me greatly if I could be your wife."

We consummated our marriage after six months, eight days, and nine hours and went from being married friends to being husband and wife.

Our love blossomed and grew for twenty-three years despite our rocky beginning, our families' meddling, our failed attempts at adoption, and our childlessness and now I sit here a widow. I wish I could go back to that day on the quad and start over. To do things different. To love John from the beginning like he deserved.

I woke up with something heavy on my chest. I was vibrating, and something soft reached out and touched me on the nose. I opened my eyes to see two bright gold marbles staring at me without blinking and I detected the faint smell of fish.

"Can I help you?" The purring grew stronger as Figaro figured he was one step closer to getting breakfast. "What time is it?" I yawned.

Mrrrrrow, the reply from Sir Figaro, the ever-hopeful.

The smell of coffee and bacon brought me fully to senses beyond the fur in my face. No one has to wave a slice of sizzling, smoked pig at me twice.

"All right, let's get up."

Figaro jumped down with a soft thud.

"Aunt Ginny is making breakfast. If you're good, maybe she'll let you have a piece of bacon."

Figaro guarded the door while I made the bed and put on my fuzzy yellow bathrobe with the cupcake pocket. Then he followed me to the bathroom to stare at me and flick his tail back and forth in an effort to hurry me up while I washed my face and brushed my teeth.

"Okay, I'm finished. Let's go." I left my room to take the back stairs to the kitchen. Figaro took his usual route under my feet while pausing every few steps to look at me to be sure I was still coming.

"Good morning," Aunt Ginny trilled.

I stared.

Aunt Ginny was wearing a floor-length, aqua-blue evening gown, long white gloves, and a sapphire-and-diamond necklace. And bunny slippers. Her hair was done up in a bun on top of her head and adorned with what looked like—yes, it was a tiara. She was removing the last pieces of bacon from the griddle with a plastic spatula. I didn't know where to begin.

"Wow! Why are you dressed so . . . fancy? Is there a breakfast ball? Do I need to go change?"

Aunt Ginny smiled at me. "Don't be silly. You're dressed fine. Some days I just wake up and want to wear a tiara. It would look silly to wear it in my housecoat."

Oh, of course. Whatever was I thinking?

"Go sit down in the formal dining room."

Ooh la la.

She had set us two places with the Royal Albert Country Roses china. A casserole of something divine sat before our plates. There was a carafe of juice chilling in a silver ice bucket next to a silver coffeepot with cream and sugar service.

Aunt Ginny followed me in with the platter of bacon, Figaro doing a sort of prancy trot at her side, his eyes fixed on the platter.

"You didn't have to go to all this trouble. Really, a bowl of Cheerios would have been fine."

She placed the bacon across from us, pulled out a chair, and sat next to me. Figaro disappeared under the table.

"Hush, child. I wanted to do it. I miss entertaining and making fancy dishes. At my age I've earned the right to do what I want and wear what I want." With that, she gave a nod of finality to the subject and started dishing out the casserole with one gloved hand.

I was not one to argue when syrup was on the line. "That smells delicious. What is it?" I took a couple pieces of bacon from the platter and put them on Aunt Ginny's plate before serving myself.

"Orange Marmalade French Toast," she said proudly. "Layers of croissant with orange marmalade and sweetened cream cheese covered with beaten eggs and cream. You sit it in the refrigerator overnight, then all you have to do in the morning is bake it. It's so easy."

I poured us both coffee and juice. "I can't wait to taste it." I put two sugars and an unhealthy dose of heavy cream into my coffee and stirred. What's a little clogging among friends and arteries? *Mmm, lovely*. Figaro peeked over the tablecloth and I could see the halfway point of his eyes. He was sitting at the table with us in the chair across from Aunt Ginny. I gave his chair a little kick for warning.

Aunt Ginny took my hand, belted out grace like a boss, then turned to me and said, "Well, dig in."

You don't have to tell me twice. I thought I would melt out of my chair as I tasted the first bites of the heavenly French toast. Sweet, flaky, that sweetened cream cheese like cheesecake for breakfast. I froze as I saw a gray paw come up and in a flash snag a piece of bacon off the platter and disappear with it under the table. If Aunt Ginny saw it she didn't let on.

"How is it?" she asked me.

"It's wonderful! You have to give me the recipe so I can make it back home." I could hear lippy-smacky noises coming from Figaro's lair. I tried to cover the sound by slurping my juice. "What is this, Aunt Ginny? I thought it was orange juice, but it tastes like tangerine."

When Aunt Ginny turned her head to look at the carafe of juice, I leaned over and tried to shoo Figaro off the chair. He swatted at me to leave him alone.

"It's a blend of juices including guava, papaya, and tangerine. Isn't it good?" Aunt Ginny took a sip of her coffee.

I shot Figaro a warning glare. "How was pottery spinning last night?"

"My teacher says I'm a natural. My vase only leaks if you put water in it." She was so pleased with herself she was sparkling like her tiara.

"How exciting!"

Aunt Ginny gave me a prim look and a shrug. "How was dinner with Sawyer?"

"She had two of the girls meet us there, and we spent the night catching up like teenagers."

A knock at the door interrupted our morning.

"I'll see who that is."

I opened the front door to a young Latina woman dressed in a gray linen business suit with her hair pulled from her face into a tight ponytail. A pair of dark-rimmed rectangular glasses sat at the end of her nose.

"Can I help you?"

She handed me a familiar business card.

"Hi. I'm Rosalind Carson from the Department of Youth and Family Services, Division on Aging." She cocked one eyebrow at Aunt Ginny, in a *you*-know-*what-I-mean* kind of rude glance. "Are you Mrs. Frankowski's grand-daughter?"

"I'm her niece, Poppy. I was going to call you later today. I have your card."

"I didn't want to take any chances that I would miss you. Your aunt has a way of giving us . . . *conflicting* . . . information, and I wasn't sure you would *really* be here this time. May I come in?"

Her insinuations fell on me like acid rain. I already didn't like this woman.

I looked over to see Aunt Ginny standing in the door-way to the parlor looking very calm and innocent. She had removed the gloves and tiara. I gave her a questioning glance, and she motioned that it was okay with her.

"Sure. Can I get you something to drink?" I led her to the parlor to sit down on the Queen Anne sofa. Aunt Ginny took a seat off to the side on the piano bench.

"No, thank you, I won't be long." She looked over at Aunt Ginny and asked me, "Could we speak alone?"

No, Lizzie Borden, we can't.

"Anything you want to say to me I'm going to tell my aunt anyway, so you may as well say it in front of both of us."

"As you wish," she clipped, and looked down her nose through her glasses. She took a manila folder out of her leather bag and opened it to a stack of yellow copied reports. "I'm here to discuss the situation of your aunt's declining mental state."

Nothing like getting right to the razor-edged point.

"We've had a few calls from concerned citizens that she may be in need of some"—she paused for a moment as if trying to come up with the right wording—"monitoring."

Aunt Ginny rolled her eyes, and I had to hold back a snicker.

"Exactly who are these people who are calling about my aunt and what kind of"—now I paused for a moment to show my irritation—"monitoring do they think my aunt needs?"

"Now, let's not get huffy, Miss . . . ?"

"McAllister," I supplied.

"Miss McAllister. I'm here out of concern for Mrs. Frankowski's welfare. Were you aware that your aunt has been seen wandering around town in the middle of the night?"

"Is walking at night a crime in Cape May now?"

She ignored me and went on. "And her style of dress indicates that she may be losing some of her faculties. We've had reports of her out about town in her pajamas and slippers, and just look at her now. An evening gown at ten a.m. on a Saturday!"

"So what. You can walk one block to the beach and find old guys wearing plaid shorts and black socks with sandals. I don't see you questioning their sensibilities."

"I'm only concerned about your aunt right now." She softened her tone. "Neighbors don't want to see her get hurt. And frankly there have also been several complaints about the condition of the house."

Yikes. Okay, she got me on the house. I was concerned about the same thing. Aunt Ginny was a little eccentric, but I liked to think of her as a free spirit, not a senile old lady in need of being monitored.

Ms. Carson continued. "The county is concerned that your aunt needs to be in an assisted living facility."

I saw Aunt Ginny grab a Hummel figurine off a shelf and prepare to hurl it. I coughed loudly, "Uh-uh!"

Aunt Ginny glared at me and put the figurine back.

"She may need medical attention for," she said, then whispered, "senility."

"There is nothing wrong with my hearing, young lady," Aunt Ginny shot from her perch across the room.

I gave Aunt Ginny a warning look and replied, "Ms. Carson, I have every confidence that my aunt is in full possession of her mental state." *No matter how cuckoo of a state it is.*

Aunt Ginny gave the social worker a smug look of defiance.

"And until it is against the law to take a walk at night or wear evening gowns in the morning I don't think what Aunt Ginny does is any of the county's business. And as to the condition of the house, we were just about to discuss how we were going to fix it up right before you arrived." *At least we are now.* "So don't let a little overgrown shrubbery concern you."

Ms. Carson gathered her briefcase and stood. "I had hoped you would be more cooperative than this. Mrs. Frankowski's case will remain under review. If she had a suitable full-time caregiver, we would consider that sufficient credence to her remaining in the home. Otherwise I must insist she be placed in the Sunset Valley Assisted Living Facility for her own safety."

Aunt Ginny shot to her feet, her fists balled at her sides. "Why, you little . . . !"

I cut her off, quickly stepping between her and Ms.

Carson. "There is no way I'm going to let that happen. I think you should leave now." I gestured to the door.

"We'll be in touch." She adjusted her glasses and headed for the door. She turned and looked back at me. "It's for the best, Miss McAllister." And with that she marched out the door to her waiting Prius.

Aunt Ginny slammed the front door and spat. "This is war, she-devil!" But then her bravado left her and she wobbled on weak knees.

I ushered her to the parlor couch Ms. Carson had just vacated.

"Why didn't you tell me you were having problems with Social Services?" I gently prodded.

"It's just so foolish!"

Figaro came over to Aunt Ginny and jumped up into her lap. She started petting him absently.

"I took a couple of walks in the middle of the night when I couldn't sleep. It's not like it's pitch-black out with all the street lights blazing. So I walked down to the beach to sit a while. What's the big deal? And I've seen young people shopping at Walmart in their pajamas. Why is it a capital crime when I go out in mine?"

"Were you having trouble sleeping because you missed Grandma Emmy?" I knew a little something about grief and would have made many a midnight walk on the beach myself if I wasn't two hundred miles away from one.

She didn't look up at me, but she nodded. "I've never been alone before." She said it so quiet I almost didn't hear her. "And I figured I'm getting old so I may as well make the most of the time I have left. So I decided convention be darned. I'm gonna dress however I please and I'm gonna do what I want when I want. At my age I've earned the right to do it and I'm not gonna stop now because the enemy doesn't approve!" A familiar spark of rebellion burned in her eyes.

I agreed and was even madder at Social Services for trying to constrain Aunt Ginny. "Aunt Ginny, we're going to get through this. I think we should call your lawyer and set up an appointment."

Preferably something for tomorrow morning. I have a six o'clock ferry to catch and I want to be on it like it's the last chopper out of Vietnam.

"That's a good idea. We need reinforcements. I'll get his number and make the call this morning."

Wanting to be very delicate with the next topic, I approached it gingerly. "I am a bit concerned about the house, however."

Aunt Ginny blushed, so I knew she knew what I was talking about. "What has been going on exactly?"

She waved me off. "I don't want to concern you about that. You have enough to worry about."

Like my schedule is so full. I'm sure Paula Deen can deep-fry butter on her own without my involvement.

"You are my concern. I want to help wherever I can." I put my hand over hers and her eyes misted up.

"The house may need a little work. But I don't have the know-how to do it myself and there isn't the money to hire someone. When Emmy was alive we had two pensions and two Social Security checks. With her gone it's just me, and the property taxes take up most of the money. I have my butter and egg money for bingo and country line dancing, but that isn't enough to put a new roof on."

Images of Aunt Ginny in cowboy boots shaking it to honky-tonk-ba-donk-adonk flooded my mind, and I had to shut it down fast. I wasn't ready to wrap my head around that just yet.

"Why don't I pay to fix the roof and get a few other

things repaired? John left me a sizeable life insurance policy."

"NO, NO, *NO*! Absolutely not! Besides, Georgina would kill you if you touch a penny of that for me. That is money for you to live on. Not for you to fix up this old house so a silly fool can stay here. One day this house will be yours and you can do with it what you want."

"Well, that silly fool stuff is just crazy talk." She gave me a shocked look, and I said, "What? Too soon?"

She swatted my arm and said, "You little brat!" I felt better now that she was acting more like her usual self and the color was coming back into her cheeks.

"Have you considered getting a new roommate?" That seemed like a reasonable idea to me. Maybe another old lady could fill the void that Grandma Emmy left and we could take care of the loneliness and the financial issues at the same time.

"Meh. Too many people irritate me."

All right, now that was definitely the Aunt Ginny I knew.

"Let's start with calling the lawyer and take it from there."

She agreed and looked down at Figaro. "What are you doing in my lap?! Boy, I have dishes to do."

Figaro jumped down and turned his back to us. That's cat talk for passive-aggressive.

We cleared the table from breakfast and I surreptitiously searched the floor for bacon bits.

"I think he ate it all," Aunt Ginny said, as she carried the dirty dishes into the kitchen.

I glared at Figaro and pointed my finger at him in warning. He responded with a bored yawn and left the room in search of a sunbeam.

Chapter 6

The moment had finally arrived that I couldn't delay any longer. It was time to try on my dress for the class reunion from hell. I pulled out the *not-so*-little black dress I bought months ago for the funeral and stepped into it. I tried to wiggle it up over my butt, but it was fighting back. How much shrinkage can we blame on the cleaners? No amount of wriggling would get it past my hips. Not even a generous application of PAM would ever get me zipped up, and there was no way I would be able to sit down and breathe, too.

I tugged off the satin-blend tourniquet and sat on the end of the bed and did the reasonable, adult thing.

I panicked.

The reunion was tonight and either I was swelled up from the salt air—doubtful—or I put on a considerable amount of weight since John died and didn't notice. Painful but most likely. Either way I would have to cry about it later because . . . I. Had. To. Go. Shopping.

Aunt Ginny was in the sunroom watching Courtroom TV and taking various notes on a steno pad. Figaro was sitting on top of the TV swatting at the judge whenever she appeared on the screen. "I'm trying to get some pointers before I have to go to court," she explained when she saw me standing there, bewildered.

"By watching *Judge Judy*?" I asked. "I'm not sure that's the same thing."

"I'm going to study *Matlock* and *Law & Order*, too." She was pretty sure of this plan of action, and I didn't want to disappoint her by introducing too much reality. It was good to keep her busy, so she didn't worry too much. Besides, I could only tackle one crisis at a time.

"I have to go out and buy a dress for tonight. Do you need anything while I'm out?"

"No, I think we have everything we need. Move your tail, Figaro! I can't see the defendant!" Figaro flicked his tail up out of the way apologetically.

I shook my head at the two of them and said, "Well, I'll leave you to it then. Be back soon."

What else could possibly depress me today?

As I was walking out the door I heard, "Get your hair done while you're out. It's all frizzy."

Oh, good. So there's that.

I parked the car at Sawyer's bookstore on the Washington Street Mall. Some things had changed over the years. The Victorian Outpost was now a Dairy Queen and Garrity's Newsstand was now Ye Olde Christmas Shoppe. But some things remained the same. Like the Fudge Kitchen. Since fudge was partly to blame for the current state I was in, I passed up their very tiny free samples and walked the block down to the Chic Boutique dress shop.

I stopped at the door and recited, "Yea, though I walk through the valley of the shadow of death I shall fear no

size tens . . . or twelves . . . or . . . fourteens . . . or . . ."
Okay, I needed to stop.

"Can I help you?" The perky size-two saleslady eyed
me, sounding like she hoped I was lost.

Yes. I need something in size round. Okay, I didn't
really say that. "I'm looking for a simple dress to wear to
a reunion." *Preferably one that comes with an invisibility
cloak.*

"What size?" she asked while looking me up and down.
I felt like the last-place heifer up on the auction block.

"I'm not really sure. If you'll show me a selection I'll
try a couple on."

She took me to the back of the store to where the
"plus-size" rack was being punished in the corner. The
options in my size range were slim pickings. Ironic.

I tugged on every single horrifying dress and not one
of them fit. They were hateful little sausage casings. Since
when were these numbers considered plus-sizes? I peeled
the last one off and wiped the tears out of my eyes. I hung
it back on the hanger and glared at it hatefully. I'd just
have to tell Sawyer I was not going after all.

"Um, I like, found this in the back of the overstock. It's
been here for a while. It must have been a special order
because we don't normally sell styles like this . . . but you
can try it on if you want to."

I looked at the dress and then at the salesgirl. She gave
me a sheepish smile, and I took the hanger from her. I
looked at myself holding up the dress in the mirror. The
question you've gotta ask yourself is "just how desperate
are you?"

Apparently, desperate enough. A lump caught in my
throat as I tugged it on and had to suck in my stomach to
get the zipper up. I did my best to avoid looking into the
mirror until the last possible second.

Nope. No way. It looks like something out of a Drag Queen Bridesmaid catalog.

I came out of the dressing room to look in the mirror under the lights. A size seven browsing a rack of skirts jumped at the sight of me, then apologized to a mannequin.

Someone had a lot of nerve making a dress this hideous. What sadist put these colors together? Then there was the belt: a black, rubbery-looking corset that might as well have been stamped with *Uniroyal*. With a buckle that would have made the Pilgrims proud.

"Oh, good, it fits." The saleslady tried to hide her disgust.

Well, good Lord. Don't act so shocked. It's not like Ringling Brothers made the dress. I wriggled out of it and checked the tag.

I looked again at the number and my heart sank. I'd gone up two dress sizes in six months. *Think about Sawyer. It's only one night, then I'm outta here.* "I'll take it."

The saleslady held up the dress at arm's length and gave it a barely concealed look of distaste before she rang it up and put it in the bag.

"You won't . . . uh . . . tell anyone you bought this *here*, will you?"

If I didn't have an event to get to, I would have told her to shove it and walked out. Instead I swallowed my pride, accepted the humiliation, and paid for the dress.

I was completely bereft of motivation and just wanted to go back to bed for the next forty-eight hours. Or years. I checked my cell phone for the time. The *Titanic* of all shopping expeditions had eaten up all my time to get my hair done. I would just have to make the best of the bird's nest. What I really needed now was a cappuccino.

And right across the street like a homing beacon sat La Dolce Vita Espresso. The universe was trying to apologize for the dress.

The smell of fresh-roasted beans met me as I opened the door and I floated into the room. There were a few highly polished wood tables and chairs in the color of espresso beans set up in the front of the shop, giving it a warm toasty feel. A pair of modern, caramel-colored leather chairs dominated the corner opposite the door, and a tall, polished wooden table with leather-topped barstools the color of cappuccino foam faced the front window so you could drink your latte while watching the kids playing in the fountain.

Note to self: Avoid the window.

Behind a polished granite-topped walnut counter a chalkboard listed the repertoire of caffeinated delights. A row of cappuccino foam barstools were lined up at the counter.

A beautiful man with piercing blue eyes and olive skin came out of the back room, drying his hands on a dish-towel. He was wearing a blue-and-white-striped dress shirt with the cuffs rolled up to the elbows, and black dress slacks, which were mostly covered by the crisp white apron tied around his waist. His dark hair curled at the collar and his temples were just starting to gray. A couple days' growth of black stubble tinged with gray covered his square jaw.

I think my eyes popped out of my head for a second, and I was horrified that he might have noticed.

"*Buongiorno.*"

The deep masculine voice poured over me like warm honey and I felt myself blush at the absurdity of the reaction at my age.

"Hi." *Did I just say that kind of dreamy? It sounded kind of dreamy to me. Pull yourself together, Poppy.* I cleared my throat.

"What can I get for you?" His broad smile made wrinkles appear around the outer corners of his eyes.

I was trying not to stare. No, that's not true. I was trying not to gawk like a slack-jawed yokel.

"Just a cappuccino, please."

"*Solo* or *doppio*?" he asked, flashing a smile that was all pure-white teeth. Darn it.

"Mmm-hmm. Oh uh, *doppio*. Please." *I gotta get out of here before I make a total fool of myself.*

"Are you on vacation?" He expertly tamped down the grinds in the portafilter and poured the shot into a warmed cappuccino cup.

"Sort of. Just visiting some high school friends." I was not going to mention I was here for a reunion for fear that he would ask which year. And oh my God, had I brushed my hair before I left the house? My eyes rolled up to the mirror behind the bar to assess the damage. I looked like I had rumbled in on a Harley. Or possibly under one.

The brief moment of attraction brought the image of the size on the dress tag flashing before my eyes, and I was ashamed all over again. Tears filled my eyes, and I tried to blink them away before he noticed.

He poured the foamed milk into the espresso with his strong olive-toned hands, jiggled the cup until a heart formed, and handed it to me. His smile vanished when he saw a fat tear roll down my cheek.

"What's the matter, *bella*? Why are you crying?"

"It's . . . nothing." I tried to laugh it away. "Just a little post-traumatic shopping disorder."

He saw the shopping bag in my hand and smiled warmly. "What did you buy?"

"The most horrifying dress in the world."

"It can't be that bad," he sympathized.

"It's a war crime in a bag. I'll look horrible."

"I don't believe that you could ever look horrible. Let me see."

I felt myself blush at his compliment and before common sense could smack me in the head I pulled out the dress and showed him.

"That is . . . No, you are right that *is* horrible." He laughed. "But you will be beautiful anyway."

Gulp. What is happening right now?

"Besides, the sexiest thing a woman can wear is confidence."

That's it, I'm not going. "Thank you. You're very kind." I smiled weakly and put the dress back in the bag.

"I am Giampaolo." He put out his hand for me to shake. "But you can call me Gia."

"Poppy. Nice to see you. I mean to *meet* you." *Oh, Lord, why am I so nervous? He's just being friendly. His hand is so strong and warm. Why am I still holding it?* I quickly let go.

"You will wear your beautiful smile and have a wonderful time at your party tonight. Tomorrow you come back and tell me everything."

I started to giggle and cleared my throat. "Thank you," I said meekly, and started to pay him.

He refused the money. "No. This one is for luck." He winked and smiled that honey smile again and my heart flipped over. I felt like a fool.

On my way back to the car I only stopped for one fudge sample—okay, it was four, but they were really tiny and it had been an unsettling day. It was only out of politeness that I felt compelled to buy a pound of fudge. I mean you can't just have four samples and not *buy* anything.

That would be rude. It was for Aunt Ginny anyway. She loved fudge.

Two hours and a half pound of fudge later I had show-ered and conditioned then blown my hair smooth and wound it up into a neat chignon at the base of my neck. I secured it with a Swarovski crystal hair clip that John had bought me a couple of Christmases past.

I poured myself into the canary yellow satin bustier, at-tached the matching toile crinoline, and pulled on the Mary Kay–pink ruffled skirt. Opening one eye I glanced at the full-length mirror to assess the damage. I looked like a giant pink-and-yellow wedding cake disaster. Des-perate, I fluffed the yellow-ostrich-feather puffed sleeves as if that would somehow help me look less like a de-ranged chicken. It didn't. I decided to forgo the belt and save it for Halloween. Didn't want to be too flashy. I sighed deeply and applied some pink lip gloss, as if that would magically tie the whole outfit together. "What do you think, Fig?"

Figaro gave me a yawn of support and swatted at a feather fragment floating to the floor. "It's the best I could do with what I have."

I sensed that Figaro was underwhelmed. *You and me both, buddy.*

I checked the time on my phone and noticed I had a text from Georgina reminding me that her gala was coming up and I still had time to lose ten pounds. *How nice.*

The doorbell rang, signaling that Sawyer had arrived to pick me up. My stomach lurched, and I considered lock-ing myself in the bathroom. On the list of things I never wanted to do in my life, going to my high school reunion fat, frumpy, and a failure was number two. Number one was running into my ex-fiancé whom I hadn't seen face-to-face since I told him I'd be faithful to him in college. Tonight I was about to do both. In ostrich feathers.

"Poppy," Aunt Ginny called me from the bottom of the steps. "Sawyer is here."

Deep breath. Just get it over with. Do it for Sawyer. I grabbed the silver clutch I used for formal occasions that held just the necessities, and descended the stairs. Sawyer was drop-dead gorgeous in a flirty little red cocktail dress. The form-fitting bodice showed off her tiny waist and perfect little curves, and the flouncy taffeta skirt made her legs look a mile long. Her chestnut hair was long and flowing and so shiny that I immediately regretted the fudge decision.

"What the . . ." Aunt Ginny stared dumbstruck at the sight of all my feathery glory.

"Oh, Poppy, wow! Look at that dress." Sawyer smiled up at me like I was Cinderella at the ball instead of runner-up for Miss Roadkill.

"Yes, just look at it," Aunt Ginny muttered to herself.

"Aw, this old thing? I made it outta the curtains this afta-noon."

Sawyer giggled. "Why, Miss Scarlett, I do declare."

"Your dress is fantastic," I told Sawyer. "Kurt's going to eat his heart out."

"I sure hope he does." She smoothed her shaky hands over her flat stomach. "I really want him to see what he's missing."

"I'm sure he knows that, dear," Aunt Ginny said, giving Sawyer a sympathetic smile. "You girls will be the belles of the ball." Then added under her breath, "Or the talk of the town." She gave another look at my dress and shuddered. "I need a drink."

We both hugged Aunt Ginny good-bye and I told her, "I'm sure it will be terribly boring and I'll be back early. I hope Figaro behaves." Of course, that would be a first.

"Don't worry. I've got my flyswatter if he acts up." Aunt Ginny made a fist at Figaro, who promptly flopped over on his side with a thud.

Chapter 7

The air hung thick like a wet wool blanket and the windows on the Corolla had a salty sticky coating so that I had to run the wipers over them before we could get going. The wind was picking up and dark clouds were beginning to form as Hurricane Mavis was making her way up the coast from North Carolina.

"Whoo, it's windy! I hope I used enough hair spray tonight." Sawyer ducked into the passenger seat and quickly shut the door. "Remember when we used to tease our hair up into a pouf and shellac it with Freeze 'n Shine?"

I checked my hair in the rearview mirror and saw it was already starting to frizz. "Oh yeah. I was six inches taller in the eighties."

"Blue eye shadow and purple lipstick. Those were the days." We reminisced all the way to the high school, both of us trying to tamp down our growing anxiety.

They say when you revisit your childhood, everything looks much smaller than you remember it. That was not my experience when I walked into the main doors by the office and what used to be the auditorium of Caper High.

The school had doubled in size since I had been there, *as had I.*

Someone I didn't recognize, sporting a yoga body and poured into a size-negative wrap dress, breezed past with a relaxed air of confidence.

My feathers fluttered. I considered throwing up but decided against it in case I decided to return those shoes and didn't want to chance any splattering.

The halls were decked out with posters and streamers welcoming the class of 1989 and the smell of floor varnish hung in the air welcoming students back from a long summer of lying on the beach forgetting everything they had learned.

There was a mural of the Caper Tiger mascot in the main foyer by the office and a long wooden table covered with peel-and-stick labels filled out with the names of everyone who had registered for the event. I noticed the "Barbie Pomeroy—Prom Queen" badge was still unclaimed.

Special program cards welcomed us to the reunion and listed several events scheduled in the east wing of A hallway.

The large gymnasium was set up for "cocktails and dancing." A disco ball had been hung from the ceiling and a DJ was blaring Van Halen's "Jump" over the loudspeakers. The smell of basketball leather and sweat clung to everything. A makeshift stage took up the far side wall and the cash bar in the corner was in full swing. Not the first time liquor had been brought into this room and not the last, I'm sure.

"It looks like Missy tried to re-create Prom Night," Sawyer said as she deftly applied her name badge to her dress while I tried to get my stick-on "Poppy McAllister" to lie flat on my rather ample chest without catching the feathers.

"Well, then a lot of people will get smashed and a couple will be pregnant before the night is over."

Sawyer scanned the gym trying to spot Kurt while trying her best to look like she was not trying to spot Kurt. "I'll go get us some drinks."

While she headed to the bar, I tried to disappear into the balloon arch when Carl Ostenheimer stumbled into me. "Hey," he slurred. "I know you. You were in my Ocean Ecology class fifth period."

"No. I wasn't Carl."

"Yesh, you were. You were blond then."

"Nope. Not me."

"Yesh, it wassh you. You sat in front of me and smelled like peaches." He took a clumsy swig of whatever concoction he was drinking and dribbled some of it unattractively onto his clip-on tie.

"Again, Carl, not me."

"Sshure it was you. I remember."

People were starting to stare. "You're mistaken, Carl. You got the wrong girl." I tried to slip away, but he grabbed me by my elbow.

"How're you so sshure?"

I removed his hand from my arm, looked him straight in his bloodshot eyes, and said, "Because I have never been blond, I have never taken ocean ecology, and we were in homeroom together."

He stared at me in confusion, then looked past me and stumbled off pointing a crooked finger at Bernadette Rogers, saying, "Heyy! I know you!"

Sawyer showed up with two ginger ales. "What did Creepy Carl want?"

"Someone to annoy." I sipped my drink and looked

around the roomful of strangers staring back at me in all my resplendent glory. I should have brought a yearbook so Sawyer and I could match up the befores and afters.

A pretty brunette with a purple streak in her hair approached us wearing a tight little red dress and four-inch leopard heels.

"Hey, girls."

I didn't have a clue who she was but Sawyer recognized her instantly. "Hi, Maryellen. You remember Poppy McAllister, don't you?"

Maryellen squinted at me and gave an unconvincing "sure I do." Then she followed up with, "Do you want to see some pictures of my grandkids?"

I blinked. Sawyer recovered faster.

"Ah . . . sure we do."

Maryellen showed us several shots of fat grandbabies on her cell phone before she saw someone she liked better and headed over to talk with them.

I gave Sawyer a pitiful look. "Now I feel really old."

"I know. I don't even have kids yet and she has grandkids."

"Yeah, but she started that brood her senior year of high school."

"True. Did you see Pete Ferguson?" Sawyer pointed to the former football wide receiver. "Fat and bald. Manages an auto parts shop now."

I was feeling better now, knowing I wasn't the biggest loser in the room. No one else had on a Big Bird suit, but they were below average in their own way.

"Oh, wow. So that's what a high school quarterback looks like in his forties."

"And over there." I followed her gaze to a very tan, very buxom blonde wrapped in a tight leopard-print halter dress. Her wrists dripping with gold bangle bracelets. "That's Mrs. Wilcott from second period History."

"What! No way. Mrs. Wilcott who's married to Coach Wilcott, the gym teacher?" I looked closer. The older woman had obviously had some work done, but this transformation would take a magic wand. "She looks twenty years younger today than she did twenty-five years ago. Mrs. Wilcott had mousy brown hair, glasses, and a lot less on top and a lot more down low."

I giggled. Okay, it was more a snort than a giggle. Maybe this was going to be fun after all.

"Uh-huh." Sawyer held up one hand and counted off, "Face lift, extensions, contacts, boob job, Zumba and um, Enrique Rojas the new Spanish teacher."

We both turned to see Coach Wilcott, the bald PE teacher and basketball coach with the beer belly standing in the corner with a plate piled high from the buffet in the cafeteria. He was dressed in gray sweats and sneakers with a whistle hanging around his neck. We looked back at the former Mrs. Wilcott and the gorgeous Latin man who looked more like a flamenco dance instructor than a high school Spanish teacher, then at each other and in unison said, "Enrique."

I spotted a very familiar-looking woman sitting at the bar in a slinky white satin sleeve of a dress. "I'm sure I know her but I can't recall her name."

Sawyer followed my gaze. "She looks just like that guy Kim dated." Then Sawyer called over to her. "Hi. By any chance are you Bruce Cole's sister?"

The woman put her drink down and replied in a husky voice, "No, I'm Bruce Cole."

Sawyer sucked in her breath, then hiccupped. "Oh-kay. Well, have fun tonight." We tried to control our giggles as we moved to the other side of the room.

I pointed to a well-dressed, handsome man with a beautiful blonde on his arm. "Who is that?"

"You won't believe me." Sawyer's eyes had a mischievous gleam.

"Who?"

We both turned to look as she whispered, "Jeffrey Rosenblatt."

"What?" I looked closer at the confident, successful man again. "Are you serious?"

"Oh, yeah." She nodded. "From AV Club Treasurer to owner of a multimillion-dollar tech firm in New England."

"Good for him." Jeffrey had spent as much time stuffed in his locker by the jocks as he did in class, so to see him so successful made me happy.

A voice like fingernails on a blackboard came from behind us. "Well, who do we have here? The lesbos have arrived." I felt a shiver of revulsion run up the back of my neck as a familiar taunting voice cackled with cheap beer and condescension.

Sawyer visibly tensed and turned pale as we both recognized the sneering unpleasantness of Joanne Junk, the prime toady of the Terrible Two. Sawyer and I secretly started calling Joanne Buffalo Gal after watching *It's a Wonderful Life* during Christmas break at Sawyer's dad's house our sophomore year. It just seemed to fit.

"And what the heck are you wearing, McAllister?"

We turned to look at the butch, former field hockey captain in her blue-jean pantsuit and were surprised to see Legally Blonde, Miss Amber Fenton herself, standing next to her.

"Cut it out, Joanne. That's juvenile." Amber took a sip of her Diet Coke and wouldn't look me or Sawyer in the eye. Amber hadn't changed since high school. Still tiny.

Still blond. Still gorgeous. Dressed tonight in a beautiful one-shoulder sea foam green minidress and silver sandals to show off her perfect little tan legs.

"Oh, relax," Joanne sneered. "I'm just helping them come out of the closet."

All through high school, Joanne thought it was hilarious to pass around that Sawyer and I were lesbians. It never made any sense since I had a boyfriend and Sawyer had a few attempts at a boyfriend, but people still laughed so she kept at it. No originality, this one.

I held my ground for Sawyer's sake. This was why I was here, after all. To back her up from the Queens of Mean, Amber Fenton and Barbie Pomeroy and their whole posse of little mean girls.

"You've had twenty-five years to come up with something original. Is that the best you can do?"

I heard a snort of appreciation from Sawyer behind me. Amber sighed as if she was already bored and had more fabulous things to do with her time.

"You got fat!" Joanne turned her piggy little eyes on me with the only attack she could come up with.

A typical schoolyard maneuver—playing the fat card.

"Or should I say fatter?"

Sawyer pushed past me and poked Joanne in the chest. "What is your problem, Joanne? Have you looked in the mirror lately?"

Why is it that bullies don't seem to understand hypocrisy? Joanne easily outweighed me by forty pounds and always had. I was pudgy as a teenager. She was pudgier. It didn't stop her from calling me Fatty. And it didn't stop me from being ashamed about it.

Sawyer went on, "Poppy is as beautiful inside and out as you are ugly through and through."

"Now, see"—Joanne shifted her weight and took a slug

of her beer—"that's why I know you two are lesbians. It's stuff like that."

At this point Amber said, "This is lame. I'm not doing this now, Jo." She turned and walked away into the crowd of middle-aged soccer moms dancing to Def Leppard's "Pour Some Sugar on Me."

All the confidence I'd been gaining by seeing I was not the only one past their freshness date in the room took control. "How *sad*."

"What?" Joanne sneered.

"*You.* You're a big sack of pathetic. After all these years you still have to be nasty to feel good about yourself."

Joanne made a face like someone was holding a dead fish under her nose and with lack of a clever comeback trotted off in search of her queen. "Amber, wait up."

"Heyy, I know youuu." He was back.

"Not now, Carl." I held up my hand and he veered off to the right.

"Well, sadly Buffalo Gal hasn't changed any." Sawyer twisted a strand of her hair around her finger while scanning the room once more. "What do you think Amber meant by 'I'm not doing this *now*, Jo'?"

I looked over to where Amber stood nursing her drink. She wore a bored expression while Joanne was poking a pudgy finger at an uncomfortable-looking Courtney Westbrae whom she had cornered over by the DJ. "Maybe she's waiting for Barbie and the big meeting. You know how they feed off of each other."

"Are you hungry? I could go to the buffet for us?"

How about instead you punch me in the face and we call it a night? If there is one thing I've never been comfortable doing in front of other people, it's eating. Spending my whole life as a pudgy kid I've always felt that every bite was being scrutinized. Every cookie was judged harshly, and I always came out looking like a glutton no matter how much or how little passed my lips. The only acceptable meals to be seen eating as a fat kid are celery sticks and SlimFast shakes. "I don't think I could eat anything knowing Tim could be close by."

"I'm keeping my eyes open for him."

I doubted Sawyer would notice Tim if he walked up and planted one full on her lips right now. She was pretty obsessed with spotting Kurt.

"I'm sure he'll be stuck in the cafeteria working the buffet anyway," she said absently.

A woman's angry whispers floated around the corner. "Just don't embarrass me tonight! I have to look good in front of these people. They idolize me."

They were met with a man's terse reply. "Look, you do you and I'll do me, like always, okay."

"I'm under a lot of pressure here. Everything has to go according to plan. Oh God, I need another drink."

The whispers were followed by none other than the Queen "B" herself, Barbie, who shoved past us without so much as a how-do-ya-do. A sharp-dressed man following behind.

I watched them disappear over by the open bar. "Well, that was awkward."

"There's Kim and Connie!" Sawyer spotted the girls across the room at the bar and waved. They saw us and broke into big smiles and headed toward us. "I can't believe she went through with it."

Kim was wearing a vintage white bustier, and a puffy white lace skirt and fishnet stockings. She had on a six-inch crucifix, long white lace fingerless gloves, and a big white bow Madonna-style in her naturally curly, dirty-blond hair.

"Kim is crazy. Of course she went through with it. I would love just half of her boldness."

"Hi! You made it!" First Kim enveloped me in a hug and then Connie. "We're so glad you're here. You both look gorgeous. Cool dress, Poppy. You're wearing it ironically, right?"

"Sure. Let's go with that."

"Kim, your outfit is awesome. I love the rubber bracelets." Sawyer was unabashedly gawking at the retro ensemble and Kim gave us all a twirl.

I felt the stares from around the room raking over my ruffles and feathers and I didn't like it at all. What was I doing here?

People crowded into the gym, clumping for group shots to upload on Facebook. The geriatric air conditioner was fighting a death match to keep up with the oppressive humidity outside. I felt a trickle of sweat run down the center of my back. Spanx had been a bad idea. All they did was push the fat around so it popped out in different places like a tube of biscuit dough, and I couldn't breathe. I tucked some side boob back into where it had popped out. There may as well have been a spotlight shining on me announcing to everyone *"this one has escaped from Jenny Craig!"*

Judging from the rumbling of the aluminum gym roof, the wind was really whipping up. I checked my watch to see how soon I could leave and go home.

We'd been here nineteen minutes.

"Can I have your attention, please?" We all turned to see a perky brunette on the little makeshift stage by the DJ holding a microphone. She was decked out in a full-length blue evening gown complete with formal white gloves and a diamond choker around her neck.

"My God, is that Missy Sparks? She hasn't aged a day

since graduation." I couldn't believe my eyes. Most of the people in the room had aged. Many had gained weight, some had lost it. Some were prematurely gray or bald. Most of the beautiful people were still beautiful thanks to 24 Hour Fitness and good DNA. But Missy looked exactly the same.

"She's still rocking that spiral perm after twenty-five years too."

"I just want to welcome everyone to the twenty-fifth reunion of the Class of 1989!" There was a round of applause, then Missy went on. "I know for me high school was the best time with the best friends of my life. Football games, pep rallies, hanging out with friends at Piro's Pizza. We were a close family at Caper High."

"What high school did she go to?" Kim whispered under her breath just loud enough for us to hear.

"I don't know what she's talking about," Connie joined in. "All I did after school was homework and chores."

Missy was out of touch with reality if she thought everyone had four years of *Ferris Bueller's Day Off.*

"We have some totally awesome events planned for tonight, including a special number from the cheerleaders. And later this evening we have a special tribute to someone who made our four years here totally rad. But first I thought we would all love reliving one of the highlights from our days here at Caper High. Our senior prom."

You could hear a collective groan throughout the crowd. Apparently, we weren't the only ones who remembered high school a bit differently than the jocks and cheerleaders.

"So," Missy gushed, "without further ado I want to bring up the Caper High Royal Court of 1989."

"Oh, brother. She's really carrying this prom theme all the way," Sawyer said.

"First, the Royal Court. Kelly Scarlito and Troy Bass."

They made their way out of the crowd to applause and took the stage. "Kristen Campbell Miller and Jerry Neal."

Kristen Campbell was poured into a stretchy aqua cocktail dress sporting about a ten-month baby bulge as she took the stage with her counterpart. I couldn't help but wonder what it must be like to carry a baby so late in life. As badly as I wanted children I couldn't imagine doing it in my forties.

"She looks like she belongs on the cover of *Maternity Vogue*," Connie said. "That is not what I looked like when I was pregnant. I think I wore a tablecloth for my third trimester."

"This is 2014," Kim laughed, "Baby bumps are a fashion statement now."

"She's the school nurse now," Sawyer whispered. "I wonder if she loses any credibility giving the safe sex talk."

"Amber Fenton and Pete Ferguson." Some of the guys in the crowd started making juvenile calls from their football days. "Fergie! Fergie! Don't drop that ball, butterfingers!"

"Then there's me, Miss Congeniality, Missy Sparks Edwards."

"Omigod," Kim said in her Valley girl voice.

Missy did something akin to a curtsy. "And Mr. Nice Guy, Paul Osborne."

Paul flounced up on the stage dressed in a very snug Marc Jacobs floral print suit and gave a big smile and waved to everyone.

"This explains his love of show tunes and Marilyn Monroe in high school," Sawyer giggled.

"Finally, your king and queen, Barbie Pomeroy and Billy Sommers."

The lights flickered for a moment and in the distance there was a crack of thunder. A beautiful blonde took the stage. Barbie was wearing a strapless silver sequined cocktail dress with a slit up to the top of her thigh. From her ears dangled teardrop diamonds that could have come off a dining room chandelier. She wore bright red lipstick and a look of derision that could derail a train.

"Speech! Speech!"

I looked around the room to see where the call was coming from. "Who in the world? Oh. It's Joanne."

Sawyer glanced over and rolled her eyes. "That figures."

Joanne caught my eye and made an obscene gesture unfit for a trucker.

Barbie gulped down the remains of what appeared to be a margarita, judging from the salt rim, snatched the microphone—much to Missy's surprise—and took over the proceedings. "Heyy, what's up, Caper High? Can you believe it's been twenty-five years? Some of us have improved with age." Barbie struck a seductive pose meant to optimize her new and improved cleavage. "I'm sure the rest of you did the best you could with what you had to work with. Good for you." She wrinkled up her nose and gave a patronizing smile directed at Kelly Scarlito.

If looks could kill, Kelly had just stabbed Barbie about twenty-six times.

"What's the matter, Billy? Don't want to join me on-stage for old times' sake?" Barbie gave Billy a pouty look and tried to get the crowd involved in pressuring him onstage.

"I think I'm gonna be sick." Kim said it but we were all thinking it.

Billy and Barbie was the closest thing we had to a power couple in high school. He was the all-American quarterback; she was head cheerleader. They were the quintessential high school sweethearts. They always wore matching outfits whether Billy wanted to or not. Voted most likely to settle down and have two point five kids and a fabulous life in suburbia. We all wanted to be them or at least be close enough to them that some of their popularity might rub off on us. When we graduated and moved on with our lives, they didn't move on together. Billy was attending the reunion with a gorgeous brunette on his arm and the sparkly engagement ring said she was there to stay.

"You enjoy the spotlight, Barb. I'll stay here with my fiancée." Billy gave a halfhearted smile up to Barbie and pulled the brunette a little closer. His good looks had only improved with age, and he was especially handsome in his slick Hugo Boss suit.

"Come on, Billy. Don't be a spoilsport. You know I only bite if you like it. But then we both know that you really, really like it, don't we?" Barbie gave a flirtatious wink and some of the former jocks broke into howls of half-loaded delight.

Missy made a lunge for the microphone but missed.

Kim and Connie were transfixed by the stage while eating trail mix out of Connie's purse. Sawyer had her iPhone out filming the catfight. "This is better than an episode of *Scandal*."

Billy wrapped a protective arm around his fiancée's shoulders when a pink flush rose up to her face.

"I see you've been hitting the open bar. What a surprise. Now I'm going show the love of my life our old make-out spot. You know the one. I caught you there with Randy Archer after homecoming."

Barbie's eyes narrowed in a menacing get-even kind of way that we'd all seen before. We'd seen it right before

Ken Turnblad came down with food poisoning the day after he didn't pick Barbie first for volleyball. Then again right before Terri Kerns had that fluke accident during a basket toss and broke her arm right after she was seen flirting with Billy. She had to sit out from cheerleading for the rest of football season.

"Uh-oh. Dead man walking," Connie said between bites.

Billy turned to lead the brunette out of the gym, but Barbie refused to be ridiculed.

"Oh, go ahead, since you're probably paying by the hour!" she said, bringing a roar from the jocks.

"Did she just imply that his fiancée is a hooker?" Connie asked incredulously.

"I believe she did," Sawyer answered in shock for us all.

"His poor fiancée." Sawyer angled her cell phone back to Barbie. There were a few uncomfortable murmurs in the crowd but Barbie kept right on strutting around on-stage. Joanne guffawed somewhere off to our right saying, "Good one, Barb." I overheard phrases like "low-class" and "so rude" from the crowd of former classmates, but I wasn't sure if they meant Barbie or Billy.

Billy stopped and turned back to the stage. "I thought you'd gone to charm school, Barb. Hope they refunded your money."

The crowd broke out into a chorus of *ooooohs*. Billy and his fiancée left the gym, leaving Barbie dumbstruck at center stage.

Missy made another lunge for the microphone but Barbie saw her coming and sidestepped her. Missy crashed into Kristen, who fell backward into Jerry. Jerry tried to save Kristen from falling but he didn't know where to put his hands around her pregnant belly so he ended up grabbing her boobs to keep himself from falling off the stage.

Barbie recovered from the blow and carried on indifferent to the chaos she had created. "You will all want to be in here later for a game I like to call . . . 'Who Got Fat?'"

Missy tried to lean into the microphone to do damage control. "No, no, we're calling it a 'Cheery Stroll Down Memory Lane.' No judgment, just fun. The cheerleaders are going to put on our old uniforms and do a routine."

"Whatever. The fact is I still fit into mine and I'm pretty sure most of you don't. Seriously, Brenda, have you even heard about Weight Watchers? Have some self-control, for God's sake."

Brenda burst into tears and her husband pulled her close and glared at Barbie.

Missy grabbed the microphone. "Now, now, let's be nice." She covered the mic with her hand and hissed at Barbie. "You promised!"

Then back to the class, "We're all here to have fun and congratulate each other on our achievements."

Barbie grabbed the microphone again. "Speaking of amazing achievements, I want to introduce my gorgeous husband, the future senator for New Jersey, Congressman Robert Clark."

"Ooh, didn't see that coming," Kim said, and nudged Connie before grabbing another handful of granola.

The Royal Court had had enough and was awkwardly leaving. Joel Miller gave Jerry a shove for grabbing his wife's boobs and Jerry's wife slapped him. Missy was trying to keep the group onstage while Barbie's husband was waving and shaking hands with the crowd like this was a whistle-stop tour. Kelly was the only one unfazed who remained onstage clapping wildly and encouraged the rest of the crowd to join in. Robert Clark put his arm around Barbie's waist and the couple flashed a pair of perfect smiles to the audience while someone took a couple of pictures from the crowd.

I had only seen Barbie's husband from the back as he rushed past me before. He was a six-foot-two stunner with wavy blond hair, a square jaw, and a broad smile of even and unnaturally white teeth. "Oh my God. She married *Ken*."

"A senator. Well, that just bites." Kim expressed the disgust we were all feeling as Barbie launched into a campaign speech, talking about what a great senator her husband was going to be *blah blah blah*.

Missy finally wrestled the microphone back and pointed for her to leave the stage.

"Okay, that's all I can stomach," I told the girls. "Let's get out of here before Missy wants to form a cheer pyramid."

We left the gym and turned right to head down the hall to the cafeteria.

The cafeteria had been converted to a candlelit formal dining room. The long lunchroom plank tables and benches were rolled up to one side of the room and small round tables were set about covered in white tablecloths with centerpieces of hydrangeas and place settings for eight. A buffet with silver covered chafing dishes was set up on the wall where we used to go through the lunch line. Former jocks were crowding in and loading up plates to be sure to get their money's worth.

Orchestral chamber music was coming from somewhere and I realized it was live. "They must be band students getting a little extra credit." I did a quick look around for a Tim sighting but the coast was clear.

"Did youse guys eat yet?" Connie asked.

"No, not yet." Sawyer looked up at me and quickly looked away.

"Well, I'm starving!" Kim marched over to the buffet table and started loading up a plate. "Do you see these shrimp? These aren't regular shrimp. These are giant cannibal shrimp that eat other shrimp for lunch! Come on."

We stood there and watched in amusement until she realized we weren't loading up plates. "What are you waiting for?" she said mid-pile.

"I don't know if I can eat a cannibal shrimp."

Kim looked at me. "We paid good money for this boo-fay. I've got my purse lined in foil and I'm taking my money's worth home."

"Oh. My. Gosh. You do not!" Sawyer eyed Kim's purse speculatively.

"She does, and she will," Connie said, picking up a plate and helping herself to a canapé. "Just be glad you've never been tricked into crashing a wedding with her."

"What? I said he was a distant cousin on my mother's side. I didn't say how distant."

Connie looked at me and Sawyer and mouthed *crazy*. We all giggled and Kim opened her purse and dumped a few shrimp in.

Sawyer and I each took some fruit from the towering watermelon sculpture while Kim and Connie filled their plates with bacon-wrapped dates, crab puffs, and lamb chops. I found us a table in the corner where I could put my back to the wall and keep an eye out for Tim. My boobs hit my chin when I sat down and I had to wiggle the bustier around some. I speared a grape with my fork and it squirted onto the front of my dress. I dunked my napkin into a water glass and dabbed at it. Now instead of a small dribble I had a big glaring water spot that screamed out "dork" for all passersby. I was about to make a break for it to go hide in the car when the table next to ours filled with the enemy.

Chapter 8

"Can you believe her? What a tramp!"

Sawyer's eyes did a full lap around when we heard
Maria Ragusa, the class secretary and voice of Caper High
morning announcements. Along with Paul and Kristen
they were in the inner circle of the popular crowd and
three of Barbie and Amber's minions. Of all the tables in
all the reunions these three had to sit at the table right next
to ours.

"Girrrl, she doesn't even know his fiancée," Paul continued. "And right in front of her own husband, too. She
hasn't changed at all."

Kelly and Kristen both laughed.

Connie leaned in and whispered, "Oh, if Missy could
hear them now."

Sawyer sat stiff as a board, like she was afraid to move
and draw their attention.

Like zombies to a fresh brain, the popular table drew
more former cheerleaders to its ranks. In between selfies
and tweets, Kelly said, "Poor Missy. Barb just steamrolls
all over her. It's got to be killing Barb not to be in charge."

Tina Winiecki joined the table. "You've got that right.

She's used to throwing money at a committee until she's the head. But we elected Missy reunion coordinator twenty-five years ago and Barb can't change that."

"Can you imagine if she was in charge of the reunion?" Paul said. "It would be one long night of Jell-O shots and pom-pom waterfalls. Instead of 'Ode to Caper High' we'd be singing 'Ode to Barbie Pomeroy.'"

Kelly took a group shot of the table on her smartphone. "Things haven't been the same with her and Billy since the incident. And I know tonight had to be hard on her, seeing Billy with another woman. She never really got over him."

Kristen waved around a lamb chop. "Please. She has more booze in her right now than a frat house on spring break. And she cheated on Billy like a dozen times. She'll have sex with anything that moves and she doesn't care who she hurts." She shoved the entire chop in her mouth up to the little paper bootie.

"Dish, girl, what do you know?" Paul prodded.

Kim swiped a crab puff off of Connie's plate and popped it into her mouth. "Now it's getting interesting."

We turned and watched the other table as Kristen picked up another lamb chop and used it to point around the room. "She slept with Kyle. Matt. Robbie."

"How can you stand to work on that campaign, Kelly? Don't you have to spend time with her?" Paul asked.

Kristen stuffed a prime rib slider in her mouth and said, "Ysmerfulfurf!" Then pounded the table with her fist.

"She isn't usually this bad. I think she's just lashing out because Billy humiliated her. Besides, she isn't there very often. She travels a lot on business for her company, Dynasty Cheer Academy, competing and scouting for Nationals. But Robert is just amazing; it's exciting to be a part of something that's going to make a difference."

"So her husband doesn't care that she slept with several of the men in here?" Another former cheerleader joined the table.

"I mean, really, I'm probably the only guy in here she hasn't been with," Paul said. "Although she has been giving me the eye. I think she wants a challenge." He glanced nervously around the room.

"If he knows," Kelly answered while handing a napkin to Kristen, "he doesn't let it affect their marriage. That's all in the past anyway. As far as I know she's been a faithful wife. They really love each other. Of course, we don't spend a lot of time talking about Barb. Congressman Clark is very busy working on his initiative to provide healthy meals and snacks in public schools for all students so they will get at least five servings of fruits and vegetables during the day. We can't help what they eat at home."

"Watch your back, Kelly," Kristen warned through a mouthful of pear Camembert tart. "They may appear to be the perfect couple but you don't know what goes on in private. You're working very closely with him and if Barb feels like you're a threat she'll make it her goal to destroy you. One of these days someone will be fed up with her enough to put a stop to her bullying for good."

"Do you think that person would want any help doing the deed?" Kim asked, but apparently, we were in the cone of silence.

Connie snickered.

"What? I'm just saying I have a couple brothers who could be bought for a hoagie."

We sat there moving our food around trying to look like we weren't eavesdropping on the other table. For a moment I caught a glimpse of Tim coming out of the kitchen to survey the buffet table and poke at one of the chafing dishes. I felt my heart drop an inch lower in my belly and had to force myself to let my breath out.

Connie saw me see Tim. "Be calm. There's no way he can see you way over here."

Tim looked really good in his starched white chef coat. What little he had aged had only been an improvement. Butterflies started thumping around in my chest, stirring up a smattering of guilt. *You have no business having butterflies or anything else with John barely gone six months.* I was relieved that Tim didn't notice me and a little hurt that he didn't even *try* to spot me. If I had been in his shoes, I would have been spying from the kitchen with binoculars.

A squeal erupted from the next table and I looked up to see that Amber had made her way into the cafeteria and Kelly was rushing over to give her a hug. "Oh, A-Bomb. I haven't seen you in forever. You're so tan! How've you been?"

"I'm good. Busy. You know, my job keeps me on the go."

"Can you believe Barbie tonight, that cow? So inappropriate!" Paul got up and pulled a chair over for Amber from the next table without asking if anyone sitting there minded.

Kristen muttered something imperceptible followed by a *harrumph* and a stab of her fork in the air for emphasis.

"I know, right." Paul must be gifted in interpretation of tongues.

"Well, some people never change. What can you do? I'll be right back. I'm going through the buffet, I'm starving."

Only a skinny girl would admit she's hungry in public.

Amber walked away from the group, which began talking about her the moment she was out of earshot.

"Are you sure that's her original nose?" Paul asked.

"I think she's holding up very well, all things considered," Kelly added.

Sawyer giggled. "It sounds just like an episode of *The Real Housewives of South Jersey*. It's just killing me not to turn around in my seat and watch."

A crack of lightning illuminated the cafeteria, reminding us that Mavis would be making an appearance tonight.

A roll of thunder was heard in the distance.

Kim narrowed her eyes and announced, "Uh-oh. Something wicked this way comes. It's a little early for our heart-to-heart, isn't it?"

"Well, now, I must have wandered into the pound because all I see is a bunch of dogs at this table." A tall, leggy blonde with long fake fingernails and glued-on eyelashes was swaying before us with one hand on her hips and the other clutching an empty shot glass. A very handsome life-size Ken doll in a tux was fidgeting behind her.

So much for Sawyer's apology theory.

"Oh my God, it's Malibu Bimbo Barbie" was Kim's icy challenge to the woman who made our lives miserable for four years. "And she's three sheets to the wind."

"What are you wearing, loser? You know there is a fine line between retro and ridiculous?" Kim just smiled a patronizing smile and refused to play Barbie's game.

"And what the crap are you wearing, McAllister? That's a dress for a much younger, much thinner woman. You look like a My Little Pony float in the St. Patty's Day Parade."

"Is this your way of saying you want to be BFFs? 'Cause it needs work."

"I don't want to be friends with you, you loser. And you"—she turned on Connie next—"1970 called, it wants its hairstyle back."

"I was hoping you wanted to make amends. High

school is over, Barbie. We don't care what you think about us anymore."

"*High school is over, Barbie.*" Barbie's mouth curled up in an ugly sneer as she mimicked Connie's words.

The Ken doll whispered, "Let's just go, dear. I feel like dancing." He gave his shoulders a little jiggle to the beat of the music in his head and glanced at Sawyer, pausing as he noticed her for the first time. His eyes roved greedily over her and he flashed a wide grin of appreciation.

Barb kept her eyes on Connie. "Shut up, Robert! Make yourself useful and go get me another drink why don't you."

"Okay, darling. Anything for my baby." Robert trotted off to the bar like a faithful cocker spaniel in search of his mistress's slippers.

Barbie turned from Connie and leveled cold, unfeeling eyes at Sawyer. "I see your ex-husband has traded up from the scrawny old model he had before."

Sawyer went pale. Barbie had gone right for the jugular.

"Of course, who can blame him?" She leaned in close to whisper in Sawyer's ear. "Rumor has it that flat-chested and frigid just didn't satisfy him. Oh, wait a minute, he was talking about you, wasn't he? Oops."

In one moment she had reduced us to being awkward fifteen-year-olds all over again. Sawyer's knuckles were white from gripping the table and she was breathing heavily. I stood up to face Barbie.

"You are so full of silicone and tequila that when you die they won't need formaldehyde to preserve your dead carcass. You know, I used to envy you. You were so pretty with so many friends. But that's not who you are anymore. I'm glad I came tonight so I could see how the prom queen grew up to be the Wicked Witch. Why don't you move on before someone drops a house on you?"

The cafeteria was suddenly silent, and I could feel people staring at us. That had come out like a threat, and my fists were balled up.

Kim interjected, "And take that flying monkey Joanne with you."

"No one here is interested in whatever you had to tell us. Not now and not later. We're over you."

"Yeah!" Kim let out a whoop of victory and Connie was nodding her head in silent agreement.

Barbie leaned in toward me and I could smell the booze on her breath. She looked me up and down with disgust. "I don't know what you're talking about and I don't have anything to tell you except that time hasn't been good to you, Poppy McAllister. It's made you fat and dumpy. It's no wonder Tim dumped you so long ago. Men don't like fat women. Especially ones that will sleep with any frat boy that comes along. How is your bastard child anyway?"

She turned to go but Sawyer was out of her seat and pouncing on her like a lion taking down a gazelle.

"You are the most hateful, bitter person I've ever known! You are as ugly on the inside as you think you are beautiful on the outside! You can take your note and shove it!"

In a split second, Sawyer had Barbie on the floor and was on top of her throwing punches. Barbie lay there whimpering, covering her face with her hot pink, manicured talons. A small crowd formed, including Amber and Joanne. Joanne looked positively gleeful for the excitement until she saw Barbie was on the bottom.

"Stop! Stop! You're hurting her!" Joanne flung herself over Barbie's body like a protective mother hen.

I pulled Sawyer off of Barbie and she was still punching at the air as Amber stepped in and screamed at me to get Sawyer out of there. "What is wrong with you all? You're acting like children."

Barbie spat out a little blood along with a string of obscenities that would make the Marines blush, while Amber pressed one of Paul's paisley silk handkerchiefs to Barbie's nose to stop the bleeding. "Kristen, can we get an ice pack and some gauze from your office?"

Barbie's husband, Robert, hadn't been much help to this point. He'd just stood there holding her vodka tonic and what appeared to be a pink squirrel. Ken handed the drinks to Kelly, who appeared right by his side and put his arm around his wife's shoulders to accompany her to the nurse's office just down the hall by the gym.

"Stay there, Robert!" Barbie violently shrugged Robert's arm off and leaned on Amber for support.

"Ooh-kay," Amber sighed as she half-supported, half-carried Barbie through the double doors out of the cafeteria with Joanne trotting dutifully behind. Kristen led the group away to put some ice on Barbie's swelling eye while I tried to get Sawyer calmed down.

"That was awesome!" Kim handed Sawyer a ginger ale. "You took her down like Pretty Boy Johnson at Madison Square Garden. She didn't even see you coming."

"Man, you really decked her," Connie said. "Have you been taking some kind of class for that?"

Sawyer was still a bit shaken up and trying to catch her breath. "No, that was a combination of growing up with two older brothers and years of pent-up rage." She looked at her hand. "Aww, I think I broke a nail."

I cocked an eye at her. "Do we need to airlift you to the hospital?"

She sipped at her ginger ale. "I got a little carried away when I heard those awful things she said to Poppy."

I patted her shoulder. "I know. It's okay."

"No, it's not. I'm so sorry I made you come tonight."

"Don't worry about it. It's just words. I don't care what Barbie thinks."

If I didn't care, then why did I feel like eating a gallon of peanut butter ice cream and crying? Barbie's hateful words did bring up a fresh wave of pain, but I didn't want Sawyer to know that. She was about to get hit by a tidal wave of her own. Kurt was on his way over with Tonia Lipinski.

Chapter 9

"Hey, Cracker Jack, are you okay?"

Sawyer sat rigid and at first I wasn't sure she had even heard Kurt. We all held our breath to see how she would handle her ex-husband, who in typical Kurt fashion lacked the common sense to leave his scantily clad, stiletto-wearing date at the bar when he came over to talk.

"We saw what happened from across the room. Hashtag best reunion ever!"

Sawyer slowly turned to look at the platinum blonde in the sheer white minidress, then looked Kurt in the eye. "I'm fine."

Then Kurt's date chimed in with a breathy "Oh, wow. You really clobbered her good. Kurt said you had a mean left hook."

Great, I see Kurt is still picking Mensa candidates for dates.

Sawyer narrowed her eyes at Kurt, "He did, did he?"

"Oh, yeah. Good for you. I'm Tonia, by the way. But nowadays everyone calls me by my stage name: Honey Moon." She offered a dainty hand that supported an enormous charm bracelet that must have weighed two pounds.

Sawyer ignored the hand and took a sip of her ginger ale. "Yep, that sounds about right."

Sawyer had played this game too many times. Their relationship had been doomed from the start. Kurt was totally committed to Sawyer. Unless she was out of his sight. Then he was totally committed to Kurt. What Kurt wanted. Who Kurt wanted. It was rumored that Kurt had slept with half of the women in Cape May County. He was charming as all get-out but couldn't keep it in his pants to save his life. It took seven years before Sawyer had had enough and their marriage finally imploded into divorce.

"Listen, Cracker Jack, don't let Barbie and her pathetic little clique get to you. They've always been jerks."

"Thanks, but I'm fine. I've got my girls here to back me up."

"I know that's right," Kim said, cracking her knuckles.

I took a protective step closer to Sawyer and shot ice daggers at Kurt.

"You can go back to your date." Sawyer gave Kurt a piercing look and his eyes turned to liquid pools of regret.

Tonia tugged on Kurt's arm. He gave Sawyer a terse nod, and they left to reclaim their table on the other side of the room.

"I need some air. I've got to get out of here for a minute, girls." Sawyer's voice quivering, she grabbed her purse and started for the double doors.

"Do you want me to come with you?" I reached for my clutch, but she shook her head no.

"I need a minute alone. I'll be right back."

Sawyer left the cafeteria, and I stewed in my helplessness. She was in pain. Wasn't this the whole reason I was here instead of home with Sara Lee? To back Sawyer up so she didn't get hurt by Barbie or Kurt. I could see my former classmates uploading the video from their smartphones.

Before I got home to Aunt Ginny's the whole town would be able to see the catfight on Facebook and YouTube. What a nightmare. I hated New Jersey.

We sat in silence for a while trying to make sense of what had just transpired until Connie broke the tension. "Who knew Sawyer was so scrappy?"

"I know, right?" Kim gushed. "I mean she seriously walloped Barbie."

"A person can only hold on to so much before they snap."

I checked the time on my phone. "She's been gone awhile. I'm gonna go check on her and see if she needs anything."

"Ask her if she needs some ice for her knuckles," Kim joked.

I left the cafeteria and walked down the hall past the nurse's office. The lights were on, but the door was closed. I passed the gym on my left, where I heard Missy giving out a Lifetime Achievement award to some teacher.

Missy. Psshh. That girl needs to get a clue. She's living in a Disney Channel sitcom if she believes life is "awesome-sauce" for everyone. In a few more hours I'll have this rathole town in my rearview mirror and I'll return to my safe little nest in Virginia. I'll get one of John's old part-ners to mediate for Aunt Ginny and this whole ugly weekend will be behind me.

One of the double doors was hanging open and a wicked wind was whipping through the foyer causing the unclaimed name tags to blow off their tables.

Still, all in all I think tonight was a success. Tim didn't see me. And we finally got to stand up to Barbie and Amber and that weasel Joanne. Too bad so many people had to see it. Although I do know a few who would like to have seen Barbie put in her place once and for all. I was so afraid I would end up looking like a loser. Thank God for Creepy Carl and middle-aged used car salesmen.

I turned down the main hall looking left and right for signs of Sawyer walking it off. Poster boards advertising various after-school clubs and sports tryouts hung on the walls above the long bank of gray lockers. Nothing down B hall. Nothing down . . . wait a minute. Who was that? Someone was lying down at the end of C hall in front of our old lockers. *Please, dear God, don't let it be Sawyer. Was she so distraught that she slipped and fell?*

I turned to walk down the dark hall toward her. Something wasn't right. My heart was pounding through my chest and a sickening fear clawed its way up the back of my neck. My heart said move faster but my legs were made out of lead.

Why is she just lying there? Why does she have pompoms?

A flash of lightning lit up the hall and I saw her eyes open and staring vacantly and the room started to spin. The crack of thunder shook the walls and lockers rattled on their hinges. It wasn't Sawyer.

It was Barbie.

And Barbie was dead.

Chapter 10

The body was lying at an awkward angle, as if someone had dragged it to this spot and left it. In front of my old locker.

Well, this won't end well.

Barbie's corpse reeked of perfume and tequila, and someone had stuffed a pompom in her mouth. *Well, that part makes sense. We've all wanted to do that for years.*

Maybe she had just passed out. I suspected it wasn't the first time she had drunk herself into a pickled coma. I grabbed the pompom and gave it a tug. A line of drool webbed from the plastic handle to her open mouth. Her head lolled to the side and I saw what looked like a giant infected hickey with a tiny black dot in the middle.

Oh my God—a puncture wound. Ding dong, the witch was dead!

Aaaaand I had just interfered with the murder scene. I shoved the pompom back in her mouth and tried to fluff it out. I quickly looked around and wondered if I had time to drag her a few more feet down to Joanne's locker.

No! That's ridiculous. Get ahold of yourself, Poppy. "Help! Someone!"

I fumbled in my purse for my cell phone to call 911, but before I had a chance to dial I heard a gasp from down the hall and quick footsteps.

Joel Miller ran up from the other end of C hall. He had discarded his suit jacket and tie and his shirtsleeves were rolled up to his elbows like he'd been working out in the yard. He was sweating and breathing heavily. He leaned in and looked at the body, eyes wide with concern. Then they narrowed to slits and shifted my way, piercing me with accusation.

I ignored his glare. "Do you know CPR?"

He didn't answer me. He stood, hands on hips, staring at Barbie, slowly shaking his head side to side.

A piercing scream nearly shattered my eardrums, and Joanne ran up panting and fell to her knees. "What have you done to her!" she lashed out at me, sobbing. She grabbed the body and let out a racking howl.

Good Lord. There was less mourning when Elvis died.

Other footsteps were coming up the hall, probably summoned by Joanne's five-alarm scream.

Amber arrived and gently pulled Joanne off Barbie's body. She checked Barbie's pulse. Her lips tightened into a thin line and her brows knit together. She slowly turned to face me and coldly asked, "What did you do?"

"*Me*? I didn't do anything. I just got here."

Joanne's eyes were bugging out and her face was scarlet with rage. "She's lying! You know she is. You saw the way she attacked her in the cafeteria! She killed her! I saw her standing over the body myself."

"I was looking for Sawyer! Joel, you were the first one here. You know I didn't kill her. Tell them."

Joel glared at me. "I don't know how long you were here. I came because I heard someone scream for help. And there was Barbie . . . and there you were standing over her, gloating. You murdered her!"

My heart thudded in my ears and felt like I was walking under water. I was most certainly not gloating. I can't say I was heartbroken, but that about covered it for me. Things were turning in a bad direction, and I tried to catch my breath but my grip on reality was swirling around me like fireflies in July.

"*Poppy*?" Sawyer called me from down the hall. She sounded a million miles away, but the sound of her voice caused tears to well up in my eyes and a sob caught in my throat. At least she was okay. "What's going on—OH MY GOD! Is that Barbie?" She ran toward us.

"Stay away from her!" Joanne shrieked. "Look what your murdering accomplice did!"

"Everybody needs to settle down and tell me what happened," Amber demanded.

Her imperious attitude went right through me. I shot back, "We don't have time for this, Amber. We need to call the police."

"I *am* the police." Amber flashed a badge she pulled out of her little silver purse.

Well, I did not see that coming.

"Nobody leaves this area," she sneered at me with a growl, "especially you, McAllister. And don't touch anything. I'm calling this in."

Amber called for an ambulance and backup, while Sawyer and I huddled together for moral support. I couldn't take my eyes off the body or Joanne sobbing next to it.

Barbie had changed into her old cheerleading uniform, probably for some hoopla Missy had planned for later. Her hair was disheveled like she'd been out in the wind and her arms were lying straight at her sides. I didn't see any signs of struggle or blood in the hall. Everything looked perfectly normal, except for, well, the dead body.

It was only moments before I heard the wail of sirens approaching from outside. Word had obviously gotten out that there was a body in the History wing, because a small crowd had formed at the end of the hall. Amber tasked Joel with pushing the gawkers back to keep the evidence intact. I overheard him say something about respect for the deceased. Before we knew it, backup crews were pushing their way through the half-drunk gaping onlookers. Every cop in South Jersey seemed to have dropped their Wawa coffee and responded, because they were swarming the area, decorating the hallway with more yellow crime-scene tape than the homecoming dance.

When the crew with the stretcher rolled up, the hall suddenly went quiet, except for the crackle of the police radios and Joanne's snorts and whimpers.

Amber was all brusqueness and business, directing several teams of officers. "Shut down all the exits. No one leaves without giving a detailed statement."

An officer placed a plastic sheet over the body, which sent Joanne into shock, and she sat on the floor against the lockers staring into space and rocking back and forth.

"Sawyer, this is Officer Benson. Go with him to give your statement." Then she turned a cold eye in my direction. "Poppy, you come with *me*."

Sawyer's grip on my arm tightened. "Can't we stay together?"

"No, I'm sorry, it's protocol." Officer Benson led Sawyer into the Psychology classroom, and she gave me a frightened look over her shoulder before she disappeared into the dark room.

"Come with me, McAllister."

Obediently I followed her into the Spanish classroom. She flicked on the lights, which came to life in stages of buzzes and clicks. Then she shut the door behind us and motioned for me to wedge myself into one of the tiny desks at the front. The room was cold and smelled like chalk dust and Doritos. Posters of Spanish-named items were decorated around the room. Someone had scratched the conjugation of "*morir*" on the top of my desk. Probably test answers.

Amber half-sat, half-leaned on top of the desk next to me.

"Look, I don't know anything," I jumped in. "I was looking for Sawyer and just happened upon Barbie. She was already dead when I found her."

Amber's eyes were cold and bore into mine. "This will go a lot easier if you just tell me the truth now. Everyone in the cafeteria witnessed the fight between you and Barbie and heard what you said about dropping a house on her. Now she's dead, and you were seen standing over the body by two eyewitnesses. It looks really bad, McAllister."

"I know how it looks, but I'm telling you *I* didn't kill her. The last time I saw her, you were taking her to the nurse's office for an ice pack. I was just looking for Sawyer, who said she needed a minute alone."

Amber had started writing notes in a little steno pad she'd pulled from her purse. "So Sawyer left the cafeteria alone?"

The minute she asked me that I knew I had made a terrible mistake. "No, it's not like that. Sawyer had just had an unpleasant run-in with her ex-husband and she needed a minute to collect herself."

"Where did she go?"

"I don't know. That's why I was looking for her."

"Did you see her anywhere in the vicinity of this hallway?"

"No! Not at all. Sawyer would never do anything like this to anyone. She couldn't hurt a fly."

"That's not what I saw in the cafeteria. She was beating the snot out of Barbie until you pulled her off."

"There is no way you could possibly think Sawyer could have had anything to do with this."

"I don't know. You tell me. I know Barbie was pretty mean to you all in high school."

Uh, what's with this "Barbie was mean" business?— Hello!

I shot back, "I seem to remember you *both* calling us names. Bullying us. Spreading lies about us. You *both* made our lives miserable."

"I'm not the one who was found standing over a murder victim."

There was a knock on the door, and then it opened a crack. Amber gestured for whoever it was to enter. An officer came in and whispered something to her, then left.

"A testimony just came in that the body is lying in front of your old locker. You want to tell me that's a coincidence?"

I should have moved that body when I had the chance. I took a deep breath before answering. "I don't think it's a coincidence, but I didn't have anything to do with it."

"Why should I believe that?"

"Think about it, Amber. If I was going to kill Barbie, I wouldn't do it in front of *my* locker."

"Where *would* you do it?"

With a sudden chill it occurred to me that her questions were just a formality. Amber was already determined to zero in on one suspect. *Moi*. Or, I guess out of respect for the Spanish class, I should say *Yo*.

"I wouldn't do it at all!"

"I have a hundred eyewitnesses that will say otherwise."

"I think it's obvious that someone's trying to set me up."

"Someone like . . . Sawyer?"

"No! Of course not!"

There was another knock on the door, and this time it was a young officer and he was carrying something. He whispered to Amber and gave her the item, which she flashed in my face.

"Do you recognize this?"

"Yes, it's my purse. I must have dropped it in the hall."

She put on a pair of rubber gloves the officer handed her, opened the silver clasp to my clutch, and carefully dug around the lining. Her eyes went from cold to icy.

"You want to explain to me why you have a hypodermic needle and alcohol pads in your purse, McAllister."

I felt panic rising in my chest like a bird trapped by a hungry cat. *Oh, no-no-no-no-no, this can't be happening*.

She pulled out one of the needles I'd used to administer pain medication to John when he was undergoing chemo. It must have been left in the inside pocket from the last black-tie event John and I had attended.

I stared at the needle in a dumbfounded stupor and tried to come up with the perfect response that would cause Amber to see that I was honest and worthy of her trust. Instead I blurted out, "Don't you need a warrant to go through my stuff without asking?"

"Not if there's reasonable cause. And we have a whole

mountain of reasonable cause out there. So now do you
want to tell me about the syringe?"

"I can explain that."

Amber's radio crackled that she was needed in another
room, and the young officer who brought in my purse
stood guard over the door while she was gone. He didn't
acknowledge me. I was left alone with just my misery to
keep me company.

Why did I come up here? Nothing good ever happened
for me in South Jersey. But not in my wildest dreams did
I ever imagine this scenario. I severely disliked Barbie. I
can't say I'd be devastated to hear she was pecked to death
by a flock of angry chickens, but I didn't hate her enough
to kill her.

This was bad. *Muy mala.* When *Officer* Amber returned,
I would have to make her listen to reason. I could have this
cleared up and be on my way home to Waterford first
thing in the morning.

Amber returned with two other officers.

"Listen, Amber, I don't know what is going on but I can
tell you that I had nothing to do with it. And I want you to
know that I'm willing to cooperate fully to help the police
find out who did."

"I'm glad to hear that, McAllister. But you'll have to do
it at the station. The medical examiner has found a puncture wound in the victim's neck that is consistent with the
syringe that was found in your belongings. You're under
arrest for the murder of Barbie Clark. You have the right
to remain silent."

The young cop who brought my purse in put his hand
on my elbow to pull me up. He closed a cold metal ring on
my wrist and brought my arm behind my back.

I couldn't believe what was happening. I could hear
Amber talking about my rights but I couldn't focus;

everything was hazy. I was handcuffed and led out into the hall, where a photographer was taking evidence pictures of Barbie's body. At the end of the hall I could hear a cacophony of muttering and the sound of cell phones documenting my shame and uploading it to social media.

In the crowd I heard Creepy Carl say, "Too bad 'dead body' wasn't on the scavenger hunt list."

I couldn't process any coherent thoughts. The events were too surreal. I was led out the main doors through a sea of judgmental faces toward a waiting cruiser.

Outside, the sky had finally opened up and a powerful rain was pelting the earth. Hurricane Mavis had arrived.

Chapter 11

I was taken down to the police station and processed. A sergeant confiscated my Swarovski hair clip and jewelry. My picture was taken and I was fingerprinted.

Then I was led to a holding cell, where two other women were already seated inside.

Everything was out of focus. I was in a state of shock, oblivious to my surroundings. When the barred door slammed shut with a loud clank, my knees gave out and I stumbled, nearly falling to the floor. One of the women put out her hand to steady me.

"Be careful, honey. That floor is concrete, and no one will come to give you first aid until your lawyer shows up."

A strong hand helped me to a cold metal bench that was bolted to the floor, and hopelessness washed over me like a tidal wave. This was not the life I had signed up for. How I desperately missed John. He was my anchor. Now I was just bobbing aimlessly in an ocean of apathy. I let the tears fall freely. My husband was dead. I never accomplished anything with my life. And now I was in jail for a murder I didn't commit. I'd probably be put away for the remaining good years I had left. Why hadn't I taken that stupid syringe out of my purse six months ago?

"You want some Juicy Fruit, honey?"

"I'm sorry, what?"

"You want some Juicy Fruit gum? I keep it hidden in my bra. The cops don't wanna look for it there, so they never confiscate it."

I looked up and for the first time began to take in my surroundings. The holding cell had two long metal benches, both bolted to the floor. The walls were painted in suicide-watch green. And, oh-my-God, there was a metal toilet just sitting in the open at the back of the room for all the world to see you do your business. I died a little inside.

I looked at the woman next to me who had offered me the Juicy Fruit. She was an older woman with beautiful long silver hair, long silver fingernails, and the longest, thickest eyelashes I'd ever seen. She was dressed in a bubblegum pink minidress and thigh-high silver stiletto boots, one leg crossed daintily over the other and she was gently swinging her top foot. She was watching me with eyes full of concern and popping a mouthful of gum.

A woman on the other side of the cell snorted. "Gum. That's *all* you got in that bra."

I looked across the cell and saw a dark-skinned African-American woman who appeared to be a few years younger than me. She was dressed in beat-up jeans and a stained gray hoodie. She leaned forward on the metal bench, her elbows resting on open knees.

"Can it, Tawnika," the woman next to me said to her, then turned back to me. "Maybe it's because I'm getting away with something but Juicy Fruit always makes me feel better when I'm arrested."

I could hear the words coming out of her mouth but

they weren't making any sense. I shook my head no. She shrugged her shoulders and went back to popping her gum.

How did my life get here? I was so full of promise. I had plans. Four-year college. Summer study abroad in Paris. Then a posh apartment in New York City, running my own bakery. I was going to call it Sassyfrass. Marriage to Tim. Two kids and a cat. Somewhere I got off track and could never seem to get back on. I never envisioned my life being this . . . disappointing. This empty. This worthless.

"What'd you do?"

"What?"

"I said, what'd you do?"

From the other side of the cell, the inmate was watching me with a mixture of curiosity and defiance.

"I didn't do anything."

She rolled her eyes and jerked her head to the side. "Oh, yeah. Us neitha. Right, Bebe?"

"I never do anything," the woman next to me said in a sweet, lilting accent. "The cops in this town just have it out for me."

"I was set up again. Ima kill that beast when I get outta here." Tawnika kicked the metal bench and it made a loud clang.

Somewhere in the distance a man's voice called out, "Knock it off in there!"

Hot tears filled my eyes. *What am I going to do? What I wouldn't give to have a time machine to go back and undo some of my mistakes. I wouldn't go to that stupid reunion, that's for sure! I wouldn't get pregnant in college or let my mother-in-law trap me in Virginia. All I want is to have a chance at some happiness. To do something with my life, to make something of myself. I'm tired of being a victim.*

"Are you okay?"

"What?"

"I said are you okay, honey? I'm Bebe."

She put out her large hand and I shook it and that was when I noticed that she had the beginnings of a five o'clock shadow peeking through a thick application of makeup.

"This is your first time, isn't it?" she asked.

"First time for what?"

"Poor thing, she's still dazed," she said to the woman on the other side of the cell. "That's Tawnika. She has connections in the Crest if you need anything . . . medicinal."

"'Sup?" Tawnika gave me a head nod. "She means you ain't neva been arrested befoe."

"Oh. No. First time."

"The first time is always the hardest." Bebe patted my hand and popped her gum. "You'll get used to it."

Dear God, I hope not. "How many times have you been in here?" I asked.

"A couple."

Tawnika snorted from across the room, and Bebe turned and looked down her nose at her.

The officer who had taken my fingerprints came back into the holding cell area.

"Heyyy, Dan."

"Bebe, what are you doing in here again?"

"The boys in blue keep targeting me. It's not fair."

"Uh-huh. I hear you keep propositioning undercover cops."

"I'm just friendly. They assume the worst." Bebe batted her eyes—the picture of innocence.

"Offica Dan"—Tawnika left her perch across the cell and came up to the metal door—"did they call my parole offica yet?"

"I'm not sure. It's been crazy out there. Hurricane Mavis is causing a lot of nine-one-one calls from scared citizens.

Mrs. Gershner's called in three times to report prowlers every time a tree scrapes against her bay window. Why?"

"This my third strike for possession and I don't wanna go back to Edna Mae. I told you guys that stuff wasn't mine this time. Moniqua planted it on me 'cause she thinks I'm steppin' out with Darrel again."

"Look, Tawnika, there's nothing I can do until your parole officer gets here. But it was a small amount of weed and if it had been your first offense you'd have been let off with community service. I'll talk to Carl and see what I can do."

"Thanks, Dan. You da best."

The officer turned to me. "You have someone trying to post bail for you, but it's taking a little time because it's the weekend and it's hard to find a judge around to sign off. Especially with you being from out of state and all."

"Someone is posting bail? Who? I haven't called anyone."

God knows Sawyer and Aunt Ginny don't have any money, and I'd let Lifetime do a reality show about my life in the big house before I'd call my mother-in-law to bail me out.

"I don't know. They didn't tell me. I just thought you'd want to know."

"Thank you."

The officer left and Bebe and Tawnika turned to me with fascination.

"You haven't even made a phone call yet?" Bebe asked, then popped her gum again.

I shook my head no.

"Why? What you in here for?"

"Murder," I mumbled.

Bebe's eyes nearly bugged out of her head and her gum fell out of her mouth and landed on the toe of her boot.

"Girrrl, who'd you ice?" Tawnika slid down on the other side of Bebe and leaned in. "Come on now, just between us."

"I'm telling you, I didn't ice anyone. I'm innocent."

Tawnika folded her arms across her chest and leaned back to size me up.

Both women, well, both *people* looked at me with skepticism. Bebe held my gaze while she unwrapped another piece of Juicy Fruit from her bra and popped it in her mouth. "I thought you were in my line of work from the way you were dressed, honey." Bebe tsk-tsked and shook her head in disbelief.

"You think I'm dressed like a hooker?" I blurted out the words before I could stop myself.

"Well, not a good one," Bebe answered defensively.

Great. I'm not even good enough to be a prostitute. Another tear burned down my cheek and I let it fall.

"Well, goodness, it can't be all that bad. A good lawyer can get you cleared with a self-defense plea." Bebe patted my arm.

"If dat don't work, you can always go for *insanity*. Judging from yo dress an' yo hair that might be the easy route if you don't mind spending a couple years in da padded palace."

My lip started to quiver and a sob caught in my throat.

"Oh, come on now, I'm just yankin' yo chain. What got you so uptight?"

"Look, I appreciate your help, I do. But my life is falling apart right now and I need this time to focus on my plan for jumping off a bridge later."

Bebe gave Tawnika a knowing look and in unison they said, "Midlife crisis!"

"You a rich white girl. How bad can it be?" Tawnika asked.

That made me indignant and I started rambling off my laundry list of grievances. "First of all, I'm not rich. My mother-in-law is. And by the way, there's a lot more to life than money. I had hopes and dreams and I flushed them away. In the game of life, my hand is a crap straight! Where is the excitement? Where is the passion? Where is the purpose for getting up every morning? I've been a good girl and obeyed all the rules and look where it got me. In prison for a crime I didn't commit. There has to be more to life than this."

Bebe and Tawnika were looking at me with matching expressions of astonishment.

"*Pshhh*. Rich people problems," Tawnika chuckled. "In my neighborhood people just want food and not getting hit."

"Honey, in my house the only hopes and dreams we had were not to be held down and burned with cigarettes when our old man came home drunk."

That deflated me. "I'm sorry, I didn't know."

"Of course you didn't. Because you're so wrapped up in your 'poor little me' script that you can't see what's going on with nobody else. You think you're drowning in an ocean of misfortune, but you're swimming in a fishbowl of self-pity." Bebe wagged her finger at me and moved her head in a little circle.

I thought facing a murder rap was the perfect time for self-pity.

"Mmmmm-mmm!" Tawnika hammered it home. "Life ain't easy for *no one*. People face very tough situations *every day*. You can keep wallowing in misery or pick yoself up and do what tough people do: fight back!" She made a fist and punched her palm. "No one else gonna do it for you. Either that or you can just let yourself drown. Up to you, girl."

"You're wasting all that emotion on depression when you could direct it into something useful like determination."

"Or an escape plan," Tawnika added.

"You need to decide, are you a quitter or a survivor?" Bebe stood up and started pacing in front of the little bench. "See me, I'm a survivor. People been trying to keep me down my whole life. Life keeps kicking me, but I'm not giving in. I just keep on getting back up. I'm fighting for what I want. No one's going to determine my fate but me. If there's a happy ending out there, I'm going to find it."

Maybe it was the desperation talking, but Bebe and Tawnika were making a lot of sense. Life had beaten them down many times and even now, in jail, they weren't giving up. I'd hermited myself away in a two-story, white brick colonial after the first curve ball was thrown at me. I thought my destiny was forever sealed the minute that pregnancy test was positive, but all I ever had to do was choose a different way. I could have stood up to Georgina. I could have chosen to go back to college. I could have adopted a child.

Goose bumps ran up my arms as realization dawned. I could choose now. The fog lifted from my brain and plowed the apathy away. Fury rose from somewhere deep within my soul and the heat burnt up the fear that had held me in bondage. Invisible chains fell away and my heart felt lighter. My shoulders rolled back and I sat up a little taller and looked Bebe in the eyes.

"You're right. I'm tired of being ashamed. I'm tired of

letting everyone else decide what I can and can't do. I'm done feeling sorry for myself. My whole life I've sat around longing for what could have been but I never got up and did anything about it. I've let fear hold me back. Things are going to be different from now on. I'm not giving up. I'm taking charge here and now!"

Bebe was hopping up and down. "Now, that's what I'm talking about. You go, girl!"

Tawnika was punching the air. "You gotta punch the system right in the neck!"

"Okay! I don't know what that means but I'm ready!"

I was caught up in their excitement. Then an invisible force sucked the energy right out of the room. There was a commotion coming down the hall and we could hear someone shouting f-bombs and threatening to get even when they got out.

"Oh, great." Tawnika and Bebe looked at each other with unspoken alarm. Then Tawnika headed over to the other side of the cell to reclaim her original spot on the bench with her back to us, muttering, "Just what I need tonight."

"Now listen, honey . . ." Bebe quickly flounced back in her seat. "Don't mess with Big Shirley, okay? She's mean. Real mean. And it sounds like she's in one of her moods. So just keep your head down and don't make eye contact."

Oh my God. What's happening? I felt adrenaline rising back up and the instinct to try to run or hide kicked in, but there was nowhere to go.

Two officers were coming down the corridor on either side of a very large white woman with short-cropped blond hair. She was wearing a plaid flannel shirt and overalls and her hands were handcuffed in front of her, but that didn't stop her from fighting against them like a rhino trying to escape the poachers.

"Get your hands off me, pig! I know the way!"

One officer opened the cell and pushed her in, then slammed the door shut.

"That's police brutality! I know my rights!" she yelled, then spit on the floor.

Bebe sat there chewing and popping her gum like nothing out of the ordinary was happening. I felt myself staring at Big Shirley, and Bebe jabbed me in the ribs with her elbow. "Eye contact," she hissed.

"What do *you* want?" Big Shirley came at me like she was looking for a fight. Which, if I were a betting woman, I'd wager was the very reason she was in there.

I felt myself staring at her, my mouth hanging open like a fish. She had an evil glint in her eyes and I couldn't look away.

"You're just begging for a beating, aren't you, Fatty? Well, you're in luck because I have one more beating left in me tonight." She cracked her neck side to side and took a step toward me. Bebe scampered off the bench and over to Tawnika's side of the cell.

No, I thought. Enough is enough. *I'm not going to be bullied. I am not powerless. No one is going to make me feel ashamed and belittled ever again.*

Feeling as if my spine had just grown superhuman strength, I stood up and put on my *I will kill* face, the one I'd only used once before when I discovered that someone had eaten the frozen Snickers bar I'd hidden in the back of the freezer.

"Let me tell *you* something, you giant sack of refuse," I growled at her.

"Oh no, she *did not* just say that," Bebe breathed.

"I've been to hell and back today and there is nothing you can do to hurt me more than life already has. Anything you can dish out, I can take it. But if you think I'm going down without fighting back you are dead wrong, woman, because I'm a survivor!"

Bebe and Tawnika seemed to gain confidence with every word I jabbed at Big Shirley's face, and now they were behind her silently encouraging me. Tawnika was motioning for me to hit Big Shirley in the kidney, and Bebe was motioning for me to duck and cover my face.

Big Shirley's expression went from confusion to shock to rage. She hunkered down and grunted like she was preparing to ram me. I steeled myself, and put my fists up to block her the best I could. Something behind me caught her eye and she stopped.

"That's enough, ladies. Don't make me tase you again, Big Shirley."

I didn't take my eyes off of Big Shirley, but I recognized the voice of Officer Amber right in front of the cell door.

"Ms. McAllister, we're not charging you at this time. We're releasing you pending further inquiries. But know that this is an open investigation and you are a prime suspect. Provisional bail has been posted so you're being released to your friend here. You're free to go, but don't try to leave town."

I slowly turned, still not trusting Big Shirley not to try a last-minute charge. Standing next to Officer Amber in a starched white chef's coat was the last person I wanted to see on the most humiliating day of my life.

Tim had come to bail me out.

Chapter 12

Awkward does not justly describe my ride home. I was humiliated to the core. Over the years I'd fantasized about running into my ex-boyfriend. I'd be skinny and gorgeous, my hair and nails would be impeccable, and I would ooze sexy. His jaw would drop as he openly gaped at my beauty, and he'd tell me he was a fool not to fight for me all those years ago.

Now here I was sitting in his stupid little black Kia, the radio tuned to the oldies station and a bikini-model bobblehead mocking me from the dashboard. The back seat was littered with fast food wrappers and an empty pizza box. I had frizzed-out hair, a broken nail, mascara streaks running down my face, and my eyes were puffy and red from crying. My dress was molting, and my belly roll had flopped over my seatbelt in a very *Here Comes Honey Boo Boo* kind of way. I tried sucking it in, but I was too tired to hold my breath very long. What I wanted right now, more than anything, was a rock to hide under.

Tim sat with his hands gripping the steering wheel at ten and two, looking straight ahead. We drove along in eerie quiet for about ten minutes, the only sound coming from the rhythmic *thu-thumps* on Route 47, until I couldn't stand it anymore.

"You didn't have to post bail. I'm sure Aunt Ginny would have come along eventually."

Tim answered, the strain in his voice evident, "I couldn't just leave you there. Despite everything . . ." He trailed off into awkward silence, then cleared his throat. After a moment he tried again. "When I heard about the murder I knew there was no way you could do anything like that. Not even to that nasty piece of work."

"I'm sure the whole town has heard about what happened by now. If not, they can watch my arrest on YouTube."

"Well, people will always find a way to gossip about what is none of their business."

I felt the heat flush down my neck. There was a definite edge to his voice. *Are we still talking about Barbie?*

Silence.

"How in the world did you come up with that kind of money?"

"I put up my bistro."

Oh my God! "You did *not* have to do that. I will pay you back." *If I can get Georgina to unfreeze some of my assets, which will be like convincing a gorilla to give up her kitten.*

"It's not a big deal. And as long as you don't try to skip town I'll get it back."

I felt like all the air was sucked out of the car. I cut my eyes to him and caught him watching me. His face broke into a grin . . . and I was sixteen again. Stupid butterflies were doing the cha-cha in my heart, as if they didn't know how ridiculous the situation was. Tim breathed out a laugh and looked away. It was small but so familiar. My mind was flooded with memories from high school: Tim trying to reassure me about a test that I thought I'd failed; Tim taking up for me after someone had hurt my feelings; Tim sitting on the porch telling me we would make the long-distance relationship work.

"Tim, you've always been so good to me. I know I don't deserve it. I'm just so sorry about . . . everything."

Silence. I'd just made it awkward again. *Way to go, Poppy.* After a couple minutes he broke the tension.

He turned to me again for a moment, his eyes soft and wistful. "Poppy, we were kids. We both made mistakes. Let's just try to put it behind us and move on with our lives." He reached out a hand and patted me on the shoulder, then shook off a stray ostrich feather.

Swallowing the lump in my throat, I tried to find the words to respond. "I don't know what to say."

"Why don't we meet for coffee later this week and catch up."

I paused, trying to let the gravity of his request sink in, but my focus was cut short by the radio and Jon Bon Jovi, belting out "Shot through the heart and you're to blame / Darlin', you give love a bad name."

I swallowed a big gulp of air and started coughing and choking on nothing. It startled Tim, and he jerked the wheel, then had to swerve the car back out of the wrong lane.

"Whoa, are you okay?"

I held one finger up and shook my head yes, still unable to speak. Tim was looking from me to the road, then back to me again.

"I'm fine," I croaked. "You just caught me by surprise."

"By inviting you to coffee?" He laughed. "Why?"

"Because of our history. Because you just sprang me out of a jail cell." *Because I look like a fat, pink-and-yellow cow.* "Because I feel humiliated. Pick one."

We pulled up in front of Aunt Ginny's house, and Tim

put the car in park. "Poppy, you have no reason to feel humiliated. It's me. Besides, I think you could use a friend right now."

A friend. Oh. How stupid can I be? He's extending an olive branch for old times' sake.

I stared dumbly. I knew I should say something, but my mind was blank. The past twenty-four hours were like a really bizarre dream.

"Do you have a cell number?"

I nodded and gave it to him.

"Expect me to call you later."

I nodded again and got out of the car. I think I gave him a finger wave good-bye. Somehow I managed to get into the house and up to my room. The barest hint of light was breaking through the dark night sky. It would be dawn in another hour or so. I knew I should start looking for a lawyer and planning my defense.

I was sound asleep before my head hit the pillow.

Chapter 13

I was walking through a crush of students in hallway D to an advanced math class. The stack of textbooks in my arms was getting heavy. I entered the classroom and took my seat. The teacher was writing complex equations on the board, and I didn't understand any of them.

Something was wrong. There was a strange vibe in the air. I couldn't put my finger on it, but something was out of place. Fear started to coil around me.

This isn't my class. I'm not supposed to be here, but I don't know where to go.

I ran out of the room leaving my books behind. Out in the hallway, so many people were pressing against me and I couldn't get through the crowd. My heart was racing. I was going to be late, but late for what? Someone poked me on the butt. I turned around to see who it was but no one was there. The crowd of students started to fade. My senses were coming back to me. I was having a nightmare. Then it happened again. A double-pat on the butt.

What in the world?

I turned over and my eyes came open.

Figaro was sitting on the bed next to me, with his orange eyes boring into mine. One gray paw aloft.

"Really? Are you actually patting me on the butt to wake me up?"

I was answered by an innocent blink, then his raised paw was returned to the bed.

I fumbled around for the alarm clock that I'd neglected to set. Almost ten-thirty.

My mind replayed the incidents from last night. I tried to change the channel, but the too-vivid memory wouldn't let me. The last words Officer Amber snarled at me were "Don't try to leave town." Unbelievable.

Go away for the weekend, they said. It will be good to get out of your rut, they said. Just two days, then I can fly back to my little nest in Waterford. It sounded like a good plan.

Now I'm stuck in hell, facing a murder rap. I pulled the covers up to my chin. *I'm never getting up. I'm staying here forever. Amber will have to take me to prison in this bed.*

So Amber is a cop now. Great. What is her deal with me anyway? She's hated me for as long as I can remember but I have no idea why. Then I remembered Bebe and Tawnika, and the steel rod I'd found for my spine last night returned. *No. No way I'm letting her pin this on me.*

I got out of bed and took a long look at myself in the mirror. "No more hiding. No more backing down. This time I choose to fight back. I can do this. Amber thinks she's got me trapped. Well, Amber, I'm not scared of you. Come at me, bro!"

Figaro must have assumed my little pep talk was for him because he jumped on the dresser and looked deep into my eyes to try his Cat Mesmer on me.

"All right, fine. I'll hurry."

Quickly I made my bed and showered. I applied some zit cream, put my hair in a ponytail, and dressed in something that was lying on the floor from yesterday. I made my way down to the kitchen and opened a can of some fancy gourmet fish heads. Fig dove in like someone had fired a starting pistol.

"Well, there you are. It's about time you got yourself out of bed. I thought you were going to sleep the day away."

Aunt Ginny had forgone the evening gown this morning and opted instead for a pair of navy woolen slacks and a buttercup yellow twinset with pearls.

"Sorry. I had a rough night."

"So Sawyer's been telling me."

"You've been talking to Sawyer?"

"She came over early this morning. We decided not to wake you. That girl has just about worried herself to death."

I groaned at the thought of Sawyer being here all morning and me being up in bed. "Where is she now?"

"I sent her back home to get some rest. We're going to meet her for lunch after we see Frank."

"Frank, the lawyer Frank? That's this morning?"

"In about a half an hour, in fact. I didn't waste any time in calling him, and he's coming in special just to see us. Frank's been this family's attorney for years. And it's a good thing, too. Because now we need a lawyer for both of us."

"All right, I'll get my purse." I reached for a blueberry muffin, then changed my mind and grabbed an apple instead.

Aunt Ginny was wrapping a peach scarf around her red beehive hairdo. "And while we're on the subject of legal matters, it's all over the news about that girl getting whacked last night."

I froze with my apple mid-bite.

"They aren't naming names yet, just saying, 'suspects were detained for questioning.' I'm only telling you this so you can avoid the news today. I don't want you to get a shock."

I nodded in acknowledgment. "Figaro, behave yourself while I'm gone."

Figaro looked up from his bowl of fish goo long enough to give me a *don't I always?* look.

We met Sawyer just after two p.m. at Mia Famiglia, a new little Italian restaurant a few doors down from her bookstore. As soon as we walked in to the stuccoed terracotta foyer, Sawyer—now wearing a blue striped cardigan with suede elbow patches and skinny jeans—launched herself at me and enveloped me in a hug that could crush the air out of a grizzly bear.

"I'm so sorry! I'm so sorry! I'm so sorry!" she cried.

"It's okay, Sawyer. It's not your fault." I patted her on the back. "I can't really breathe like this."

"Oh, I'm sorry." She let me go. "I've been so worried. I should have never made you come up here. And if I hadn't insisted on walking out alone so no one could see me cry, you would never have . . ." She put a hand over her mouth and started crying again.

"Relax," I said, hearing the new confidence in my voice. "I'm not taking this sitting down. And by the way, you have a lot of nerve looking so cute in skinny jeans the day after we were interrogated for a murder."

Sawyer stepped back, eyes wide, and took me in. "Wow. Who *are* you?"

I giggled at her look of shock.

"Could we sit down and do this? I'm starving," Aunt Ginny interrupted, barreling up to the hostess who seated us at a starched white linen–covered table, in a quiet corner in the back. The Chairman of the Board was belting out "The Way You Look Tonight" from a speaker hidden behind some hanging ivy.

After we got Sawyer settled down and swapped seats twice because Aunt Ginny thought she felt a draft in the first two spots, we finally looked at the menus. I desperately wanted the Pasta Carbonara, but with new resolve, I managed to order a salad with grilled chicken. Sawyer ordered the same and Aunt Ginny tried to order a Sanka with her minestrone. We had to explain to the waiter exactly what Sanka was. Then we had to talk Aunt Ginny off the ledge because no one has Sanka anymore, and convinced her to try a French press. She, of course, resisted because she'd gotten along her whole life without it and had done just fine and didn't want to change now. The waiter offered to let her try some for free and she finally agreed—with a wink to me and Sawyer. After her second cup she decided that it was "purty good after all, even if it was pretentious."

"So how did the meeting with the lawyer go?" Sawyer asked.

The meeting with Frank had left me less than optimistic. He said the cops were anxious to put the case to rest and one in particular was gunning for me. Gee, I wondered which little blond cop that would be? Proving my innocence would be an uphill battle, but I had to do it both for my sake and for Aunt Ginny's. I was fighting for two now. Fighting to keep myself out of prison, and fighting to keep Aunt Ginny from being forced out of her home.

"Well, as far as Social Services versus Aunt Ginny, he said cases like this come up from time to time as people are dealing with senior citizens who don't have family around to assist them. If the state feels the quality of life of the aged . . ."

Aunt Ginny hurled a roll at my head. "Who you calling 'aged'? You watch your tongue, missy!"

I caught it and raised my other hand in surrender. "I'm not saying it. Frank said it. If they feel the feisty senior has lost their faculties, they will step in and require them to move into an assisted living facility for their own protection."

"Poppycock!" Aunt Ginny banged her fist on the table, making the silverware jump.

"Aunt Ginny has clearly not lost her faculties," Sawyer crooned.

"I always did like *this* one," Aunt Ginny crowed, jabbing a thumb in Sawyer's direction.

Sawyer grinned from ear to ear. "What about you being here though? You said Social Services steps in when there is no family around to assist."

"I live too far away. The state will say that I'm not actively involved in Aunt Ginny's life to properly assess her needs. But that's minor compared to the problem of my viability."

"What's that? What's *viability* mean?" Sawyer asked, looking from Aunt Ginny to me.

"Thanks to the events of last night and my arrest, the lawyer thinks the state will reject me as a proper guardian for Aunt Ginny."

"If I ever get my hands on that little Rosalind Carson

I'll turn her over my knee for this!" Aunt Ginny balled up her fist and shook it at a lady a couple of tables over.

Startled, the lady turned to look, and appeared rather alarmed to see no one behind her.

Sawyer and I exchanged amused expressions. "Okay, settle down, Sugar Ray. Let's not make matters any worse. Frank said it's vitally important that I get a good lawyer who can defend me if I have any hope of keeping Aunt Ginny in her home."

"Can't Frank represent you?"

"He's not that kind of lawyer. I need a criminal lawyer; he does family law. And we're running out of time. This Social Services agent is pushing hard to move proceedings along. We have a competency hearing in just a couple of weeks."

"That means *to see if I'm crazy*," Aunt Ginny supplied.

Sawyer put a hand to her chest. "Well, oh my goodness. How can they even question that?"

"I'd like to know who determines *their* competency!" Aunt Ginny smacked the table and clipped the edge of her spoon, which went flying. It landed on the table behind us next to a toddler who promptly picked it up and used it as a catapult to launch peas at the passing waiter. "But that's enough about my problems. I want to hear about last night. I got Sawyer's side this morning while you were sleeping. Now I want to hear it from you."

With some detail, we filled Aunt Ginny in on the events of the reunion and the UFC championship brawl through the period of time leading up to my arrest. Officer Benson had released Sawyer from the History room across the hall after I was cuffed and led to the squad car. But she was still a person of interest since they hadn't ruled her out as an accomplice yet.

"What are we going to do?" Sawyer asked.

"Well, I've made a decision," I announced.

They both looked at me expectantly.

"I've lived my whole life ashamed. I've been pushed around by high school bullies, Georgina, even the number on the scale. I've let fear keep me from trying things because I was afraid of what people would think. While I've been sitting back numbing myself with food and television, dwelling on what could have been, half my life has passed me by. I don't want my past mistakes to paralyze me from taking chances anymore.

"Amber is determined to pin Barbie's murder on me and someone may or may not be trying to frame me for it. This time I'm not going down without a fight. I need to find out who murdered Barbie and clear my name. It's time I took charge and turned my life around."

Aunt Ginny nodded her head. "I couldn't agree more. We can't just sit back and let the cops handle it. We should conduct our own investigation like on *NCIS*. . . . And I'm glad to see you finally got yourself a pair."

I stared at her, shocked. "A pair of what?"

"I don't know," she said, shrugging. "They said it on TV and I think it means *chutzpah*."

Sawyer giggled at Aunt Ginny and asked, "You mean we're going to interview witnesses and dust for prints?"

"Not exactly," I began, "but . . ."

"We need to find out what the DNA evidence points to," Aunt Ginny said with authority. "See who saw what and what they know."

Oh, Lord. It was time to rein in Aunt Ginny before someone found her going around the neighborhood in a trench coat, wearing a spy recorder, trying to interview suspects. "Aunt Ginny, I don't want to pull you into this. It's my problem."

Sawyer scooted in closer. "We could do it. We know a lot of people in town and I've stayed friends with a few from school."

Aunt Ginny gave a whoop of excitement. "There you go! We can prove you're innocent before that mean little cop has a chance to plant evidence or bully you on the stand."

"Exactly," Sawyer agreed.

I shot Sawyer a look. "Would you stop encouraging her?" I jerked my head toward Aunt Ginny. "*We* can't afford any. More. *Crazy.* The county is watching you, just looking for a chance to put you away. *Got it*?"

Aunt Ginny's mouth went into a pout.

"But that's just it," Sawyer pleaded. "So much is at stake for both you and Aunt Ginny. How can we afford not to?"

Aunt Ginny put on her best lost puppy expression. "I could be put in a home if you're convicted. You don't want me in a home, do you?"

I looked at Sawyer, who was nodding emphatically in agreement. Aunt Ginny wasn't the only crazy one at the table.

"All right, fine," I agreed. "You can *both* help. But Aunt Ginny, you're staying way in the background. No midnight sleuthing in back alleys or going through people's trash."

Aunt Ginny clapped her hands and giggled, and Sawyer gave us both a big grin.

"Why am I sure I'm going to regret this?"

Chapter 14

"So, who are our suspects? Who would have wanted Barbie dead?" I asked.

We were back at Aunt Ginny's place, seated in the sunroom again. Figaro had come to add his two cents, *mrrrowwww-ing* now and again as if in support.

"Who *wouldn't* want Barbie dead?" Sawyer responded, and rummaged around her hobo bag for a notebook and pen. "She was mean to everyone. You heard the awful things she said onstage. Billy looked furious when Barbie humiliated his fiancée. I think the only people she didn't offend were Amber and Joanne."

"Everyone sitting at the table next to us was pretty disgusted with her. Especially Kristen. At least, I think she was. It was hard to understand what she was saying half the time."

Sawyer started scribbling a list. "The gist was that Barbie sleeps around. Maybe a jealous wife killed her."

"Or her husband," Aunt Ginny said. She'd dragged out glasses and a pitcher of sweet tea, and a plate of millionaire bars she'd whipped up the night before that I was feverishly trying to ignore. "I remember this one time I thought my *fifth* husband, Danny, was catting around.

I wouldn't stand for that. Nuh-uh. I'd definitely write that down."

Sawyer wrote down "catting around" and underlined it. "Plus, her husband is running for office," Sawyer added, biting the cap of her pen while she was thinking. "He may have wanted to get rid of her before a scandal breaks out about her infidelity."

"A murdered wife is a pretty big scandal," I said.

"It could get him a lot of voter sympathy," Aunt Ginny said. "As long as he could make it look like he was a poor widower, only carrying on because it's what his dear late wife would have wanted." She put the back of her hand to her forehead and feigned distress.

"Okay," Sawyer went on, "we know that Amber, Kristen, and Barbie went to the nurse's office with Joanne."

"Right."

"And we know that thirty minutes later Barbie was dead."

"Right."

"Did you see or hear anyone in the nurse's office when you walked by?" Sawyer asked me.

"No, but the lights were on."

"That doesn't mean anyone was in there," Aunt Ginny said.

"True," Sawyer and I agreed.

"Did you see or hear anyone in the halls?" Sawyer asked.

"I heard Missy onstage, giving out an appreciation award. Other than that there was no one in the hall. But I did notice that it was windy in the foyer and one of the doors was open."

"So someone must have just gone in or out," Aunt Ginny said.

"Right. And I didn't see anyone else until I saw Barbie's body in front of my old locker with a pompom shoved in her mouth."

"Do you think that's what killed her?" Sawyer asked. "Did she choke on the pompom?"

"Well, she had a puncture wound in her neck, so I think that probably had something to do with it. I heard Amber discussing toxins with the paramedics, but I don't think they know exactly what did her in."

"The police would have to order a toxicology report to determine the cause of death," Aunt Ginny dispensed more of her *NCIS* knowledge. "They'll test blood and tissue samples and do a full autopsy to discover if a toxin was used on the vic."

Turning to me, she winked. "That means *victim*."

I rolled my eyes.

Sawyer gave a low whistle. "How long does that take?"

"It can take weeks," Aunt Ginny said, "but on TV someone usually orders it to be expedited so they can wrap up the show in an hour. For all the cops know, the perp shanked the vic and shoved the pompom in her mouth afterward to throw them off the scent." Aunt Ginny sat back with a self-satisfied expression and tapped Sawyer's notebook with her fork. "Write that down."

I stared at Aunt Ginny for a beat. "Do I need to put a parental lock on the True Crime Network? Yer killin' me."

Aunt Ginny answered by sticking her tongue out at me.

Sawyer tapped her chin with the pen. "Do you know why they took you in for questioning and not me or someone else?"

"They found an old syringe in my purse."

"What in the world did you have that for?" Aunt Ginny asked.

"Nothing anymore. It was a Demerol shot for John's pain management, from when we went to the Bar Association gala a couple months before he died. I've only been out of the house dressed up once since then and that was for the funeral. I didn't even know it was in there."

"That should help us though, shouldn't it?" Sawyer directed the question to Aunt Ginny, who gave a confident nod. "I mean they will test it and see that it isn't what killed Barbie."

"As long as it doesn't have her DNA on it," Aunt Ginny said, then looked me square in the eye. "It won't, will it?"

"No. Why would you think that?"

"It doesn't hurt to ask," she shrugged, acting offended that I'd take offense.

"Let's keep going," Sawyer intervened. "You were the first one to find Barbie's body?"

"Yep."

"Who was there next?"

"Joel, then Joanne."

"Joel Miller? That's interesting," Sawyer noted.

"Why is that so interesting?"

"Joel is Kristen's husband, and he volunteers as a part-time coach during basketball season. So he would have had a lot of alone time with Barbie before and after team and cheerleading squad practices—if you know what I mean."

"Where are you going with this?"

"We all know Barbie was a man-eater. Maybe Joel was coming to meet Barbie for a little rendezvous and Kristen found out about it and killed her. I mean, he did show up quickly. Why?"

"Sorry. I just can't see an eight-months pregnant woman killing someone and dragging them through the hall, can you?"

Sawyer's face fell. "No, I guess you're right. But Kristen was pretty upset with Barbie at the reunion, and she *was* one of the last people to see her alive."

"That's mighty fishy," Aunt Ginny said. "Write that down."

Sawyer wrote down "Joel," and drew a fish next to his name. "Maybe Kristen and Joel are in it together."

"I would move them to the top of the list." Aunt Ginny tapped Sawyer's notebook with her fork again.

"I agree." Sawyer made a notation to move them up due to "greater fishiness."

"So our prime suspects are Billy and his fiancée, Kristen and Joel, a mystery jealous wife, and Barbie's husband, Robert. Is that right?" Sawyer asked.

"It's a start at least," I agreed.

"You should go to that school tomorrow and see if they have security tapes that could have caught the whole thing," Aunt Ginny suggested.

"Ooh, that's a good idea." Sawyer wrote it down in her notebook.

"Okay, I'll see what I can find out," I said.

"I wish I could go with you but I have to cover the bookstore tomorrow," Sawyer said.

"That's okay," I said. "I'll come and have coffee with you after and tell you everything I find."

"And while you're there maybe try to question Kristen," Sawyer added.

"She's not going to talk to me," I protested.

"Then we'll make her talk!" Aunt Ginny kicked the coffee table and some of my coffee sloshed out of my cup.

Sawyer and I stared at Aunt Ginny for a minute before going back to the list to finalize our plans. Sometimes I wondered if Aunt Ginny just might be crazy after all.

Chapter 15

The next morning, after Aunt Ginny and I had coffee—
and after I dug Figaro out of the trash can where he was
licking plastic cupcake wrappers—I powered up my cell
phone for the first time since the reunion.

I had forty-six voice messages. Half of them were from
a distraught Sawyer. Most of the rest were from Connie
and Kim. One was from Georgina asking me where I was,
when would I be home to help her coordinate the swag
bags, and had I lost any weight yet. One voice message
was from Aunt Ginny who said, "Poppy, it's Aunt Ginny,
pick up. Pick up, Poppy. I can't tell if this dang doohickey
is working or not. Poppy! Pick up!" And then twenty minutes of Aunt Ginny muttering to Figaro about how much
she hated newfangled technology.

I texted Connie and Kim that I was okay and we should
get together later and I would fill them in on everything. I
ignored Georgina.

I called the referral Frank had given me for a company
to begin cleaning up Aunt Ginny's yard. Shorebird Landscapers were coming out to trim the bushes, prune the
trees, collect the leaves, and mow and winterize the grass.

Aunt Ginny was worried that they would dig up her peonies, but I assured her that her peonies were safe.

Then I placed a call to Handyman Haven to arrange for a contractor to come out and repair the front gate and a broken window on the second story, and replace the rotten wood around the porch. Frank was going to get some estimates for me by next week for having the outside of the house painted.

Aunt Ginny handed me a slip of paper with a phone number scrawled in purple ink. "I have one more call I want you to make."

"Who is it?" I asked.

"Well now, don't get mad."

"Why would I get mad?"

"I asked my friend, Mrs. Dodson, to give me the number of a doctor her daughter goes to for the depression."

"A psychiatrist?"

"No! Not a headshrinker. I can do that for you myself."

"You can shrink my head?" I said with mock horror.

"Quit being fresh." She swatted me on the arm. "This is a different kind of doctor. One that doesn't use traditional medicine unless you really need it. She uses herbs and potions and stuff."

"So—a witch?" I teased.

"Girl, don't make me get my yardstick to your behind."

"Yes, ma'am."

"Now, this doctor did a lot of good for Charlotte, and I think she can do a lot of good for you, too. I want you to give her a call."

"Okay."

"I want you to call today."

"Today?"

"Yes, today. With all the stress that's been added to you with taking care of me and this house and now the murder charges you'll probably need a potion to keep yourself from falling over dead."

"Well, no one wants to fall over dead."

"Poppy Blossom McAllister—I'm serious. Now please give her a call."

Ooh, pulling out the middle name. "Okay, I will. But don't get your hopes up. It takes time to get an appointment with a doctor."

Well, I was wrong about that. It turned out that Dr. Melinda was not a witch but in fact a holistic naturopath who could also prescribe medical tests and prescription drugs when needed. At least that's what her receptionist told me.

"I guess I'll give it a go."

"You won't be disappointed."

"When is your next available?"

"How about this evening at five o'clock?"

"This evening? As in tonight?"

"You are Ginny Frankowski's niece, aren't you?"

"Yes," I said with growing suspicion.

"Your aunt called in this morning and said it was an emergency."

That sneaky little devil. No wonder she told me not to get mad. "I can be there at five, no problem."

"Okay, we'll see you then."

Aunt Ginny had mysteriously disappeared.

Before leaving, I left her a note that I was going to the high school and would be back tonight to glare at her menacingly.

Chapter 16

I pulled up in front of Caper High and parked in a visitor spot. School was canceled for the students on account of the incident over the weekend. I signed in with the security guard at the door and he gave me a temporary pass. I was about to enter the office, when I heard a ruckus down the hall.

"What's going on down there?" I asked the guard.

He rolled his eyes. "Some nutcase is trying to set up a memorial where that woman got killed the other night."

Well, this I gotta see. I walked down the hall and found a shrine laid out in Barbie's memory. Battery-operated candles were lit everywhere. A spray of flowers in the shape of a cross sat in front of a row of lockers and a portrait of Barbie hung on the door to the Spanish classroom.

Missy was frantically trying to wrestle a three-foot-tall teddy bear away from Joanne. "You can't leave this here. The kids will be back in school soon!"

"Don't you tell me what I can and can't do! This is where Barbie died, and this is where I'm setting up a proper tribute in her honor!"

Joanne saw me standing there. Instantly she lunged for

me, but her foot caught on the cross and she tripped. "You! This is your fault! Returning to the scene of the crime!"

Missy grabbed the teddy bear and tucked it under her arm. "Joanne! I will have you banned from this school if you don't calm down."

"Under whose authority?!" Joanne snarled, picking herself up.

"I am acting chair of the Alumni Association and liaison to the principal. You don't want to push me, Jo."

I raised my hands in surrender. "I had nothing to do with Barbie's death, Joanne."

She started to cry. "You're a liar! I will see to it that you're put away for life for this."

Missy gave me an exasperated look. "It's probably best that we get you to the front office right now."

With a backward glance to Joanne, who was resettling her candles, I followed Missy to the office.

Colorful posters advertising lunch menus and school activities hung on a bulletin board, while a large portrait of the school superintendent graced the opposite wall. Missy deposited the stuffed bear behind the long counter that separated the waiting room from the administrative area in the back.

"Joanne's having a tough time with Barbie's death. They were very close."

"Sure." *Some would say too close.*

"I'm surprised you're here. The last time I saw you, Amber was putting you in a police cruiser."

"Well, I wasn't charged with anything and it's still an open investigation. I'm looking for evidence that will prove my innocence."

She thought about that for a minute. "I understand. I would probably do the same thing in your position."

"That's why I'm here. I was hoping to see if there are security tapes from Saturday night that might have caught something."

"I think the police already have them, but you can ask Mrs. Wyatt, in the office. If anyone knows what's going on around here, she does."

"I'll do that, thank you."

Missy gave me a long, appraising look. "I'm a pretty good judge of character and you don't strike me as a killer."

"I'm not. Well, except for spiders. They give me the heebie-jeebies." I followed her out to the security guard desk by the entrance.

"Let me know if you need anything and I'll help you as much as I can." She gave me a reassuring smile. "I'm up here most days volunteering on one committee or another. Athena's a sophomore this year and I want to stay involved. I want her to love Caper High as much as we did."

Uh-huh. "Sure you do."

"It's just so unsettling that someone who was at the reunion killed Barbie. She could be very difficult at times, but she had a good heart. She was wonderful with the cheerleaders. I just can't believe that one of our friends could do something so heinous. The class of '89 is a family." She wiped a tear from her eye.

"Oh, yeah I know." *The Capones were a family too.*

"Well, I have to run. I was just up here dropping off Athena's Shakespeare project when Principal Hinkler asked me to try to reason with Joanne. I'm meeting Kelly to help with the arrangements for the memorial service Wednesday evening."

Wow, that was fast.

"Poor Robert. He's just distraught, as you can imagine. He and Barbie were perfect for each other. He's not even sure he wants to continue the campaign. Says his heart can't bear to go on without his beautiful wife at his side." She wrote her phone number on a Post-it and handed it to me. "Let me know if the security tapes were helpful. And call me anytime you need to talk." She signed out of the visitors' log, gave a backward wave, and in a flash was out the door.

"Athena?" I said to the security guard.

He rolled his eyes and went back to his newspaper.

Mrs. Wyatt was estimated to be about 101 years old. Okay, not really, but good Lord, the woman was ancient when I was in high school, and that was twenty-five years ago. Thin as a rail and more scalp than hair, she had a pair of cat-eye glasses she wore on a chain and she'd put them on the edge of her nose to read. She was looking down her nose at a logbook when I said hello.

"What can I do for you?" she asked without looking up.

"Hi. My name is Poppy and I'm looking for information about the crime that happened the other night."

"Mm-hm." She still didn't look up.

"I was wondering if there was security tape footage from Saturday's reunion."

"I already told the other one. We only run the cameras outside at night. Nothing inside the building."

"The other one?"

"Yeah, the little blond cop."

So Amber had already asked about the tapes. "Why do you only run the outside cameras at night?"

"Because we only expect people to be murdered during the day when the students are here." She looked down her nose at me. "After hours we keep track of the grounds and parking area where the kids like to come back and see what they can vandalize."

"I see. By any chance were these tapes reviewed from Saturday night?"

"Yep."

"Aaaand do you know what was on them?"

"Yep."

"I don't suppose you could tell me."

"I don't know. My memory's all hazy. Prescriptions are getting mighty expensive these days. Medicare just doesn't cover as much as it used to."

Are you kidding me? Was I actually being shaken down by someone's sweet little grandmother? I took out twenty dollars and passed it to her. "I would hate for you to not have your prescriptions."

She took the twenty, squinted through her glasses at it, and tucked it under her bra strap. "That should help."

"So what did they see on the security tapes?"

"They got nothin'. Too many people coming and going because of the reunion. Walking around, making out in the bushes worse than a bunch of hooligans. Nothing around the time of the murder. If anyone came in or out of the building to do the deed, they managed to avoid the cameras."

"Do you think that's a coincidence?"

"Doubtful."

Interesting. "Thank you, Mrs. Wyatt."

"You betcha."

I left the office and started for the exit when I had another idea. I turned right instead and headed toward the nurse's office.

Chapter 17

Pregnancy-chic Kristen was long gone and had been replaced by grouchy, Goodyear-blimp Kristen. She wore her hair in a bun on top of her head with a pencil sticking out of the side of it and had on a pair of dark, rectangular glasses. Her sexy aqua cocktail dress had been exchanged for a pair of sensible brown maternity slacks and a billowy blouse. And she wore a white lab coat with NURSE MILLER monogrammed over the breast pocket and a scowl. She looked to be inventorying bandages and cotton balls when I knocked on the door.

"Come in." She looked me up and down for a moment without expression. "I can't write excuse notes to get your child out of P.E. You'll have to go to your family doctor for that."

"Oh, I don't have a child . . . in school here." *I don't know why I added that last part.* "I just wanted to talk to you for a moment."

She scrunched up her nose and tilted her head back to look at me through her glasses. "Do I know you?"

"Yes," I repeated, "it's me, Poppy. Poppy McAllister." She kept staring at me blankly. "Have we met?"

I sighed deeply. Some things never change. "Poppy McAllister from the class of 1989."

Nothing.

"I was the one arrested Saturday night for—you know." I made a slicing motion with my finger across my throat.

Her eyes grew wide with alarm. "It's you."

"What? I didn't do it."

She appeared to be very nervous and moved behind a metal desk covered with three-dimensional models of various organs and began fiddling with a model of a five-pound blob of fat. "What do you want?"

I sat down on one of the plastic orange chairs in the waiting area. I looked around the room hoping to see something that looked like an obvious clue but nothing jumped out. The room smelled of antiseptic and something chemical-y. Painted in off-white, it was pretty cheerless except for a box window hosting a row of flowerpots. Orchids, Venus flytraps, and other exotic plants I didn't recognize. A door on the left was open and I could see an exam bed covered with a roll of protective paper. There was a tall cabinet behind the desk that I assumed was filled with first aid supplies, because it had a large red plus sign on the front.

"I was hoping you could help me with something."

"Why should I help you with anything?"

"I'm trying to help find Barbie's killer and I need some information. That's all."

Her eyes narrowed. "Information about what?"

"What happened in here Saturday night when you brought Barbie in for an ice pack?"

"What do you mean what happened? I gave her an ice pack."

"Did anything unusual happen?"

"No." She sat down in the chair behind her desk and

pressed against the side of her belly to get comfortable. "Not when you consider who was in here."

"Was it just the four of you? You, Barbie, Amber, and Joanne?"

"Amber wasn't in here. She dropped Barbie and Joanne off at the door and went to call her captain to report the catfight you and your friends instigated."

Okay. I'm gonna let that go. This time. "So she wasn't in here the entire time you treated Barbie?"

"No, but I didn't treat her for very long. After Amber left, Barbie lashed out at Joanne, who ran out of the office in tears. I gave Barbie an ice pack, which she threw back at me a minute later and told me to shove it somewhere. Then she stormed out."

"What did she say to Buffalo—I mean Joanne—to make her leave crying?"

"I don't know. Probably something mean. Joanne worshiped Barbie. She always has. But Barb only indulges her when she feels like it. Ever since Amber and Barb had the big fight, Barb has been trying to repair the relationship any way she can. I think Barb thought Amber was going to stay in here with her. Once Amber left, Barb quit the damsel-in-distress act and bit Joanne's head off."

"What was the big fight about?"

"No one knows. But I'm sure it was something Barb did. She didn't care who she hurt. She'd lost a lot of friends since high school."

"Why?"

"We'd all grown up but she was still as vain and immature as ever. Frankly, I'm surprised someone didn't go off the deep end and kill her sooner. No offense."

"None taken. Do you know anyone who would want to kill Barbie?"

"A lot of people who knew Barb probably wanted to

kill her. She ruined lives and broke up marriages. She'd go after your husband just to prove she could get him." She turned away quickly and wouldn't look me in the eye.

"Did something happen between Barbie and your husband, Joel?"

Kristen's nostrils began flaring wildly and her cheeks turned pink and splotchy. She balled her fists at her side. Her belly didn't seem to be a hindrance all of a sudden, as she lunged at me. "What do you know about that?!" she demanded. "Who have you been talking to?"

I reared back to avoid getting belly punched. "Whoa, relax, okay. That can't be good for the baby. I haven't been talking to anyone. I overheard you and your friends talking about how Barbie sleeps around and you said she goes after husbands. I'm just putting two and two together."

"Well, you're wrong. Joel and I are perfect. He would never cheat on me. We have a wonderful marriage, and now a precious baby is coming to make our family complete." She rubbed her belly and waddled back to her seat.

Wow. Okay. Talk about poking the bear! I asked as nonthreateningly as I could, "What did you do after Barbie left your office? I didn't see you come back into the cafeteria."

"I was exhausted. I lay down in the exam room and fell asleep. I didn't even know Barb was dead until Joel came to get me after he gave his statement."

"So you were alone?"

"Not that it's any of your business, but yes, I was alone," she snapped.

"I'm just trying to establish a timeline."

She narrowed her eyes at me again. "Look, Amber is very good at what she does. If you're guilty, she'll find out."

I just hope she's good enough to see that I'm innocent.

I thanked Kristen and left her office. I started taking my visitor's badge off to return it to security when I heard my name.

"McAllister, what are you doing? You can't be here!"

Amber was standing in the hall, hands on hips, just outside the front office. And she was far more intimidating in uniform than she was in her green cocktail dress. Joanne was standing next to her looking smug.

"This is an open investigation and you're a prime suspect. You can't return to the scene of the crime. Do I have to put you in seclusion?"

I steeled my shoulders and stood my ground. "Since I'm free and there are no court orders in place, I actually think I can go just about anywhere I want, Amber. And I was just asking some questions."

Amber looked surprised at my bold response. *Good. Let her be surprised. This is the new me and she'd better get used to it.*

Not put off, she walked over to get in my face. "Questions about what?"

"Questions about what happened when *you* took Barbie to the nurse's office with Kristen." Okay, maybe I shouldn't have been admitting this to the cop who wanted to pin the murder on me, but Kristen was going to tell her anyway.

"McAllister, have you lost your mind? You weren't charged last night, but that doesn't mean you're in the clear."

"At this point, no one is," I replied, staring her down.

"I could haul you back to jail right now for interfering with my investigation."

"I'm not interfering. I have every right to ask questions. Why do you have it in for me?"

She opened her mouth to bark out another order, but I cut her off.

"I didn't kill Barbie. I hadn't even seen her for twenty-five years until last night. With as many people as I hear hated her, don't you think someone who she's had recent contact with is far more likely to have done it?"

"Do you think I'm an idiot? What do you think 'open investigation' means? We're still tracking down leads and gathering evidence. But right now it doesn't look so good for you."

"Did you know Joanne and Barbie had a fight after you dropped them off at the nurse's office?"

Joanne had a crazy look in her eye. "That is a lie! Who told you that? Barbie and I were best friends!" She balled up her fist and was preparing to strike, but Amber stepped in.

"Settle down, Jo. I'm not discussing the case with you, McAllister. Now get out of here before I regret not keeping you in that holding cell longer. And I don't want to see you on the premises again. Is that clear?"

"I was done here anyway."

With that, I pushed past her and tore off my visitor's badge. I returned it to the security desk. While I was signing out, though, I read through the list of visitors for that day. Kristen's husband, Joel, had signed in that morning and signed out just twenty minutes later. I made a mental note to tell Sawyer and Aunt Ginny.

Outside, I realized that I probably just increased the wrath of my enemy. The little bowl of cereal I'd had that morning had worn off long before, and I was starving. What I really wanted more than anything was a cappuccino from a certain little café.

If the café had a dreamboat barista it was entirely coincidental, and I hadn't noticed.

Chapter 18

I parked around the back in Sawyer's parking spot. She walked to work, and it was vacant since this was the off-season. During tourist season someone would invariably sneak in there the moment it was free. I checked my hair in the rearview mirror and decided that it was beyond my abilities and needed professional resuscitation. I fixed my makeup and put on some lipstick. I wasn't trying to impress anyone. It's just good manners to look your best in public. Besides, he might not even be there.

"*Buongiorno, bella.* I am glad to see you again."

I could feel the heat rising into my cheeks. Traitorous genetics.

"You were so good the other day, I had to come back for more." *What did I just say?* "*It* was so good—the cappuccino . . ."

He gave me a warm smile. "What can I make for you today?"

I took a deep breath. "A cappuccino, please. A *doppio*."

"In Italy we don't drink cappuccino after ten-thirty. It is just for breakfast." He was trying to make small talk.

"Well, in America we don't eat cake for breakfast, so I

guess we're even." *What am I talking about? Why didn't I just go to Starbucks?*

"Ah, so you have been to Italy?" Using a straw, he drew a kitty-cat face in the foam and topped it with a chocolate syrup bow.

"Yes, once. Just Rome, Florence, and Venice. Oh, this is so cute!" I admired the latte art, and he seemed pleased.

"*Parla italiano?*"

"No, I don't speak Italian."

"Are you sure?" he said with a laugh.

"No. Well, I mean I speak *that*. I just only know a little."

"Well, maybe one day we will practice together."

Did I just have a stroke? I feel like I just had a stroke. "I . . . don't think . . . you need . . . any practice." I stumbled over the words.

He laughed a hearty laugh and I felt weak in the knees. "You are funny, *bella*. How was your party? Were you as beautiful as I imagined you would be?"

I accidentally snorted some of the foam up my nose and had to wipe it off. "Umm, it was okay. Until someone was killed and the cops arrested me for the murder." *Well, that will scare him off for good.*

He gave me a sideways look. "You are joking, no?"

"I wish I was kidding. I spent the night in jail and they finally let me go because they didn't have enough evidence to hold me."

His jaw dropped. He took the apron off from around his waist and placed it on the counter. "Come. Sit. I want to hear about this." He motioned for me to take a seat in one of the leather chairs and walked over to lock the door and turned the sign around to CLOSED.

Before I could stop myself, I was singing like a canary on bird crack to this beautiful man and he was listening intently as if I wasn't a crazed lunatic. I filled him in on the whole reunion debacle, right down to the arrest.

"I feel like my whole life has been an array of bad choices and their consequences. I haven't been in the driver's seat. I've been tied up in the trunk. I should be home in Waterford right now, but instead I'm stuck here in Cape May trying to clear my name."

Gia smiled at me and nodded. "I understand, *bella*. My life, too, has taken a few wrong turns. But each day is another chance to get it right. We don't give up. Perhaps God has you stuck here so we can help each other."

I smiled back and our eyes met. I felt a strange tug somewhere in the vicinity of my chest and I forgot to breathe. I felt giddy and ridiculous at the same time. Maybe that foam had gone all the way up to my brain. Then someone was knocking on the front window and the moment was broken. It was Sawyer and she was waving madly at me.

"I will let your friend in so you can talk." Gia opened the door and gave Sawyer a kiss on each cheek, then retreated to the back room.

"As soon as my customer left I ran right over. Isn't this coffee shop wonderful?"

"So good. Thank God for espresso."

"And the owner, Gia, he's so sweet."

I felt myself blush. And then a thought occurred to me. Sawyer worked right across the mall from him every day. They'd probably talked hundreds of times. If he was going to be interested in anyone, of course it would be her. I felt like a fool. He was just being friendly.

"What's the matter? You're frowning."

"Nothing. I have to tell you about my visit to the school."

"Tell me everything. How'd it go?"

But before I could tell her, a customer headed into her shop and she had to run back over.

I gulped down the rest of my coffee, tried to pay for it, but was denied again.

"This one is on the house. You're having a rough weekend."

"Are you sure? The last one was on the house too."

He smiled and shrugged. "I am the boss."

I thanked him and floated across the mall to wait until Sawyer was free again.

Through the Looking Glass was adorable. Sawyer had invested her life savings plus a small inheritance that her grandfather had left her into buying the shop. The décor was inspired by *Alice in Wonderland*. The walls were powder blue with swirly quotes from the book painted around the room. The back corner had a children's area with tiny, overstuffed wing chairs to make the kids feel like they had grown large from the cake that said "eat me." On one wall she had painted just the eyes, grin, and stripes of the Cheshire Cat. She had a second-story open loft with the words "Down the Rabbit Hole" painted in a spiral on the ceiling. This was where she kept the grown-up books in mystery, science fiction, fantasy, and literature. There were two comfy chairs in the shape of fat seashells in the center of the loft, where you could sit and read and just enjoy the space. Her romance and chick-lit section was at the front of the shop in a pink and red "Queen of Hearts" alcove. One Saturday a month she hosted a tea party and all the books were discounted by ten percent. It was a lovely bookstore.

I went to my favorite area while I waited for her to finish ringing up a purchase of *Anna Karenina*. In the corner opposite from the children's books was a section marked by a life-sized Alice painted on the wall with the words CURIOUSER AND CURIOUSER swirled around her head. This was the area dedicated to scratch-and-sniff and pop-up books.

"I knew you would find your way over here."

"I want to see if you have anything new." I was spinning the tornado in a *Wizard of Oz* pop-up book.

"I have a new *Winnie-the-Pooh* pop-up in the back I've been holding for you." She brought it out and I *oohed* and *aahed* over it. From the moment I pulled the tab and Christopher Robin pulled Pooh Bear out of the honey tree where he was stuck, I knew I had to buy it.

We spent the next couple of hours in between customers going over the details of my visit to the school.

"The killer knew how to avoid the cameras."

Sawyer joined me in the loft on a seashell chair. "It would have to be someone who works there, or at the very least was there often enough to know where the cameras were located."

"Well, that casts some doubt on Billy and his fiancée. They were from out of town like me."

"How'd it go with Kristen? Did you learn anything?"

"Apparently, there was a big fight in her office when they got there. Joanne left crying because of something mean Barbie said to her."

"Do you think Joanne should be a suspect?"

"I doubt it. I think Joanne was the only person who truly liked Barbie. You wouldn't believe the shrine she was setting up to her where we found the body."

"Oh, my Lord."

"Oh, and when I was signing out I noticed that Joel Miller had signed in that morning as a visitor."

"What do you think that was about?" Sawyer asked.

"I don't know. Maybe nothing. He *is* Kristen's husband. Maybe he was just visiting."

"Why would he be visiting his wife right after she got to work? Wouldn't he have just seen her at home or called her?"

"You would think."

"Maybe he wasn't just visiting. What if he was picking something up, like some evidence to get rid of?"

"He could have been dropping off her lunch or anything else."

"Well, I think we need to check it out. Given that his wife had a big fight with Barbie the night she was killed, we need to find a way to question him."

"How do you propose we do that?"

"Maybe we can go to where he works. Let's see what he does for a living." Sawyer opened the alumni directory that everyone had received at the reunion.

"You won't believe this! He's a plumber. Why don't we call him to come fix something?"

"Do you have something that needs fixing?" I asked.

"No. Let's just make something up."

"No need," I replied. I knew a place that needed a lot of fixing up.

We called his office and set up a service call for tomorrow morning at Aunt Ginny's. With all the exterior work being done on the house it seemed the most logical place to have the fake emergency. Then I said good-bye to Sawyer and headed out to my cockamamie holistic doctor's appointment in Court House, where I was sure to be told I needed my chakras cleaned or some such nonsense.

Chapter 19

I expected incense and New Age music and one of those electric fountains that makes you have to pee, but Dr. Melinda's office was very modern and bright.

The room was painted creamy yellow with eggplant-colored Barcelona chairs and oak hardwood floors. One wall was dedicated to white built-in bookshelves that hosted a bevy of materials on natural remedies, organic cooking, and holistic medicine. There was a row of dendrobium orchids in pots along a box window and a table hosting *Alternative Medicine* and *Paleo Magazine* issues.

I checked in with the receptionist and she gave me a stack of papers to fill out that was thicker than my first mortgage application. When I was done chronicling my life and health history and the contact information of everyone I knew three times, she offered me some green tea. Which I accepted. And then didn't drink, because it was disgusting. It tasted like someone cooked green beans, then poured the water into a cup and said, brightly, "Drink this, it's good for you."

I was irritated that Aunt Ginny had tricked me into coming here. I didn't have time to have my chi realigned by some swami, I needed to catch a killer. I pulled out my phone and googled "how to kill someone with a hypodermic needle." Air embolism, poison, chemical warfare, puffer fish venom. There were a lot of scary people on the Internet. I was going to search deeper into "death by bee pollen" when Dr. Melinda came out and introduced herself.

Against my better judgment, I liked her immediately. I had expected a hippie Earth Mother type, but she was more like a girlfriend you'd love to go shopping with. Long, thick honey-brown hair surrounded a pleasant oval face. Brown eyes smiled at me behind rectangular black-rimmed glasses with hip-looking red flames on the sides. She was wearing a white turtleneck and brown slacks and had on the cutest pair of chocolate brown wedges with four-inch heels.

Her exam room was a total disappointment from my perspective. There wasn't a crystal pyramid or shrunken head in sight. It was like sitting in a cozy living room. There was a comfy, Rowe Rockford love seat and matching chairs. Instead of anatomical charts there was art on the walls. Except for the exam bed, you would never know you weren't in someone's house.

"Look, I'm sorry my aunt put you up to this, but I really don't have a lot of time for anything too metaphysical."

She blinked at me. Then laughed like she thought I was joking and gestured to a chair for me to sit down. She radiated calm. Looking over the paperwork I had filled out, she asked, "So why don't you tell me what's going on?"

"Well, let's see," I began, "I'm tired all the time and have no energy. But then I also have insomnia. I swell up every time I eat something. Of course, I mostly eat cookies, so . . ." I trailed off.

She took some notes down while nodding. "What's changed in your life recently?"

"My husband died, I've gained sixty pounds, and I was arrested for murder a couple of nights ago at my high school reunion. Oh, and I keep getting this weird eye twitch. What do you think *that's* about?"

Dr. Melinda's pencil lead snapped off and flew into the African violet next to her. Taking a slow breath, she picked up her coffee mug and took a slug from it. "When did the eye twitch start?"

"When I arrived in Cape May for the reunion."

"How long ago did your husband die?"

"Six months."

"When did you start gaining weight?"

"Two minutes after I got home from the funeral, I guess."

"Did you commit the murder?"

"Nope. Hadn't seen her for twenty-five years."

"Why do they *think* you did it?"

"Because I had the misfortune of finding the body."

"That's it?"

"That, and the fact that we were enemies. But you can't throw a rock in this town without hitting one of her enemies."

She nodded and gave me a long look. "Tell me what happened at the reunion?"

I filled her in on the events up to the squad car. "Now I have to try to prove my innocence and figure out who the real killer is before I'm charged with the crime."

"What was determined to be the cause of death?"

"I don't know for sure, but I saw a puncture wound in the victim's neck and I think it may have been some kind of poison. Other than that I'd say she died from pure meanness."

"Okay, it sounds like you've had some traumas. Grief and anger may be a root cause for some of your physical problems. But—since the murder investigation is the most pressing—let's go there first."

I liked her. Okay, so she might be right about emotions affecting my health. But I wasn't going to be mixing tofu and sprouts in my food anytime soon—I was sure she'd try to slip that in—but she did have my attention.

"There are a lot of poisons," she was saying, "but not a lot of them are easy to get a hold of unless you work in a laboratory or travel to South America."

"Most of the suspects I've come up with are local," I chimed in. "Except maybe her ex-boyfriend and his new fiancée. I don't know about foreign travel, but none of them work in a lab. Most of them work at the high school."

Dr. Melinda's eyebrows shot up. "Isn't there a chemistry lab at the school?"

"I hadn't even thought of that."

"Someone with access to a chemical lab can easily create a deadly poison if they know what they're doing." She cocked one eyebrow and tilted her head. "How were you at chemistry?"

I met her look with a cocky one of my own. "I dropped out in the first quarter. I was more of a vo-tech kinda gal."

"You seem very calm, considering the amount of chaos in your life. How do you usually deal with stress?" She went back to taking notes.

"Twinkies. Sometimes Ho-Hos."

"Now, *that* stuff is poison."

"Hmm, maybe someone injected Barbie with snack cakes."

"Murder by cream-filling. That would be a first. I like it."

We both laughed, and I relaxed. Maybe she wouldn't be so bad after all.

"Tell me about the insomnia."

About an hour later the exam was complete and she gave me an execution list. "Um, this may as well say don't eat anything you like ever again."

"I know. It seems difficult right now, but you'll get used to it. Our bodies weren't designed to live on the standard American diet. Stay away from the five fingers of death: sugar, soy, dairy, wheat, and corn. And of course, no artificial anything."

"What will I put in my coffee?"

"Do you *need* coffee?"

"Do you *need* air?"

"Okay. Point taken. Try stevia. It's a natural herb that you can use as a sugar replacement. From now on I only want you to eat real food. Think like a caveman. What did our ancestors eat? If it comes from a factory, you don't eat it. If it doesn't exist in nature, you don't eat it."

"Can't I be a caveman who had a cow and made her own cheese?"

"Uh . . . No. Maybe later you can have some grass-fed dairy, but for now I want you to cut it out. We need to repair the damage to your immune system first. I want you to throw away all harsh cleansers in your home. Use only organic and natural cleaning supplies, beauty creams, shampoos. If you eat it, drink it, breathe it, or apply it to your body, it has to be chemical-free."

She gave me some probiotics from a small refrigerator

to "repopulate my gut bacteria"—whatever that meant—and a bottle of gluten-free digestive enzymes to help with the "leaky gut reaction," which was one of the most disgusting things a doctor had ever said to me.

"One last thing," she said, "we need to address the stress you've been under. I want to you start doing yoga for relaxation. And I want you to make sure you get at least eight hours of sleep a night. Not in the morning, when it's daylight, but at night when you are supposed to be sleeping. Do you have any questions?"

"I don't have to drink any more green tea, do I?" *I mean even I have my limits.*

She laughed. "It's so good for you."

"It tastes like grass."

"Then just drink filtered water with lemon. No sweeteners. But one day it may become my personal challenge to change your mind about the green tea." She gave me a big smile.

Then she wrote something on a little doctor's pad and handed it to me. "Here's a script for some lab work. I want to check your thyroid."

She handed me a book on the Paleo diet. "Read this and try some of the recipes. The chicken enchiladas in coconut tortillas are one of my favorites."

"That sounds good."

"And as for your other problem, be careful. If the cause of death was poison, then the murder was carefully planned out and prepared for. A cold-blooded killer won't think twice about coming after someone who gets too close to the truth."

"Thanks, I'll be careful."

"Call me if you need anything."

I made my follow-up appointment and went to the car

with my new Nazi food regime, bag of supplements, diet book, and list of yoga positions and studios in the area.

This diet may as well say "no more happiness." But I had made a vow to change my life, and that included taking better care of myself. So I was determined to put on my big-girl pants and just deal with it.

All the way home I entertained thoughts about how I was going to repay Aunt Ginny for sending me to a doctor who took away pasta. The best form of revenge, I decided, was to make her do it all with me.

Chapter 20

"Why do *I* have to be punished?" Aunt Ginny protested.

"Because it was *your* idea," I countered. "And *you* conned me into going in the first place."

"I didn't know she was going to take away cheese. That's like taking away oxygen. How are we supposed to live without ice cream? What are we, animals?"

I inhaled the cheeseburger and double onion rings I'd picked up on the way home, part of my "dead man walking" last meal. I would have to put on my big-girl pants—starting tomorrow.

"There are recipes in the book she gave me to make ice cream out of coconut and bananas."

Aunt Ginny picked at her fries and *harrumphed*. I almost felt sorry enough to let her off the hook. Almost.

"If I have to do this Barbarian Diet with you . . ."

"Caveman Diet," I corrected.

"Whatever. Caveman Diet. Then you're going with me to my class at the senior center tonight."

"Sure. What is it? Knitting? Water aerobics?"

Aunt Ginny gave me a look like I had lost my mind.

"Water aerobics? That's for old people. Tonight we're taking salsa dancing lessons."

I almost choked on my vanilla malt. "Salsa dancing! I don't know how to do that."

"That's why we take the class." She cleared our empty wrappers and paper bags and put them in the trash for Figaro to inspect later. "Now, go get your duds on. We're leaving soon."

I stomped upstairs to my room and threw open my closet. Aunt Ginny had conned me into something again. Unbelievable. On the other hand, maybe a little social interaction would keep her from prowling the neighborhood in her pajamas again.

I didn't have anything that officially classified as "duds." The only dress clothes I'd brought with me didn't fit. My dress from the reunion was quarantined in the hamper, disgraced after its night in lockup. "I don't have any duds!" I yelled to Aunt Ginny.

Figaro had come in to watch, and I swore he was laughing at me. He sat on the bed watching me ransack the dresser, his whiskers twitching in amusement. The best I could come up with was a pair of black yoga pants, a white Empire waist blouse, and my silver flats. I dressed and tried to tame my hair flat. I presented myself to Fig and he gave me a judgmental cat look that said, *So that's what you're wearing? I wouldn't wear that to a neutering.*

"You're impossible, Fig."

I waited for Aunt Ginny in the front parlor. When she emerged from her room, she was wearing a blood-red wrap dress and a pair of matching low-heeled dancing shoes. A square-cut black onyx surrounded by diamonds hung around her neck and she had a black fringed shawl draped across her shoulders. My eighty-something-year-old great-aunt was officially sexier than I was. I may have just hit rock bottom.

The salsa class—and I use that term loosely—had already started when we arrived. We could feel the *thump thump thump* of the beat from the parking lot, and Aunt Ginny was already rolling her shoulders and shimmying on the way up the sidewalk.

The seniors out on the dance floor were being led by a silver-haired man in tight black tuxedo pants and a crisp white ruffled shirt that was open to the waist showing a patch of gray chest hair. The very debonair Mr. "Shake-your-bum-bum" Ricardo was demonstrating a move he called "the Copa."

When he saw Aunt Ginny enter the room, he lit up. "Ah, my favorite partner is here!"

I watched Aunt Ginny blush and give Mr. Ricardo a coy little wave. She caught my raised eyebrows and answered with a prim sniff. Mr. Ricardo shook his bum-bum all the way over to take Aunt Ginny by the hand and lead her back to the dance floor. I watched in amazement as she shook her bum-bum and followed him out there.

From what I could tell, everyone was pretty much doing their own thing. Mrs. Dodson was in the center of the room shuffling her feet side to side with a look of abject seriousness while pumping her cane in the air to the beat. Mr. and Mrs. Spisak were dancing what looked like a fast waltz. Thelma Davis was off to the side by herself, windmilling her arms and marching back and forth.

A hunched-over little man with a head full of white hair was hanging on to a walker that sported three tennis balls on its metal feet. He shuffled over to me and asked, "Wanna dance, Cookie?"

Before I could answer him, I was swept away by Mr. Glostner, who grabbed me by the hand and twirled me out to the dance floor. "You can thank me later," he said, winking.

I looked around for Aunt Ginny to come rescue me, but she was shaking her hips with Mr. Ricardo and swinging her black fringed shawl around her head.

The little walker man shuffled past me and called out, "He won't hold on to all his hair."

Mr. Glostner tried to dip me, but halfway into the maneuver he cried out in pain and dropped me to the floor. "I'm so sorry, miss. Won't be but a moment." He groaned and stepped away gingerly. "Just let me go take my back pill and I'll be ready in two shakes."

He lumbered off, and the little walker man shuffled back again. "How do ya like me now?"

I picked myself up and looked for a corner to hide in, but Mother Gibson grabbed both my hands and started pedaling them up and down in time to the music.

Mr. Spisak lost control of Mrs. Spisak and twirled her into a potted palm. She didn't seem to notice and kept dancing with the palm until Mr. Spisak retrieved her.

Much to my relief the song ended. "Mamma needs to go put another nail in the coffin. Be right back." Mother Gibson snuck off to the bathroom to smoke, and I tried to make a break for it.

I had a moment of terror when I caught Mr. Ricardo trying to pick up Aunt Ginny for a lift. Thankfully, they abandoned the idea.

There was a tap on my shoulder, and when I spun around a little Indian man bowed to me. "I am Mr. Raj Patel. Would you do me the honor?"

"Oh, why the heck not."

I let Mr. Patel lead me around to "Mambo Italiano."

He wasn't bad. He twirled me past a couple of ladies pouring contents from a silver flask into the punch bowl, and I overheard something interesting.

"I heard she made a fool of herself over the Sommers boy again. He swore she would regret it someday. It looks like that day has arrived."

"It took him years to get over the humiliation of it. He was so ashamed he had to leave town. But I don't think he's capable of murder, do you?"

I tried to get closer to hear more, but Mr. Patel swung me off in another direction and I lost them. I searched the crowd for the ladies but they had disappeared.

When the dance free-for-all was over, I was exhausted and ready for bed. Aunt Ginny and her friends decided, however, they were having too much fun to go home.

Ivey Spisak knocked on her hip with her fist. "I paid a lot of money for this titanium. Let's go see what this baby can do."

"I know a great little club in Wildwood called Caliente," Mr. Ricardo offered. "Let's move the party there."

"I'll be breaking curfew," Mrs. Dodson said, looking at her watch fob pinned to her blouse. "But what is Charlotte going to do, ground me?"

"Aunt Ginny," I asked. "What do *you* want to do?"

Aunt Ginny looked at Mr. Ricardo, then back to me. "It's only eleven. It's early yet. I remember when we used to go out dancing till breakfast." Mr. Ricardo gave her a beaming smile.

"Maybe fifty years ago," I muttered under my breath.

Aunt Ginny looked so excited that I agreed to go with them to Caliente. So much for Dr. Melinda's instructions to go to bed early.

We all piled into two cars. Aunt Ginny and the Spisaks

went with Mr. Ricardo. The widows, Mrs. Dodson, Mother Gibson, and Thelma Davis, went with me.

"Poppy, did you go to that doctor I told Ginny about?"

"Yes, Mrs. Dodson. Thank you for the referral."

"Sure thing, honey. Nasty business that depression stuff. Did she give you anything disgusting to drink?"

"Just some green tea in her office."

"She gave Charlotte a protein smoothie that could peel paint off the wall."

"So what's this about you being arrested?" Mother Gibson got right to the point.

"Lila!" Mrs. Dodson's head snapped around in shock.

"What? We all know she was arrested Saturday night. It was all over the senior center by Sunday afternoon. Let's get it out in the open."

"I don't mind," I told them.

"Well in that case, give us the skinny." Mrs. Davis ignored the reproving look from Mrs. Dodson.

I told them about the reunion and the history between "us" and "them." Us being the B crowd and them being the popular kids who made our lives miserable for years. I described the crime scene, and finding the body, finishing with the story of my arrest and spending the night in jail.

Mother Gibson shook her head and said, "Oooh, child." Mrs. Davis was clutching Mother Gibson's arm and fanning herself out of overexcitement by the time we got our table at Caliente.

"I know Kristen Miller's mother," Mrs. Dodson said, "and I can't believe that girl would have anything to do with this, even if she is having a change-of-life baby to save her marriage."

"Save her marriage from what?"

"Well, I normally don't tell tales out of school," Mrs. Dodson said with practiced gravity.

Thelma snickered. "Since when?"

"Oh, yes you do," Mother Gibson added.

Mrs. Dodson ignored both of them and went on. "Save it from divorce. Kristen suspected her husband had an affair about a year ago and it nearly did them in."

"She just suspected it?" I asked. "She doesn't know for sure?"

"She didn't ask. Her mother said she had all the proof in the world, except catching him in the act. Phone records, florist receipts, hotel bills, e-mail, you name it. But she never questioned him. Just told him she wanted to work on their marriage and have a baby."

"Like that's gonna help anything." Mother Gibson rolled her eyes. "These young kids don't know what they're doing nowadays. Babies are hard work. Not accessories like those little dogs in purses."

"I'd love to have a little purse dog to carry around with me." Mrs. Davis cradled an imaginary dog in her arms.

"Thelma! You already have three cats. If you get any more animals I'll call the health department on you myself!" Mrs. Dodson warned.

Trying to steer the conversation back to Kristen and Joel, I asked, "Does she know who he had an affair with?" I fully expected it was Barbie.

"Oh, yes," Mrs. Dodson said, nodding. "She knows. But if she told her mother, the woman wouldn't tell me. And believe you me, I tried to get it out of her."

"We believe you," Mrs. Davis giggled.

"And this baby wasn't easy to make, either. They didn't do it the old-fashioned way. Nuh-uh." Mrs. Dodson looked at the other ladies and they were all nodding in agreement. "She had the doctors do that in-vee-ter-o."

Mother Gibson frowned. "Honey, that's a lot of needles."

"Needles?" I asked.

"Oh, yes. You have to give yourself shots. At home," Mrs. Dodson answered sagely.

"Can you imagine doing something like that to yourself?" Mrs. Davis asked. "Things sure have changed from when we were young. If we couldn't have a baby we just had to live with it."

I thought about the two ladies I overheard at the senior center. "Did something happen between Barbie and another boy? Possibly Billy Sommers? Something humiliating?"

The ladies didn't know of anything, but Mrs. Dodson said she would check with her contacts at the Christian Women's League. "If anyone knows what happened, they will."

Mr. Ricardo spun Aunt Ginny by the table. "What are you all doing just sitting there? Life is too short to sit in the corner when you could be dancing."

Aunt Ginny looked at me and said, "Nobody puts baby in the corner," then Mr. Ricardo cha-cha'd her away again.

The widows got up to dance, but I was preoccupied with rumors. Could Billy have killed Barbie? Was this revenge for some past humiliation? Or was Joel trying to cover up an affair? I would have to find a way to question Joel about Barbie when he came to the house in the morning.

Chapter 21

Every muscle in my body ached. Aunt Ginny had me out salsa dancing until two a.m. Note to self: Start taking whatever vitamins Aunt Ginny is on.

I started my day with a mugful of hot water with lemon and a fistful of pills that would intimidate Keith Richards. Then I went to the lab to have what was surely a record-breaking amount of blood drawn for all of Dr. Melinda's tests.

On the way home I stopped at the market to shop for the grass-fed meat, wild-caught fish, and free-range eggs on the whole foods shopping list. I loaded up on everything sold in the green aisle for the house. Next, I made a quick visit to the farm stand to load up on organic produce. My old grocery list read like a Who's Who of culinary stars. Ben & Jerry, Marie Callender, and Mrs. Fields. Ah, the good old days! Shopping was a lot faster sticking to the perimeter of the store, I'd give Dr. Melinda that.

When I got home I ate a bowlful of raspberries, while throwing away or boxing up for charity everything in the refrigerator and pantry that was not whole foods compliant. Which turned out to be just about everything. I thought

Aunt Ginny would need a slug of the thirty-year-old scotch she kept hidden in a hollowed-out thesaurus in the library when she saw the peanut butter go in the trash. Figaro was furiously batting around a loose bouillon cube and generally getting in the way.

Sawyer rushed in, out of breath, and put the ginormous tote bag she called a purse on the kitchen counter. "Did I miss anything? Where is Joel?"

"No. Mr. Plumber is late." I boxed up the last package of pasta for the food bank donation and made us a pot of herbal mint tea.

"Well, don't that beat all." Sawyer plopped down on one of the avocado vinyl chairs at the Formica table, where we'd spent hours playing Trivial Pursuit and Monopoly in high school. "And I rushed over here thinking I was the one who was running behind."

"What are we saying is broke?" Aunt Ginny joined Sawyer and poured them both a cup.

"We told him there's a problem with the water heater, so we need it to be convincing."

I watched them sit at the table conspiring together and enjoying their herbal tea. I considered joining them, but more than anything I wanted a cookie. I was starving. I looked at the trash bag where I knew I had thrown a box of Nutter Butters, but decided I had too much pride to dig through the trash and had a handful of almonds instead.

A knock at the door signaled the arrival of our interrogation victim. Aunt Ginny and Sawyer were fighting to peel off of the vinyl chairs.

"Relax, I'll get it," I told them.

Joel gasped when he saw me open the door. I smiled and his eyebrows raised farther into his hairline. He looked down at his work order and back up to me.

"Mrs. Frankowski?" he asked nervously.

"I'm her niece, Poppy." I put my hand out, but he just stared at it, then at his work order.

"Won't you come in?" I stood back and gestured into the foyer, where Aunt Ginny and Sawyer had appeared, standing suspiciously close to each other and staring at Joel like he was an alien species. Figaro sauntered into the room, his face covered in yellow dust and smelling like chicken soup.

Joel looked side to side nervously, then down at Figaro in alarm. "Oh my God, what is that?"

Figaro froze in his tracks looking up at Joel, then flopped over on his side with a thud.

I shook my head at the pitiful chicken-dusted feline. "That's just my cat."

"Well, is it okay? It looks like it just had a stroke." Joel was watching Figaro curiously.

"He's fine," Aunt Ginny said as she nudged Figaro with her foot and pushed him a couple of feet off to the side and into the library. He slid into the room without resistance and just lay there.

"Why don't I show you the water heater?" I offered.

Joel followed me down the hall toward the kitchen and into the mud room, his neck craning to keep his eyes fixed on Figaro as long as possible. Figaro lay there unmoving and stared back until we were out of sight.

"So what's wrong with the water heater?" Joel took a pen out of his pocket to make some notes on the work order.

"It's making a *glug-glug-glug* sound," Aunt Ginny demonstrated.

"It's more like *blerg-blerg*," Sawyer added.

"No, it's a clanging, bubbling sound like *glerggping—glerggping—glerggping*."

Joel was blinking at the two of them. Aunt Ginny tapped on Joel's clipboard. "Why aren't you taking notes?"

I gave Aunt Ginny and Sawyer a look that said, *what the heck is wrong with you two?* "Why don't you just take a look," I suggested.

Joel squatted down and checked gauges and tapped pipes, listening.

"Oh, it's been acting up something awful, hasn't it?" Aunt Ginny said to Sawyer.

Sawyer nodded vigorously. "Oh my, yes, it's just been so loud we can hardly talk in here. Isn't that right, Poppy?"

Oh, Lord. Don't drag me into this. "Oh, yes," I mocked them. "Because you two do so much visiting here in the mud room."

Joel moved down the pipeline with a flashlight, tapping and looking for problem areas.

"It's a wonder we have any water at all with all the noise it's been making." Aunt Ginny was pouring it on thick.

"Well, here's your problem." Joel shone his flashlight at the pipes on the backside of the water heater.

"What?! What problem?!" Aunt Ginny shoved Joel to the side to see behind the heater. "What do you mean here's your problem?"

Sawyer's hand flew up to her mouth in surprise.

"Well, yeah," Joel answered, looking at each one of us in turn. "You have a leak in this pipe behind the water heater. You can see it dripping from here." He shone his flashlight behind the unit, and sure enough there was a slow drip and a puddle of water.

Aunt Ginny retreated out of the mud room, and sat at the kitchen table to drink her tea and calm down. She continued to stare at the back of Joel's head, her eyes narrowed, muttering darkly to herself.

We discussed how much the water heater would cost to fix and Joel went to his truck to get some tools and parts.

Sawyer craned her neck to see the puddle and sighed. "It's always something."

While Joel was making the repairs, I tried to casually introduce some of the questions we had thought up earlier.

"So, I was wondering, how did you get to the murder scene so fast the other night?"

Joel was lying on his back around the water heater. He dropped his wrench with a loud clang. "What?!" He sat up so fast he hit his head on a pipe running to the washing machine.

"You were the first person to arrive on the scene after me, and I was just wondering how you got there so fast."

"Like I told the police," he growled, "I was inside the little gym on the other end of the hall where I'd been shooting hoops with Pete and Troy. I opened the door to get some air for a minute and heard a scream, so I ran in to see what was going on. That's when I saw you standing over Barbie's body." He frowned at me and I froze.

Sawyer jumped in to break the tension. "I hear congratulations are in order. You and Kristen are expecting."

"We are. She's due any day now."

I recovered and asked, "I'm told your baby is pretty special. That you and Kristen went through a fertility clinic?"

Joel went back to working on the pipes, but he kept one eye on us. "Yeah. We tried for years to get pregnant on our own, but it just didn't happen. Then we decided having kids just wouldn't be for us. Kristen works with kids every day and sees the problems they face, so we figured maybe we didn't have one of our own for a reason."

"What made you decide to have a baby in a test tube?" Aunt Ginny startled me. She had snuck back into the room and was hovering behind us.

"It's a little more complex than that," Joel chuckled. "But my wife just woke up one day and said she wanted to have a baby and we were running out of time. So she made us an appointment to see a fertility specialist."

He had removed the old copper pipe and was attaching a new fitting with some smelly glue.

I decided to throw what little tact I had out the window; my freedom was on the line here. "Has pregnancy helped Kristen forgive you for having an affair with Barbie?"

Joel didn't move. His hand was frozen on the wrench around the old copper pipe. We all held our breath waiting to see how he would react. I watched Aunt Ginny's gaze move from Joel's hand on the wrench up to her rolling pin on the wall and back again. Joel put down the wrench, reached for a blowtorch, and fired it up.

"What are you talking about?" His voice was artificially cool.

"I heard that this baby was a way to save your marriage."

Joel slowly put the torch to the new fitting and fired it.

"I'm sorry. I thought everyone knew. Maybe I should just go back to Kristen and ask her."

Joel remained silent.

Aunt Ginny took a step toward the rolling pin.

Joel sat up and began collecting his tools. "I don't know where you got your information, but I have never been with anyone other than Kristen since we met freshman year. We're high school sweethearts."

Yeah, and I'm a flying nun. "That's so strange. The way Barbie's friends were talking about it at the reunion, it sounded like fact."

"Well, there's your first mistake. Barbie didn't have any friends. Except maybe that weird one that always followed her around. You can't believe anything you hear from that group of—"

"Watch it, sonny," Aunt Ginny warned. "I don't allow no cussin' in this house."

"That group of *gossips*," Joel substituted. "Sooner or later, Barbie burned every friend she ever had. It's probably what got her killed. But I'm guessing you probably already knew that."

"Did you notice anything suspicious the night of the reunion?"

"There was plenty suspicious. Everyone was getting drunk and the cheerleaders with that ridiculous pep rally."

"I mean with Barbie in particular. How about anything during the weeks leading up to the reunion?"

He thought for a minute. "She had a lot of secret meetings with Coach Wilcott, and he always looked shifty about them. He was very stressed when she showed up, and he tried to avoid her as much as possible."

"Wouldn't it be normal for her to meet with the basketball coach seeing as how she was the cheerleading coach?" Sawyer asked.

"Well, yes and no. Barbie wasn't a school employee. She was a volunteer, like me. She had her own cheerleading program and she led cheering camps and competitions, so she worked with a couple of different schools. She was here a lot, working with the cheerleaders. But unless they were doing something special, she'd have no reason to coordinate with the coach."

"What made you think the meetings were secret?" Sawyer asked.

"The way the coach kept looking around, checking to see if anyone was watching them. The way he would rush Barbie into his office and shut the door and pull the blinds. He looked like a man trying to hide." He wrote out an invoice and handed it to me. "I'm not going to lie. You did a lot of people a favor the other night. But don't get cocky and start nosing into other people's business."

I paid him for the plumbing repair and we watched him leave.

"Do you think he was telling the truth?" Sawyer asked.

"Definitely not," Aunt Ginny said.

"How do you know?"

"His eyes shifted to the left when he told you some things. That means he was lying or holding back. I learned that on *Matlock*!"

"Some of it was true. Some of it we'll have to dig deeper to find out," I answered.

"One thing is sure," Aunt Ginny said. "He didn't tell you everything."

Chapter 22

After grilled-steak salads for lunch, Sawyer left to go back to her bookstore to take over for her assistant, Bethany. I was just about to head out to the school to talk to Coach Wilcott when Aunt Ginny called me from the sunroom.

"The pho-one is for you-u," she sang out. "It's a bo-oy."

What *boy* would be calling me? I took the phone from her. "Hello?"

"Hey, gorgeous . . . Hello?"

I was suspicious from the word *gorgeous*. "Who is this?"

"What do you mean who is this? It's Tim! I told you I was going to call."

My heart did a little flip. "Oh, hi."

Aunt Ginny was hovering over me like a crazed lunatic, making me even more nervous. I tried to wave her away but she swatted back at me. "I thought you were just being polite, given the circumstances."

"Don't be ridiculous. I meant what I said. I want us to get together."

"O-kay." My stomach was trying to decide if this was

excitement or dread, so it churned up both to cover all bases. "When would you like to meet?"

"I was thinking, why don't we go to lunch on Thursday? I can have my *sous-chef* cover the restaurant for the afternoon."

Aunt Ginny was hopping from side to side in excitement. Figaro, seeing this, thought we were playing a game, and came over to spin in circles at her feet.

"Sure, I think Thursday would be fine. Do you want me to meet you somewhere?"

"No, I'll come pick you up at one o'clock."

"That sounds like a date."

I regretted the word as soon as it left my mouth. *Why did I just say a date?* What had I done?

"Would that be okay with you?"

"Um, yeah."

"O-kay. I'll see you on Thursday."

Aunt Ginny was dancing a little jig, and Figaro was looking from her to me expectantly as if surely this was a treat-giving kind of situation.

"You have a da-ate," she said gleefully.

"It's not really a date, it's just lunch."

"It sounds like a da-ate."

"I think I'm going to be sick."

"Now calm down. It's not a big deal. Where is he taking you?"

"I don't know. We're going to lunch."

"See, relax. That's like a mini-date. More than coffee, but less than dinner. No pressure."

"Where are you getting these rules?" I eyed her speculatively.

"*Sex and the City.*"

Oh boy. "I'm going to go check out Joel's alibi with

Coach Wilcott. I'll be home in a little while. Don't forget we have our first yoga class tonight with Sawyer."

"I'm going to call the Interfaith Food Bank to come pick up these boxes. On your way out, take those bags out to the curb before I change my mind about this cocka-mamie diet and eat the cookies out of the trash."

I left for Caper High, marveling at how similar Aunt Ginny and I were.

I stopped at Stauffer's Bakery to buy a box of encouragement for the security guard. He'd said he wouldn't allow me in the school after my last run-in with Amber. I was on a "banned" list and I couldn't cross the imaginary line past his desk.

Security is a noble profession. An impenetrable force, sworn to protect and uphold the directives of local law enforcement. And after two jelly and one cream-filled doughnut they draw a darn good map to where the coach parks his car in the back lot and leaves the building around four-thirty. God bless 'em.

I parked my Corolla by a Dumpster where I still had a line of sight on the back door to the little gym and waited. About five minutes after the four-thirty bell, the coach emerged, right on schedule.

"Coach Wilcott—do you remember me?" I asked nervously.

He squinted at me and gave me a once-over before recognition dawned on his face. "Joy Peterson? Is that you?"

"Um, sure. Why, yes, it is me. Joy Peterson. Who else would I be?" *Let's see where this goes.*

"How long has it been?"

"Oh, I don't know. How long do *you* think it's been?"

"Gosh, at least fifteen years. Are you still playing volleyball?"

"No. Not these days." *Or ever.* "I see you're still a gym teacher. How is that going?"

"Good. We have a good basketball team this year. A lot of potential."

"Oh, good, good. Hey, I had a couple of friends here at the reunion the other night, and they were telling me about the incident involving the cheerleading coach, Barbie Clark. Were you here when that happened?"

His jovial demeanor was instantly replaced by a mistrustful scowl. "What are you, a reporter now or something?"

"Me? No. Don't be silly. One of my friends was very close to Barbie, and is very broken up about the whole thing. I was wondering what happened. Do you know any of the details?"

"I don't know anything. I was in my office the whole night." He tried to push past me to a more-rust-than-paint red Trans Am that looked like it would be more comfortable up on blocks in someone's front yard.

I moved to the left to block him. "That's a shame. You didn't even get to sample the buffet?"

"Nothing. I had paperwork that I had to finish before Monday's away game."

Really? What about that plate of wings we saw you scarfing down like they were about to be added to the endangered species list?

"That's too bad. I hear it was really good. Did you see Joel Miller at the reunion at all?"

He stopped trying to get around me and gave me a level stare. "Are you sure you're not a reporter?"

I put my hands up in surrender. "I promise. Not a reporter."

"Or a cop?" he added.

"Nope. Just trying to help a friend."

"What friend?" He narrowed his eyes and leaned in till I could smell Jack Daniel's and Doritos duking it out on his breath.

I had to think fast. "Do you know Joanne Junk?"

"Yeah, I know Joanne." He visibly relaxed. "Great field hockey player. She would have been a great phys ed teacher."

We actually had a bet about that in high school. "I'm only looking for some information so an innocent person doesn't go to jail." Well, that *was* true.

"Yeah, Joel was here. He was in gym B with some of the guys shooting hoops."

"Was he there all night?"

"I don't know. I wasn't watching him. Why? Do you think he had something to do with what happened?"

"I don't know. What do *you* think? What kind of relationship did Joel have with Barbie?"

"It used to be pretty chummy from what I could see. They were always flirting. It's not my place to judge but it was courting disaster, what with his wife being the school nurse and all. I tried to warn him to stay away from Mrs. Clark but he told me to mind my own business."

"Did they have any kind of falling-out recently? Any arguments?"

"Something happened but I don't know what. About the time Mrs. Miller announced that she was pregnant things cooled off between Coach Miller and Coach Clark. You could feel the tension all the way across the gym."

"Do you think Mrs. Miller suspected something was going on?"

"All I know is there was electricity in the air when the two women were together. Like two cats before an alley fight."

"How about you? You worked with Coach Clark. How was your relationship?"

"Fine. We didn't talk much."

"Doesn't the head coach work pretty closely with the cheerleading coach?"

"She wasn't technically part of my department, but she ran a couple of ideas by me from time to time about things she wanted to do with the cheerleaders when it included my boys. Running through banners and nonsense like that. Otherwise she was on her own."

"Did she run any special plans by you recently?"

He hesitated. "No. Nothing for this school year." He pushed past me and grabbed the door handle on his car. "Look, I gotta go. I got a meeting to get to."

I hope it's an AA meeting. "Sure. Hey, one more thing, how's your wife, Mrs. Wilcott? We all thought you two were such a cute couple."

His face flushed and he looked away as he got in the car and started the engine like he hadn't heard me, so I turned to go.

"Joy. Joy. Joy."

Oh, that's me. "Yes?"

"Tell Joanne I said to take care of herself, okay?"

"I will. Thank you, Coach."

He gunned the Trans Am with the vanity plate that said GLRYDAZ and tore out of the parking lot. As he left, I saw his eyes watching me in the rearview mirror.

Chapter 23

Talking to the coach creeped me out enough to need some coffee, so I drove over to the Washington Street Mall for no other reason than because I needed an espresso. It's not my fault the owner is so hot. Sometimes people just be needing coffee. Don't be so judgy.

"*Buongiorno, bella.*"

I giggled. *Get it together, Poppy.*

"You look frazzled. What's going on?"

I sat down at the bar and sighed. "I just tried to interview a couple of suspects and they both lied to me."

"That makes them look more guilty, no?"

"Oh, definitely. But I only need one person to be guilty as long as it isn't me."

"You want a cappuccino?"

"No. I can't have the milk anymore. It's kind of like a food allergy. Can I just have a *doppio*, please."

"You got it." He readied the shot. "No more dairy, huh?"

"No. Among other things."

He raised his eyebrows at that and I felt myself blush. "F-food things."

"Ah." He placed a small glass of sparkling water in front of me.

"What is this for?"

"To cleanse your palate for the espresso."

Oh. How fancy. I took a drink of the water and waited. He nodded his approval.

He poured two shots and placed one in front of me. I picked it up and went to gulp it, as per usual.

"What are you doing?"

"I'm drinking my espresso."

"No." His eyes twinkled with merriment and I put my cup back down.

"First, stir." He stirred his cup, and I followed suit.

"Then, smell." We both breathed in the rich aroma.

"Next, toast." He tapped my cup with his. His eyes never left mine. "*Chin-chin.* Now, sip."

We both took sips of our coffees. There was something seductive and intimate about the ritual. That must have been some high-octane caffeine, because my heart was racing.

"Was it good?" He was watching me with intensity.

My voice caught and I squeaked out, "Uh-huh."

He must've been very pleased with my sad little answer because he grinned from ear to ear. "Good."

He turned away, and I realized there was another lady who had come into the shop while I was preoccupied with my espresso. She was standing at the counter, staring at me with wide eyes. Then she turned to Gia and said, "I want that too."

Chapter 24

"Which one do we want to try first?" Sawyer had the list of yoga studios Dr. Melinda had given me. We were trying to pick one that had a class for beginners. Was there such a thing as a class for pre-beginners, where you lay on a yoga mat and just watched and snarfed Cheetos?

"How about this one called 'The Golden Lotus.' That sounds authentic."

We were waiting for Aunt Ginny to finish getting ready so we could leave. Sawyer and I were each dressed in traditional yoga pants, or as I called them, pants. Hers were gray, mine were black. And we each had on a ribbed tank top. Hers was pink, mine was black. Sawyer looked adorable. I looked pale and puffy and my upper arms were the consistency of cold oatmeal.

"I'm ready." Aunt Ginny breezed into the sunroom wearing flowing white cotton pants and a matching white short-sleeved cotton T-shirt. She had a psychedelic scarf wrapped around her head like a turban. She was either going to yoga or a Grateful Dead concert.

Sawyer stared at the bold, tie-dyed rag on Aunt Ginny's head. I recovered a little faster.

"So whatcha got there?" I asked.

"This is my yogini head wrap. We used to wear them a lot in the sixties."

"Uh-huh. You planning on wearing that out tonight?"

"You better believe it."

Sawyer and I looked at each other. "Okay then," Sawyer said. And I could hear every word she *wasn't* saying. "Let's go."

The Golden Lotus was in a little strip mall that didn't have much going for it besides a bicycle rental shop and an Italian water ice stand. I pushed open the industrial glass door covered in faded blackout paper to an eruption of thick white smoke, heavy with sandalwood and body odor. Through the dimly lit studio we saw an Indian statue with six arms in one corner and a brass gong the size of a washing machine drum in the other. Overhead played a series of low metallic hums and I saw Aunt Ginny reach up and adjust her hearing aid.

"Whoo-whee, it's hot in here." Sawyer fanned herself with the studio list. "It must be over a hundred degrees."

"It is precisely one hundred and five degrees."

An anorexic-looking Indian man dressed in an orange diaper had appeared out of nowhere. At least I think it was out of nowhere. The incense smoke and the sweat was stinging my eyes. "You are here for the class? Come. Come."

His bony hand grabbed my wrist and was pulling me inside where a handful of people were writhing around on thin mats on a parquet wood floor.

Aunt Ginny clutched her right arm with her hand and rolled her eyes back in her head. "Um. Oh, no. My right arm. I think I'm having a heart attack," she intoned flatly.

"It's the left arm," I hissed through gritted teeth.

"I mean the left arm. Oh, it's both arms," Aunt Ginny said. "It must be a double heart attack."

Sawyer put her arm around Aunt Ginny's shoulders. "Why, this isn't the emergency room. I think we made a wrong turn. Come, Granny, let's get you to the hospital."

"Ooohh," Aunt Ginny moaned. "I just hope we're not too late."

I released myself from the man's bony grasp and felt for the door. "Sorry, can't stay. Granny's sick."

We got back to the parking lot and deeply breathed in the cool night air. Aunt Ginny, miraculously recovered from her near-death experience, fast walked to the car and called, "Shotgun."

"What's next on the list?" I asked Sawyer.

Sawyer consulted the printout and announced, "Zen Mania has a beginner class starting in thirty minutes."

"This better not be another hinky setup like that last one." Aunt Ginny gave me a warning look, and I prayed that the next studio would be a little less . . . transcendental.

Zen Mania was a pleasant contrast to the Golden Lotus. Brightly lit with a calm interior and birchwood floors, it was located down at the Point and had a huge picture window overlooking the ocean and beach. Soft music accompanied by the sound of ocean waves created an atmosphere of tranquility. There was a row of brightly colored rubber mats rolled up on one side of the room next to a bowl of lavender mat-cleansing towelettes. A low shelf housed a collection of colored foam blocks and straps.

I looked around warily for signs of anything that would set Aunt Ginny awhirl again, but saw no gongs or diapered men in sight.

Wasn't yoga supposed to relax you? I felt edgy.

"This one looks good," Sawyer said. "What do you think, Aunt Ginny?

But Aunt Ginny wasn't there. She was pulling out an aqua-colored mat and wiping it down.

"Oh, I guess she approves," Sawyer chuckled.

A lithe woman with white hair cropped very short and spiky like a hedgehog approached us carrying a clipboard. Judging from her baby blue unitard I'd say she had about minus-two percent body fat.

"Hi, I'm Skye. Is this your first time at Zen Mania?"

I told her it was and she gave us some forms to fill out. I filled Aunt Ginny's out for her since she was sitting cross-legged on her mat with her eyes closed and her hands up in the air making *okay* signs.

"My aunt's a little eccentric," I warned Skye when I caught her watching Aunt Ginny with curiosity. "I hope that won't be a problem."

Skye gave me a big smile. "I think it's wonderful. You're all going to have a great time tonight. Just go at your own pace and modify the moves to your personal level." She excused herself to go help someone pick out yoga blocks and a strap.

Sawyer grabbed a handful of lavender towelettes. "Come on, let's go grab our stuff."

We got our gear and rolled our mats out at the back of the room. Skye called the class to order and instructed everyone to take their "easy seat."

Sawyer and I looked around to see what an easy seat was so we could copy it.

"Now I want everyone to practice your *pranayama*. Breathe in and out, with your hand on your belly." Skye whispered out the commands in a hypnotic tone and the class began some kind of deep-breathing exercise.

I tried to copy them, when Sawyer nuked my attempts at bliss by jabbing me sharply in the side.

"Ow."

The lady on the Day-Glo pink mat next to me gave us a cautioning look. "Shhh."

I mouthed, *Sorry*, to Ms. Pink Mat and hissed, "What?" to Sawyer.

She jerked her head toward the doorway. "Look who just walked in!"

"Who?" I turned to look and Sawyer hissed at me again. "No! Don't look right at them."

"How am I supposed to see who it is if I don't look at them?"

Skye softly cleared her throat. "That's good. Now everyone stretch your legs out in front of you and touch your toes. Use your strap if you need it."

Sawyer grabbed her strap and looped it around the balls of her feet. "Okay, look, but don't look like you're looking."

I reached around for my strap, but discovered Ms. Pink Mat had taken it. How could that be a good-karma thing to do? I was met with another angry look. I casually glanced to the front of the class. "Ohmygosh! It's Kelly."

"I know!" Sawyer gave me a new strap and reached for her toes with her hands. "What's she doing here?"

Kelly had brought her own mat and was rolling it out in the front of the room. She sat on her mat and bent over until her forehead touched her knees . . . then went through her knees right to the floor.

"I don't know but it looks like she comes here a lot." One end of the strap escaped my hand and snapped the man in front of me on the butt. He turned to glare at me, and I mouthed another apology.

Skye cocked her head to the side to peer at me and

Sawyer. Her voice was somewhere between the divine bliss of Krishna and the growing wrath of Shiva the Destroyer. "Everyone doing okay in the back?" she said through gritted teeth.

Sawyer and I both nodded a vigorous *yes* and tried to disappear into the birchwood floor. Aunt Ginny saw us lurking in the shadows and loudly dragged her mat over to join us.

"What are you doing back here?" she whispered loud enough to be heard next door.

"Shhh. Sit down," I hissed. "The girl that just came in was one of Barbie's best friends."

"Okay, let's move into cat-and-cow position."

We moved to our hands and knees while Aunt Ginny looked around to see who we were talking about and in another "whisper" said, "The little blonde in the peach top or the chunky lady in the yellow spandex that's screaming for help?"

The lady in yellow spandex gasped and frowned at Aunt Ginny.

Sawyer tried, without much success, to stifle a snort.

Skye looked up from her cat-and-cow position and gave us another aggravated look. "Let's all move into downward dog. Remember to *relax* and just be one with the ocean waves. Let all your stress *melt away*." Her terse commands hinted that her aura of calm was now on shaky ground. I suspected she wanted to shove something in our *asanas*.

"Aunt Ginny!" I whispered lower. "The little blond one."

Kelly was a few spaces in front and to the right of us. I was relieved that she hadn't noticed us yet.

Skye cleared her throat more loudly this time. "I want to welcome Poppy McAllister, Sawyer Montgomery, and Virginia Frankowski. They are *just visiting* us tonight."

"Well, she knows we're here now," Aunt Ginny said dryly.

Sawyer sucked in some air and started choking. I raised my hand in a halfhearted wave to the rest of the class, most of whom seemed pretty irritated for people who were supposed to be Zen. Kelly swung her head through her knees to gape at us so fast she pulled a hamstring and had to sit out for the next few minutes and stretch.

The next hour was full of grunting and sweating in contortionist positions. It was impossible to hang upside down and still see what the instructor was doing.

"I think my spine is fused into a straight line. I have no bend." Aunt Ginny was looking at me from a ninety-degree angle where we were supposed to be touching our toes in a forward bend.

"I thought this was a beginner class," I grumbled to Sawyer.

She gasped, "I didn't know breathing could be so hard."

Sawyer got a side cramp during triangle pose and fell over, causing me to lose my balance and knock Aunt Ginny down. Skye was looking more and more frazzled as the class went on. She had sweated through her unitard, and her once serene expression was now tight and blotchy. A woman with a pinched face and a nose like a hawk on the other side of Aunt Ginny moved her mat a few inches farther away with a *humph* and a haughty eye roll. Finally we reached what Skye called corpse pose. It was a lot like just lying there but with someone commanding you to relax.

I tried to let all my tension go as Skye directed, but I felt painfully awkward about doing a corpse pose a few feet away from a woman whose friend had recently done a final corpse pose of her own, what with me being the prime suspect and all.

"How am I supposed to soften my eyeballs?" Sawyer whispered to me.

Aunt Ginny quietly snored and I snapped my fingers next to her ear. Her eyes popped open and she said, "Squirrels."

"We're in yoga," I whispered.

"Still?" she answered back.

Skye folded her hands in a prayer position and bowed to the class. "Thank you everyone. *Namaste*."

I would have bowed, but I couldn't move. When she came back up, she looked at us with an expression that was anything but tranquil.

"I think I sprained something, but I don't know what it is." Sawyer groaned as we wiped off our mats and began rolling them up.

Skye handed me a schedule for the rest of the month. "I hope you enjoyed your first session. Why don't you come back next week and try out the *silent* yoga class."

We thanked her but before we could get out the door we were accosted.

Kelly trapped us by the bulletin board. "Poppy, Sawyer, hi. I can't believe I ran into you here."

"Hi," I answered her while trying to plot an escape route. "We're just as surprised as you are."

"How is Robert holding up?" Sawyer asked, making conversation.

Kelly put a hand over her heart. "He's devastated, of course. But he's making it through. He's keeping busy with the campaign."

"He's still running for office?" I tried to sound non-chalant.

"Oh, yes. It's what Barbie would have wanted. She cared very deeply about the issues as much as Robert did. They were really going to make a difference together. Now

Robert has dedicated the rest of his campaign to Barbie's memory. He truly has a servant's heart."

Aunt Ginny cocked an eyebrow and looked at Kelly skeptically, then rolled her eyes and looked away while muttering, "Told ya."

"Isn't he concerned about the scandal?" Sawyer asked. "I thought the husband was always a suspect."

"He's not a suspect." A look of indignation crossed Kelly's face and was quickly replaced with her familiar saccharine smile. "The police cleared him right away. Along with being an upstanding member of higher society, Robert was generously answering questions from his constituents, in the cafeteria. In fact"—she looked at me—"I think you are their main suspect."

Aunt Ginny balled her fist and narrowed her eyes at Kelly.

Sawyer stepped in to buffer and prevent a very un-Zen-like incident from happening at Zen Mania. "The investigation will prove that Poppy's innocent. The police are already focusing on other leads."

"I was just in the wrong place at the wrong time." I smiled weakly and we all waited for a few irritated yoga students to walk past on their way to the exit before continuing. "Do you know of anyone who would have wanted to hurt Barbie?" I asked Kelly.

"No, not at all. Why ever would someone want to hurt her? She was a pillar of society. Everyone loved her."

Sawyer and I looked at each other with skepticism, remembering a very different Barbie.

"She selflessly gave her time to oversee several charities: the PTA, Alumni Association, PETA. Every spring she ran a fundraiser for underprivileged kids to go to cheer camp. Those kids really counted on her."

Kelly's voice trembled as she went on. "I don't know how Robert does it, but he just keeps going for the sake of the people who depend on him. He just needs to get through the memorial service tomorrow afternoon so he and Tiffany can move on, and begin to heal."

"Who is Tiffany?" I asked.

"Tiffany is Robert and Barbie's daughter. She's a sophomore this year, and just made head cheerleader, just like her mom. She's the youngest student to become cheerleading captain since Barbie." Kelly sniffled and wiped invisible tears from her eyes. "Thank God for Missy. She's put together a scholarship on behalf of the Alumni Association in Barbie's name, and Tiffany will be the recipient this year."

"That was nice of her," Sawyer said to Kelly, then looked at Aunt Ginny and shrugged.

"It was very important to Robert and Barbie that Tiffany go to the best college to cheer competitively."

"Sure," I offered, not really knowing what else to say.

Kelly pulled a smartphone out of her lululemon yoga bag. "Okay, I have to get back to work. Robert and I have a strategy meeting to discuss the post-memorial fundraiser. People are more generous when they know you're grieving. You two should probably not come since you're suspects in the murder case. But here are some invitations to give to your friends. It's only a hundred dollars a plate, but they'll have to pay at the door since the event is last-minute. I could have done a lot more if I'd had time to plan in advance."

She handed me a stack of engraved invitations that read "You are Cordially Invited to a Fundraiser to support Congressman Robert Clark in Memory of his late wife, the beloved Barbara Clark." When I looked up, she was on her cell phone and exiting the studio without a backward glance or wave good-bye.

"How exactly was she going to plan a memorial fund-raiser in advance?" Aunt Ginny asked.

I looked at the invitations in my hand. "Or did she?"

Chapter 25

I hit the snooze button for the third and final time. If I couldn't find a way to prove my innocence, my days of lounging in bed and getting up whenever would be over very soon. I'd be doing a long stint in a women's prison. A few months ago that thought would have had me paralyzed with fear. But I was done letting circumstances drag me through life. The events of the past week had taught me that life is what you make it. Problems are going to come whether you live life to the fullest or numbly hide from the world. I was choosing to live. And part of my new life included taking better care of myself.

So I made my bed and washed my face with the thirty-year-old Noxzema. Note to self: Buy skin care products today. Then I put on my yoga outfit from last night. Note two: Buy decent workout clothes. I got out my yoga posture sheet that Dr. Melinda had given me and attempted the positions. Chair pose, forward bend, downward dog, plank—nose to nose with Figaro.

"Can I help you?"

Mrow.

Cobra pose, breathe. "I'm sorry, sir, but breakfast will be served when I am finished here."

Mrooooow.

Child's pose, breathe. Gentle nudge on the head.

"Not yet."

Mrow.

Roll over, corpse pose, breathe. I went over Skye's words from last night. "Breathe in relaxation, breathe out tension. Let it go. Let yourself sink into the earth without a care. Breathe in renewed energy, breathe out stress."

Hhhhuh, hhhhuh, hhhhuh.

"Figaro! Do not hock up a fur ball when Mommy is in relaxation pose!"

Hhhhuh, hhhhuh.

The spell was broken.

I got off the floor and glared at the cat, who suddenly felt fine, then went to take a shower. Note three: Buy decent hair products. In fact, I would get my hair done today. I had a date with Tim tomorrow, unless I chickened out and drove to Peru. Was Peru an extradition country? No, too risky. *Better get my hair done just in case.*

I dressed in another pair of yoga pants. Note four: Buy some new clothes. I'd been waiting twenty years to lose weight to get a decent wardrobe and it hadn't happened yet. Time to bite the bullet and accept myself the way I was right then.

My cell phone rang the flying monkeys tune from *The Wizard of Oz* and the Wicked Witch's picture popped up. Great. Georgina must have sensed there was money about to be spent.

"Hello."

I was greeted with brusque commands. "When are you coming home? I thought this ridiculous reunion was only for the weekend. You know I signed you up to fill the swag bags."

"Georgina, something has come up."

"What is more important than the Waterford Historical Society luncheon and keeping your word to me?"

"Georgina, there was an incident at the reunion. A woman was murdered."

"If she's dead, then there's nothing you can do to help her now. I want you to leave at once. This is important to me."

"Georgina, I am not able to leave town while the police are investigating the crime."

"Don't be ridiculous, Poppy, of course you can leave town. Only a suspect would be detained. . . . Oh my God, you're a suspect! What did you do now? Poppy, so help me God, if you bring any more shame on this family I will see to it that you are removed from John's trust fund."

I rolled my eyes. This was the very reason I had avoided Georgina in the first place. Everything was about money and control with her. How she ever convinced John to put his life insurance in trust I'd never know.

"I didn't do anything. It's an open investigation and I can't leave New Jersey until they close it. You will have to get someone else to fill the gift bags. Why don't you ask Esmerelda?" *Poor Esmerelda. Wait till she finds out I just threw her under the bus.* Georgina's maid already deserves combat pay just for working in that house day after day.

"That silly girl will just do it wrong. Now I'll have to do it all myself. Oh, why does everything happen to me? You'd better make sure you are home before the Knicker-bocker charity event next Friday. I'm counting on you to fill a seat so my table is full. After all I've done for you it's the very least you can do for me."

"Sure, Georgina."

"Now, how is the diet going? Has it produced any results yet? I've heard there is a new diet shake that is getting positive results as long as you don't eat any solid food between eleven a.m. and midnight. You should look into it."

"I have to go, Georgina. My battery is about to die."

"How many times have I told you to plug—"

I ended the call before she could finish the sentence. Figaro's ears were flattened to his head and he was flicking his tail.

"Relax, she's two hundred miles away. Come on, buddy. Let's go to the kitchen and get you some nasty cat goo."

Aunt Ginny was decked out in an eye-blinding, hot-pink track suit with matching pink jacket and pink Reeboks. She was wearing a pair of white plastic, round earrings, a matching white plastic bracelet, and a pair of white-rimmed sunglasses.

"Hello. Are you going out for a walk?" I opened a can of chicken livers and dumped it into Figaro's bowl.

"No." She got a cantaloupe from the counter and started slicing it into wedges.

"Why are you wearing sunglasses?" I got out the eggs and a glass mixing bowl.

"Because they match my outfit." Aunt Ginny looked at me like this should have been obvious.

"Oh. Okay." I broke the eggs in the bowl and whisked them until frothy. Then poured them into the ceramic frying pan I had heating on the stove. "I'm going to go get my hair done today."

"Oh, thank God!" Aunt Ginny said, with more enthusiasm than I thought necessary. She walked over to the trash can and hurled the cantaloupe peels with such force she knocked the lid off. Then she seized a couple plates and flung the cabinet shut, grabbed a couple forks, and marched over to the table and slammed them down.

"What's the matter?"

"Apparently, it's against the law now to wear roller skates."

I flipped through the Rolodex of my mind to find a

possible scenario to match with Aunt Ginny's words and came up empty. "Says the 1970s police?"

"Says that busybody socialist lady."

"The Social Services lady?"

"That's the one."

"Did she catch you wearing roller skates in the house?"

Aunt Ginny paused and looked at me like I was crazy. "No. What are you, some kind of nut? I was on the boardwalk. Why would anyone wear roller skates in the house?"

"Why would anyone wear roller skates on the boardwalk?"

"Because they don't have a skateboard."

"Oh, well, of course, if you don't have a skateboard then roller skates make perfect sense."

"She wrote me a ticket."

"Like a parking ticket?"

"Like a 'you're an old lady and could break a hip' ticket. It arrived this morning in the mail."

Aunt Ginny pulled a crumpled-up ball of paper from her pocket and chucked it at me.

I smoothed it out and saw it was another letter from Social Services, pleading with Aunt Ginny to submit to a psychiatric evaluation before she hurt herself. She had been spotted on the boardwalk deemed to be involved in "reckless endangerment to self and others."

"That also says my house isn't fit to be lived in and should be condemned."

"Well, that's a gross overstatement. We need a couple repairs and a good sprucing, but it's not ready for the wrecking ball."

"Why is this lady coming after me? We aren't the only house on this street that needs a coat of paint."

She was right. Was there something else behind this assault on Aunt Ginny? I plated the scrambled eggs and we sat down to eat. "That's a good question. And we'll get to the bottom of it. Don't worry."

I reminded Aunt Ginny that the landscapers were coming back today to plant some fall annuals and clean up the flowerbeds, and that I'd left a check on the desk for them. Then we discussed our encounter with Kelly last night over breakfast and agreed on one thing.

"I should attend the memorial service to see if I can overhear any chatter about the investigation." I texted Sawyer, Connie, and Kim to let them know my plan, and they texted back that they would join me. Given the circumstances, we thought it was better to not draw attention to ourselves, so we decided to go incognito and keep to the back.

Aunt Ginny was so excited that I was "beautifying" as she said, that she insisted I leave right away and she would clean up from breakfast. "You got to get there early so they have enough time to do what they gotta do."

"Good Lord, Aunt Ginny! How much do you think they have to do to me?"

She looked at my hair and looked away. "Just go now."

I took my litany of supplements, got my keys and purse, and headed out the door. A vase of lavender roses had been set on the porch. I looked around to see if the person who left them was still here. There were a couple of neighbors who were standing at the mailbox across the street, pointing at Aunt Ginny's house. When they saw me, they quickly turned away to investigate an oak tree in the yard. *Hmm. Nothing suspicious about that at all.* I picked up the vase and read the attached card.

I remembered the purple ones are your favorite. I can't wait to see you. Love, Tim

I put them on the side table in the foyer for safekeeping until I returned, and smiled all the way to the salon.

The historic white clapboard Chambers Mansion now houses the Radiance Day Spa. Late-season roses were still in bloom and lined the brick path to the front door. The plush lobby was decorated in pale pink to match the roses outside. Pan flute music was playing softly overhead. I signed in and sat on an overstuffed white love seat to wait for an opening. Luckily, they took walk-ins, and this being the middle of the week I didn't have to wait too long. A young woman with short black hair that had bright blue tips walked over and introduced herself as my stylist, Courtney. She had a nose ring and both arms were covered in colored tattoos up to the shoulder where they met a black satin bustier.

"Are you Poppy McAllister?"

"Yep, that's me."

She sat next to me on the edge of the love seat and gushed, "Are you the same Poppy who was arrested for murder the other night?"

I sighed. "Yep, *that's me.*"

"Ooh, that's all everyone's talking about. Come on, let's get you back to the consultation area and you can fill me in on your side of the story."

Oh, goody.

After a quick discussion about the condition of my hair, and the possibility of entering the *Guinness World Records* for greatest number of split ends, a picture was taken for the spa's "Before" wall.

"People would never believe us if we told them how you walked in here so we need the picture for proof."

Well, gee, that's not offensive at all.

Then Courtney had me draped in smocks, basted my hair in bright pink goo, and wrapped it in tin foil.

"You know, she was in here the day she died."

"Barbie was here?"

"Oh, yeah. Came in to have the works done before the big reunion. I did her roots. She'd made the appointment months in advance."

"Did she say anything about an invitation she'd sent, or a special meeting with some girls she used to know?" *And bullied to within an inch of their sanity.*

"She didn't say anything to me about an invitation, but she was very determined to look her best for someone she hadn't seen in a long time. An old rival maybe?"

"Did you catch a name?"

"She never used a name, but she said she was planning to make them suffer."

"Suffer how?"

"I don't know, but she was scary intense. She said that success and beauty were the best forms of revenge. So I asked her, 'Aren't these people your friends?' And I swear her skin turned ice cold and she said, 'My only friend died a long time ago. Now I just have a bunch of people who want to use me.'"

"Wow, that's . . . creepy. Did you ask her about what she was planning?"

"I got the heebie-jeebies after that and gave her a magazine. She didn't say anything else about the reunion, but I only did her hair. You should ask Charlemagne. She did her body wrap."

Courtney sat me under the dryer and let me stew in my thoughts about Barbie. I wondered who she was planning to make suffer. If she hadn't seen the person in a long time, it couldn't be Joel or Kristin, could it? The smart money was on Billy. If she was planning to make him jealous over her "success and beauty," I bet it threw a wrench into her plan when he showed up as the owner of a Fortune 500 company with a beautiful fiancée. So much for rubbing his face in it. I needed to talk to Charlemagne and see if Barbie said anything to *her* about what she was planning.

"Let's see how you're doing under there." Courtney lifted the hair dryer and opened a foil packet. "You're good. Let's go rinse you out and cut off those split ends now."

Two hours later I was a new woman. My hair had been cut, colored, and deep conditioned. I had golden highlights that brightened my face, and my hair was bouncy and smooth.

"It looks fantastic, Courtney."

"I've been known to work wonders. Miracles will run you a little more," she said, winking.

"I don't suppose Charlemagne is here today, is she?"

"Yeah, she's here. You interested in a facial or a body wrap?"

What I wanted was a chance to ask her about Barbie.

Courtney leaned in to examine me. "I recommend a facial. Your pores are crying out for help."

I squirmed in my seat. "I don't know that I have time for that."

"Come on, your skin really needs it. What is your beauty regime like?"

"Um, does washing my face with soap count?"

"Oh, honey, this *is* an emergency."

I was taken to a locker room and given a thick terry cloth robe that seriously needed to rethink its "one-size-fits-all" policy. Then I stored my belongings in a locker and went to the quiet room to wait.

I was perusing a much-pawed-through issue of a gossip magazine when a gal who was surely an Olympic dead-lifter in her free time, dressed head to toe in white, busted through the door. "Where's the emergency facial?"

I was a little afraid and without words, so I meekly raised a finger. Charlemagne seized me by the wrist and led me to a treatment room to get situated, while she went to "heat up the rocks."

"What are the rocks for? And how hot are they going to be?" I called after her billboard-sized back, but she was already gone.

When Charlemagne returned, she tied a terry cloth belt around my head and shined a confession spotlight in my face.

"Let's get a look at those pores."

She covered my eyes with two wet cotton balls so I wouldn't suffer further retina damage. "So, you're the one who they say killed the politician's wife."

"I have been unjustly accused of that, yes."

She poked at my face with a metal stick for a few minutes, then finally turned the light off, removed the cotton balls, and massaged some rose-scented cleanser onto my face.

"Courtney said you saw Barbie the day of the reunion."

"Mrs. Clark was a regular. Once a month she came in for a facial and body wrap."

"Were the two of you friends?"

Charlemagne wrapped my face in a warm, rose-scented washcloth so only my mouth was exposed, and gave a hearty laugh. "Not for all the hoagies in South Jersey. That one was mean as a snake and a lousy tipper. Ten percent for having to wrap her naked cellulite in mud and Saran Wrap month after month. Huh."

She massaged a grapefruit-scented cream into my skin. I fought the urge to lick some of it off. I was starving without my morning fix.

"Did she say anything during her last treatment about her plans for the reunion?"

"I know she had something up her sleeve, because she booked an extra-long seaweed detox wrap. We also call that the 'look great naked wrap,' because it flushes about ten pounds of fat and water from the body for forty-eight hours."

File that bit of information away for another day. "Did she ever talk about any old boyfriends or new lovers?"

Charlemagne had washed off the grapefruit cream and was gently massaging a gritty, vanilla-scented paste on my face. "No, but then she was married to a politician, so she had a lot of events where she had to make appearances. She never said anything directly about cheating on him, but when she talked about her husband there was always disappointment in her tone. I don't think her marriage was a happy one."

"They looked like the perfect couple at the reunion. Like they were madly in love."

"People are rarely what they seem. Most of my clients are here because they want to hide something from the world. Cellulite, wrinkles, age spots, tiny veins busted by too much boozing. Not many people have the nerve to let it all hang out and let people see who they really are."

I thought that might be directed at me and my "before" picture out in the lobby. I wanted to protest, but I was distracted by the chocolate-scented masque she was applying. I was thinking about getting a spoon. . . .

"Did Barbie ever mention having any enemies? Maybe having a score to settle with someone?"

"Not to me. Mrs. Clark was more concerned about her appearance than anything else. I just chalked it up to her being in the public eye what with her husband's campaign for Senate starting. She was also very proud of her cheerleaders. She was working with them to compete at the National Championships in the spring."

Charlemagne ordered me to relax and, apparently, that meant *be quiet*. After a few more creams were applied and removed, she collected the hot rocks and used them to massage my shoulders and back, and I lost the ability to form sentences. By the time I was able to collect myself, she was applying the final layer of moisturizer and the appointment was over.

I finished getting dressed and met her back in the quiet room. She handed me a list of items to buy to keep up the skin care regimen at home. Most of them could be found in the lobby conveniently placed by the cash register, but a few things had to be picked up at the beauty supply store.

When the receptionist was ringing me up, I asked her how much a hair appointment, facial, and seaweed wrap each month would cost. Whew! Barbie was spending a fortune on spa treatments each month. I wondered how she was able to afford such luxury while her husband was spending huge amounts of money campaigning.

I left with two bags full of lovely smelling beauty products. Shampoo, conditioner, mousse, gel, vitamin hair masque. Facial cleanser, exfoliant, toner, moisturizer, brightening mask, eye cream, day cream, night cream.

"What happens if I get them mixed up?" I asked the receptionist. She said she wasn't sure and I should call the emergency hotline number if it happened.

I drove over to the strip mall in Rio Grande to the beauty supply superstore to pick up the rest of the items on Charlemagne's list. Rows and rows of every froufrou beauty product advertised in glamour magazines. When teenage girls dream of heaven, they dream of this store.

Things sure had changed since the last time I'd bought beauty gear. I didn't know where to begin. Finally I chose a new ceramic hair dryer, a set of hot rollers, and some new ionized hair brushes. The makeup counter was leagues beyond Cover Girl and I picked out a brand called Smashbox. I bought primer, tinted BB cream, finishing powder, an eye shadow palette called "Rock Star," mascara guaranteed to make me look like I was wearing false eyelashes, and a lip gloss that promised to give me lips like Angelina Jolie. *Because surely that's the feature on Angelina Jolie that men are drawn to.*

Before I left, I picked up one more item of indulgence. A bottle of Coach Poppy perfume. It already had my name on it. How could I refuse?

A couple stores down, there was a plus-sized boutique so I made a stop and bought myself a few new outfits, some workout clothes, and a whole new wardrobe of what Aunt Ginny called "unmentionables."

I'd spent a fortune today. Georgina would need a double martini and a Valium when the bill came in. I had never spent this much of my allowance in one day before. It felt good to do something for myself for a change. I just hoped it wasn't all in vain. If I was convicted, I couldn't take any of it with me.

Chapter 26

I pulled up in front of Aunt Ginny's to find a team of landscapers huddled around the birdbath while Aunt Ginny marched back and forth waving a broom in the air.

"What's going on?" I asked whoever would answer me first.

One of the landscapers approached me with his ball cap in his hand. "Your grandmother is crazy, ma'am. The workers are afraid to get too close."

Aunt Ginny whacked the steps with the broom. "Scram, ya rodents!"

"Aunt Ginny? What ah . . . what are you doing?"

"There's a wild pack of chipmunks living under the porch, and I know they're the thieves responsible for gorging on my tulip bulbs." She whacked the lattice-work running under the wraparound porch. "Get out, freeloaders!"

I looked from Aunt Ginny to the landscaper who had approached me, and he circled his finger around his ear and mouthed, *Loco*.

"Aunt Ginny, the workmen can't get to the flowerbeds because they're afraid you might hit them."

"I said I was sorry. How was I to know he was right next to me?"

I looked back and saw a workman with a bag of frozen peas on his eye. He waved.

Just then a chipmunk came tearing out from under the porch and galloped across the yard. Aunt Ginny tried to take off after it, but I put my arm around her just in time. "Whoa! Okay, why don't we go inside and have some tea. I'll show you the new clothes I just bought. How does that sound?"

"What about the chipmunks?"

I began to lead her up the steps. "Let's get some peanuts and a feeder for the corner of the yard so they'll leave the tulips alone."

"Or," she countered, "let's put the peanuts in Old Man Murillo's yard. That way they'll eat his begonias and leave my bulbs alone."

I nodded to the landscapers and they got back to work cleaning up the flowerbeds, while we entered the house. "That's another good plan."

I settled Aunt Ginny, then went back out and relieved the car of my shopping haul, lugging the bags inside to the sunroom. Figaro jumped from bag to bag, checking for treats and inspecting each one for enemy intruders. Aunt Ginny nudged a bag with her foot and he shot out of it and tore up the stairs to safety.

"Ha. Some guard cat you turned out to be," she called after him.

From upstairs, we heard the sound of Figaro flopping over onto his side.

She turned to me and gave me an appraising once-over. "You done got your hair did. Looks good."

As I showed Aunt Ginny my new clothes, she nodded approval for each item. I went upstairs to put them away and changed into a black A-line skirt with a burgundy chiffon blouse and tall, black leather boots for the memorial. When I came back to the sunroom, I found her covered in green goo with cotton booties on her hands and feet.

"This moisturizer burns. I'm not sure it's working right."

I looked at the bottle. "That's not moisturizer. It's a purifying clay masque."

"Oh. How long do I leave it on?"

"Till about five minutes ago."

"Okay." She toddled to her bathroom to wash off the clay and I put away the beauty creams before she could do any more damage.

The doorbell rang, so I grabbed my checkbook prepared to pay the landscapers—but it was Rosalind Carson, Everyone's Favorite Social Worker and Darth Vader's mentor.

"Ms. Carson," I said, trying not to grit my teeth. "What can I do for you?"

Behind me, Aunt Ginny hollered, "I want to try a different smelly cream on my face. Where'd you put them?"

I sang out sweetly, "We have company, Aunt Ginny. The social worker"—by which I meant the Cold Clammy Hand of Death—"is here."

Aunt Ginny, not taking the hint, appeared behind me wearing a pink bathrobe and pink bunny slippers, and she had her hair pulled back in a pink terry cloth headband. She took one look at Ms. Carson, loudly muttered, "Bah!" and walked away.

Ms. Carson shook her head and tsk-tsked. "Bathrobe in the middle of the day. Still confused about what time it is." She took out a little notebook and started writing.

I did not invite her in. "Did you need something?"

She looked down the end of her nose at me. "I'm just here to tell you that Mrs. Frankowski's hearing has been set for two weeks from today. I want to implore you, once again, to talk some sense into the dear woman. The transition to the Sunset Valley Assisted Living Facility will go much smoother if she goes . . . voluntarily." She handed me a copy of the pronouncement.

"Mrs. Frankowski has no intention of moving anywhere at this time. As you can see, repairs on the house are underway and the yard is looking beautiful."

She continued in a sugary tone, "I do hope I didn't give you the impression that a little cosmetic clean-up was all that was needed to appease the state, Miss McAllister. Mrs. Frankowski needs supervision. And I'm afraid that due to the events of last week, you will no longer be considered a suitable guardian." She gave me an insincere smile and wrote something in her notebook.

Where is a flamethrower when I need it?

Since I had a yard full of landscapers and a couple of nosy neighbors watching, I decided to take the high road and not drag Ms. Carson to the ground by the bun on her head.

"Ms. Carson, I appreciate your visit, but we have everything under control on our end and we'll be ready for the hearing when it arrives. Can I send you home with some flowers from the garden today? As a token of our appreciation for your looking out for Aunt Ginny?"

Aunt Ginny snorted from the other room. "That'll be the day. I hope she gets stung by a bee."

I shut the door a little more and gave Ms. Carson a weak smile. I picked up the pruning shears to cut her a bouquet of lavender and white spikes.

Her eyes grew wide. "Surely you're joking." She dropped

the sweetness act and scribbled another addition to her notebook. "That's foxglove, and it's poisonous. A confused old lady shouldn't even have that in her yard."

She stormed down the sidewalk in a huff, slamming the gate behind her and calling back to me, "Get your act together, Miss McAllister, or you won't even have visitation rights once your aunt is in the system. I'll make sure of it!"

Chapter 27

I instructed the landscapers to please remove the foxglove and anything else that was potentially poisonous, and replace them with something less controversial. I reheated the vegetable soup I had made for dinner last night, and Aunt Ginny and I ate in the kitchen while we discussed Ms. Carson's visit.

"Why is she so hell-bent on putting me in a home? I've been doing just fine without *supervision*. *Meh*."

"I don't know, but we have less than two weeks to remove any obstacles to getting a favorable ruling."

"Then you probably shouldn't have offered her a poison bouquet."

"Yeah, well. Hindsight."

Figaro hovered and begged until I opened a can of minced fish guts, only to have him turn his nose up and refuse to eat them.

After dinner I steeled myself for what lay ahead. I had to be out of my mind—but I also had to do this. Sawyer, Kim, and I had decided to go to the memorial incognito to limit our chances of being thrown out, so I put my hair up in a bun and put on the blond wig I'd bought from the party store, hoping it didn't look too cheap and obvious. Then I donned the pair of white-rimmed sunglasses that Aunt Ginny was wearing the other day.

"How do I look?" I asked Aunt Ginny.

"Like Sophia Glickman."

"Is she a spy?"

"No. She plays Texas Hold 'Em at the senior center on Tuesday nights."

I waited for the other shoe to drop.

"Those were her glasses."

The glasses slid down my nose and I peered over the rims at Aunt Ginny, who looked very guilty.

"I won them fair and square."

"Does Sophia Glickman know that?"

"Don't ever go all-in on a pair of fives at the flop."

"Oh, Lord."

The doorbell rang.

"That must be Kim. She's driving me to the memorial, since my car has Virginia license plates."

Kim's curly hair was tucked into a short black wig and she was wearing a simple black dress and black Mary Janes. It was the most boring outfit I had ever seen her in.

"I borrowed it from my mother," she responded to my stunned silence.

"Aunt Ginny, I'll be home in a couple of hours. *Try to stay out of trouble*," I muttered as I walked out the door.

My stomach was churning up nerves. I had to pull this off without being recognized. Amber had already threatened me to stay away from the investigation. If I was discovered, it could seriously jeopardize my case.

This was going through my head as I caught sight of myself in the mirror by the front door. I wished I'd sprung for a wig that didn't look like it had been through a zombie apocalypse.

* * *

Evoy's Funeral Home was a two-story white Colonial with black shutters, located in the heart of North Cape May. It sat behind a large pond graced by a pair of swans. Several tastefully decorated rooms filled with Queen Anne sofas were separated by collapsible partitions. Today they were packed wall-to-wall, and all the partitions were open to accommodate the large crowd. Kim and I split up since we'd stand out less by ourselves than with each other.

I grabbed a Kleenex as camouflage, pretending to dab my eyes as I began milling about the room. There was a huge portrait of Barbie on a golden tripod at the front. It was surrounded by sprays of pink roses and white lilies, and numerous baskets and wreaths of flowers were lined up around a podium. People were mingling, speaking in hushed tones.

I searched for familiar faces. Coach Wilcott was sitting quietly in a wing chair in the room across the partition. He appeared to be alone. Kristen and Joel were seated together in the back. Connie and her two girls were there to pay respects to their cheerleading coach, just like we'd planned. She gave me a slight chin nod. Amber was nowhere to be seen.

"He isn't just *not here*. He's disappeared entirely." Paul Osborne, dressed in black slacks and a silver button-down was holding court with Tina Winiecki and Maria Ragusa over by a tray of chocolate chip cookies.

"What do you mean he's disappeared?" Tina pulled out a cell phone and was feverishly tapping out a message on the screen.

"I mean, *poof!* Vanished! He's wanted by the police for questioning and they can't find him anywhere."

Who are they talking about? I looked around the room for Robert Clark and didn't see him. *Did he skip town before his wife's memorial?*

"I know they have a brutal history, but I didn't think he would be so cold as to miss her funeral."

Courtney Westbrae rushed up to the group, tapping on her cell phone. "Well, can you blame him? She humiliated him at the reunion."

Robert entered the room from a side vestibule followed by a young teenager. The girl stood uncomfortably at his side with one arm wrapped around her back holding her other arm.

That must be Tiffany, poor thing. To lose a parent at such an important age is so painful. I would know. But if Robert is here, then who are the police looking for?

Maria picked up a cookie and sniffed it. "He used to love her."

Paul took the cookie out of her hands and put it back on the tray. "That was before she stood him up at the altar. Twice!"

Standing on the other side of Robert was the attentive Kelly. Dressed in a dark green pantsuit she held a clipboard and was wearing a wireless mic headset. Every so often she touched the earpiece and spoke into the microphone.

Missy entered from the back of the room dressed head to toe in black, her eyes red from crying. She sat in the back.

Kelly whispered something to Robert, and she and Tiffany took their seats in the front row.

Robert took the podium first. "I want to thank you all for coming. It means a lot to Tiffany and myself that so many of Barbara's friends and colleagues would continue to show us their support at this difficult time. I have no doubt that the parties responsible for my beloved wife's brutal murder will come to justice. It's one of the things that I promise I will fight for when I am elected to represent this great state of New Jersey in the office of the Senate. I am fully committed to a greater crackdown on violent criminals."

I felt as if every eye was going to turn and focus on me.

"On the very day that my lovely wife was taken from us, she said to me, 'Robert, running for office is going to be tough. No matter what happens, promise me that once you enter the race you will *stay* in the race, for my sake.' Well, honey"—Robert came out from behind the podium and looked up to the ceiling—"I'm doing this one for you." He blew a kiss to the ceiling and sat down next to Tiffany.

I tried not to choke on the absurdity of his speech, while Kelly took the podium. She wiped invisible tears from her eyes and asked if anyone else wanted to say a few words about Barbie.

I have a few, I thought, *but they're more like graffiti than a eulogy.*

Joanne approached the front and began to sob. Through gulps of air she said that Barbie was her best friend and an angel sent to earth. I fought the urge to put my finger down my throat and gag.

Then Missy took a turn and said what a good friend Barbie was, and that her and Athena's hearts went out to Robert and Tiffany. She encouraged them to stay strong. Then she announced the cheerleading scholarship the PTA had put together in Barbie's name and how all the cheerleaders could be recipients of said scholarship when the time came. I didn't hear everything she was saying because an old woman with a cane was gesturing to me from the next room.

I looked around to see if there was someone behind me she might be calling to but, no, she was calling *me* over. As I got closer she grabbed my arm, and with a lot of strength for a feeble old woman, she pulled me into the coatrack.

"*Shh!* It's me."

"Sawyer?"

"Yes."

"Wow. I didn't recognize you at all."

"I had Jimmy Mokey do me up. He does hair and makeup for the community theater. Listen, did you hear about Billy Sommers and his fiancée yet?"

"Is that who's missing?"

"Yes. The police haven't been able to find either of them for questioning since the reunion."

"Do you think something happened to them?"

"Either that or they're on the run."

"Did you know that Barbie and Billy had been engaged?"

"Yeah. Everyone knows that."

I gave Sawyer a look.

"Well. Okay, everyone who didn't *move away* knows that."

"She stood him up at the altar?"

"Twice. It was all the news fifteen years ago. Hey, that's probably why they had so much animosity between them."

"Ya think?"

Sawyer gave me a sheepish grin.

My cell phone buzzed and I fished it out of my purse.

"Poppy! Poppy! Can you hear me?"

"Yes, Aunt Ginny, I can hear you. What's wrong?"

"They're all over the house!"

"What?"

"I told them to wait until you got home but they ignored me and pushed in anyway!"

"Who's all over the house?"

"The cops! They're tearing everything up!"

Amber! That's why she wasn't at the memorial. I could feel my heart pounding in my ears.

"They have a search warrant! Hurry up and get home before they start planting evidence. Young man! Put that—" The phone went dead.

"I have to go. The cops are searching my house."

We exited the coatrack to find a very startled Joanne Junk, who was reaching for a flannel jacket. She looked from Sawyer to me and then her piggy little eyes narrowed to evil slits.

"What are you two doing here?"

I didn't have time to be detained right now. "We're just paying respects, like you."

Joanne pulled out a pink-leopard-clad cell phone from her pocket. "We'll see what Amber has to say about you two being here."

But before she could find Amber's face on her display, Sawyer *walloped* Joanne in the shin with her cane. "Oops. So sorry."

Joanne went down to one knee, and Sawyer took off running for the door.

Joanne yelled, "The killers are here!" and a commotion headed my way.

I calmly backed away from Joanne and slipped into the crowd. I grabbed the funeral director and said, "A lady fell down over by the coatrack. I heard her say something about a lawsuit." He ran toward Joanne and I slipped out the side door. Kim was waiting with the car running.

"What happened? I heard Joanne squeal so I knew it was time for the getaway car."

"Thank God. Amber has a CSI team tearing up Aunt Ginny's house as we speak."

I took off the blond wig and let my hair out of the bun.

Kim took the corner on two wheels.

"Whoa, Danica Patrick."

Kim shrugged. "What? All the cops in the county are at your house right now."

"That's a good point. Floor it."

"Did you at least get anything good in there?"

"Billy's missing."

"Get out!"

"Since the night of the reunion."

"Dude."

"How about you?"

"There's a campaign fundraiser at the Moose Lodge on Friday."

"See now, that's weird. Would you still run for office if your spouse had just been murdered?"

"If someone I loved had been murdered, I don't think I could get out of bed for days—let alone kiss babies and shake hands."

Kim nodded. "Yeah, something doesn't add up with that. He should be more distraught. Even Kelly seems far more interested in getting Robert elected than in the death of one of her best friends."

"You think maybe they're in it together?"

"I don't know. Maybe they killed Barbie to get the insurance money for the campaign."

I tried to compute that. "But what would be in it for Kelly after the election?"

"Maybe Robert is going to give her a job as one of his staff."

We turned the corner on Aunt Ginny's street and saw an entire SWAT team combing the yard. Eight police cars, an officer with a police dog, and seven nosy neighbors were parked at the curb. Before I could get out of the car, Amber was in my face.

"McAllister! What the hell have you done?!"

Chapter 28

"What's going on here, Amber?"

She shoved a search warrant in my face. "Item one! I have the authority to seize all cleaning products and items of a chemical nature. You want to tell me how you are the only house in the county that doesn't have one single chemical! Not even a bottle of Windex! And every cleaning product you have is brand-new and unopened!"

Jiminy Freaking Great. "We've gone completely green. Doctor's orders. I'll get you her number so you can ask her yourself."

Amber turned a deeper color of rage. "Well, isn't that convenient. And item two!" She stormed over to the yard waste bags and dumped one out. "I have the authority to search the grounds for organic material of a poisonous nature! And you just happened to tear up the yard and dispose of the evidence, *today*!"

Aunt Ginny flew out of the house with a war cry when the clippings hit the grass. "You little gnat!"

With a leap, I grabbed Aunt Ginny by the waist to keep her from committing a felony against Amber's head.

Through gritted teeth I said, "Aunt Ginny! The neighbors are watching."

Kim took Aunt Ginny by the hand and led her back to the house, but not before Aunt Ginny threw her arm out to point a menacing finger and an icy glare in Amber's direction.

A uniformed policeman came out of the house carrying my bags of skin care and beauty supplies.

"No! I just bought those items this morning!" I fished through my purse and pulled out the receipts and shoved them at Amber. "Look at the time stamp."

She begrudgingly took the slips and examined them. Her mouth pressed into a thin line. "Take them back in the house, they're clear!" She thrust the receipts back at me. "Someone has been on a spree."

I should have known primping would be the death of me.

"We're just living our lives over here. Shopping and doing the yard work had nothing to do with hiding evidence, because we have nothing to hide."

Amber gestured to the other cops on search and seizure detail. "Bag and tag it all, and take it back to the lab."

The cops started loading the van with the bags of yard clippings. I thought of the foxglove I'd told the landscapers to get rid of and said a prayer that God would supernaturally turn it into petunias.

Amber folded her arms across her chest and shook her head. "You always did get away with everything, didn't you? Little Miss Goody-Goody. Teacher's pet. Well, not this time. I will find a way to nail you to the wall for this."

I took a step toward Amber. "You have been gunning for me from the start. What is your problem? Haven't you done enough to hurt me?"

"What *I* did to *you*? That's how you want to play this?

My name's Poppy McAllister and I'm always a victim. Poor little ol' me. You gotta lotta nerve."

I watched, speechless as she got into the driver's side of one of the cruisers and pulled away from the curb, lights flashing. *What in the world is she talking about? What did I do to her?*

Three sets of eyes were staring at me from the front window. The orange pair saw me look back and flopped over. On the other side of the street, a pack of nosy neighbors began to disperse back to their game shows and weather channels. This incident had given the gossip mill enough fuel to run on for weeks.

I thought about Aunt Ginny's hearing and wondered how much this could hurt her case. It was time to find out exactly what the neighbors had been saying to Social Services. I decided that first thing tomorrow morning I was going to find out.

I woke the next day with a determined sense of purpose. Quickly I made the bed and rapid-fired through my yoga postures like a yogini on speed. I locked Figaro out, so as not to have a repeat shakedown like the day before. Then I showered and schmeared on all my new beauty supplies. Only my hair wouldn't cooperate. I tried to do the same steps Courtney did at the salon, but my hair had a mind of its own and mocked me.

Then I dressed for my first date in over twenty years. I was terrified. I tried on all my new clothes and nothing worked. Everything that looked so good in the store now made me look like a frumpy cow. Stupid store mirrors! I considered calling Tim and telling him I had terminal acne or the Ebola virus and had to cancel, but I knew if I did there'd be hell to pay with Aunt Ginny. I was finally too exhausted to try anything else on so I went with a short green plaid skirt, a black T-shirt, a pair of black wool tights, and tall black boots with silver buckles up the back.

Getting Poppy 2.0 ready took considerably longer than the old *roll over and fish a cookie out of the couch* routine of version 1. Even Figaro was getting impatient and was *shk-shk-shk* scratching at the door.

I had decided last night that the best way to soften up the neighbors was to take them muffin baskets. And since there is no way that I have enough self-control to stay out of the muffins once they're baked, I chose to make muffins that were compliant with my Paleo Diet.

I fed Figaro another can of the exact same fish goo he refused yesterday and today he dove in like it was his favorite meal ever. Then I put on one of Aunt Ginny's "Donna Reed" aprons, opened the Paleo cookbook Dr. Melinda had lent me, and turned to the Paleo Blueberry Muffin recipe.

I got out the almond meal, coconut flour, honey, eggs, blueberries, and other ingredients and preheated the old Magic Chef oven to 350. It felt good to be in the kitchen again. I'm always my most comfortable when I'm baking. It's my own private therapy. I needed to get my mind off of my date with Tim this afternoon and plan my questions for the neighbors.

Yesterday I learned that Billy and his fiancée were missing. That seemed like a pretty big red flag that he was either guilty of something or the killer had more than one victim. Yet the cops chose to ransack *my* house. What could I possibly have done to Amber to make her target me? And what could she be looking for in my yard? *Please, dear God, not foxglove.* I would be so up the creek if Barbie was killed by digitalis. The cops were looking for something poisonous that grew in the yard, and chemicals in household items. Did that mean the plant item was also in the cleaning supplies? Or was the poison made up of multiple substances?

I stirred together the batter and gave it a taste. Dr. Melinda's recipe was good but it needed a pinch of nutmeg.

And what about motives? Barbie had burned a lot of people in her life and that made narrowing down the suspects tricky. Robert and Kelly had the campaign angle. Joel and Kristen had the adultery angle. Billy had the forefront on revenge. And they were all behaving oddly enough to cast doubt on their innocence. Even Coach Wilcott lied repeatedly about the reunion and his relationship with Barbie. Why? What could he possibly have to gain? Or hide?

I folded in the blueberries, then gently filled the paper cups and put the tins in the oven. I had fifteen to twenty minutes before the muffins would be ready, so I called Dr. Melinda's office and left a message for her to call me about the investigation as soon as she could.

Washing the bowl, I repeated the recipe, this time using strawberries instead of blueberries, and I scraped a vanilla bean into the batter in place of the cinnamon and nutmeg.

There was still the question about how the killer was able to make the poison. Did they make it in the kitchen or in a lab? Kristen, Joel, and the coach all worked at the school and had access to the chem lab. But I doubted Kristen would be messing around with chemicals in her condition. She wouldn't want the baby to be born with flippers or six toes. And what about the suspects who didn't work at the school? How would Billy or Robert cook up a poison and fill a hypodermic needle without a lab? Were syringes that easy to get a hold of? I'd only had mine left over from John's cancer treatment.

Wait a minute. Amber never gave me back the needle

from my purse. It's in police custody as evidence. Or is it?
A terrifying thought occurred to me. What if Amber was
behind all of this? She and Barbie had some kind of
falling-out. She was one of the last people to see Barbie
alive. And she sure had made it to the crime scene awfully
fast. Not to mention how determined she'd been to pin this
on me from the start. She wasn't even looking at other
suspects and there were so many blindingly obvious motives out there. She had the alleged murder weapon and
could dip that needle into any substance found in Aunt
Ginny's house to frame me.

I ran to the computer and started searching. I was desperate to find evidence to clear my name before Amber
showed up to arrest me again. In the state of New Jersey,
you need a doctor's written prescription to buy a syringe,
but there were medical supply stores online that would sell
you a hundred of them on the honor system.

So the killer either had syringes because of a legitimate
illness, or bought them online, in which case there should
be a record of the sale. I already knew Kristen had access
to needles. She had to inject herself with hormones for her
in-vitro procedure. Not to mention she was the school
nurse. She would be able to order whatever medical
supplies she needed without suspicion. I would have to
visit her again.

After the muffins had cooled, and I ate one of each to
make sure they were good, then a third one to calm my
nerves, I made up the baskets and headed out for the
neighbors.

First I visited Mr. Winston directly across the street. I
had seen him and Mrs. Sheinberg pointing at the house the
other day when the roses arrived.

"Hi, Mr. Winston. Remember me? Ginny's niece, Poppy
from across the street?"

"Of course I remember you. I'm not senile you know."

Mr. Winston was in his late seventies with a bushy white mustache, courtesy of Mother Nature, and bushy black hair, courtesy of Just for Men. He was hard of hearing, but he refused to wear a hearing aid so things tended to get lost in translation.

"I brought you a muffin basket."

"No, thanks. I just bought Thin Mints from that shyster down the street."

"It's a *gift*, Mr. Winston."

"A gift! Oh, why didn't you say so?" He took the basket and headed into the faded, pink Victorian. "Come on in here and set a spell, Little Red."

Mr. Winston's front room could have been featured in *Victoria* magazine: Home Edition—Pre-Demolition stage. Knickknacks as far as the eye could see lined the faded floral-print walls. I sat on the threadbare, pea-green settee next to a stuffed cat on a pillow.

Mr. Winston unwrapped a blueberry muffin and broke it in half. "Whiskers was the best cat I ever had. Didn't even scratch up the furniture."

I stifled a gasp when I realized that Mr. Whiskers wasn't a toy stuffed cat, but an actual taxidermist-stuffed, used-to-be-alive-and-climb-trees-and-chase-birds kind of cat. One of Whiskers's eyes was loose and dangling in my direction. I tried not to look more than twice, but I couldn't stop myself from glancing his way.

Mr. Winston wiped the crumbs off his red flannel shirt. "So how is Ginny these days? Lots of doin's over there lately."

"Aunt Ginny is great! You may have noticed that we've been sprucing up the place."

"Moose? There aren't any moose for hundreds of miles. They only live up north."

"No, not MOOSE. SPRUCE. She's SPRUCING. The yard is looking beautiful, and the painters come soon."

He nodded in understanding. "Sprucin', huh. I thought about sprucing this ol' girl, but she'd lose a lot of her charm that way."

I looked up at the four cuckoo clocks on the wall across from me. One had a cuckoo permanently ejected and hanging upside down by one claw. "Have you seen much of my aunt lately?"

"Seen her? Oh, out and about here and there." He unwrapped a strawberry muffin and took a bite.

"Have you noticed anything unusual about Aunt Ginny? Like maybe her clothes?"

He put one foot up on the ship's wheel coffee table. "If she has a problem with her toes she should get her a pair of these orthotics. Best decision I ever made."

Sigh. "No, Mr. Winston. HER CLOTHES. THE WAY SHE DRESSES." I fluffed my skirt out as a visual aid.

"Yes, that is a pretty dress. You must get your good taste from your aunt. She's always been a snappy dresser." Mr. Winston popped the rest of the strawberry muffin in his mouth and gave me a wink.

"Mr. Winston, have you talked to anyone from Social Services about Aunt Ginny?"

"Who?"

"Social Services?"

"Who's that?"

"THE LADY FROM SOCIAL SERVICES. HAS SHE BEEN BY?"

"No. No one's been by. 'Cept my daughter Judy comes by once a month to bring me some frozen dinners and crossword puzzles."

"Someone has been complaining about Aunt Ginny.

Now the state wants her to move to an assisted living facility."

"Bull hockey! Ginny's one tough broad and if anyone can take care of themselves it's her. I wouldn't take on that grizzly bear for nothing." He laughed at his own joke. "Of course, the person you should ask is Nell."

"Why is that?"

"I seem to recall her saying that she had some trouble with Social Services a while back. She had to go to court over it."

My heart was beating a little faster with this new information. I stood to go. "Thank you, Mr. Winston, I'll give Nell a visit."

"She's not home right now. Today is the day she baby-sits those two young'uns next door to Ginny."

That would be the home of Clarissa Dorsey, who just moved up to next on my list. I gave Mr. Winston a hug. "Thank you for the visit."

"Come back anytime you want to bring baked goods. I haven't had homemade goodies since Vera died eighteen years ago."

I promised him I'd come back as soon as I could and managed to refrain from saying "as long as I'm not in jail." I gave one more look to Mr. Whiskers, shuddered, and shut the door.

I walked across the street to the Dorseys' lemon-and-lime sherbet, Italian Gothic–style home. Clarissa answered the door with Ian in her arms and Colin wrapped around her leg.

"Clarissa, hi. I'm Ginny's niece, Poppy."

Clarissa put out her hand to shake mine. "It's nice to meet you. Your aunt has told me so much about you. She misses you terribly."

Leave it to Aunt Ginny to lay a guilt trap through unsuspecting strangers. "I brought you some muffins."

Ian and Colin took off with the muffin basket before Clarissa could get ahold of the handle. "I'm sorry about that. Those two are a handful. They just love Mrs. Frankowski. My mom lives in Colorado, so they hardly ever see her. Your aunt has become a stand-in grandmother to them."

"I know Aunt Ginny loves spending time with them. In fact, the reason I'm here is to help Aunt Ginny."

"I hope nothing's wrong." Somewhere inside the house came a crash. "Colin! That had better not be my Tiffany lamp!"

Then came a muffled, "It was Ian."

Clarissa turned back to me. "I'm so sorry. What's going on with Mrs. Frankowski?"

"Well, it seems someone has been telling a Social Services worker that Aunt Ginny can't take care of herself anymore. I was looking for Nell to see if she knows anything that could help us. I was told she is usually here today."

"Mo-om!" came a call from somewhere in the house.

Clarissa yelled over her shoulder, "What?"

"Ian's in the peanut butter!"

"Ian, get out of that peanut butter right now! Nell babysits the boys while I go shopping and run errands, but she is leaving today for a two-monthlong trip down the Amazon. We switched our days this week because of her travel plans."

A boomerang smothered in peanut butter came hurtling out of the front door and missed my head by inches.

Clarissa turned and yelled through the open door, "Colin! What have I said about playing with that thing in the house?"

"You said not to."

"Then why did it just come flying out the front door?!"

"I don't know."

"I'm sorry, I have to get in there before they destroy something else. I've never heard anything negative said about Mrs. Frankowski by anyone. As far as we're concerned, she's a saint. If she needs anything we'll be there for her."

"Thank you, I appreciate that."

"I think Nell was going over to Mr. Murillo's this morning to drop off her keys. He's going to take in her mail and water her plants while she's gone. We volunteered to do it, but she insisted she didn't want to trouble us."

There was a loud thud from inside the house, followed by, "Mo-om!"

"I'm sure she appreciated the offer." *She was probably terrified to let Baby Kong and Godzilla Jr. in her house while she was gone.* "If you think of anything that could help Aunt Ginny, please let me know."

"I will." She gave me a warm smile and went in to deal with whatever carnage Colin and Ian had created.

I was getting desperate. Mr. Murillo said that I had just missed Nell, but she was on her way to Mrs. Colazzo's. He also said that Aunt Ginny was the first neighbor to welcome him and his wife to the neighborhood when they moved in years ago and if there was anything she needed to let him know and they would be there.

Then Mrs. Collazo said that Nell had come by earlier to drop off the last of her garden tomatoes, and that she was heading over to the Sheinbergs' house with her cockatiel, Max. Then she offered to give me the phone number of her nephew, Dino. In case Aunt Ginny needed someone *whacked* or I was free for dinner Sunday afternoon.

The case against Aunt Ginny was looking more and

more strange. None of the neighbors had spoken with anyone from Social Services. In fact, they all thought so highly about Aunt Ginny that none of them had noticed any unusual behavior. So where was Ms. Carson getting her information? I had to talk to Nell, if only I could catch up with her before she flew off to the jungle.

I rushed over to Mr. and Mrs. Sheinberg's house. Mrs. Sheinberg was a tiny woman with steel gray hair and sharp black eyes like a bird. She was brown as a walnut and had a perpetual hump in her back from years of working hunched over a counter filling rugelach in her family's Jewish bakery in Philly.

We sat in her black-and-white kitchen at a little white Formica table, drinking glasses of iced tea.

"Nell should be along in a little while. You made these muffins yourself? They look good."

"Mrs. Sheinberg, I couldn't help but notice you and Mr. Winston out front the other day."

"Yeah, Harry's a good guy. His wife, Vera, and I used to play pinochle together before she passed, God rest her soul." She tapped her mouth with the side of two fingers. "Toi toi."

"I saw you and Mr. Winston pointing at the house. I was wondering if you saw anything wrong with it."

"Wrong? No, nothing was wrong. We were trying to figure out what those men were looking at the other day. But then you came out to get your pretty flowers and we didn't want you to think we were yentas. So, you got a boyfriend? Is that who the flowers were from?"

"No, just a friend. What men are you talking about?"

"You know, the men who were out a couple weeks ago. They were taking the pictures."

"When was this?"

She shrugged her shoulders. "I don't know." Then she

leaned back in her chair and called into the other room, "Sol!"

"What!"

"When were the men out looking at Ginny's house?"

"Last Tuesday, I think. Or Monday."

She leaned back into the table and rolled her eyes. "He don't know. I think it was Monday morning. They pulled up in two cars like they were meeting there. They were wearing them fancy suits." She leaned back in her chair again. "Sol!"

"What!"

"Weren't they wearing fancy suits?"

"No! I think one of them was wearing a sport coat."

"Bah!" She leaned back in and made a grimace. "He don't know. They took a bunch of pictures on their doo-hickeys."

A little white-haired man with a fifteen-strand comb-over and a bulbous red nose came in. "I do too know. It was a Monday. They were talking about the house and pointing around like they were discussing it."

"Yeah. That's right. Then they left. They didn't look like tourists so Harry and I were trying to figure out what they were looking at, but everything just looked normal to us."

The Sheinbergs' phone rang. It was an old-fashioned tabletop model with a rotary dial that *tk-tk-tk-tk'd* when you turned it. Mr. Sheinberg picked it up.

"Yeah. Yeah. Yeah. Yeah. Okay then."

Mrs. Sheinberg gave him a shrug. "What?"

"Nell's running late. She's taking the bird to Clara's. I gotta schlep it over here later."

Mrs. Sheinberg patted my hand. "I'm sorry, *bubala*, it looks like you waited for nothing. Maybe you can catch her at Clara's."

Seriously?

I said my good-byes and promised to come back soon. Clara Pritchard's house was my last chance to catch Nell before she flew off to the toucans and pink river dolphins and I had to face my date with Tim.

Please, dear God, let me catch her. I'll never ask for another favor again. Okay, that's not true, but still . . .

Mrs. Pritchard lived in the blue, Dutch-style Victorian right next door to us. It was like a big blue barn turned sideways. Her yard was always neat as a pin.

She was short and round, with pink cheeks and white hair. I guessed she was somewhere in her late seventies. She would be the perfect Mrs. Claus.

I handed her the muffin basket.

"Oh, honey, you're a peach. But you just missed Nell. She caught a cab from here to take her to Newark Airport."

I deflated like a Macy's balloon at the end of the parade. More accurately, like someone who was probably going to the iron country club for a long time.

No one else had been able to shed any light on why Aunt Ginny was being targeted by DYFS. Nell was the one person who might have information to help us fight back and now she was gone. Mrs. Pritchard had to be my last interview of the day because my time was up. I hoped she could give me something useful.

"You want some limeade? I just made a pitcher."

"I would love some."

"Why don't we sit out here on the porch since it's such a lovely day?"

It was actually a bit chilly, but Mrs. Pritchard took a lot of pride in her rosebushes and was forever trying to force people into seeing them.

She came back with two glasses of limeade and sat on a yellow metal glider. "Mr. Lincoln won first place at the garden show this year." She pointed to a beautiful red rosebush.

"Wow, congratulations. He's beautiful."

I took a sip of my limeade and my eyes crossed. It was so tart you needed a shot of Novocain to drink it.

Mrs. Pritchard took a sip of her limeade and smiled broadly. "I see Virginia has done some work on her yard lately. It looks good."

"Thank you. We're also doing some repairs and re-modeling so the place will be good as new before you know it."

Mrs. Pritchard looked next door at Aunt Ginny's. "Virginia has a lovely home. It must be nice to have something stay in the family for so many generations."

"We're very blessed. I just wanted you to know about the repairs so you wouldn't worry about Aunt Ginny. She's doing really well."

She turned to me with surprise. "Why in the world would I worry about Virginia? She isn't sick, is she?"

"Well, no. She's very healthy. I just know some of the neighbors have been concerned lately." I took a very small sip of my limeade and braced myself for the shock.

"Honey, no one is concerned about Virginia Frankow-ski. She can take care of herself. We're all worried about you."

I gasped, and sucked in a whole mouthful. I started choking and Mrs. Pritchard got up to get me a napkin.

I quickly tossed the rest of my limeade on Mr. Lincoln before she came back.

Mrs. Pritchard returned and handed me a paper towel folded in half, then looked down at my glass. "My good-ness, you drank that fast. Let me get you some more."

"No! Thank you. I am . . . so full. It was . . . really delicious."

She sat back down. "It's a secret family recipe, you know."

"That is one you need to keep a secret, for sure."

She sat up a little straighter. "Oh, I agree."

"What I really want to hear about is why the neighbors are worried about *me*."

"We all know what happened at the high school the other night. None of us believe you to be capable of murder. We've known you since you were a child. We're worried that you won't be able to prove it."

"So when you were all standing out front watching the police search the yard?"

"We were making sure they didn't plant any evidence. Did they ever find the condo viarta majory?"

"The what?"

"The *condo viarta majory*."

"What in the world is that?"

"I was hoping you would know. Before you arrived we overheard the cop with the K-9 say that's what they were looking for outside."

"I've never heard of it, but I'll ask a couple of my friends." *Like my friend Google.*

"Do they have any other suspects?"

"I don't know if *they* do, but I have a few."

"I saw you had a visit from Joel Miller the other day. Is he a suspect?"

"Well, I don't think I should . . ."

"He's been bad news since day one."

"Bad news how?"

She looked away and shook her head sadly. "He got Dianne Hoag's grandson hooked on that mara-wanna."

Now, Meatballfist Hoag was the biggest pothead at Cape May High back in my day. So the chances were pretty strong that if there was a drug problem, he was the regional manager of Weeds-R-Us. But I couldn't tell that to sweet Mrs. Pritchard.

"Oh, I'm sorry to hear that."

"We were all sorry to see a nice girl like Kristen marry a boy like that."

I nodded along.

"But then that Barbara Pomeroy, if anyone knew how to screw up a wedding it was her."

"I just found out that she almost married Billy Sommers."

She tsk-tsked. "He was such a good boy, too. Smart as a whip. He got a scholarship to go to that fancy technical school in Georgia, you know."

"A football scholarship?"

"No, goodness me. He won some big science fair award."

I was dumbfounded. "No, I did not know that."

She took another sip of her limeade and rocked in the glider. "Oh, yeah, his grandma was so proud. He has his own tech company now. He's some kind of corporate high muckety-muck. It's a shame he couldn't give a job to Meatballfist Hoag."

That made me laugh—hard.

"Just think, that Barbara could have married him instead of letting him get away."

"Mrs. Pritchard, have you spoken with Rosalind Carson from the Department of Social Services about Aunt Ginny?"

She thought for a moment. "No. I haven't spoken to anyone from DYFS. Why?"

"They said the neighbors are complaining about her."

"No one on this street has ever said an unkind word about Virginia Frankowski. I would know."

I stood to go. "Thank you so much for the visit, but I'm afraid I have to get going."

"Come back anytime. I'll bring over some of my limeade for Virginia later."

"Oh, she will just *love* that. Thank you."

I waved good-bye and as I walked home I tried to google "*condo viarta majory*." Google didn't have any idea what I was talking about, so I asked Siri. Siri tried to make me a restaurant reservation at the Lobster House. I would have to ask Dr. Melinda.

I texted Sawyer to find out what entry caused Billy to win the science fair. If it was chemistry-related we might have just zeroed in on our killer.

Chapter 29

Aunt Ginny was in the library when I got in. She had a feather duster in one hand and a lit cigarette in the other. She was swishing the feathers at the middle row of books, and Figaro was batting wildly to try to catch them. "The doctor called while you were out."

"Thank you. Why are you smoking?"

"Don't I always smoke?"

"Not since I was a kid."

She looked at the cigarette between her fingers like it was a loaded gun. "I found it and I thought I must have started again."

"Not that I know of."

Aunt Ginny smashed the cigarette into a cork coaster on the end table. "Oh, thank God. That was disgusting."

Figaro jumped at the feather duster and knocked over a marble bust of Edgar Allan Poe the size of a wine bottle. The statue hit the marble fireplace mantel and Mr. Poe's nose broke off like a disgraced pharaoh. Aunt Ginny swatted Figaro with the feathers. "What did I tell you about that?"

Figaro froze in position, his eyes wide and dilated from the game. Then he flopped over and fell off the end table.

"Serves you right." Aunt Ginny picked him up and set him back on the table, where he proceeded to take a bath.

"Oh, before I forget, Mrs. Pritchard is bringing you some homemade limeade later."

Aunt Ginny scrunched up her nose and stuck her tongue out. "Blecch. We can use it to peel the paint off the front porch."

I returned Dr. Melinda's call and her receptionist put her through. "Great timing, I'm in between. How are you feeling?"

"Detoxing is hitting me hard. I've had a headache for two days. I can't believe the sugar withdrawals are this bad."

"Sugar hits the brain just like cocaine. I know it can be hard but hang in there. It passes in a couple of days. I got your test results back and, just as I suspected, they were positive for Hashimoto's."

"So I'm a ninja?"

"It's an autoimmune disease of the thyroid that is causing a lot of your symptoms like the fatigue. I'll send over some information and we'll set a follow-up to check your levels again in a few weeks. You just need to be sure to keep avoiding gluten, soy, and dairy."

"Ugh."

"I know. And stress management is more important now than ever. Would you say your stress levels are improving?"

"Umm . . ."

"What happened?"

"Well, the cops searched my house last night."

"Oh, no. What were they looking for?"

"Chemicals. Mostly in the form of cleaning supplies.

Which, by the way, you may be getting a call to ask you about my recent decision to go green."

"I am so sorry. What horrible timing."

"They were also tearing up the yard. Do you know anything about poisonous plants? Especially one called *conviarta majory*? Or something like that."

"Hmm. I haven't heard of that, but I know there are a lot of common plants that are poisonous. Do you know anyone with an exotic flower bed?"

I had no idea what people's houses or yards looked like around here. All I remembered was a lot of houses with crushed seashells strewn about in the place of grass. "No, but I can ask around."

"I have an old textbook here somewhere that covers herbology. I'll call you if I find anything."

I thanked Dr. Melinda and hung up. I checked my phone for texts from Sawyer. Nothing.

A black Kia Soul pulled up in front of the house.

Aunt Ginny came tearing down the stairs, followed by Fig. "He's here! He's here!"

"Oh, God, I'm going to be sick. I just know I'm going to make a fool of myself."

Aunt Ginny patted me on the shoulder. "You're going to be fine. Take a deep breath."

"Do I look okay?"

"You look fantastic. Don't worry."

I reached to open the door but Aunt Ginny stopped me. "Not yet. You don't want to appear too eager."

"How long am I supposed to make him wait? He's just standing out there."

"Slowly count to ten. Then open the door."

This seemed ridiculous, but Aunt Ginny had five husbands to back up her methods, so I started the count. At ten, I opened the door just as he was about to knock a second time. "Hi."

Tim was wearing faded blue jeans and a white cotton shirt with the sleeves rolled up to just below the elbow. His blond hair fell in waves around his face and curled out at the collar. Years of living at the beach left him with a permanent tan and laugh lines around his eyes. He was the walking embodiment of surf sexy.

"Hey, beautiful. Long time no see." He leaned in and kissed me on the cheek.

I went all light-headed. "So you're sure you want to do this?"

"I've thought about this moment for almost twenty-five years. I'm sure."

I took a deep breath to calm myself. Why do men look better with age but women just wrinkle and sag? Life isn't fair. I felt myself staring all moony-eyed at him.

Aunt Ginny saved me. She put her hand on the back of my shoulder and gave me a push toward the door. "Okay, now. You kids have fun."

"I'll have her back before you know it." Tim waved good-bye to Aunt Ginny.

Aunt Ginny called after us, "You can keep her."

That is not helping, Aunt Ginny.

Tim just laughed. "She is still a riot."

"Oh, she's a pip all right."

Tim took me to a little French restaurant in West Cape May called Le Bon Gigi. "You will love this. The chef here is a friend of mine."

His "chef friend" was a cute little thing in her late twenties with long blond hair worn in a ponytail and about ten percent body fat. She came bouncing out in her tiny little chef coat and Tim leaned down to give her a hug.

She stood with one hand on his shoulder while she spoke to me.

"It's so nice to meet you. Any friend of Tim's is a VIP here."

"Geej is into the farm-to-table movement. Everything on her menu comes from local sources."

"Geej" smiled adoringly at Tim. "I think it's important to support local farms. Just about everything in my kitchen is organic including the milk, cream, and eggs."

"Oh. That's . . . very nice." *I guess. What do I know? Everything I know about organic I learned a few days ago from Dr. Melinda.*

Tim asked Gigi, "How's your turnover?"

"Good today. Smooth. Last weekend we were slammed. I was in the weeds every night. A bus of Wheel of Fortunes pulled up and wanted a dollar menu. How were you?"

"My salamander's down until tomorrow so I'm pushing the scampi and two of my servers were no-shows."

"*Gah*. What is it about this time of year everyone goes nuts?" Gigi turned her big brown eyes on me. "Are you a chef too?"

Oh, good. And I was afraid this would be awkward. "Nope."

After an uncomfortable pause, Tim pulled out my chair. "Well, why don't we sit down?"

The heel of my boot caught on the carpet and I stumbled onto my seat. I recovered quickly only to knock my fork on the floor.

Gigi removed the menus, and my clumsy fork, from our table. "I'll send a waiter over to get your drinks. Don't worry about ordering. I'll take care of everything."

She flounced back to the kitchen before I could even form the word *gluten* in my brain. *Please, God, don't let me die today from either embarrassment or bread crumbs.*

Tim and I locked eyes. "So, alone at last."

I once met Steven Tyler after an Aerosmith concert and I wasn't nearly as starstruck then as I was right now. I spent years dreaming about this scenario. A dream that usually did not include Gigi. I tried to cover my nerves, but still rambled, "Tell me everything. I want to know all about college and work and how did you start your own restaurant? And your mom, does she still hate me?"

Tim gave me a broad smile and I felt the heat rise up to my cheeks. "Yes. But to be fair, she hates most people."

I giggled.

"Poppy, I've been wanting to tell you something for years."

I swallowed hard. "Yes?"

"I owe my whole career to you. You're the reason I became a chef. If you hadn't pushed me into going to culinary school, I wouldn't be where I am today."

"Then I bailed on you."

He shrugged. "That's all in the past. We were kids. What matters is today."

"I'm so sorry things went the way they did. I made a mistake that derailed our entire future together."

"I made some mistakes of my own. I should have tried to stop your wedding. Make the grand entrance and yell, 'I object!'"

"Why didn't you?"

"I didn't have the guts. Plus, my brother got me drunk just in case I worked up the guts."

"If you had crashed my wedding, I probably would have run off with you."

We sat in silence for a moment. The weight of what could have been hung heavy between us.

"Were you happy?"

"I was. Until John got sick and died. He was a great husband."

"Did you love him?"

"Not at first, but I grew to love him very much. Did you ever get married?"

"Almost. Twice, in fact."

"What happened?"

"It didn't work out. They both eventually said the restaurant was my first love and they couldn't compete with her. But they were wrong, because you were my first love."

It was one of those moments where you feel an invisible pull between two hearts right before something wonderful happens. It was interrupted by butternut squash bisque.

Gigi had come from the kitchen to serve us personally. *Goody.* "How is everything so far?"

I suspected Gigi was there more to spy on Tim than to do quality control, since we hadn't tasted anything but water. "Good."

Gigi flounced back to the kitchen and I watched Tim watch her go. The moment was broken between us.

"So fill me in on what the heck happened at the reunion. I was in the kitchen most of the night, but I heard bits and pieces."

I told him all the gory details that I knew.

"So that congressman was Barbie's husband?"

"Didn't you know that?"

"No. He comes into my restaurant a lot but he has a different woman with him each time."

"Really?"

"And by the way he was acting at the reunion, I figured he was with Kelly."

Once again Gigi appeared at Tim's side. "Next we have a summer salad of fresh tomatoes and white corn with rosemary and a homemade garlic butter–soaked crouton."

Tim smiled at Gigi. "I love your croutons."

Gigi smiled back. "I know you do."

Is crouton *a euphemism for something I need to know about?*

When Gigi had reluctantly returned to the kitchen and we were alone again, I asked, "What do you mean 'the way he was acting'?"

"When I came out of the dining room, to check the chafing dish levels, I saw them looking very cozy in the corner. Kelly was whispering something to the congressman and he definitely looked like he was into it. It wasn't too long after that the police were locking the place down. I tried to find you, but Connie said you had disappeared to look for Sawyer."

He reached for my hand. As if pulled by an invisible beacon, Gigi materialized. It seemed the closer Tim and I got to connecting, the faster Gigi appeared at his side to break it up.

To her credit, Gigi served five courses of amazing small plates. After the bisque and the salad there was a mini broccolini-and-gruyere napoleon. The main course was broiled lamb chops with garlicky roasted beets and purple fingerling potatoes. I was starting to think all the garlic was another attempt to sabotage our date. But then she brought tarte tatin with homemade maple ice cream for dessert, and I was temporarily pacified. I knew in my heart that none of it was gluten-free, but I ate it anyway. I was having serious doubts about my ability to stick to Dr. Melinda's diet.

And then there was Gigi. Next to Tim. With her hand
on his shoulder. Again. "How was everything?"

Crowded.

"Fantastic, Geej! You are one gifted chef. Everything
was so fresh. What's the secret to your broccolini? How
do you get it so tender?"

"Harvesting at the right time. My produce guy doesn't
harvest the plant too early like most farms. He waits until
it is perfectly ripe and at the peak time to cook it. And you
don't want to cook it where the farmer cuts it off at the
dirt. Trim the pieces off where they are tender."

An image of the windowsill in Kristen's office flashed
before my eyes. She had rows of orchids, lilies, and other
exotic plants. *And one of the pots has stalks of something
cut off at the dirt.* My heartbeat started to pick up the pace.
Amber was looking for exotic plants in my yard and Kristen had some right out in the open in her office. And
Kristen worked down the hall from a chemistry lab, plus
she had access to needles.

"Isn't that right, Poppy? Poppy?"

Tim was asking me something and I had no idea what
it was. I nodded. "Mmm-hmm."

Tim turned to Gigi. "See. Poppy would love to take
some cooking lessons from you sometime."

Oh my God! What? No, I wouldn't!

Gigi gave me a tenuous smile. "Sure. Call me anytime
and we'll set it up."

"That sounds good." *Almost as good as an indictment.*

Gigi handed me a business card with the restaurant information. "Tim has my cell number. You can get it from
him if you can't get me at work."

Well played . . . Geej.

Tim paid the bill and chatted with Geej—a small part
of me died each time I heard that name—for a couple

more minutes while I made a plan to pay another visit to Kristen as soon as possible.

By the time we pulled up in front of Aunt Ginny's, I was up to my neck with "farm-to-table." It had been an afternoon of mixed signals and missed opportunities. I was disappointed, but at least I hadn't done anything humiliating.

I said good-bye and reached for the door handle.

Tim spun me around to face him. He had a look of such intensity in his eyes, one that I hadn't seen in a very long time, and I was afraid to breathe and break the spell.

He leaned in and kissed me—and twenty-five years dropped away in moments. There was something familiar, yet exciting, about being in his arms and I never wanted it to end.

I found myself in the foyer, and didn't know how I got there. Tim may have said he would call me later. I may or may not have said good-bye. All I knew for sure was that whoever said you can't go home again had never been kissed like that.

Chapter 30

I waited for the final bell to ring. When the pack of students swarmed the parking lot and bus line, I was on the move. I donned a pair of mirrored sunglasses and grabbed a ball cap that was sticking out of a backpack as it walked past me. I shoved it down on my forehead and tucked my hair inside. The security guard was occupied with harassing a couple of freshmen who were still getting the hang of high school protocol and I slipped past him and down the hall to the nurse's office.

Kristen was packing up her belongings, ready to go home for the day. A bottle of water, an orange, a cell phone. I could see the row of plants on the window behind her. The one with the cut stems was gone but a brown ring stained the wooden ledge where it had once been.

Kristen's face twisted into a frown when she saw me. "What are you doing here? I thought you were banned."

"I brought you something." I pulled the peace offering from my bag and placed it on the desk in front of her.

She looked at it warily. "You brought me a Snickers bar?" Then she grabbed the bar and tore off the wrapper like it was the last crab leg on the all-you-can-eat buffet.

Her mouth was full of peanuts and caramel, but I could just make out, "What do you want?"

"I want to talk to you about getting pregnant."

"What?"

"I've been thinking about having a baby. My late husband and I were never blessed, and now my time is almost up. If I'm going to do this I need to do it now. I heard you had in vitro to conceive."

She was suspicious but the sugar was kicking in, so I had about twenty minutes of mellow before she crashed.

"Have you picked a donor yet?"

My mind flashed on Tim and I suddenly felt giddy.

"Whoa! I'll take that giant blush you're showing as a yes. You need to get started right away with a fertility doctor. It takes several rounds of hormone therapy before your body is ready to receive a viable embryo. And at our age it can be hard to get the pregnancy to take."

"How often did you have to give yourself injections?"

"Every day for two weeks, and you might have to repeat the process for months until you get enough eggs harvested."

"That sounds painful."

"It's not fun, but it's worth it." She rubbed her giant belly.

"Don't you have to fill the needles at home? You're a nurse, so I'm sure that was easy for you, but I don't know what I'm doing."

"No, you get prefilled disposables."

"What happens to them when you're done?"

She stopped rubbing her belly and furrowed her brow. "What do you mean what happens to them? You throw them away in a sharps container."

"You can't reuse them for something else?"

"No. Why would you want to?"

"What if you had no choice and it was an emergency? Could you reuse them then?"

"They would be contaminated. They would have to be boiled and sterilized, then disinfected with a strong bleach."

Bleach. Like what Amber was looking for in Aunt Ginny's kitchen. Now it made sense why the police were looking for both a chemical and a plant. The bleach would kill whatever was in a syringe the first use and the plant must have been poisonous.

She stared at me for a moment, then her face flushed red. "Wait! You don't want to know about in vitro, you're nosing around about the investigation."

Uh-oh! Chocolate must be wearing off. "No, I'm really interested in getting pregnant. But since *you* want to talk about the investigation, I *guess* we could."

"Wait. I don't want to talk about the investigation."

"Then why did you bring it up?"

"What? I didn't mean to."

Wow, we used to do this to Barbie's clique in high school. We called it "The Wabbit Season." I couldn't believe it still worked.

"But you are *so* right. Barbie was killed by an injection of some kind. Do you think the needles could have come from this office?"

Kristen looked like a bikini model trying to figure out calculus equations, but she went on with the conversation. "Everything in this office has a very strict sign-out procedure."

"Have supplies ever gone unaccounted for? Like maybe an aspirin or a syringe?"

"Never." She walked over to a locked cabinet and opened it. "Look, here is the med locker. There is nothing stronger than Benadryl in here, except for some of the students' insulin and EpiPens. And here is the sign-out sheet. Nothing leaves this room without my signature."

"Does anyone else in the building have access to the medical supplies?"

"Not in here. Of course, the coach has his own supply of emergency first aid for away games. He could have an EpiPen or insulin shot in there."

"So you think the coach killed Barbie?"

"What? No, I don't."

"But you just said that." I was talking in circles to make her think she'd given something away. "Why would he do it?"

She put her hand to her forehead and sat back down. "I know she was probably sleeping with him. They sure had enough private meetings together."

"Your husband said the same thing."

"When did you talk to my husband?"

"The other day when he was at my house."

Her eyes widened. "For-for what?"

"He didn't tell you? We were talking about Barbie." The blood drained from Kristen's face and for a moment I felt bad about tricking her. I got over it.

"What did he say about her?"

"Nothing you don't already know."

"So he admitted it."

Now we're getting somewhere. "Do you mean he admitted the affair or he admitted he killed her?"

"The affair, dummy. Joel didn't kill anyone. Why am I even talking to you about this?"

"You need to talk to someone."

Kristen started to cry so I handed her the tissue box on the waiting room table. She waved it off.

"Those things are like sandpaper. I have some in my desk that are better."

Okay, I guess I'll get those for you. I opened her desk and looked around. Instead of office supplies her desk looked more like a cosmetics counter. Assorted lotions and powders, tweezers and makeup brushes, a giant jar of wrinkle cream, and a well-worn copy of *What to Expect When You're Expecting*.

I handed her the box of Puffs. "How did you find out about Joel and Barbie having an affair?"

"Barbie sent me pictures of them together . . . doing . . . you know. Then I found receipts and phone records."

"What did Joel say when you confronted him?"

"What makes you think I confronted him?"

"Didn't you?"

She wiped her eyes. "He doesn't know I know."

"Well, *I* asked him about the affair."

"You had no right! That was none of your business. . . . What did he say?"

"He denied it."

"That figures."

"So you two didn't talk about it. Didn't discuss the root problems or demand that he break it off. You just picked up and kept going like it didn't happen?"

She put a protective hand on her belly again. "The affair was a mistake and it's over. Now that we're expecting he has to stay with me."

O-kay. That's not twisted logic at all.

"The word on the street"—*at least the street that leads to the senior center*—"is that this baby is an attempt to save your marriage."

"We were so happy together when we were younger. A baby was all that was missing."

She was zoning out on me and to be honest, I was a little afraid of her. She needed some counseling and possibly lithium. It was time for my Hail Mary pass and then get the heck out of Dodge. I stood as if to go. "Those flowers on the windowsill are beautiful. You have quite a green thumb."

"Thank you. Most of them came from the Ecology Club."

"It looks like one is missing—what was that one?"

"Just an orchid. It needed to go back to the greenhouse for some TLC."

"I've been thinking about getting an orchid. Do you ever cut those and put them in a vase?"

She snorted. "Not unless you want them to die really fast. Dendrobium orchids don't live long off the root. You're better off enjoying them as a plant."

"You ever make anything with the flowers?"

She yawned. "What, like a bouquet?"

"I was thinking more like perfume."

"No. I wouldn't know how to do something like that."

I left Kristen's office and went to the gym to talk with Coach Wilcott. The gym was empty so I went around back to the staff parking lot. The Trans Am was gone. I went back inside to the coach's office. It was dark inside and the door was shut. I knocked quietly. "Hello?" No answer. I tried the doorknob and to my surprise, the door swung open. I quickly looked around to make sure no one was watching me, then I ducked into the office and shut the door.

The smell of sweat socks and unwashed uniforms punched me in the face. I felt like I was back in the fifth grade when boys were gross. Whatever athletics budget the school had, it was not being spent in here. One 1970s-era metal desk. One army-green metal filing cabinet. A whiteboard covered with circles and X's and arrows diagramming some sport's play took up one wall. Motivational posters like "There is no I in team" and

"If you can dream it, you can achieve it" were hung around the other walls.

I checked the coach's desk. Nothing exciting there. Office supplies and a giant container of salted peanuts. The file cabinet was full of students' records and insurance forms and one nudie magazine in the back of the top drawer. *Yuck!* For a guy whose entire fashion sense was comprised of matching the color of his plastic whistle to his sweatpants of the day, the coach was surprisingly organized.

I was about to give up when I spotted a black duffel bag under the lone visitor chair in the corner. I pulled the bag out and tried to open it but it was locked. There on the side was a luggage-style combination dial. *Great.* Then I had an idea. I rolled all the numbers to zero and the lock opened. *Pssh, men.*

Jackpot! This was the med kit. I used a ballpoint pen in my purse to push around the contents. It was full of bandages, ibuprofen, and ice packs. Alcohol swabs, wound cleaner and gauze pads, and one lone EpiPen. I took a couple of pictures of the contents with my phone and locked it back up.

At that exact second, I heard footsteps and the jingle of keys coming toward the office and started to panic. Shoving the bag under the chair I looked around for a place to hide. I tried to cram myself under the desk but my rear was sticking out. The footsteps stopped right outside the door. In a pathetic attempt to hide my butt, I pushed open the middle drawer from under the desk and it rested on my rear.

The doorknob jiggled and the door cracked open. I held my breath and said a prayer. Nothing. Then the lights were turned out and the door was shut.

Footsteps faded into the distance.

I could breathe again. It must have been the janitor. I lifted my hips, scooted the drawer back in, and backed out from under the desk. I popped my head up at eye level and peered around the room. That was too close. I am not the kind of girl who sneaks around and goes through other people's belongings.

I cracked open the door and looked out. The coast was clear. I left the office through the gym as fast as my size eight boots would carry my size eighteen behind.

I was heading home when I got another idea. I gave Missy a call.

"Hey, you. How is the investigation going?"

"Fine. I have some leads. I have a question for you."

"Sure, anything. I want to help any way I can."

"Who is the Ecology Club teacher?"

"Mr. Nelson. Why?"

"I was just wondering. I want to get an orchid for the house and I was hoping he could give me some pointers on how to keep it alive. I seem to have a black thumb."

"Oh, well, you will have to wait a couple of weeks. Mr. Nelson is on medical leave until mid-October. Something about a minor surgery. I don't know for sure but I hope it was to have that giant mole removed from his nose. No matter how hard you try it's impossible to keep from staring at it when he talks."

"Oh, that's too bad. I guess the orchid will have to wait."

"Why don't you just ask the parent volunteer?"

"The *what*, now?"

"Every club has a teacher overseer and a parent volunteer. You know, in case the teacher can't be there. It encourages parent involvement."

"I did not know that. Who is the parent volunteer for the Ecology Club?"

"Hold on while I check the staff directory. . . . Oh, dear, it was Barbie."

Alarm bells were ringing in my head, but I couldn't decipher just why.

"I guess you'll have to wait for Mr. Nelson. Of course, you could just Google it." She laughed.

"Oh, of course. *Duh*. Why didn't I think of that?"

"Sorry I couldn't help you more. Are you holding up okay?"

"Yeah. You know, taking it one day at a time."

"Well, you're in my thoughts and prayers. Let me know if you need anything."

I thanked her and hung up. *Do I need anything?* Both the coach and Kristen had access to needles and knowledge of the security cameras, and worked down the hall from the chemistry department. But neither one of them seemed like making a poison in a chem lab would be their forte. Joel had a strong motive and could get the needles from the coach's bag and the plant from his wife's office. But would he know what to do with them? And what about Billy? Strong motive. Science award. Mysteriously missing. But he'd been gone from the area for years and the motive was weak. I was missing something important, I could feel it. I thought what I needed right now, more than anything, was a miracle.

And maybe a latte.

Chapter 31

I drove back over the bridge into Cape May. It was really too late for caffeine, but I had a killer detox headache that only espresso could cure. Plus, I had a quiet night in with the girls planned for later, and that should be a lot more lively than lying around in pajamas watching *Law & Order* reruns.

When I walked into the espresso bar, two ladies were sitting at the front window drinking iced coffees, and a very serious-looking little boy with blond hair was sitting at the counter. He was wearing khaki shorts and a navy sport coat with a crest over the pocket. Through his thick glasses, his eyes were the size of quarters.

"Hi. I'm Henry. I'm lactose-intolerant."

I had to tamp down a giggle. "Hi, Henry. I'm Poppy. I'm gluten-intolerant."

"What's glue-in?"

"It's the stuff that makes bread and spaghetti and cookies."

He gasped. "Oh, no!"

"I know, right?"

"Do you have special cookies and sketti you can have?"

"Not yet."

"I hope you get some. I have special milks, so I don't have to feel left out."

"That's good. It's no fun to feel left out, is it?"

Henry shook his head *no*.

"How old are you?"

He held up four fingers. "I'm f-ree." He switched to one finger. "But I'm going to be four soon."

A giggle escaped, and I sat down on the stool next to him. I looked over at the ladies who were engrossed in conversation and not watching Henry at all.

"Ooh, a birthday. Do you have any special plans?"

Henry nodded and his glasses bounced on his nose. "We're going to the zoo to see the kitties."

"I love kitties."

"They go, *mrow*."

"Which kitties do you want to see?"

"The ones with the polka-dots."

"Mmm. Leopards. Nice."

Henry nodded. He was very serious like a little old man, and my heart just melted.

Gia came in from the back room carrying a giant bag of coffee beans slung up on one shoulder. His blue-and-white striped shirt was open at the neck and his sleeves were rolled up to his elbows. My heart melted some more.

"*Buongiorno, bella*. I see you have met my son."

I was stunned. I looked from Gia to Henry, who was watching my reaction closely. I smiled. "Yes, we've been talking about kitties."

Henry nodded. "Poppy can't have skettis."

Gia smacked his forehead with his palm. "Oh, no! *Non pasta, e una tragedia!*"

Henry looked at me and giggled. "My dad likes to talk like that."

"Yes, I know." *And I'm trying real hard to keep from throwing myself at him.*

"Daddy, could she come with us to see the kitties?"

Oh, boy. Poor Gia—put on the spot. "Aww, that's not—"

"Yes."

"Say *what*, now?"

"Yes, *bella*. Come with us for Henry's birthday on Saturday."

Hmm. Who exactly is "us"? I was racking my brain to remember any signs of wedded bliss. *Have I seriously been flirting with a married man this whole time?* I looked at Gia's hand. No ring. Still . . .

"Are you *sure*?" I looked to Henry, and saw those giant eyes pleading with me. I couldn't help but smile. "I would *love* to go."

Gia's smile lit up the room. "It is settled then. We will meet here at eleven, and we'll go to lunch after."

Did I just get asked out? I can't tell. Now I'm going to obsess about this.

He started to whistle a little tune, and pulled his cell phone out. He said something in Italian, then hung up.

"Nonna is ready for you now, so go on over. I'll watch you."

Henry jumped down from the stool and adjusted his sport coat. "We're making *waveeoowee* today."

I looked at Gia, and he mouthed, *ravioli.*

"That sounds yummy. I almost forgot to ask you, what do you want for your birthday?"

He answered without hesitation. "Cake."

A boy after my own heart.

Gia walked him to the front of the store and gave Henry a hug. "Be good for Nonna."

Henry looked back at me and curled his fingers in a little wave. "Bye, Poppy."

I curled my fingers and waved back. "Bye, Henry."

I watched him walk across the courtyard to an older woman wearing an apron. They went into the Italian restaurant I had brunch in last week.

"That is my mother, Henry's *nonna*. She keeps him for a couple hours in the afternoon before the dinner rush until my evening barista comes in."

Okay, Poppy, just be cool. Be the kind of girl who holds her cards close to the vest. Poker face. Mysterious. "Are you married?" The words flew out of my mouth with reckless self-abandon.

Gia froze mid-stride. His face broke into a slow grin. "No. I'm not married." He took his place behind the bar and readied a shot. "Henry's mother left us soon after he was born."

"Oh, I'm sorry. So it's just the two of you?" *Too obvious?*

"I wouldn't say that. My mom does a lot for us. And I have big family who is always around. Whether I want them to be or not."

He pulled a thick, sweet shot of espresso.

"That must be nice. I'm an only child and my father died when I was young." *Okay, now I'm rambling.*

"I am sorry, *bella*. My father died when I was just a boy living in Roma. I know how hard that is." He pulled a little container out from the under-counter fridge, poured the contents into a frothing pitcher, and warmed it.

"Henry is adorable."

Gia grinned. "He's so serious. Four going on forty."

"Does he get that from you or his mother?" *Okay, now that was definitely too obvious.*

He laughed. "Not his mother." Gia poured the shot into

a warmed cup and topped it with the heated mixture. Then he sprinkled cocoa on top and placed it in front of me. "Try this."

I tasted the drink. "It's very good. Rich and sweet. But it's not milk. What is it?"

"You said you were not allowed to have milk anymore so I made you up some of what I make for Henry. It's a combination of coconut and almond."

"You remembered that I can't have dairy?"

He shrugged and made a face that said it was nothing. "I hoped you would like it."

"I love it. I made some gluten-free muffins this morning out of almond and coconut flour. I never would have guessed that you could make milk out of them too."

"You should bring some in tomorrow. I would love to try them. I've been wanting to expand my selection for people with allergies. My mom makes most of the desserts in my case but she is old-school. She doesn't do gluten-free. She thinks I'm making it up."

"She sounds like my aunt. I would love to. I'll bring some in the morning."

"Good." He smiled like he had just gotten away with something. He started to whistle again and wiped down the counter.

"Good." I wondered what he was up to and drank my coconut cappuccino while he waited on a customer who had stopped in after work for a flat white to go.

When the customer left, Gia came back over. "Now tell me, how is the investigation going? What have you found out?"

"I found out that the police are looking for chemical cleaners and a flower that could be poisonous."

"Really? That must be the cause of death."

"I think so too. I remembered that Kristen had exotic plants on her windowsill so I dropped in on her today."

"And?"

"A plant was gone."

"Do you think she was getting rid of evidence?"

"I don't know. With Kristen and Joel it's hard to say what's going on. Is one of them the killer? Or is it both of them? And they both keep pointing fingers at the coach."

"What would be their motives?"

"Kristen found out that Joel was having an affair with Barbie."

"Jealousy is a strong motive. How did she catch him?"

"Barbie sent Kristen pictures of her and Joel together."

"Oh, *Dio mio*. What a way to find out."

"The weird thing is, Joel doesn't know he's been caught. Kristen never confronted him."

"Then they couldn't have killed her together. How would Kristen explain it to Joel, what they were doing?"

Huh. Why didn't I think of that? "You make a good point. But Joel could have killed Barbie to cover the affair. To keep Kristen from finding out."

"Or maybe he wanted to call it off and she threatened to tell his wife."

"That makes sense too. If he wanted out of the affair and Barbie refused, he could have killed her to keep her quiet."

"Who is the coach they both keep pointing fingers at?"

"He's the high school gym teacher and basketball coach. They were both volunteers under his oversight."

"What would his motive be?"

"I don't know yet."

"Have you questioned him?"

"Once, the other day. And he lied to me. I tried to talk

to him again today but he had already left the building, so I kind of . . . snuck into his office and looked around."

Gia stood up straighter and ran a hand through his hair. "Oh, mama! Please do not get caught."

"I was careful." *Except for the whole butt-sticking-out part.* "And I was desperate. I am quickly running out of time."

Gia put one warm hand over mine. "Don't worry. We will figure this out." I felt my insides go all squiggly.

A beautiful young girl came in from the back room. She had long black hair and red fingernails that matched her red stiletto boots. She was tying an apron around her size two black leather hips. She came over and smacked Gia playfully on the butt. He smiled and pulled her into a hug.

Be calm. Be aloof. "Well, look at the time. I guess I'd better go. I have to go see . . . people . . . some people about . . . stuff—stuff with friends."

Bumbling, I dropped my purse on the floor, then I laughed like a maniac.

Pull yourself together, Poppy. I picked up my purse by the wrong end and dumped out the contents. I was shoving items back in as fast as I could. "See you tomorrow, muffins. I mean, *ha-ha*, see you tomorrow *with* the muffins. Okay, bye."

I can't believe he has a girlfriend. I was so stupid. And why do I even care? After that kiss from Tim I have no right to be jealous. I raced out to my car in the back lot. I'd left them both wide-eyed and stunned. Boy, do I know how to make an impression. *Why did I ever agree to bring in muffins tomorrow? I could have never stepped foot back in there and spared myself the humiliation. Ugh. Always with the big mouth.*

Chapter 32

Tonight was my chance to relax and de-stress. Just a quiet night with the girls. No investigating. No humiliation. No accusations. Just sitting around, talking about old times. Sawyer had set the whole thing up.

Connie lived off the island in North Cape May. It was an old neighborhood, where the houses were aluminum siding, backyards were surrounded by chain-link fence, and keeping up with the Joneses meant having a carport and an above-ground pool.

Connie's house was a typical East Coast Colonial, with baby-blue siding and white shutters. Pots of bright orange mums were placed on either side of the front door and the girls' bikes were sitting in the front yard.

Sawyer met me at the door decked out in tight, acid-washed jeans, neon orange leg warmers, and a hot pink sweatshirt cut off at one shoulder. She had big white plastic triangles dangling from her ears and a giant bow in her teased-up hair.

"Is there something you want to tell me?"

Sawyer flashed her million-dollar smile. "We have a surprise for you."

"I can see that."

Kim called from the back room, "Get her in here!"

Sawyer grabbed my arm and dragged me through the living room where Mike and Emmilee were watching college football.

"Hi, Mike."

"Good luck in there."

Emmilee giggled in an ominous, conspiratorial kind of way.

The girls were in Connie's kitchen surrounded by every hair and makeup product on the market, and they were dressed like an '80s cover band. Connie had spiked up her hair Billy Idol–style. She was wearing white pants, a light blue T-shirt, and a white blazer with the sleeves pushed back. Her daughter, Sabrina, was applying a thick layer of bright blue eyeshadow in long streaks across Connie's eyelids.

"It's eighties night at the karaoke club."

"No."

"We're all going."

"No."

"Oh, come on," Sawyer pleaded.

"You know I have nothing to wear to this."

Kim was wearing a sleeveless, gold foil minidress, a red Members Only leather jacket, with matching red heels and red lipstick. She handed me a stack of clothes. "We got you covered."

My heart sank. *What happened to relaxing? Don't people just sit around and talk anymore? This day just keeps getting better and better.* I did the forced march up to Connie's bathroom like a condemned prisoner. Prison might be a step up from the week I'd had.

The girls had gotten me a hot-pink push-up bra, *Like that was really necessary.* A sleeveless pink minidress with a black mesh belly shirt. A pair of black half-calf fishnet capris and black ankle boots. I wiggled into the outfit and stared at myself in Connie's mirror in shock. I looked like a giant box of Good & Plenty.

Returning to the kitchen, I was greeted by the girls' squeals of delight. Even Sabrina was in on it.

"You look great, Aunt Poppy."

Connie pulled out a chair for me. "Sit down and Kim will do your hair. Sabrina will do your makeup."

I flopped on the chair. "I feel I need to curb your expectations that I'm planning on singing at this club."

Sawyer sat across from me. "Don't be ridiculous. We're all going to sing. And I happen to know that you have a beautiful voice. We were in choir together."

"That was a lifetime ago." *I have to find a way to get out of this.*

Kim was teasing my hair to within an inch of its life. "Just wait till we get there and you hear the rest of us. You have nothing to worry about."

"Sawyer, did you find anything out about Billy Sommers's science fair project?"

"Not yet. I'm still waiting to hear back from one source."

I reached for the hand mirror and Sawyer snatched it away. "Not yet. Hey, how was the big date?"

"It was okay. The date itself was uneventful but the kiss at the end was amazing."

The girls all made "ooooh" noises, and Sabrina giggled.

"How are you enjoying cheerleading, Sabrina?"

"I love it. At least I did before what happened to Coach Clark."

The room grew very quiet.

"The cheerleaders must really miss her."

"She just got us all new uniforms and equipment from one of her secret donors. And she was preparing some of us for her all-star team that competes nationally."

"Just some of you?"

"Coach Clark owns Destiny Cheer Academy, and she handpicks the best girls from the public schools to represent her. She said if I kept working on my extension that I'd be a definite."

"Very exciting. Did she have a partner who can take her place?"

"We haven't heard yet, but I think it will be announced this weekend at our All-State Competition. Do you want to come watch me cheer?"

"I'd love to."

Sabrina grinned and went back to applying blush to my cheeks.

Connie was applying another layer of mascara to her already tarantula lashes. "Whatever came from Amber's searching the house? Did you find out what she was looking for?"

"I'm pretty sure she was looking for a poisonous plant."

"What makes you think that?"

"She took all the yard clippings with her. She was also bent out of shape because we didn't have any chemicals."

Sawyer was killing brain cells with a toxic amount of hairspray. "What kind of chemicals?"

"Household cleaner kind of stuff."

Connie started packing up the hot rollers. "Does this mean Barbie died from a poisonous cocktail of Windex and petunias?"

"I don't know. I went to Kristen's office to follow up on a lead about the plants."

Kim was finished ripping my hair out, so it was Sabrina's turn to do my makeup. *Lord, help me.*

"Did she say anything helpful when you questioned her?"

"Well, I did the 'Wabbit Season' on her."

Sawyer smacked the table. "Get out! And it worked?"

"Just like it used to."

"What'd you find out?" Connie asked. Connie turned to Sabrina. "Bean, you are sworn to secrecy. Anything you hear can't be repeated outside of this room, okay?" Connie held up her pinkie.

Sabrina hooked pinkies with her mom and said, "I promise."

A pang of envy shot through me. How wonderful would it be to have a daughter to make pinkie promises with?

"She said that you would have to sanitize needles in strong bleach if you planned on using them again, and, that Coach Wilcott had a lot of secret meetings with Barbie and she thought he had needles in his med kit."

Sabrina was putting blush on me with a giant puffy brush and stopped mid-swipe. She had a strange look in her eyes.

"So I snuck into the coach's office and searched the med kit."

The room went silent.

Sawyer was the first to speak. "You did what?"

"What choice did I have? He's been ducking me. I questioned the coach the other day and he lied about even *eating* at the reunion and we all saw him there."

Kim sat down and pulled her chair closer. "Did you find anything?"

"I took some pictures on my phone. I only found an EpiPen, but he had a lot of alcohol wipes like you would have to prep for injections. What do you suppose those were for?"

Sabrina had been watching us very closely. She was growing paler by the minute.

Connie asked her, "Bean? What's going on? Do you know something?"

"Well. I don't want to get anyone in trouble."

"If you know something that could help Aunt Poppy, we need to hear it."

We all waited expectantly.

"Last year, Coach Wilcott was arrested during fourth period."

Sawyer gasped. "Oh my God! For what?"

"Nobody knows. But he was back the next morning and it kind of gave him some street cred, so nobody cared."

"And nothing ever came of it?" Kim asked.

"Not that I know of. He's still the gym teacher and basketball coach, so I guess not. But then a couple months later, my boyfriend, Mark, started getting sick."

"Your *boyfriend*?"

"Mo-om."

"We'll talk about that later."

"Go on, hun," Kim encouraged her.

"Mark said he was working toward taking over the starting point guard position since Chad Nickels was graduating soon. The coach was giving him something to give him an edge, only it was making his face break out really bad and he was having trouble concentrating in his classes."

"Giving him something like *what*?" I asked.

"He said he wasn't allowed to talk about it. He wanted to stop taking it, but he was afraid he would lose his place on the lineup. The coach was really pushing the team to improve."

We were all stunned.

Connie was the first to speak. "It has to be steroids."

"Aren't they *illegal*?" Sawyer asked.

"Oh, you bet they are," Connie said.

"Mom, you can't say anything. I promised," Sabrina pleaded with Connie.

"Maybe that was what all the secret meetings with Barbie were about," I said. "Maybe she found out about the steroids, and was threatening to tell on the coach so he killed her."

"But how do we prove it?" Sawyer asked.

"I'll call Amber in the morning and tell her what we found." I looked at Sabrina. "I won't say how we discovered it. At the very least it might cause her to consider other suspects."

I picked up the hand mirror that Sawyer forgot she was keeping from me and looked at myself. Rainbow eyeshadow, thick black eyeliner, and fuchsia cheekbones. "I want this to be my prison headshot if I'm booked."

Chapter 33

Hotlipz was the hottest karaoke bar in Cape May. The club was set up lounge-style. White leatherette armchairs set around glass mosaic coffee tables facing a wide stage bathed in purple light. The giant screen on either side of the stage displayed song lyrics so the audience could sing along. A bar stretched along the back wall where only losers and drunks worked on tomorrow's hangovers.

The night was just picking up and the room was all spandex and hair gel as far as the eye could see. Two middle-aged guys with beer bellies, dressed head to toe in yellow leather, were on stage destroying Tears for Fears's song "Shout."

Sawyer was bouncing with excitement. "I'm going to go sign us up for a couple songs."

Kim led the way to a reserved table for four. "Sign me up for 'Girls Just Want to Have Fun.'"

The girls ordered drinks, club soda with lemon for me, and Sawyer returned. "I wanted to do 'Eternal Flame,' but there were already four people ahead of me signed up for it."

"So what did you take?" I asked.

"'Total Eclipse of the Heart', and I signed you up to sing something, Poppy."

"What?"

"I knew you wouldn't do it yourself and you need to relax."

"Relax. By singing in front of all these people?"

"Don't worry, you get to pick the song when you get up there."

"Oh, that makes me feel much better."

The DJ motioned to Sawyer. "I slipped the DJ a twenty to jump the line. Come on, we're up."

I started to panic. "All of us."

Connie was pulling my arm. "Yeah, come on. It'll be like old times."

Before I could fake an alien abduction or pull the fire alarm, I was onstage knee-deep into the Go-Go's "Our Lips are Sealed."

Okay, so I had more fun than a fat girl at Hershey Park. The crowd was generous and the applause was heady. Except for one lone voice from the bar with their back to us, booing.

"Who is that?" Kim looked like she was going to go postal on the boo-er and Connie held her back. "That is not proper karaoke etiquette, dude!"

The person at the bar responded, "Neither was that sucky song."

"That's it." Kim got away from us and marched over to encourage the rude guest to be more polite by way of going all "Jersey girl" on him.

Then the guy spun around on his barstool.

"Joanne?"

I stopped short and Sawyer crashed into the back of me. There she was, Joanne Junk. Dressed in David Bowie glam and three sheets to the wind.

"Why are you losers here anyway? Ssshouldn't you be out hiding evidence or copping a plea?"

"Oh, boy." Connie motioned to the bartender. "Can we get some coffee over here, please?"

Joanne started crying into her shots. "She was the only friend I had. No one else liked me until Barbie. Then you took her away."

"Joanne, please believe me. I didn't kill Barbie." I sat on the stool next to Joanne and spoke to her softly. "I know you're hurting, and I'm so sorry for what you're going through. I would feel the same way if something happened to these girls."

"I saw them, you know."

The girls and I made eye contact with one another to see if any of us understood what Joanne was talking about. None of us did. "Saw who?"

"He didn't deserve her either."

"Who, Joanne?"

"Robert. He was cheating on her. She told me she knew."

"What did she say?"

"That it served her right for all the terrible things she'd done."

Kim muttered, "Well, that's probably true."

Connie jabbed Kim in the side. "What else did she say, Joanne?"

Joanne didn't answer directly. She was in a drunken fog. "She should have left him like I told her to."

The bartender brought Joanne's coffee, and I encouraged her to drink it. "Did she know who he was cheating with?"

"It was Kelly, you idiot. I saw them the night of the reunion."

"Saw them where?" I asked.

"After Barbie was hurt by Sasquatch over there"—
Joanne glared over at Sawyer—"she lashed out like she
does when she's embarrassed."

"Uh-huh." *Just when she's embarrassed. Okay, let's
go with that.* "That's when you and Barbie had the fight
Kristen mentioned?"

"It wasn't a fight. Barbie said some mean things she
didn't mean and I had to go out for some air. I went out
the front door and saw Kelly and Robert making out by the
gymnasium emergency exit."

"Are you sure it was them?" I remembered Tim saying
he saw them in the cafeteria getting cozy.

"I'm not an idiot you . . . idiot."

Kim pushed the cup and saucer closer to Joanne. "Here,
have some more coffee. Your retorts are getting weak."

"Joanne, I've been trying to find out who killed Barbie
that night. Anything you know could help bring the true
killer down." I put my hand on Joanne's shoulder. "I know
you want that more than anyone. Now, are you sure it was
Robert and Kelly?"

Joanne started to sniffle again. "It was definitely Robert.
But I didn't see the blonde's face. I might have thought it
was Barbie if I hadn't just left her with Kristen, but I'm
sure it was Kelly."

"Where was Amber?"

"In the main office on her phone."

Sawyer asked, "What did you do after you saw them
together?"

"I was so upset I ran. I had nowhere to go so I just circled the building. Until I heard idiot number one here
scream." Joanne tilted her head in my direction.

I guess I'm idiot number one.

The DJ called up "Jo-Jo Smooth" to do a number, and the crowd started chanting, "Jo-Jo. Jo-Jo."

"That's me. I'll be right back." Joanne slipped off the barstool and took the stage.

We couldn't wait to see what Buffalo Gal was about to perform. Especially since she was in no condition to do much of anything right now.

But Joanne sang the heck out of Queen's "Bohemian Rhapsody." When she hit the final note, the crowd erupted and stood to their feet.

Joanne politely bowed and left the stage like this was nothing new for her. She sat back down on her barstool. "So what have you idiots found out with all your nosing around?"

"Joanne. That was amazing," Sawyer said.

"Whatever," Joanne grunted in reply.

"No, really, Joanne," I said. "You are really good."

Joanne narrowed her eyes at us. "Are you making fun of me?"

"We are not making fun of you. We had no idea you could sing like that."

Joanne shrugged it off, but we could tell she was pleased with the compliment. We invited her to join us at our table. Then we were shocked when she agreed. We talked a little about the investigation but gave nothing away. Who knew what Joanne would be like when she sobered up?

"Poppy McAllister, *you're on*!"

I thought I'd faint dead away when the DJ called my name. I had totally forgotten about Sawyer signing me up to sing when we arrived.

Who knows. I could be in prison this time next month. My list of regrets is long enough without adding "failure to let go at karaoke." The old Poppy wouldn't even have been here in the first place. The new Poppy decided to suck it up and sing.

It's hard to find a song that represents the rebellious, wild days of our youth that isn't currently being used to sell fiber bars, razor blades, or sexual aid drugs, but I picked a song that truly epitomized my current place in life. The anthem of the '80s generation, "Livin' on a Prayer."

The secret to good karaoke is that the more the audience drinks, the better you sound. I gave it my all, and thank God and Jon Bon Jovi, the entire bar sang along with me.

Sawyer had me ready to try out for *American Idol*, but my favorite compliment came from Joanne.

"You didn't suck. In fact, you sounded pretty good— in every key you were in."

When I got home, high on adrenaline, I could feel that something was off. I found Aunt Ginny sitting by herself in the kitchen in the dark.

"What's the matter?"

She snuffled. "Six generations of McAllisters have lived in this house and I'm going to be the one to lose it."

I sat across from her. "What are you talking about?"

"They're coming for me. I don't know why and I can't stop them."

I put one hand over hers. "Hey. We'll figure something out. Let's not give up hope just yet."

Aunt Ginny gave me a wan smile. "I know you're trying."

"Not just me. Frank is working on the legal end. And all of the neighbors want to be character witnesses."

"Well, that is something."

"See. We'll get through this. And if all else fails we can have Mrs. Pritchard bring some of her homemade limeade to the hearing. That'll get the heat off of you in no time."

Figaro sauntered in, eyed us both speculatively, and flopped over on his side.

Aunt Ginny grimaced. "Lord Jesus, help us."

Chapter 34

I woke up with Figaro breathing on my face. Sometime in the night he had climbed on top of me and was closely watching for signs indicating he would be fed.

I rolled around and made a good effort to attempt my yoga poses. When I had given up all hope, I hit the shower. I had to wash my hair three times to get all the hairspray and gel out. I think the eyeliner was permanently tattooed under my eyes. Ah yes, the price of beauty in the '80s.

I got dressed in jeans and a black T-shirt that said, "Come to the Dark Side, we have cookies." Then blow-dried my hair smooth and put on just enough makeup to not look like the Crypt-Keeper.

It was time to make Gia's muffins. I was dreading the moment I had to walk into Signore Hot Stuff's coffee shop. I made a fool of myself in front of him and his girl-friend last night and I didn't need a reminder of the shame. I had been out of the dating pool, and every other pool that didn't involve the couch and the TV, for so long that I con-tinued to underestimate my ability for humiliation.

I whipped up some gluten-free lemon blueberry muffins and baked them in giant Texas tins. They were the equivalent of three regular muffins, but no one bought the small ones anymore. When they were done baking, I made a batch of gluten-free strawberry muffins, but I baked a dollop of sweetened cream cheese in the middle. I couldn't have dairy but I could live vicariously through Gia's customers.

"You're up early." Aunt Ginny entered the kitchen wearing a blue jean skirt and a pink short-sleeved checkered shirt tied up at the waist in a knot. She had on pink cowboy boots and atop her head sat a matching cowboy hat.

"I couldn't sleep any longer."

"Mmm, something smells good. Whacha cookin' in here?"

"I'm making gluten-free muffins for the coffee shop. You look like you're going to a hootenanny."

"Why?"

"Because you're dressed head to toe like Daisy Duke."

"No. I mean why are you making the muffins for the coffee shop?"

I stopped arranging the muffins in the basket and looked at her. "That's the part you needed clarified?"

"Well, I know what a hootenanny is." She picked up a strawberry muffin and sniffed it.

"Gia wants to offer allergy-friendly bakery items and he asked me to bring in gluten-free muffins to try them today."

"This one's good. What is it?"

Aunt Ginny had taken a bite out of the muffin.

Okay, I guess I'll deliver eleven muffins instead of twelve.

"That one is Strawberry Cheesecake. What do you think?"

"It's purty good." Aunt Ginny reached for a blueberry muffin. "Let's try this one."

"I think they'll be a hit but I still have to get them approved by Gia and his evening barista-slash-girlfriend."

"What time will you be home? We have that Moose Lodge fundraiser to crash."

"Is that why you're dressed for the Wild West?"

"They're moose, not buffalo."

"Oh. Silly me." I had two baskets packed with the muffins and it was time to face the espresso.

But before I left, I needed to fill someone in on the dirt we uncovered about Coach Wilcott. I called the police department's non-emergency number and asked for Officer Amber.

"Fenton here."

"Amber, it's Poppy."

"Make it fast."

"I just want to give you some information."

I heard her heave a disgusted sigh. "What is it, McAllister?"

"I got an anonymous tip that Coach Wilcott has a stash of needles in his med kit, and he has an arrest record. He worked very closely with Barbie and there is no small amount of suspicion that something sneaky was going on between those two. We all saw him at the reunion, so you may want to investigate his alibi."

"McAllister, I pity you. Of course we know about Coach Wilcott's record. What do you think we're doing over here? And it isn't anything related to the murder investigation. Now just stay out of it. Your days of freedom are limited. Better quit nosing around and enjoy them while you can."

The line went dead.

So that went well. I shoved my phone in my back pocket, and grabbed the muffin baskets on my way to the car.

It was early, and Cape May was just waking up. Kids

were waiting for the school bus, shops were unfurling whimsical flags and lifting metal gates, and joggers were wearing a trench into the boardwalk.

La Dolce Vita opened early to accommodate locals on their way to work. When I arrived, Gia was blasting Dean Martin and dancing with an imaginary partner while setting up the tables and chairs. Today, I was determined to remain casual.

"Good Morning, *bella*." He sniffed the air. "What did you bring me?"

"Gluten-free muffins as requested."

He took the baskets, said, "These look wonderful," and set them down on the counter. He got out the container of coconut-almond milk from the mini-fridge and heated a pitcher of it, then pulled two shots of espresso into warmed cups. To one he added the milk and moved it closer to me, the other he left straight. Then he gave me a wink and cut a blueberry muffin in half.

On his first bite he looked very thoughtful, considering, but only for a moment. Then he gave an approving nod and said, "This is delicious. I would never have guessed gluten-free."

Aunt Ginny had said the same thing that morning, but when she said it I didn't feel all giddy inside.

"I'm going to put these in my pastry case with a gluten-free sign and see how quickly they move. How much do I owe you?"

"Nothing. You haven't let me pay for a single coffee yet. I'd say we're even."

"No, your time is important. I say one dollar per muffin on top of expenses."

"That's too much. You'll lose money."

"Then I'll add free coffee for life as long as you bring the muffins in every day."

"How is that supposed to be better?"

He had a sneaky smile on his face and he shrugged.

"What if they don't sell?"

"Pssh. Of course they'll sell! They are delicious. But even if they don't, they are still worth every penny."

"Gia, this is a terrible deal for you."

"Time will tell."

I was the one making out in this deal, but he got that silly cryptic grin on his face and started to whistle again, so I had that feeling like he was somehow getting exactly what he wanted.

I was still contemplating Gia's motives when little Nancy Reagan came into the shop. She appeared to be early twenties, wearing a red power suit with a smartphone glued to her ear. She bounced up to the counter.

"I know, I know, right?"

Gia stood patiently and politely smiled.

She put the phone down and fluffed up her brunette bob with the red streak underneath where Gia could see it. Then she struck a seductive pose. "Heyyyy. I'm April."

"What'll it be, miss?"

"Okay, I want a twenty-four-ounce, nonfat, sugar-free, extra-hot Milky Way Latte, extra whip. And ohmigod ohmigod one of those gluten-free Strawberry Cheesecake muffins. I could die."

She got right back on her phone, furiously tapping on her screen with both hands. "Hey, can I leave one of these posters in your window for Congressman Robert Clark? I'm like so supposed to be out hanging them up all over town before the fundraiser today, but if I don't get a mani-pedi I'm literally going to die right here."

Gia gave her a warm smile. "You can leave it on the counter there."

She laid down a large poster that had ROBERT CLARK FOR SENATOR in big, white letters.

"Ohmigodyouaresoawesomesauce." Her phone vibrated and she snatched it up. "Yes, Kelly, Hi. Yes. Yes. Yes. I'm hanging the posters up right now as we speak. Yes, I agree. Very sympathetic. Yep, his wife died here. I'm on it." She hung up, then dialed. "Kim, it's April. Can I come in for a quick mani-pedi like right now? I'm meeting Ashlee there, but I have to be quick because my boss is being a real Cruella. Thanks, you're the best."

Gia rang her up and took her credit card. She tore into the muffin. "Omigod. This is the best thing I've ever eaten in my life. Forrealzez."

"That beautiful lady over there made them." Gia pointed in my direction and I looked behind me for the beautiful lady.

April raised her voice and spoke slowly like she thought I was dimwitted or hard of hearing. "These are really good!"

"Thank you. Your nails are beautiful, where do you get them done?" I couldn't even see her nails, but I needed an excuse to ask some questions about Barbie and the campaign, forrealzez.

"Oh, thank you. I go to Nailed It! on Beach Drive. It's just around the corner."

"I'll have to try them."

April turned back to Gia and made a face that I thought was supposed to be sexy. "And you, cutie, call me anytime if you want to hang." She wrote her number in lip gloss on one of La Dolce Vita's napkins and passed it to him.

Gia smiled politely and said, "Have fun getting your nails done."

When she was gone, he rolled his eyes and tossed the

napkin in a box by the register that was full of similar scraps.

"You get a lot of phone numbers?"

He shrugged. "Some. You know, kids. Tourists. Summer residents."

I had a feeling that list could keep on going for a while. "Well, it looks like I'm going to get my nails done if I want to eavesdrop on April and Ashlee."

"That's sure to be riveting. I'll see you tomorrow?"

"Where else am I going to get a coconut-almond cappuccino?"

That made him smile halfway around his face.

Chapter 35

Nailed It! was a storefront salon facing the ocean, placed between one touristy shop selling beachwear and another touristy shop selling beach towels.

The bright red-and-gold room had a row of pedicure chairs with foot Jacuzzis on one side and a row of manicure tables on the other. Several bamboo plants were strewn about and one wall was covered with a rainbow display of nail polish.

April was already seated next to another young woman I assumed to be Ashlee, and they were both wearing plastic baggies on their hands.

A little Asian lady named Pearl greeted me, looked at my hands, and tsk-tsked. "Oh, honey, you haven't had one a'dese in long time. You need deep treatment on your cuticles."

"Okay, if that's what I need." I started to head over to sit next to April, but Pearl had me by the wrist and dragged me over to a pedicure chair.

"We do spa pedicure. Very nice. Sit, sit."

I looked longingly to where April and Ashlee were in deep discussion, probably about the campaign.

"Well, I was just going to do my hands today."

"No. Spa pedicure very good. You like."

She began to run water into the foot bath, putting in some blue crystals that smelled like gardenia but looked like the stuff in the bottom of an aquarium tank.

"Um, I'm not sure I have time today."

"No. Sit. You like. Not too long."

Somehow she had me sitting in the chair with my shoes off. I don't remember rolling up my pants, but there they were around my knees. I had a bottle of water and the chair was kneading my back. Three other Asian women wearing matching purple smocks were standing in a row, smiling at me. Pearl was scraping my foot with what looked like a cheese grater and it was half a size smaller when she was finished. A fifth woman approached from out of nowhere and said, "You pick out a color."

"Pink?" I asked.

"No. Too light. You need red. Red very pretty. You have boyfriend?"

"No, no boyfriend," I replied. I craned my neck to try to hear what April and Ashlee were talking about, but the water in the footbath and the hum of the massage chair were too loud. *Didn't April say she was getting a mani-pedi? If I just wait it out they should be joining me over here.*

"This will get you boyfriend. Red very lucky."

"Okay." The massage hands of the chair and the bubbling water were lulling me into compliance.

I was drifting away when Pearl asked me, "You want eyebrow wax?"

"What's wrong with my eyebrows?"

Pearl squinted at my face while massaging my calf, then wrinkled up her nose and shook her head. "We do eyebrow wax. Your new boyfriend will like."

There was talk of further waxing that my boyfriend

would like, but no amount of chair massage was going to make that happen today.

What was taking April so long? She had both of her hands resting inside of glowing boxes.

Finally, the noises were off and Pearl shoved the foam version of brass knuckles between my toes and applied the red lacquer.

I could just barely make out April saying, "I have to get to the Moose Lodge to set up the tribute movie for the fundraiser. Kelly will kill me if I'm late."

Pearl tapped my leg. "Pedicure all finished."

I jumped up and duck walked over to the manicure table, but Pearl caught me and swung me around. "We do eyebrows now."

"But I don't . . ."

Pearl must have learned all she knew about pampering while guarding hostages during the Vietnam War. She dragged me into a back room. "You lie down." Then she shined a spotlight in my eyes and applied something sticky like honey under my eyebrow with a popsicle stick.

"Are you sure this is necessary? *YEOW!* Does the Geneva Convention know about this?"

Pearl got five swipes. Two over the eyebrows, two under the eyebrows, and one in the middle. Then she rubbed a cotton ball of lotion over the angry pink welts as some kind of apology.

I stumbled over to the manicure station and sat next to Ashlee. As soon as my butt hit the chair April and Ashlee stood up and moved across the room to the pedicure chairs. *Are you kidding me?*

"She must be thrilled that Mrs. Clark is finally out of the way."

"That's a horrible thing to say!"

"What? She's been pining for him for months. Here's her chance to make a move."

"*Pining* may be too strong a word."

"You're the one who said she won't leave his side."

"I'm sure all campaign managers come out of the office buttoning their blouses at one time or another."

"Now you're just proving my point."

April's and Ashlee's technicians started the water in their chairs and I had to lean back to hear them.

"She may be the campaign manager from hell, but I don't think she's that low-class to move in on him before the ink on the death certificate is dry."

"We'll see soon enough, won't we?"

Pearl tugged my arm to pull me closer and gave me a big smile. "Your hands will look very young. This will get you boyfriend."

April and Ashlee had changed the topic to Rob and his lack of commitment when a sharp pain seared up my finger. I looked down and saw I was bleeding. Then up at Pearl, who met my eyes and smiled showing two rows of even teeth. "Oops. You have very bad hangnails. Come to the back. I fix."

"Come to the back of what?"

Pearl had a death grip on my middle finger and she pulled me into a back room full of first aid supplies. She tsk-tsked and applied several potions and creams to my hand. Then she wiped it all off and stopped the bleeding with a squirt of superglue.

"That can't be good for you."

Pearl smiled and showed me both rows of teeth again. "See, I fix." She dabbed oil on each cuticle with a basting brush and commanded, "Go wash your hands."

By the time I returned to the front of the salon, April and

Ashlee were gone. Their technicians had started manicures on two new clients.

I washed the lotion and oil off my hands. When I turned around, Pearl was immediately behind me. "Now we do the color."

I'd already lost all opportunity with April, so I would have to question her at the Moose Lodge. I picked a pale pink and got it past Commandant Pearl.

"You finished. You pay now."

I paid Pearl for the services. She tried to get me to make an appointment to come back in two weeks.

"I don't know my schedule that far out and my next availability might be in ten-to-twenty."

Chapter 36

I parked in front of Aunt Ginny's and ran into the house trying not to touch anything with my wet nails. Figaro raced me up the stairs only to flop on the top one. I had to hop over him at the last second or he would've been smushed.

"Aunt Ginny, I'm getting dressed for the fundraiser now," I called out.

It had gotten hot and muggy since the hurricane had swept through and taken the lovely breeze up the coast to Maine. I peeled off my slacks and changed into my brown skirt and a flowy peacock blue blouse. I slipped on my chocolate brown boots and freshened up my makeup. I tried to tame my hair down but it fought back. I hate New Jersey humidity. I went downstairs to wait in the foyer for Aunt Ginny. Figaro ran alongside me and dodged across me at the bottom step.

"What is your problem today, Fig?"

Mrooow.

He rubbed against my leg and I picked him up around the middle. "Do you miss me? You're used to me being home all the time, aren't you, buddy?"

"If he's telling you he's hungry, don't believe him. I just gave him a can of tuna at lunchtime."

Aunt Ginny had changed into a red satin dress with a pencil skirt and a low neckline.

I put Figaro down and he tried to lead me toward the kitchen.

Aunt Ginny was pulling on black leather driving gloves. "Figaro, don't be a glutton."

Figaro flattened his ears to his head and presumably began working on plan B, which most likely involved pooping in Aunt Ginny's shoe.

I locked the front door and started to head toward the Corolla.

"Why don't we take Bessie?" Aunt Ginny was holding her keys up and dangling them.

Bessie was Aunt Ginny's 1958, cherry red–and-white Corvette convertible with whitewall tires, and she was in pristine condition. Bessie had never been in an accident. Not because of Aunt Ginny's driving, which was horrendous, but more likely because the car was so exquisite that no one dared hit it and mar its beauty. Everyone got out of the way when they saw Aunt Ginny coming.

"Um, sure. You want me to drive though?"

Aunt Ginny marched out to the detached garage in the back. "No, I've been wanting to take the old girl out for a spin."

I said a silent prayer for protection and got in the passenger seat.

Aunt Ginny put the top down, then backed Bessie out of the garage and peeled out down the gravel driveway to the street.

Mr. Winston was out getting his mail. When he saw Aunt Ginny, he dropped his circulars in the grass and ran for the front porch, shouting, "*Ginny's behind the wheel! Take cover!*"

Aunt Ginny ran up over the curb and backed into Mr. Winston's mailbox, tilting it to a forty-five-degree angle. Then she put the car in drive and swerved out into the lane. She overcorrected and rammed the Sheinbergs' trash cans. One of the lids flew up into the hydrangea bushes. Aunt Ginny tapped the horn and gave a little wave to Mrs. Sheinberg as she drove by, dragging the other trash can lid behind us.

"I just saw Mrs. Sheinberg make the sign of the cross. I didn't know they were Catholic."

Aunt Ginny adjusted her rearview mirror to check her lipstick. "They aren't, they're Jewish."

"Aunt Ginny, you know you just blew through a stop sign?"

"They don't apply to me."

"What do you mean?"

"Everybody knows my car and they always give me the right of way when they see me."

I said a second silent prayer because I was having doubts that the first prayer was enough to cover me.

"Did you remember to bring your checkbook? This shindig costs a hundred dollars a plate."

"I've got it. Robert could feed a third-world country just on what Barbie spent at the spa each month, but every time you turn around he's having another fundraiser. What's that all about?"

"Maybe he's too cheap to spend his own money on his campaign."

"Do you think maybe he needs the life insurance money to pay off debt?"

Aunt Ginny blew through a red light at an intersection and we were narrowly missed by a truck hauling produce.

"My first husband, Jimmy Ray, nearly lost everything we had to the gambling bug. One time he came home from work with a bunch of low-quality paint-by-numbers he took instead of a paycheck for working in some Greek restaurant. I had to borrow money from your great-grandfather to keep the electricity on."

"What did he do with all the paintings?"

Aunt Ginny took a narrow corner on two wheels. "Hocked 'em for money to bet at the track."

We came to a screeching halt in front of the Loyal Order of the Moose, Cape May branch. Aunt Ginny reapplied her lipstick. I tried to loosen my grip on the door handle and checked to see if I'd peed a little. *Prison probably isn't so bad. I bet they even have a book club. A book club could be nice.*

Sawyer opened my door and touched me on the shoulder. "You're here. You're still alive."

"Aunt Ginny is driving Bessie."

Sawyer pulled me gently up by my elbow. "I know, honey, come on."

The Moose Lodge was a one-story wooden beast of a building the color of, well . . . a moose. I guess it was a theme with them. The inside was pretty utilitarian. Long rows of tables with folding chairs. A stage area with a microphone. The kitchen was in the back and there were windowed openings where food could be served buffet-style or expedited for servers. The most impressive thing in the room was the massive bar at the front, which looked to have every kind of hooch known to man, and a couple of homemade ones.

April was stationed at the door collecting checks for the "donation" that was required to get your dry chicken and soggy green beans. Robert and Kelly were at the front by the stage, spreading the campaign promises like manure in a cornfield. I pointed them out to Aunt Ginny.

We got in line to question Robert in the guise of greeting him and were stonewalled by Kelly. "What are you doing here?"

Aunt Ginny raised her voice to be heard by those around us. "We made a donation, young lady. Don't tell me the congressman doesn't have a minute to talk to an old lady?"

Kelly began backpedaling as fast as her Jimmy Choos would take her. Matching Aunt Ginny's volume, she tried to sound light but her voice came out high-pitched and tight. "Of course! The congressman always has time for his constituents of all ages." Then she growled at me, "You are not here to make another scene, are you?"

"No, of course not. We're supporters of Robert's campaign."

Robert was shaking Aunt Ginny's hand, but he was devouring Sawyer with his eyes. She was dressed pretty simply in a short-sleeved navy blue dress with white polka dots and a flared skirt. It was Donna Reed without the pearls and Robert was all but drooling.

Kelly noticed, and the irritation showed on her face.

"So Kelly, what are your plans when the election is over?"

"What? I don't know yet. Consulting? Maybe go back to event planning. Why?"

"I was just wondering if you had a position in Robert's staff if he won."

"We've talked about it but haven't really decided anything." She took Robert's arm and gave him a pointed look. He let go of Sawyer's hand that he had been holding for far too long and gave Kelly a vacant smile. "I'm sorry. We need to keep the line moving."

"Hey, one more thing. My aunt was thinking about making a large donation to the congressman's campaign. She was so saddened by his recent loss, what with Barbie dying so suddenly and not because of me at all, that she was thinking about matching her donation to the amount of Barbie's life insurance."

"Oh, that's very . . . generous. But why the life insurance?"

"Robert's speech moved us how it was Barbie's last wish that he carry on if anything happened to her. Such devotion."

"Mm-hmm, right."

"And we want to honor Barbie's memory. Whatever she donated to the campaign, through her life insurance, Aunt Ginny wants to match it."

Kelly looked over to Aunt Ginny, who was now drinking a free cocktail and schmoozing the reporter from the *Star*. Aunt Ginny threw her head back and laughed, then looked at Kelly and waved.

"Well, Barbie didn't donate anything to the campaign. Her life insurance went into trust for Tiffany, her daughter."

"All of it?"

"All twenty-five thousand. She didn't have that much."

"We had assumed she had a much larger policy. Aunt Ginny will be so disappointed."

"No one expects to die in their forties. I guess life insurance wasn't a priority to her. But don't let that stop you from honoring her memory by donating to the campaign. Robert would be so honored to have your aunt on his team. We've had our eye on a TV spot."

"You know what, I've been hogging you this whole time. Just look at the line of people behind me. I don't want to be selfish. We'll talk."

I grabbed Sawyer away from Robert and we caught up with Aunt Ginny to fill her in.

Kelly was whispering something to Robert and he was nodding. She had him by the elbow and introduced him to the next person in line.

"I don't get it," Sawyer said. "One minute he's asking me up to his hotel room and the next he's all over Kelly."

"He asked you to his hotel room?"

Sawyer wrinkled her nose and gave me a frown.

"What did you say to him?" Aunt Ginny asked.

"I was stunned so I said, 'I was a friend of your wife.'"

"What did he say?"

"He said his wife didn't have any friends."

I looked back at the door we entered through and noticed April was alone. "I'll be right back."

I walked over to the front podium and April gave me a big smile that didn't quite reach her eyes. "Hello."

"How did your nails turn out?"

She squinted at me. "Pardon?"

"Your nails." I flashed my hand. "Did you get them done?"

Understanding dawned. "Oh, *shhh*. I don't want anyone to know about that."

I whispered back, "I understand. Bosses can be such a drag. Am I right?"

"Oh, you don't know the half of it."

"Yours seem to be pretty flirty with each other too. What's the deal there?"

April looked up at the stage where Kelly had her hand on Robert's back. "Let's just say, some of us have better compensation packages than others."

"Don't you think it's kind of surprising since his wife just died so recently?"

April straightened up and suddenly looked very nervous.

"You're not with the press, are you? You're required to tell me."

"What, me? No way. I'm only here because my grand-mother wanted to come." I pointed to Aunt Ginny, who was drinking another free cocktail and dancing what looked like the Charleston.

April was satisfied with our lack of professionalism. "Just between you and me, I'm pretty sure it started before she died. I mean she was a real bi-otch. Everyone hated it when she came into campaign HQ. Including Con-gressman Clark. He used to play Kool & the Gang's 'Celebration' every time she left as a signal for us to come down off of high alert. He's really pretty cool like that."

"Can I have your attention please? If you'll all take your seats, Congressman Clark would like to say a few words."

The speech was pretty much a copy of the one from the memorial with a few campaign promises thrown in.

Somewhere between better schools and lower taxes, Aunt Ginny forgot where we were, mistakenly thought she was in a nightclub, and wandered up onstage during Robert's speech to put a fiver in his waistband.

"Why, thank you! This gives me an idea for another fundraiser."

The room cheered for his quick thinking. Aunt Ginny thought the cheers were for her and tried to go back on-stage, but I grabbed her by the waist.

"Oh, no you don't."

"But I forgot to get change."

When the speech was over, Robert approached me and I thought he was coming to kick us out. Then he grabbed my hand and handed me a key from the El Dorado Motel—Room 4. "Give this to your friend."

In light of Aunt Ginny's antics I asked, "Which one?"

Robert leered at Sawyer and winked. It was time to go.

I drove Bessie and Aunt Ginny home and made us some coffee in the French press.

Aunt Ginny had her forehead resting on the table. "How many of those cocktails did I have?"

"I counted at least four."

"I used to be able to hold my liquor better."

That was probably true. I didn't have the heart to tell her that the "cocktails" were nonalcoholic. She'd stuffed cash in a congressman's underwear "drunk" on fruit juice and ginger ale.

Chapter 37

Aunt Ginny had bet me that Mick Jagger was in his seventies and still touring and I said no way. I lost the bet. Now we're going to Zumba.

Aunt Ginny was waiting for me downstairs in bright orange sweat pants and a lime-green T-shirt. She had matching lime-green athletic shoes on.

I dressed in my go-to black yoga pants and a black tank top. Then I decided to live a little and changed into a pink tank top. Then I felt self-conscious and put the black one back on. I chastised myself that I was done living with body shame and put the pink one back on again.

By the time we got to Zumba I was too tired from getting dressed to work out, but Aunt Ginny insisted that she'd won fair and square and I was going to "shake it."

The workout was all Latin music and hip shaking and stomping. Out of all the exercises I had tried, this was definitely my favorite. But then maybe I just had more energy from better eating and sleeping this week. In fact, I hadn't had insomnia once since coming to New Jersey. My days were too full of activity, mostly trying to stay out of jail, but we were making headway. If anything, we had too many suspects.

Joel, Kristen, Coach Wilcott. *Hey. I think that's Mrs. Wilcott on the other side of the room.* I tried to shimmy across the room in time with the music.

"Mrs. Wilcott?" I asked while doing a fast box step.

She answered me while doing a body roll. "I used to be. Who wants to know?"

"Poppy McAllister. I used to be in your twelfth-grade English class."

She did some fist pumps to the music and shook her shoulders. "What can I do for you?"

We were back to the body roll. "Can I ask you a personal question?"

More fist pumps. "You can ask."

Two steps to the right. "It's about Coach Wilcott." Two steps to the left. "Is he in any kind of trouble that you know of?"

Two steps to the right. "What kind of trouble?" Two steps to the left.

Body roll. "There are rumors that he may have been mixed up in something with Barbie Clark, the cheerleading coach." Double foot stomp.

Mrs. Wilcott grabbed a towel and wiped her face off. "Why are you asking?"

"He's being implicated in her murder and I'm trying to find out the truth."

"No way. Charlie wouldn't hurt anyone. He doesn't have it in him."

"Did he say anything to you about problems with Coach Clark? Meetings with her?"

"Nothing to me. But we mostly talk about alimony payments and maintenance on the house."

"Was there anything unusual about his behavior at all?"

She tilted her head to the side and thought for a moment. "Now that you mention it, he did say that he was having some money problems and he's been late with my alimony checks for the past few months."

"Do you know why he was having money problems?"

"He didn't say. But it was something that really shook him up. He seemed scared. Charlie was not a go-getter. His only motivation was on the basketball court. It's one of the things that caused our marriage to end. Whatever it was, Charlie was not the initiator of it."

"Are you aware that Coach Wilcott has an arrest record?"

She paused. "I am. But how are you?"

"Apparently, he was arrested during school hours. The students think it gives him 'street cred.'"

Mrs. Wilcott began to pack up her bag. "Charlie is a good guy. He just has some issues."

"Issues that would get him arrested?"

"Look, it's nothing I can talk about, I'm sorry I couldn't be of more help."

She picked up her Zumba gear and darted around me.

Well, that was pointless. I collected Aunt Ginny from the juice bar, where she was drinking something tall and green, and we headed home. When we pulled up to the house, we could see something sitting on the front porch.

"What is that?" Aunt Ginny asked.

I got out of the car. It looked like a bouquet of flowers. "Maybe it's from Tim."

"I bet you're right. Men usually send flowers after a date when they want to see you again."

I felt myself getting excited. I picked up the pretty white flowers and breathed deeply. There was something famil-iar about the scent. Then I turned on the porch light and froze. My heart started thumping in my chest and my hands started to shake.

"What's wrong?" Aunt Ginny came over to get a closer look at the bouquet.

"Those aren't from Tim."

"How do you know?"

"Because he wouldn't leave a note that says 'Back off or you're next.'"

Chapter 38

"I will knock someone flatter than a flitter!" Aunt Ginny snatched the note off the plant. "No one comes after my family!"

I tried to will myself to go call the police and report the harassment, but I just stood there staring at the note.

Someone was actually threatening to kill me. And I had no idea who it was.

"Poppy. Poppy Blossom! Snap out of it!" Aunt Ginny was holding the phone out to me. "We're calling the cops."

"But what if they send Amber? She could just spin this as more evidence against me."

"Then tell them to send someone else."

I dialed 911 and reported an imminent death threat.

"No, there is no assailant right in front of me. No, I am not being held captive. Yes, I'll hold."

"Officer Rogers speaking."

Oh, thank God. I told the officer what was going on and he said he'd be right over. Aunt Ginny and I went into the library to wait. After about twenty minutes of rage pacing, Aunt Ginny went to make us some tea. Finally the doorbell rang.

I was flooded with relief until I threw the door open to find Officer Amber. She was out of uniform and dressed for a social visit in jeans and a Phillies jersey.

"What happened to Officer Rogers?"

"He alerted me to your 'threat,' and I said I would come check it out since I'm the lead on the case."

Oh, lucky me.

"You did interrupt my plans for the night. Can I come in?"

I stood to the side, and waved my arm for her to enter. Figaro sauntered around the corner, sensing something was up I'm sure, and sat at the foot of the steps to give Amber the stink eye.

Amber tapped her foot and looked around the foyer. "So where is it?"

I led her to the library. "In here."

Aunt Ginny walked in carrying a tray with three cups of tea. "What is *she* doing here?"

"She came for Officer Rogers." Aunt Ginny and I shared a look of *what else could go wrong tonight?*

I sat on one end of the couch and Aunt Ginny sat on the other. In her most gracious tone, Aunt Ginny offered, "Would you like to sit down?"

Amber sat in a wing chair in front of the fireplace. Figaro jumped up on the mantel and glared at her like a gargoyle fending off evil juju.

"So. Tell me what happened."

"We came home from"—I felt the heat rise to my face—"an outing. And we found this on the front porch."

Amber took out her cell phone to take a couple of pictures of the plant. "I'm guessing you touched everything and mucked up any evidence we might have found."

"I'm sorry," I said with obvious irritation, "I should

have been thinking about fingerprints instead of being stalked by a killer."

Aunt Ginny cleared her throat loudly. Amber rolled her eyes and took notes in her flip book.

"I'll take the flowers and note into evidence and see if we can pull anything off of them, but I suspect we'll get nothing. Let's pretend for a minute that you didn't set this up to try and throw suspicion off of yourself."

"God, I knew you would go there!"

Amber ignored my outburst. "Who have you been talking to lately? Who might you have stirred up?"

"No one really. Just Kelly and Robert. Joanne, Kristen, Coach Wilcott, Joel, some people at the farmer's market, the Moose Lodge—"

"Okay, I get it. You've been running your mouth all over town. Great. That'll really narrow it down."

I balled my fists up and had to shove them under my knees. "Why can't you see that this proves I'm innocent? Why else would someone send me a death threat?"

Amber closed her flip book and bagged the note. "It's not hard for me to believe someone could hate you enough to want to kill you, if that's what you're asking."

Figaro flicked his tail and knocked a figurine of a girl on a swing off the shelf. It hit Amber on the head and she jerked her neck around to see where it came from.

Aunt Ginny started to laugh but quickly covered it with a cough. Then she chastised Figaro by cuddling him off the mantel and cooing at him. "That was a very bad boy. Let's get you some tuna."

The two of them went to the kitchen and I feigned an apology. "I'm sorry about that. He's just a really good judge of character."

"Uh-huh." Amber stood to go. She took the plant and

the bagged note. "You're pretty cocky for someone about to be charged with murder."

I was silent, because I knew if I responded, it would be with a fist.

Amber spoke with measured calm. "In less than seventy-two hours, my final report will come in from the crime lab. If it matches all the other evidence and the eyewitness accounts like I think it will, I'll be back. And we'll both go for a little ride downtown."

"This is Cape May. There is no downtown."

She smiled a cruel smile that narrowed her eyes to slits. "You know what I mean! Now, I'll go question the neighbors to see if someone saw something, but I don't expect it'll turn anything up. And quit nosing around town. If this really did come from outside, you've made another enemy. And this time your little friends won't be able to back you up."

I watched her go. I'd obviously touched a nerve with someone and that someone was a killer. I just wish I knew which someone it was. Staying out of jail was now priority number two. Priority number one was not getting killed.

Chapter 39

My life is over. A psycho wants to kill me, Amber wants to put me away for a hundred years. And now I'm having chest pains. I think I'm dying. And I have terrible breath. When did I eat sardines?

Mrrrrow.

"Oh, it's you."

Figaro had me pinned to the bed. He was either very compassionate about my circumstances or completely impervious to my pain.

"If you love me you'll go fetch me a cookie." I'm finished with this stupid diet. I don't want to die and regret not eating at the Fudge Kitchen one more time.

Figaro laid his head down on my chest, settling in for a long pity party.

How many hours of my life did I waste watching cooking shows? I should have been doing research like watching *Orange Is the New Black* and *The Shawshank Redemption*. They would have come in handy now.

My cell phone rang the Wicked Witch theme. Figaro growled and jumped off the bed. I thought about ignoring it, but seeing as how my life was at an all-time low, how much worse could it get?

"Hello, Georgina."

"Oh, my God. Are you still there?"

"Yes, Georgina."

"The fundraiser is in six days. You need to get home."

"I probably won't make it."

"Don't you dare let me down, Poppy."

"Someone wants to kill me."

After a moment of silence Georgina responded, "Don't be so dramatic."

"If I'm not dead I'll be in jail, and Friday is too soon to count on parole."

"I'm calling Jim. You should have called him days ago. Honestly, you can't do anything for yourself."

"I didn't want one of the partners to know John's wife was arrested for murder."

"Why? It's not like they'll be shocked."

"That's nice. I gotta go now, Georgina." I felt like every bit of the new Poppy I'd become since the night in jail with Bebe and Tawnika had just been beaten out of me by Amber and my mother-in-law.

"You just be ready when Jim calls you back. I mean it. You drop whatever ridiculous—"

"There goes my other line. I gotta take this. Bye, Georgina."

I hung up and threw the cell phone on the other side of the bed, then pulled the covers up over my head.

Every kilowatt of energy went out of me.

What felt like a few minutes later, someone was tapping on my forehead.

"Who is it?" I asked from under the covers.

"It's me."

"Figaro?"

Aunt Ginny pulled the covers off my face. "Very funny. When are you getting up?"

"Never."

"You can't just lie in here and hide. We need a plan to fight back."

"I'm not fighting back. I'm done."

I was in a funkier funk than the funk I was in before I came here to get out of my funk. Awesome. Back at home I only had to expend energy to get up and get cookie dough out of the fridge. Now I felt like I had to climb an ice-covered slope up an invisible mountain to prove my innocence . . . with no handholds. Game over.

"We've come too far to give up now. Besides, I'm an old lady and you promised to help me fight Rosalynn Carter."

"Rosalind Carson."

"Who?"

"Rosalind Carson. You said . . . never mind."

Aunt Ginny tottered out of the room, then turned back and said, "Don't make plans for tonight. We're going somewhere."

I hope it involves fake passports.

I flung the covers off and sat on the edge of the bed. What I needed right now more than anything was a pack of raspberry coconut Zingers. I grabbed my cell phone and threw it in my purse. Forget the makeup, forget the yoga, forget the new outfit. Who was I kidding anyway? This is the beach. Wearing leggings and a long T-shirt I fit right in.

I put on my flip-flops and headed for the Corolla. Aunt Ginny and Figaro were on the front porch sitting on a wicker love seat. They didn't try to stop me but I heard Aunt Ginny say, "Uh-oh," as I went by.

I drove to the nearest Wawa and bought two packs of

Zingers and a Hostess lemon pie and ate them in the car with the oldies station playing "Bad Moon Rising."

There was a *tap tap tap* on my window, and I jumped and spilled mochacchino all over my T-shirt. *Oh, good. It's Tim. I vote suckiest day ever.*

I rolled down the window and turned off the radio. "Hi."

"Hey, gorgeous. Breakfast of champions, I see."

"It's been a rough week."

"I bet. How about we get your mind off of things and go for coffee."

"I'm kind of busy right now." *You know, wallowing in shame.*

"I can see that. How about Tuesday, then? After my weekend shift."

"Sure. Sounds nice." *In fact let's get married on Tuesday because that'll happen too.*

"Great. I'll pick you up at ten."

"Will Gigi be joining us?"

Tim's face broke into a knowing grin. "Not this time."

"Okay, then."

I rolled the window up and was about to put the car in reverse to get the heck out of there when my cell phone beeped that I had a voice message. It was from Sawyer.

"Poppy, help! Can you please come over? AAAHH! It's an emergency."

I didn't even call her back. Just put the car on the road and drove right to her.

Sawyer lived in a condo a block off the beach. It had been her father's until he retired and moved to Hilton Head, South Carolina. Then he rented it out for the summer for a couple of years. After her divorce, Sawyer moved in.

I parked in front of the sand-colored, three-story complex. Most of these condos were full of late-season guests and snowbirds who hadn't made the trip back south yet, but a few of them belonged to year-round residents. Many of the balconies had beach towels and bathing suits draped over railings, making flapping noises in the ocean breeze.

I ran up the three flights of steps and threw Sawyer's door open. "I'm here!"

The condo was a small studio meant for only one or two people. What it lacked in size was more than compensated for by the coziness Sawyer had lovingly created for herself. Instead of the typical lighthouse/seashell theme, Sawyer went with beach cottage white and aqua with accents of coral. The living–dining–kitchen area was about the size of my bedroom in Virginia, but it had a large balcony overlooking the Atlantic Ocean that made up for it. Right now the sliding glass door was open and you could hear the crash of the surf in the distance and the call of seagulls wafted in on the salty breeze.

Sawyer was sitting on top of her granite counter with her legs dangling over the edge, drinking a cup of coffee.

"Aren't those your pajamas?"

"Sawyer, what's the emergency?"

Then I got the shock of my life, as who should walk in from the bedroom but Kurt. "Hey, Poppy, how's it going?"

Sawyer gave me a weak smile. "A bird flew in through my door."

Kurt had something cradled in his hands. He walked over to the open balcony with it.

I mouthed to Sawyer, *And you called* Kurt?

Sawyer sipped her coffee and wouldn't meet my eyes.

Kurt opened his hands and a little sparrow flew out the door. "There you go, Cracker Jack. You're all safe."

Sawyer put her coffee down and jumped off the counter. "Thanks for coming right over. I didn't know who else to call."

Excuse me. Chopped Liver, party of one.

"Hey, anytime." Kurt looked at Sawyer like he wanted to say more.

I watched the awkward moment between them as long as I could, then I kicked an issue of *Real Simple* off the coffee table.

Kurt picked up his keys and turned for the door. "I guess I'd better go then."

I said, "Bye, Kurt."

Sawyer gave him a silent wave.

When he had left, Sawyer and I started talking at once.

"Are you out of your mind? Why would you call *him*?"

"I know, I know, but I was really freaked out and you didn't answer your phone."

"It took me like five minutes to get here."

We stared at each other for a beat.

"Why is your face getting so puffy?"

"I'm swelling up from eating snack cakes."

"What happened to your Paleo Diet?"

"I don't want to talk about it. What was the big emergency? Your killer pterodactyl incident?"

Sawyer blushed. "I got that text from my source that I'd been waiting for, about Billy Sommers."

"Finally." This could be it. The clue we've been waiting for to blow the lid off this whole thing. "And?"

Sawyer shook her head no. "He won the engineering award for making a solar-powered hot-dog cooker."

I was gutted. "Solar-powered what? That's an award? You could literally cook the hot dogs in the package if you stick them in the sun. Why would you need an invention for that?"

"What can I say, solar power was a big deal back then."

I sat on her couch, sulking. My face was starting to itch

and my stomach was expanding. I didn't realize how much better I had been feeling until now.

"So I guess you're going out dressed like that?"

"Going where? I'm not going out."

"You promised Sabrina you'd go to her cheer competition this morning."

"Oh, crap. I forgot all about it."

You know, back in Virginia I was too far away for people to ask me to do things. That had a lot of appeal. I was also very lonely, but you gotta pick your battles.

"Do I have time to go home and change?"

"Not really. But you should at least comb your hair. And maybe wash it first. Let me get you a towel."

Thirty minutes later, we pulled up in front of the Wildwood Convention Center. The arena was buzzing with teenagers doused in glitter and bows, all atwitter about competing. Floor mats were set up in front of a row of judges and a backdrop had been constructed courtesy of sponsors. The largest sponsor in the middle was for the Dynasty Cheer Academy.

I found Connie and Kim with other Caper High Cheer parents.

Connie pulled me into a mom hug that reinforced my fear that I looked like crap on a cracker.

"Our girls are up next."

The team was announced and the lights dimmed. The numerous loudspeakers began to boom out club music. Flashing strobe lights set to the bass line gave the feel of being at a rave. So I'd been told.

The cheerleaders exploded onto the stage and went right into tumbling passes and jumps.

Connie explained what we were watching because none

of us had ever been a cheerleader. Or been friends with a cheerleader. Or been around a cheerleader without being humiliated.

"Now they're doing their lifts. Good girl, Sabrina. She's the one on the top there."

Kim was clutching her cell phone, recording everything. "Don't fall, catch her, there you go."

"This is the synchronization portion. They have to perform their jumps perfectly timed."

I was amazed at the athleticism of the young kids as they did their stunts. "Sabrina is really good."

Kim beamed, "I know, right?"

"In fact, they're all really good."

Sawyer pointed to the girl on the far end. "Except that poor little one over there."

Connie sighed. "That's Athena."

I watched Athena for a minute. She tried really hard, but she was always just a little off. *Story of my life, honey. Get used to it.*

"Sabrina told me they put her on the end in hopes that the judges don't notice her as much."

Down in the front there was one cheerleader with her back to us, jumping on the sidelines doing all the moves with the girls.

"Is that Barbie's replacement?"

Connie shook her head. "Nope. Coach Wilcott had to step in and represent the girls today."

Coach Wilcott was down at the judges' table looking awkward from his black whistle to his white sneakers. Anger rose up to the roots of my red hair. I got that death threat not long after being in his office. What if he'd seen me, and instead of attacking me right then and there decided to terrorize me?

The routine was over and the lights came up. I marched

down to the floor to question Coach Wilcott, but the sideline cheerleader cut me off. It was Missy. Dressed out to match the team.

"Weren't they wonderful?"

"Missy. Hi, yeah. They were great."

"Did you see Athena? She was the one with the power moves on the end."

"I did see her." She was like a train wreck. She caught your eye every time she messed up. You tried to look away but you just couldn't do it.

"Hey, since you're here." Missy hauled a purse up from the bleachers that was big enough to smuggle a refugee in. "Let me give you one of these."

"A flyer about the alumni bake sale?"

"It's tomorrow."

"Yes, I see that. But I don't know if it's a good idea that I attend, do you?"

"Oh, I don't want you to attend."

"You don't?"

"No. I've been stuck with the job of heading it up, what with our dear friend's passing and all. I want you to donate something."

"Well, that's very generous." *Of me.*

I was starting to get a headache from the sugar. Maybe eating pie for breakfast wasn't a great idea after all.

"I think it could also help your character witness too, you know?"

"I guess—"

Missy cut me off. "Great. Have it to the school by ten a.m. Don't be late. Now where is that girl? I'm so proud of her."

Something had begun to stir inside me while she had blathered on about the stupid bake sale. Everyone in town knew I was under the interrogation lights—and at this amazing moment in my life, Missy wanted me to *bake brownies*? I felt a thread of anger rising like smoke from a smoldering fire inside me.

Missy was looking around me to find her daughter. "Oh, there she is. I'm going to go congratulate her."

Athena was standing off to the side, not part of the group. The rest of the cheerleaders had moved like a pack of meerkats to the side of the arena to await their scores. I felt sorry for her. I remember very well what it was like to not quite fit in.

Then I saw someone who made the smolder inside burst into flame.

Coach Wilcott stepped away from the judges' table, and I grabbed him by the whistle.

"Can I talk to you for a minute, please?"

"Joy Peterson?"

"Who?"

"Isn't that your name?"

"No. But I think you already know that."

I pulled the coach away from the competition to the empty bleachers. "Did you threaten me?"

"What? No. What are you, some kind of lunatic?" The coach looked around nervously, but there was too much noise from the next cheer group for anyone to notice us.

"Look, I know you lied about being at the reunion the other night because I saw you."

"I don't know what you're talking about." His eyes darted side to side, looking for a way of escape.

"And I've had sources tell me that you were seen colluding with Barbie Clark on several occasions—something else you lied about."

"So. What does that have to do with anything?"

"I think you killed Barbie at the reunion."

He sputtered at that. "Wh-what? That's ridiculous. Why would I do that?"

"Because she was blackmailing you. She found out you were giving the basketball players steroids."

The blood drained from his face, and he looked like he was going make a run for it.

"How did you find out?"

"The secret meetings, your recent money problems, it all adds up. Barbie threatened to turn you in for dosing the team."

"You're wrong. She threatened to turn me in *if they lost*. The steroids were her idea. She wanted a winning season to showcase her cheerleaders. Better scores meant better turnout and better turnout meant more exposure for the teams, both hers and mine. She wanted me to keep giving out the steroids, and she had secretly recorded me agreeing to use them. She said she'd go to the police if I stopped."

The coach started to cry. "Look, I don't have much left, I had to buy all those steroids on the Internet, and that blond witch bled me dry making me buy all new mats and equipment for her cheerleaders, but I'll give you what I can to keep quiet."

"Oh no! I'm not going to jail for a murder you committed, buddy."

"What? I didn't murder anyone. I mean I'm not sorry she's dead, either, this gets me out of a real jam. But I didn't kill her."

"You had a motive, you were at the reunion, and I know you have syringes in your med kit so you had access to the murder weapon."

"No, I don't!" He yanked open the med kit. "Here, check. I don't have anything like what you're talking about."

"Then how do you inject the steroids?"

He pulled out an old Excedrin bottle and opened it. "They're pills. See."

Oh. Whoops. "Well, if you didn't kill her, then why would you lie about being at the reunion?"

His lip started to quiver again. "Please don't tell anyone. I can't afford another strike. I was only spying on Francie to keep her safe. She started dating that imposter, Enrique. He's not even Spanish. He's from Hoboken."

Where is this going? "Go on."

"Then she caught me and got a restraining order. I can't be within fifty feet of her except when we're at work."

"*That's* why you were arrested?"

"She's having a midlife crisis, and when it's over and she sees him for who he really is, she'll come back to me."

Sure she will. Who could pass all this up? "So where did you disappear to the night of the reunion?"

"I saw Francie and Dwight—that's his real name, *Dwight*—I checked. I saw them leave the gym together and I followed them out to the back lot."

"And you spied on them?"

He nodded and sobbed out a hiccup. "Going at it like a couple of teenagers in that polyester playboy's Chevy Impala."

I handed him a tissue from my purse. He could be lying, but it was hard to fake that level of pathetic. The coach was a dead end.

Connie was waving me over from across the arena. Sabrina had rejoined the girls and I wanted to praise her for how well she had done.

"You were wonderful!"

"Thank you. I'm not as good as Tiffany, but I'm working on it. Aunt Poppy, you're kind of a mess. What happened?"

Connie turned scarlet. "Sabrina!"

Sabrina looked away from me and fiddled with her bow. "Well, she is."

"I had a rough night." I pulled out my phone and showed the girls the picture I took of the plant before it was taken into evidence. "Someone sent me this with a nasty note attached."

"*Convallaria majalis*," Sabrina said.

"What did you just say?"

"*Convallaria majalis*," Sabrina repeated. "Lily of the valley. It's poisonous."

"How did you know that?" Kim asked.

"It's on my biology test. We're doing botany this quarter."

Sawyer pulled out her cell phone and Sabrina spelled it for her. "Lily of the valley. Extremely toxic if ingested."

I was stunned. That's what Mrs. Pritchard had been trying to tell me. "This is what the police were looking for in my yard the other day."

Kim took the cell phone from Sawyer. "They didn't find any, did they?"

"Not that I know of. I've never seen it before last night. But now I know why it smelled so familiar. I thought it was Barbie's perfume the night of the murder. She had a faint floral scent about her."

So the killer sent me a threat attached to more evidence against me and I turned it over to the police. I may as well have begged Amber to arrest me.

Chapter 40

I felt sick to my stomach. Not just from the realization that I'd given Amber more evidence incriminating myself, but from the sugar rush in my breakfast tantrum. I had to go home and lie down.

Aunt Ginny was dressed in a netted pith helmet and safari khakis and she was spraying the rosebushes by the front gate. I would have said something, but my hair was frizzed out with angry thoughts, I had lemon pie filling and coffee stains on my pajamas, and I could feel a zit beginning to form on my forehead.

We stared at each other for a couple of seconds, then sighed and each went on our way.

I had to peel my pants off, because they were cutting off my circulation now. How can something that tastes so good make you feel so bad? I lay down and started to cry.

I thought about Bebe and Tawnika, and wondered what they would say about my "Rich White Girl" pity-party.

Figaro came in to sit on the bed to grieve with me.

I dozed off and woke up sometime later and thought I was having a hot flash. Figaro was sleeping on my head like an ushanka hat. I scooped him down to my arms and cuddled him. He nuzzled me, purring until he heard Aunt Ginny's call.

"Here, kittykittykittykitty!"

Then he shot out of my room like he was headed for the last lifeboat on the sinking *Titanic*. So much for loyalty.

I sat up and spied a wrapped present sitting on the dresser. That wasn't there before I fell asleep. I opened it and found a beautiful little watercolor of an ugly caterpillar forming a cocoon. The caption read: "Rewrite Your Script." It was signed "GinnyMac."

It took my breath away. Aunt Ginny had painted it for me. I was the ugly little caterpillar and it was my choice if I wanted to stay that way or go through the pain of change. I put it on the mirror until I could frame it. I took a look at my reflection. "Just keep trying," I told myself.

I took a shower and conditioned my hair. I schmeared all my beauty products on my skin and face and applied my makeup. I blow-dried and styled my hair and applied a de-frizzing finisher. Then I put on a blue maxi dress and silver sandals. After a spritz of my new perfume I headed downstairs.

Aunt Ginny was in the sunroom with Figaro on her lap. I walked over to her and gave her a hug.

"What's that for?"

"My beautiful present. I love it."

Aunt Ginny blushed. "Just a little doohickey for you."

I made us some water with lemon and mint, took all my supplements that I had ignored that morning, and we sat in the sunroom to take stock of our situation.

I handed Aunt Ginny a glass. "I think we can rule out the coach as a suspect. He's guilty of giving steroids to minors without their parents' consent, but I don't think he killed Barbie."

"What makes you so sure?"

"He was spying on his ex-wife making out in the back parking lot at the time of the murder."

"Did anyone see him out there?"

"Joanne was walking off a verbal assault from Barbie. I can ask her."

"Well, let's hope she saw something useful. What about Mr. Plumber?"

"He definitely had an affair with Barbie. Kristen knows about it. But he said he was in the other gym shooting hoops when she was murdered."

"Who was he playing hoopies with?"

"I think he said Pete and Troy."

Aunt Ginny took out a little brush from a side drawer and started to run it through Figaro's fur. Fig opened one eye like he was trying to figure out just what was happening, then he gave up on it and went back to sleep. "You need to give them a call. What about the wife? If she knows about the affair, do you think she killed her?"

"His wife had all kinds of access to syringes what with her fertility treatment and being a nurse and all, and they are both at the school every day and know where the security cameras are. Plus, they could use the chem lab at the school without encountering much suspicion. But she's nine months pregnant. I mean—come on."

"If she's crazy enough to have a baby to save her marriage, she's probably crazy enough to kill to save it too. I personally would have killed the husband for cheating on me before I went after the other woman, but that's just me."

Hmm. What did happen to Aunt Ginny's third husband,

Uncle Gush? I forced that thought back to the recesses of my brain.

"Billy is still missing, but his science fair award was a dead end. We need to know what happened between him and Barbie. There were a lot of rumors flying around about something unforgivable that happened, but I haven't found out what it was yet. Mrs. Dodson still hasn't gotten back to me either."

"You'll see her tonight."

"I will?"

Aunt Ginny nodded. "When we go out."

"So we still have Robert and Kelly as suspects."

"That Robert is a catbird if you ask me."

"What do you mean?"

"He is definitely not the grieving widower. He's too . . . handsy. He was all over Sawyer like ants at a Fourth of July picnic."

"Yeah, but Kelly watches over him like a hawk. I thought they might be in it together for the insurance money, but it turns out Barbie had very little and it was left to Tiffany."

"If one or both of them were the murderer, it wasn't for the money. Maybe Kelly did it to get Barbie out of the way. So she could get her hooks into Robert."

"That's possible. She does seem to worship him. Kelly said Robert was in the cafeteria answering questions about the campaign when Barbie was killed, but Joanne said she saw Robert and Kelly kissing outside at the time of the murder, and Tim said he saw Robert and Kelly getting cozy in the cafeteria during the murder."

Aunt Ginny put the brush away, took out a pink bandana, and tied it around Fig's neck. "That's three different alibis. They can't all be right."

"What if the events are all right, but the timing is

wrong? Maybe Joanne saw them coming back inside from the scene of the crime."

"Then Tim saw them after they'd returned, while you were standing over the body?"

"That could work."

Figaro sat up, sniffed the bandana, and gave me an alarmed look.

"Are you sure the cop isn't behind it all?"

"Something happened between Barbie and Amber to destroy their friendship. I need to find out what it was. For that matter, what is Amber's problem with me? I never did anything to her. We were never even friends."

"She sure thinks you did something."

"We're missing something big, I can feel it, but I don't know what it is."

Figaro shook his head back and forth and tried unsuccessfully to back out of the pink bandana. Then he shot off of Aunt Ginny's lap and galloped sideways down the hall trying to outrun it.

Aunt Ginny threw her head back and laughed. "You'll get some juicy information tonight. Just wait."

Chapter 41

Aunt Ginny's big night out was bingo at the fire department, a big white building with red lettering that said CAPE MAY POINT FIRE STATION NUMBER ONE. The front was dominated by the three bay doors for their distinctive blue and white fire engines. The American flag flapped proudly overhead in the offshore breeze.

Firemen are special everywhere, but even more so in South Jersey. We have over twenty-one firefighter-themed museums, and we host one of the largest annual firefighter conventions with an annual Fireman's Parade every September.

Firemen were especially special in my family. My grandfather was a fireman. So was his father, his grandfather, his brother, and his uncle. So if we had a chance to support the fire department, we did it. If that meant a night of soft-core gambling, we were willing to fall on that grenade. And these seniors were serious contenders.

Bingo was set up in the dining hall. Long rows of tables ran side to side in the large room and two flat-screens were hung on the wall at the front where the winning numbers were displayed. One table was set up in the back selling refreshments and bingo paraphernalia.

Aunt Ginny and I each bought a book of cards. I got us some of the world's worst coffee, and we joined Mrs. Davis and Mother Gibson at their usual table down at the front. Mrs. Davis slid her purse over to fill the empty spot next to her to save the seat for Mrs. Dodson, who was running late.

A small gray-haired sergeant of a woman marched over and barked out that there was no saving of seats allowed.

Mrs. Davis would not be put off. "I'm not saving a seat, she's in the bathroom, you old bat."

"If she's not here in the next five minutes, I'm coming back to confiscate that spot."

"Come right on over. I had cabbage for dinner tonight and I'm so gassy I could blow the roof off the place. But you're more than welcome to sit downwind of me."

The gray-haired sergeant mashed her eyebrows down and puckered her lips up until the two almost met. Then she thundered off to be someone else's little ray of sunshine.

Mrs. Dodson ran in the front door out of breath with her bingo cards waving in the air. "I'm here. Don't let her have my spot! I was in the can!"

We settled into our seats and after Mrs. Dodson caught her breath, she turned to me. "Poppy, honey, how are you holding up?"

"I'm getting a little frazzled. We're quickly running out of time to prove my innocence."

"Did that lead I gave you help any?"

"What lead, Mrs. Dodson?"

"Didn't I tell you about the big blowup between Barbie and Billy Sommers?"

The hairs on the back of my neck stood up and I got goose bumps up my arms. "Did you find out something?"

"Well, good Lord, honey, I thought I told you already."

Mother Gibson took out a box of contraband jelly doughnuts for the "gals" and placed it on the table. "Edith, you need to get yourself some of that ginkgo I told you about. You'd forget your address if it wasn't pinned to your hat."

Mrs. Dodson helped herself to a doughnut. "I know, but every time I get to the health nut store I forget what I'm looking for."

Mrs. Davis giggled and dunked her doughnut into the oil slick the VFD called coffee. "It's health *food* store, you nut."

I was getting worried Mrs. Dodson would forget about me entirely. Apparently, so was Aunt Ginny.

"Focus, Edith. Barbie and the Sommers boy."

Mrs. Dodson looked like she was trying to figure out what we were talking about.

"You said something about a blowup?"

"Oh, yes. It was all the do around here years ago. My friend at the Christian Women's League told me that the two were engaged right out of college. Her family sprung for a half-page spread in the *Inquirer* announcing it. The invitations went out, the gifts came in. The day of the wedding, Barbie didn't show up."

I was a bit disappointed with what the Christian Women's League considered gossip.

"Well, that happens." *It almost happened to me. If Georgina hadn't held the proverbial shotgun, John and I would never have gotten married. Accidental pregnancy or not.*

"Oh, just wait. That's not the whole story. The real scandal begins a few months later when they got engaged again. The families tried to play off the previous embarrassment as a joke."

Mrs. Davis cut in. "That's right. The invitations all said 'Second Time's the Charm,' didn't they?"

Mrs. Dodson turned to Mrs. Davis, "Thelma. This is my story."

Mrs. Davis rolled her eyes and took another doughnut. "Continue."

Mrs. Dodson turned back to Aunt Ginny and me. "Then the night before the wedding, it was called off again."

Aunt Ginny poked at the powdered sugar with her finger. "No."

"Ummm-hmmm."

Mother Gibson lit up a cigarette under the NO SMOKING sign and hid it in a secret ashtray she kept under the table. "Tell her the rest."

Mrs. Dodson leaned in closer and lowered her voice. "It was spread around that Barbie had cold feet and called the wedding off again, but her gran tells a different story after a couple glasses of root beer schnapps. The night before the wedding, Billy caught Barbie having the honeymoon behind the Milky Way with his best man."

Okay. Now we have a motive.

"Her parents were so mortified when he called the wedding off they told everyone that Barbie did the dumping because *Billy* was unfaithful."

Aunt Ginny whispered to me, "Guess who just rose up to number one on my suspect list?"

A member of the Fireman's Auxiliary Club called the evening to order and the first game began.

Anyone who thinks that life slows down as a senior citizen has never watched a roomful of grandmas run a table at bingo. Twenty cards can be covered at once with an ink stamp and the rapid-fire execution of a World War II Browning machine gun on a call: *Bapbapbapbapbapbapbap!* You had to see it to believe it.

At one point Mrs. Davis thought she had bingo, but it turned out she had a schmear of jelly from her doughnut on I-19 that made it look like 1-18 and the pot went to the gray-haired sergeant.

I tried to keep up with my cards, but I was so tired the numbers were moving around on me. Plus, it took all my willpower to leave the doughnuts alone. I had to smack Aunt Ginny's hand once when I caught her trying to sneak one when she thought I was in the ladies' room.

We never did get to the final jackpot because Mother Gibson got her cigarette too close to Mrs. Davis's wig and set it on fire. Mrs. Davis had enough AquaNet in it to spontaneously combust in the full sun, so all we saw was a blue flash and then a puff of white smoke. It caused so much chaos that we had to evacuate the bingo hall. Sister McGradey, who is nearly a hundred years old, mistook the smoke for a sign that we'd elected a new pope.

The firemen weren't too pleased being called in to put out a fire in their own station. Eddie Shoemaker gave a stern lecture to Mother Gibson about the no-smoking policy in public buildings. (Which, of course, she knows about, but she lights up anyway. If anyone challenges her, she taps her ear and says her hearing aid isn't working.)

I went to pick up the car so Aunt Ginny wouldn't have to walk and found Pete Ferguson standing next to a green Oldsmobile out at the curb. In high school, Pete Ferguson was a wide receiver on the football team, which made him Caper royalty. But in junior high, he was my next-door neighbor, and I knew him more for being able to fit six beans up his nose at one time. This was my chance to check on Joel's alibi.

"Hey, you. How's it going?"

He took a long drag off a cigarette. "Long time no see, Red."

"Well, I was at the reunion the other night."

He gave me a sly grin. "So I hear."

"I didn't see you much."

"Nah, that's not really my scene anymore."

"What'd you do all night?"

"You know. Jumped through a couple of Missy's hoops. Grabbed some wings, then played ball with the guys. What'd you do?"

"You know. Same."

He laughed.

"I wanted to ask you something about that night."

"Shoot."

"Did you play ball with Joel Miller?"

"Yeah. He was there."

"Was he there the whole time?"

"Yeah. Why wouldn't he be?"

I guess I can cross Joel off the list.

"I mean, except for when he stepped out to get some air."

"Did anyone go with him?"

"No. We were too busy competing to see who has the best jump shot."

"How long was he out there?"

"'Bout twenty minutes."

"Twenty minutes! Are you sure?" That was plenty of time to run to another hall, kill Barbie, and be back in the gym before being noticed.

"Yeah, it was a little while. Troy and Mike played a whole game of twenty-one while they waited for him. I figured he got the munchies and went back to the buffet."

"And you never went to look for him?"

"Didn't think about it. He's a big boy. Why are you asking?"

"Just trying to figure some stuff out. You didn't by any chance see Coach Wilcott at the reunion, did you?"

"He walked through once. Carrying a plate of food, I think. Didn't see him after that."

About that time, the little gray-haired sergeant marched up to the car. "Take me home, Peanut. That's enough excitement for tonight."

"Peanut" opened the passenger-side door for the sergeant. "Okay, Nana. Let's go." Then he turned to me. "Take care of yourself, Red. Keep your head down."

I smiled back at him. "Let me know when you work up to seven beans."

Pete laughed and got in the car. Nana stuck her tongue out at me as they pulled away.

Aunt Ginny was dancing a jig by the car when I returned, her eyes sparkling with delight. "I won two hundred dollars."

"Good for you. Why do you have powdered sugar on your lips?"

Aunt Ginny's hand flew up to her mouth. "Whaaaat? How did that get there? I bet it was when Lila started that wig fire. I *had* to save the bingo cards and the box of doughnuts."

"Oh, of course. You gotta have priorities."

"And then there was that big fan I walked past. It probably blew some of the powdered sugar on my face."

"Uh-huh."

I let Aunt Ginny go on like that all the way home. She was a good distraction from my nagging fear about what we would find on the porch tonight. Would I live to tell about it tomorrow?

Chapter 42

I was busy Sunday morning making Paleo muffins for Gia's shop. The first batch sold out yesterday and people had been requesting more. Today I'd fiddled with two new recipes: Cherry Chocolate Chip, and Banana Walnut Coconut.

I found special allergy-friendly chocolate chips in the health food section of the ACME, so I bought enough bags to make some Paleo-friendly chocolate chip cookies for the alumni bake sale later.

After yesterday's disastrous fall off the wagon, I was trying really hard today to stick to my diet. At least for the next twenty-four hours. After that I might be on whatever regimen the county lockup prescribed.

Figaro was being supportive by batting around the empty bag of walnuts, every now and then stretching up to my elbow and patting my arm to get my attention. I showed him the cookie dough, which he sniffed and then lost interest.

Aunt Ginny padded into the room following the smell of baked cookies and French-pressed coffee.

I poured her a cup, and brought her a sample of each muffin. "I splurged and bought some Ethiopian Yirga-cheffe for us. I don't know how much longer I'll get to enjoy it."

Aunt Ginny sipped her coffee. "I don't want to hear any more of that nonsense. You're not going anywhere and neither am I. We can do this." She gave me a frail look of concern. "Don't you think so?"

My heart went out to her. "Of course we can." *Dear God, I hope so.*

Aunt Ginny reached into her pocket and handed me a business card. "Before I forget, I made you an appointment at that fancy-schmancy spa for a massage."

"You did?"

"I appreciate all you've done for me these past few days and I want you to have a little pampering. I made it for today at four o'clock because I didn't know if you'd be able to make it after tomorrow."

I swallowed hard.

"I know we'll prove your innocence, but in case we have to do it from prison, I wanted you to have this sooner rather than later."

I hugged Aunt Ginny and packaged up the cookies into baggies of four and made a sign that said GLUTEN-FREE—CONTAINS NUTS. Then I packed up the muffins and took the lot out to the car.

I thought today might be my last day to drool over Gia, so I dressed especially nice. Only Gia wasn't there, his girlfriend was.

She looked me up and down when I came in and she did not look impressed. "Are those our muffins?"

"Just as promised." I put the baskets up on the counter and told her about the two kinds. "I made little signs for them so the customers would know just what they are."

She picked one of them up and sniffed it, then curled her nose up. "I don't know why he's making such a big deal about these."

"They're gluten-free, so hopefully they'll bring in some new customers."

She picked up the baskets and shoved them on the back counter. "Whatever. They're still fattening. You don't look like this by eating that."

Oh. Okay then. Shamu, out.

"I hope they sell quickly for you."

She went back to filing her nails. "Bye."

I turned to go and she said, "Oh, wait a minute. Gia wanted me to give you this."

She was holding out an envelope.

I thanked her and took it out to the car to open it. There was a note inside.

> *I missed you yesterday.*
> *G.*

Missed me? Missed me as in *I was longing to see you and you didn't come in*? Or missed you as in *Hey, I must have left before you got here. Sorry, bro*?

I put it in my purse, so I could sleep with it later. *Cough.* I mean read it later.

There were signs advertising the bake sale lined up all along Route 9 leading up to the parking lot at Caper High. Outside, tables were set with baked goods donated by different teachers and alumni. Missy had organized the tables by category. When I checked in with her at the front of the lot, I could tell by her scowl that she was obviously very grateful that I was participating.

"You're late!"

I gave her a cheery smile. "Only by ten minutes. There are a lot of cars turning in here."

Missy wasn't exactly her usual perky self. She seemed a bit overwhelmed. "That's because I advertised in all the papers and letters went home to all the parents."

"That was a really good plan on your part."

"I know. What have you got?"

"Chocolate chip cookies."

"What does that sign say?"

"Gluten-free."

"Table fifteen."

She pointed down a long row of tables lined up under white tents. I passed several tables of muffins, cupcakes, cakes, fruit pies, cream pies, whoopie pies, cookies, bar cookies, and brownies to table fifteen, marked OTHER.

There were three more entries on the table. Chocolate fudge, homemade granola bars, and Rice Krispies treats.

Joel Miller was manning the table and he wasn't happy to be there or to see me.

I put my box of cookies down. "I guess table fifteen is for the rejects."

"Looks that way."

"Why are you here?"

"Those are Kristen's Rice Krispies treats. It's all she knows how to make."

"They look good."

"Thank you. I'll tell her you said that. Missy strong-armed her into running a booth, but she's having Stevie Nicks contractions so she stayed in bed, and now I'm here instead."

"You mean Braxton Hicks?"

He shrugged. "I have no idea."

I looked around us and no one seemed inclined to walk all the way down to our spot in bake sale purgatory, so I sat down next to Joel.

"I talked to Coach Wilcott the other day."

"Good for you."

"You were right about him."

"Right about what?"

"The secret meetings with Barbie."

"I told you."

"You also told me you were in the gym all night playing basketball."

"I was."

"See, now that's funny. Because Pete said you were gone for about twenty minutes."

"What? No way."

"Hey. I'm just telling you what he said."

"What's your point?"

"You know my point. Someone else killed Barbie and they're trying to frame me."

"And you think it was me?"

"You had a motive."

"What motive?"

"You had an affair with her. Maybe you wanted out and she said she'd tell Kristen so you killed her to keep it a secret."

Joel had picked up a Rice Krispies treat and was squeezing it until the plastic package burst. "What makes you so sure I had an affair with anyone?"

A battle raged within my soul. It went against everything in me to give up a confidence, but in less than forty-eight hours I would be in jail if I didn't find the real killer. *Forgive me, Kristen.*

"I know you had an affair with Barbie because Kristen told me. She has . . . evidence."

Joel's face flushed with rage and he pounded the Rice Krispies treat into the table, smushing it flat. He sat for a couple of minutes breathing heavy, and I was glad to have so many people around us as witnesses.

He picked up the smushed snack and chucked it across the lawn.

"Damn Barbie. The infertility almost ruined my marriage. Kristen blamed me because the doctors couldn't find anything wrong with her. She was consumed with having a baby and angry that I couldn't give her one. Barbie came along when I was weak."

"Let me guess. Barbie said she understood you, she told you how great you were and how lucky your wife was to have you. She was lonely and you two didn't mean for this to happen. Blah blah blah."

Joel looked me in the eyes, and I could see his pain. "I wish I could say you were wrong, but you're not. I regretted it right from the start, and told Barbie I was ashamed of what we were doing, because I still loved Kristen, I always have, and I wanted out of the affair."

"I take it things didn't end well?"

Joel pounded another Rice Krispies treat into a pancake. "She was furious. She threatened to tell Kristen everything if I ended the relationship. She said she'd ruin my marriage."

"People do some awful things in the name of love."

A lady with two small children approached the table. "My son has celiac disease and I was told you have something gluten-free over here."

She saw all the bags of destroyed Rice Krispies treats, then looked from Joel to me. I gave her a small smile. She quickly bought four packages of the gluten-free cookies without further conversation. When she left, Joel continued.

"Love had nothing to do with it. Barbie couldn't stand being second. She always had to be better than everyone else and she would lie, cheat, or steal to get there. If I ended the affair, it would mean Kristen won. I even threatened to tell Robert and she laughed in my face and said, 'Go ahead!'"

"Why didn't you just confess to Kristen?"

"I didn't want to lose her. I think she could eventually forgive me for having an affair. I'm just not sure she could forgive me for having it with Barbie."

"Were you still having the affair at the time of the reunion?"

"Absolutely not. Barbie broke it off when Kristen announced we were pregnant. Said she got tired of me but I know something must have happened for her to think she won. I know you're looking for someone else to blame, but I'm not your guy. I didn't kill her."

"You don't have any alibi for the time of the murder. What were you doing for the twenty minutes you were out of the gym?"

He sat quietly and looked around to see if anyone was in earshot. "All right, fine. You can't go to the police with this and if you do I'll deny it. Got it?"

"Yep."

"I was around the corner smoking a joint, okay? I'm freaked out about having this baby. I'm afraid I'm going to break it or something. And I'd been keyed up waiting for Barbie to pull some stunt with Kristen. I just needed to get the edge off, you know what I mean?"

"Well, if smoking a joint is anything like eating a pint of Heath Bar Crunch, then yes, I know what you mean."

"Look, can you just be cool about this and not tell anyone? I've got enough to deal with now that I have to talk with Kristen about Barbie."

Gah! It was high school all over again. Be cool and don't tell I was getting high. Be cool and don't tell I was sleeping around. Why did we buy into the lie that the jerks were popular and we had to be like them? I didn't even like these people twenty years ago.

I left Joel smashing Rice Krispies treats at the reject table and started walking back to my car. There was a table set up for Congressman Robert Clark and they were giving out packaged bakery cookies—for a donation, of course. April was at the table handing out "Vote Clark" buttons and brochures.

"Hi, April."

"Hi . . . you."

"Where are Robert and Kelly?"

"Oh, they're around here somewhere. Shaking hands and networking, I'm sure."

The last table I passed had beautiful little fairy cakes for sale. Miniature works of art covered in rolled fondant with little animals and unicorns and flowers. One was decorated with purses and shoes. All made out of gum paste.

"Who makes these? They're beautiful!"

"Who wants to know?"

That was a voice I would know anywhere.

"Joanne? Are these yours?"

She smacked my hand. "Don't touch them! You'll smudge the luster dust."

"I didn't know you were so talented."

"There's a lot you don't know about me, McAllister."

Joanne was a lot less friendly than I'd expected. I thought we'd bonded over Bon Jovi.

"Hey, do you have a minute?"

"No."

"Joanne, please. I need to ask you something."

She huffed. "Fine. Carl, watch my table, please."

We walked a few feet away from the bake sale to get some privacy.

"The night of the reunion, did you happen to see anyone else outside when you were walking around? Other than Robert and Kelly?"

Joanne made a face and started to walk away.

"Where are you going?"

"I'm not talking to you about this."

I ran to get in front of her. "Why are you being like this? I thought we got past some of the hostility the other night."

"What other night?"

"You know. Hanging out at karaoke?"

"I don't even remember karaoke."

Of course you don't. Because that would make my life too easy.

"You'd been drinking . . . a lot. We hung out."

She looked skeptical. "We hung out?"

"I was just as surprised as you were."

"Well, I don't remember."

"Okay. Look, I'm sorry you don't remember. But can you please help me. I'm desperate."

She stopped walking away. "Yes."

"Yes what?"

"Yes, I saw someone outside when I was walking around."

"Do you know who it was?"

She mimicked me. "*Yes, I know who it was.* It was Charlie Wilcott."

"Where was he?"

"In the back parking lot keeping an eye on . . . some of the cars."

"Might one of those cars have had his ex-wife Francine in it?"

She gave me a sideways look. "It might have."

That's the coach's alibi.

"Hey, you didn't happen to see Joel out there, did you?"

"No."

Oh well, it was worth a try.

"But he was probably behind the greenhouses getting high."

"What would make you say that?"

Joanne shrugged. "Because he smelled like weed when we were being questioned by the police."

"Joanne, you've been a big help. Thank you."

"Whatever." Joanne started back to the bake sale.

She is always a surprise. I guess that crosses Joel off the suspect list. That just leaves Robert, Kelly, and Billy.

I went to the car but I couldn't find my keys. I checked my purse and both of my pockets. Nothing. I must have left them with the cookies.

I went back to the table to search for them and Joel had disappeared. All that was left was a cash box and the remains of a few Rice Krispies treats. All my gluten-free chocolate chip cookies were gone. They must have been a big hit. And there were my keys sitting next to the box.

When I got closer to the box I saw a note.

"I told you to BACK OFF! You were warned!"

Chapter 43

This time I didn't touch it, but I scooped it into a plastic bag that was sitting on the brownie table. I asked table fourteen if they had seen anyone leave the note. They hadn't been paying attention.

Maybe I crossed Joel off too soon. I put all the items with the note in my car. I sat there trying to calm my nerves and figure out what to do next. I dug the sample bag of cookies out of my purse that had been for Gia. Since he wasn't at the coffee shop, they were mine now.

I ate all four of them in record time, but I was still shaken up. I refused to spend my last few hours of freedom obsessing about prison. Instead, I was going to push my fear straight into denial.

Shoes. I'll go buy shoes.

I drove to the Washington Street Mall and tried on shoes at the Shoe Shak. I felt a little better after I bought a pair of four-inch hot pink heels with leopard spots. They reminded me of *Josie and the Pussycats*. They didn't match my outfit, but I wore them out of there anyway.

It was time for my massage at the Radiance Day Spa. Aunt Ginny had booked the appointment and paid for it—

God bless her—and I didn't want to let her down by missing it.

I walked into reception and signed in. There was another lady waiting ahead of me. Our eyes met. She gasped, then quickly covered her face with a magazine.

"Kelly?"

The woman got up, magazine in place, and ran through the door into the treatment area. When I looked into the room after her, she was gone.

Why is she acting so weird? I walked back over to the sign-in book, but the name above mine was "Felicity Johnson."

I asked the receptionist, "Excuse me, do you know who that lady sitting on the love seat was?"

She looked at the sign-in book and said, "Felicity Johnson."

Gee, that was helpful. "What is she having done?"

"I'm sorry, but we're not allowed to give out information about clients' Botox treatments."

"Sure, I understand. It's good to keep that information top secret."

She nodded somberly.

"Let me ask you something, for myself. What kinds of services do you offer here that involve injections?"

She cocked her head to the side and rolled her eyes up to her forehead. I think I smelled a brain cell burning out.

"Hmm, let's see. There's Botox, Juvéderm, Restylane, vitamin B12 shots . . . Yep, that's all of them."

"What if I wanted to have one of those, say, Botox. Could you do it today?"

"Let me find out."

She disappeared for a few minutes. When she returned, she held the treatment doorway open. "Evan will take you now."

I was taken to a small clinical room and instructed to lie down on the table. After a couple of minutes, a young man dressed all in white, with a bushy tuft of blonde hair on his head, came in to greet me. He was carrying a little silver tray draped with a cloth. He put the tray on the counter.

"Vell, let's see how ve are doing today. You want ze Botox, yes?"

"Yes, is that it there?"

"Yes, ve are all ready. Let me just check your face."

Evan grabbed my chin and turned my face side to side. "No, dis is no good."

My voice was muffled from Evan's holding my jaw. "What's no good?"

"Zere aren't enough wrinkles for ze treatment. You are too full of ze natural Botox."

"What is the natural Botox?"

"Your face is too chubby. You look too young."

Well, that was the first time in my life being chubby was a good thing.

"Too bad I already mixed it. Oh vell, it von't go to vaste." Evan looked in the mirror and examined his face. Then he picked up the Botox and gave himself the injection on the side of his left eye. "Bye-bye crow's-foot."

He put the needle back on the tray, turned to me, and said, "You have more to do today?"

I nodded. "A massage."

"Okay, go vait in ze quiet room. I'm sure Ginger vill be along soon."

Then he left. HE LEFT. I watched the door close and I looked at the syringe on the silver tray. I looked at the door then I looked at the syringe. I took out my phone and took some pictures of the syringe. Then I went to the quiet room to think.

I didn't want a massage. I didn't like the idea of lying there naked under a sheet and being poked. But it only took about two minutes to go from being ashamed of my body to wanting to put Ginger on permanent retainer. The stress melted away and gave my mind a chance to plan.

I had three strong suspects left, and one of them had regular appointments where needles were left out on silver trays for the swiping. It was entirely feasible that Kelly had the means and opportunity, but what about the motive? The insurance money was a bust and getting Barbie out of the way to go after Robert was just vague rumors. I needed something more concrete.

I paid for my massage and left Ginger an exorbitant tip to show my appreciation. All the way home I mulled over my suspect list. The problem was, Barbie had made a lot of enemies and any number of people had a valid motive.

I pulled up to Aunt Ginny's house. There was a man and a woman standing in front of the house taking pictures. There was nothing especially unusual about this since tourists did it all the time. But then the man took out a tape measure and ran it along the front yard.

"Hi there."

They were startled to see me. "Oh, hello."

"It's a beautiful house."

The woman gushed, "I know it's just perfect for a bed and breakfast!"

"Sure, I can see that. Many of the houses in this neighborhood are bed and breakfasts."

The man chimed in, "Oh, we know. We've done all our demographics. This one is especially perfect because it's a corner lot."

"What were you measuring for just now?"

The woman showed me a drawing of Aunt Ginny's house with a wishing well in the front yard. "We were making sure there was enough room for this. We want to call it 'Wishes Come True.'"

I looked at the couple. Their enthusiasm was apparent by their eager, smiling faces flushed with excitement. "That's a really good name for a B&B, but why are you looking to do it with this house?"

The wife gushed some more, "We have it on good authority that this house will be on the market soon."

"Cameron!" The man grabbed her hand. "We have to go now."

The two argued under their breath across the street to their car. I walked down the block a little before returning home so they wouldn't see me go into Aunt Ginny's house.

I had to make a couple phone calls when I got in. I had a very strong suspicion I knew who their hot tip was coming from. I just had to be able to prove it.

Chapter 44

I tossed and turned all night, weighted down with fears of cavity searches and plastic lunchroom trays carved into shivs. The first morning light announced my last few hours of freedom. The girls were having a special luncheon for me today to buck up my spirits and, I suspected, to wait with me until Amber came to haul me off to the slammer. We decided to do it at Aunt Ginny's house so there wouldn't be a bunch of videos of my second arrest going up on YouTube from another public confrontation.

I made the Paleo Enchiladas that Dr. Melinda said were her favorite. They were missing something. Probably a few pounds of cheese. But since I was back to breathing freely from the Zinger incident I didn't want to push it. The least I could do was a few more hours of being healthy.

Sawyer brought some lemonade made with stevia for us, and Connie made a fruit salad. Kim said she googled the Paleo Diet and made the one dish she figured the diet revolved around. She brought three pounds of bacon. Figaro didn't leave her side all afternoon.

Sawyer pulled a large black book out of her tote bag. "I thought it would be fun to look at our old yearbook."

Kim placed a folder on the dining room table. "And I brought my pictures from the reunion. I had them printed out so I can scrapbook them later. I thought we could go through them together."

Neither of them were fooling anyone. They were both trying to keep me distracted from thinking about what was happening. Even Aunt Ginny kept sighing and leaving the room. I tried to force myself to relax, but it was impossible. I picked up the stack of pictures Kim brought and thumbed through them to at least keep busy. I had to relive my awful lemonade ostrich dress. Ugh.

Wait. What was that?

"Hey. Look at this picture."

The girls and Aunt Ginny crowded around me. Connie was the first to speak. "It's a picture of me with Janet Riley before you two got into it with Barbie."

I pointed to a figure slightly out of focus. "But look in the background here. Isn't that Robert?"

Kim took the picture and held it farther away. "It is. And he has his hand on that blond cheerleader's butt. Is that Barbie?"

Sawyer took the picture. "It isn't Barbie. See here, her hand is showing and she has a French manicure. Probably fake nails. Barbie had bright pink nails the night of the reunion. I remember seeing them when I was on top of her."

I smiled to myself. "I saw them too, when I was pulling you off her."

Aunt Ginny cocked one eye. "Well then, who is it?"

"It has to be Kelly. Everything points to the two of them being a couple. I think we need to show this to Kelly and see what she says."

"Before you do that," Connie said from the other side of the table, "you'd better look at this."

We all moved down to where Connie was thumbing through the yearbook. "Look what I found."

It was a picture of the Ecology Club. Barbie was holding up a lily of the valley and the caption read, "Barbara Pomeroy discovers poisonous plant growing at daycare center."

"The article goes on to praise Barbie for her discovery and her knowledge that the plant was poisonous. It says she may have saved some kids' lives by removing it."

An idea came to me. "Show me the different scholastic clubs."

Connie thumbed through and we looked at the different club group shots.

"What are you looking for?" Sawyer asked.

"Every one of these clubs has Barbie listed as the club president. Look, Pep Club—Barbie Pomeroy, President. French Club—Barbie Pomeroy, President. Key Club—Barbie."

"Whoa, look at this one." Kim pointed to another club group shot. "Ecology Club—Barbie Pomeroy, President. Kristen Campbell—Vice President. And they're all in there. Joanne, Amber, Missy, even Billy is in Ecology Club."

Alarm bells were ringing in my head. Kristen told me she got those exotic plants from Ecology Club and that she didn't know how to take care of them. She said she sent them back to the greenhouse to get TLC.

"If she was the vice president of Ecology Club, surely she knows a little about taking care of plants."

Aunt Ginny shot one fist into the air triumphantly. "You bet your sweet bippy."

"The killer has to be one of these. Kelly, Billy, or Kristen. Since Billy is still missing, I can't do anything with him. But I can question the other two."

Connie looked at the time on her phone. "Kristen might

be at the PTA meeting at seven tonight. We could catch her there."

I thought about my weird encounter with Kelly yesterday and the syringe that was left in the spa room. "I want to question Kelly first. We've got a picture of her with Robert. That could prove motive."

The flashing of blue lights bounced off the dining room mirror and suddenly my mouth went very dry. "They're here."

Sawyer teared up and let out a whimper. Connie and Kim were motionless and silent.

Aunt Ginny took charge. "Go out the back. Take Bessie. We'll stall them here. Kimberly, you go out the window in my bedroom, and when you hear my signal get in your car and peel out down the road in the other direction. Got it?"

I grabbed the photograph and yearbook and did as Aunt Ginny said, slipping out the back just as I heard her say, "Good afternoon, officers."

I eased Bessie around the garage, through the back yard, and through poor Mr. Murillo's hedge. Then I tore down the side street and didn't look back. For a brief second I was tempted to just keep going. Forget about Kelly and Kristen and Amber. But then I would be leaving behind everyone I loved. I was better off going to prison than losing Aunt Ginny and Sawyer.

I raced over to the campaign office. It was an unimpressive storefront operation. Just a big room full of desks, phones, and computers, surrounding an enormous poster of Robert.

I parked Bessie out front and ran in with the pictures. "Is Kelly here?" I held my breath.

April was sitting at the front desk playing Candy Crush. "She's in the back. You want me to—"

"No, I'll find her." I raced to the back to an office door

marked KELLY SCARLITO and flung it open. The room was empty.

Come on karma, cut me a break already. Then I heard Kelly's voice coming down the hall. She was standing in her doorway with a colleague holding a file and staring at me.

She turned to the guy. "Could you excuse us, please?" Then she shut the door behind her and came toward me. "I was afraid of this."

"I don't want any trouble, I just want to talk." I backed away from her.

"I can't hide it any longer. Now you know."

I stood behind the desk. "I shouldn't go to prison for something I didn't do."

Kelly stopped moving. "What?"

"What?"

"What are you talking about?"

"What are *you* talking about?"

"I'm talking about being embarrassed because you caught me at the spa getting Botox treatments."

I blinked. "Me too."

"In my line of work, image is everything. If Robert has an old lady representing him, he loses the appeal of the younger generation. I have to keep myself young-looking."

"I'm much more interested in your personal relationship with Robert."

"My personal relationship? What do you mean?"

"I know Robert and Barbie weren't the happy couple no matter how you keep trying to sell it."

I pulled out the photo of Robert and her, and slapped it on the desk.

She looked closely, then sat on one of the chairs behind her. "What are you going to do with this?"

"Do you recognize who's in that picture?"

She looked at it again and shook her head. "No."

"It's you."

"Ah, it's not me."

"What do you mean it's not you? Blond hair in a pony-tail, cheerleading uniform, who else could it be?"

"Any number of people. Missy had all the cheerleaders put on their old uniforms to reenact some stupid home-coming routine. Why would you think it's me?"

"I know you're having an affair with Robert. Three different people saw you very cozy together at the reunion."

Kelly breathed out a laugh. "That's rich. I might be the only woman in Robert's life who he isn't sleeping with. I spend half of my time trying to keep him out of trouble, and the other half covering it up when he finds it anyway."

I still wasn't sure she was telling the truth. I looked at Kelly's hands. Her nails were painted deep red and they were badly overdue for a refill.

"When was the last time you got a manicure?"

She held up her hands to show me her fake nails. "The week before the reunion."

Another dead end. "This really *isn't* you in this picture, is it?"

"I have no doubt that people saw Robert behaving in-appropriately at the reunion with someone who wasn't Barbie, but it wasn't me. It probably wasn't even the same woman each time. Robert is a sex addict. Whoever is in that picture, it's one of the other girls who could still wear the outfit." Kelly looked at the book I was holding. "What is that?"

"Our old yearbook." I turned to the Ecology Club page. "What do you know about this?"

"Oh, I remember that day. It caused a huge fight and almost destroyed Barbie and Kristen's friendship."

"The story says Barbie found the lily, but everyone looks miserable in the picture except for Joanne."

"That's because Kristen found the plant. Barbie wouldn't know a poisonous plant if it bit her on the nose."

"If Kristen found the plant, then why is the article about Barbie saving those kids?"

"Because Barbie always had to be in the spotlight. She was constantly taking credit for the things we did. This story should have been about Kristen."

"Why did you all stay friends with her if she was so terrible to you?"

"We were dumb kids and Barbie wielded a lot of power over us. If anyone crossed her, she made them an outcast. Remember Tina Agliono?"

"No."

"See. She stood up to Barbie once. Now no one even remembers she existed. The one thing Barbie was truly good at was cheerleading. She was the captain of the squad from sophomore year to graduation. But if any one crossed her, she got even. She put Cindy Parlett on top of the pyramid, then persuaded David Eegan that it would be hilarious to drop her. Cindy broke her ankle and was out of cheerleading for the rest of the year. She was that vicious."

Kelly handed the yearbook back to me.

"You know she was accepted to be a cheerleader for the Eagles after college."

"Really? What happened?"

"She got pregnant with Tiffany."

"I didn't know you could be a professional cheerleader if you were married."

"She wasn't married. She knew Robert from her Politics class at Princeton. They had a marriage of convenience. Barbie's family helped Robert get his seat in Congress, and Robert married Barbie to cover up the pregnancy. There are rumors that Tiffany's father was Amber's fiancé, Douglass."

And that must have been the "incident" between Barbie and Amber.

"Don't say anything, because Tiffany has no idea."

That poor girl. My cell phone vibrated and I got a message from Aunt Ginny. Hurry up – we can't hold them off any longer. They've put out an APB for Bessie. LOL.

LOL? I wondered what she thought that stood for?

"I appreciate your help, but I have to run."

"Sure thing, please keep what we talked about between us. I wouldn't want it getting out that I use Botox."

"My lips are sealed."

Kelly was a dead end. And I couldn't believe it, but it was looking more and more like Kristen could be the killer. I kept defending her, saying there was no way a pregnant woman was capable of murder. But the evidence was stacking up against her.

Chapter 45

The parking lot at Caper High was mostly empty. There were a smattering of cars from a few teachers working late and a couple of clubs having late meetings, but no cop cars patrolling the area.

I parked Bessie up front in Mr. Wiseman's spot, put my head down, and fast walked into the building. There was no security this late in the day, so I passed the sign-in desk and went toward the cafeteria looking for the PTA meeting to find Kristen.

As I was passing the nurse's office I heard what sounded like the air being let out of a stack of tires. "Shhhhhhhh shhhhhhhh hahhhhhhh."

I craned my head in the doorway and there was Kristen with her feet up against her desk, her knees bent to the ceiling and her hands on her belly.

"Hhhhheeee hhhhheeee hhhhhooooo."

"What in God's name are you doing?"

"I'm in labor, you idiot!"

"Why aren't you at the hospital?"

"Come over here and dig your hand into my back for me."

"Eww, why?"

"Didn't you ever help any of your friends when they were in labor?"

"No one ever asked me." I was nervous as all get-out so I did what I do when I'm panicking. I started rambling.

"I was only pregnant once and I had a miscarriage. I had to have an emergency hysterectomy and then couldn't get pregnant anymore so people tended to stay away from that subject with me."

Kristen's eyes bored into me while I was talking. "Shhhhhhhh shhhhhhhh hahhhhhhh."

I dug my fist into her back where she showed me. "What's with all the weird noises?"

"It's Lamaze breathing. It's supposed to distract you." Then she let out a war cry—"AAAAAHHHHH!"

I dug my fist in harder. "Is it working?"

"No!"

"Should I call an ambulance?"

"No! Joel is on his way. What did you want anyway?"

"Ummmm."

"Spill it! Hhhhheeee hhhhheeee hhhhhooooo."

With my other hand I opened the yearbook to the Ecology Club page. "What's going on in this picture?"

Kristen started panting like a dog. "Heh heh heh heh. Barbie is taking credit for someone else's achievement. Again. AAAAHHHHH!"

"Oh my God. What do I do?"

"Hold my hand!"

I took Kristen's hand. "Like this? OW THAT HURTS!"

And then Kristen turned into the devil. "DON'T TELL ME WHAT HURTS! Hhhhheeee hhhhheeee hhhhhooooo."

I was terrified.

"So you found the poisonous lily of the valley and

Barbie took the credit for it? And that's why you look so miserable here?"

"No. Shhhhhhhh shhhhhhhh hahhhhhhh. I didn't find the plant. Missy did. Missy was the smart one. She was just always number two at everything. Look at the clubs."

"I'm losing feeling in my arm. That can't be good."

A sudden crash splashed to the floor. "What was that?"

"My water just broke."

"Eww. That's disgusting. It's all over my new shoes."

Kristen twisted my hand. "Do you see what I'm going through here right now?!"

Okay, I'll just burn them.

"All right, I'm sorry." I turned the yearbook back a couple of pages. "In just about every club that Barbie was president of, Missy was vice president."

"Except for Ecology Club. I won that office fair and square."

"How did that happen?"

"We waited until Missy was absent to do the elections. Hhhhheeee hhhhheeee hhhhhooooo."

I had been so blind. The pieces did fit together perfectly. Missy was always at the school. She was in Ecology Club and she definitely knew the lily was poisonous. But she was so nice. She kept wanting to help me with the investigation. Could she be the killer? There was only one problem.

"Missy couldn't have killed Barbie because she was onstage giving out the Lifetime Achievement Award when Barbie died. I heard her."

"It was prerecorded."

I felt like all the air was sucked out of my lungs. "What?"

"Missy prerecorded the award video so she could change her clothes into her cheerleading uniform. She introduced the award, then the lights went down, and she slipped offstage and the recording came on. She wasn't onstage."

Joel rushed in, eyes wide with panic. "The paramedics are here. They're coming in the door right now.

Kristen let out a howl. "AAAAHHHHHHEEEEE!"

I thought I felt a bone crack in my hand. I fell to my knees. "Joel, take over."

Joel looked at the death grip Kristen had on my hand and the look of pain on my face. "Uh-uh. No way."

Kristen screamed, "Joel!" and Joel rushed to her side.

Kristen let go of my hand when the paramedics helped her onto the stretcher. They wheeled her out of the room with Joel right behind. I was left alone. With something horrifyingly disgusting on my brand-new *Josie and the Pussycats* shoes.

Missy Sparks? Miss Congeniality? Reunion coordinator. The one person who knew I would be at the reunion outside of my friends. Missy who worked in the school and could use the chem lab and avoid the security cameras. Missy who looked like she hadn't aged a day since graduation, perhaps from an unhealthy amount of Botox.

I left Kristen's office and turned left down to the cafeteria. The PTA meeting was over and Missy was packing up her tote bag.

"Hi. What are you doing here?"

"I came to see Kristen."

"I think she's gone."

"She is."

I stared at Missy. She stared back. She looked at my hand and saw the yearbook open to the Ecology Club picture of the lily discovery and her expression changed. The plastered-on smile disappeared and her eyes became cold and hard.

"So, I figure you made the poison in the chem lab after school one day? Sterilized the needle with industrial-strength bleach from the janitor's closet? Sound about right?"

Missy dropped the binder she was holding onto the table with a loud smack. "I don't know what you're talking about."

"Oh, I think you do. Barbie was top dog around here and you've been waiting twenty-five years to finally get some appreciation."

Missy's face crumbled. "She deserved to die. You know she did."

"Is it a fluke that Amber has been targeting me, or did you set me up to take the fall?"

Missy took on a manic look. Her eyes dilated to pinpoints and her speech became a quiet, measured hiss. "It's nothing personal. I'm sure you're a very nice person. But Barbie hated you and your little clique. You four were the most obvious to look guilty."

"How did you know I would have a hypodermic needle in my bag?"

Her laugh was high-pitched and unnatural. "That was luck. I had no idea you'd have a needle. If I'd known, I wouldn't have had to drag Barbie down the hall to your locker. I knew one of you was bound to get into it with her at the reunion. That's why I made sure there was an open bar."

"You thought we would get drunk and cause a scene?"

"I didn't know about you, but Barbie was a functional alcoholic. I knew she'd hit the booze. And once she was drunk she would pick a fight with one of you. I just had to wait for it to happen."

"That was a pretty big gamble on your part. I almost stayed home."

"That's why I sent you the letters."

"Those notes from Barbie saying she had to tell us something were from you?"

Missy had her hand inside her tote bag. "You were all supposed to meet in front of your old locker and find the body together. That way one of you would be a suspect. She almost ruined the whole plan with that ridiculous injury she faked. Then Kristen had to go and give her an ice pack. I waited in the janitor's closet for ten minutes for her to come out. I had to move my timetable up a bit but it worked out. I was able to get her down to Home Ec to change into her uniform. That's when I finally got her to shut up."

"You planned all this, because she lied about finding a plant?"

Missy's nostrils flared. "And saving a daycare full of kids!" She tried to calm herself. "Barbie always had to steal my glory. Barbie married a congressman. My husband left me for another man. Barbie's daughter gets the best of everything. I have to scrape by just to give Athena the things she needs. Barbie didn't love this school, yet she bought her way onto every committee just to outdo me. Just like in high school. I should have been club president. I should have been captain!"

There was an eerie tone to Missy's words, and I knew I wasn't dealing with a person who was totally inhabiting planet Earth.

Missy pulled something out of her bag and hid it behind her arm. She took a step toward me.

"I've made sure there is enough evidence against you

that I will never be a suspect. When Amber finds you with the murder weapon, she'll put you away for good."

I tried to move away but my back was against a table.

"I want Athena to have everything I had *and* the things I didn't. I want her to have the popularity, the glory, the adoration. And someone is always standing in her way, stealing the spotlight. Do you know who that someone is?"

I took a step to the side. I wanted to call for help but my cell phone was in Bessie out front. I was trapped in here with Crazy Mary. "I'm guessing Tiffany."

"I would do anything for my daughter. Barbie was never going to let Athena on that all-star team and Athena has to get a cheerleading scholarship."

Missy lunged at me with a hypodermic needle in her hand. I dodged to the side like in Warrior II Pose.

"Athena has to go to a good college to make more out of her life than I did. I settled for the first guy to come along."

Missy lunged at me again and I ducked down into Chair Pose.

I never thought all that yoga would come in this handy.

"Now I sell used cars in the Villas. The Villas! And I do it for her to have a better life. There is no way I'm going to let you ruin that."

Missy was right in front of me, but I had nowhere else to go. My back was against the lunch counter. She lunged again and I felt a scrape on my cheek. I grabbed a lunch tray off the stack on the empty lunch line counter. "You know what Athena has that Tiffany doesn't?"

"What?"

"A mother who wasn't murdered."

Her eyes went wild and she stepped back to make a final lunge.

In the half moment she paused I swung the tray as hard as I could and whacked Missy on the side of her head. She crumpled to the floor like a paper lantern.

"Everybody freeze!"

Officer Amber had busted in through the crash bar with two other officers, guns drawn. She took one look from me to Missy and returned her gun to her holster.

"At ease, everyone. Nice job, McAllister. I figured you'd be the one in a pile right now."

Amber spoke into her radio and called for an ambulance.

"Kristen called us from the delivery room. She figured out that Missy must have murdered Barbie and you would probably stick your nose into it and get yourself killed instead of letting us do our job."

"So far your job has only been to try to prove my guilt. If you'd been trying to prove my innocence I might have stayed out of it."

Amber laughed. "Right. Like you stayed out of it at Senior Prom."

"What are you talking about?"

"I'm talking about Shane Gerraro."

"Shane?"

"You knew I liked him and you convinced him to go with you instead of asking me."

"You're as crazy as Missy, you know that. I went with Shane because my boyfriend had already graduated and had to work. We were in Drama together and the whole club went to prom as a group. We only paired up for the pictures and the corsage. And by the way, he was a real jerk the whole night. Don't tell me that's what this has been all about. You've been holding a grudge against me because of a guy you liked?"

"No. How petty do you think I am?"

"I don't know, let's find out."

"That. That right there is the problem."

"What?"

"All through high school you and your little friends made fun of me. You bullied me for not being as smart as you were."

"Am I in the Twilight Zone? I—bullied *you*?"

"That's right. You made fun of me for being a cheerleader. You tricked me into eating grasshoppers. You loved to embarrass me. You always had something smart to say and I never had a comeback because I'm not as quick as you."

Excuse me while I pick my jaw up off the basement floor.

I stared in disbelief. All those years, Barbie and Amber bullied us and made our lives miserable and their perception was that we were the bullies.

A catalog of the gross unrealities here flipped open in my head.

Barbie. The prettiest, most popular girl at school, had no real friends, a loveless marriage, and became an alcoholic who lived in fear of losing her outer beauty.

And Missy. Voted Miss Congeniality, the nicest person in the class. A crazed lunatic who murdered one of her friends so her daughter would have an edge over another kid and she could finally be in charge of a committee.

It was so important for these girls to be popular that they gave a piece of their soul away. They lost all self-respect because of their obsession with respectability.

And as far as fears went, I'd been no better. Hiding out from the world, afraid of being judged for not being pretty enough or thin enough or successful enough. Barbie and Missy attacked other people, whereas I'd been attacking myself.

"Amber, I'm sorry if I ever made you feel humiliated, or like you weren't good enough somehow. Please forgive me."

Amber looked stunned like she didn't quite know how to take what I was saying. Then she narrowed her eyes and the wall went back up behind them. "Very funny. Just stay out of my way, McAllister."

I guess we can't expect everyone to be ready to change when we are.

Chapter 46

"I'm so glad you finally came to your senses and chose to do the right thing." Rosalind Carson took a seat at the dining room table and opened her briefcase. "Mrs. Frankowski will get the best care at the Sunset Valley Assisted Living Facility, you can be sure of that."

I joined her at the table. "You were right. Aunt Ginny can't be alone or she will hurt herself or someone else. I just don't want that burden resting on my head."

"Nor should you." Ms. Carson gave me a sympathetic nod and took out a stack of papers.

Aunt Ginny sat at the other end of the long mahogany table, looking forlorn and pitiful.

"I've taken the liberty of drawing up a contract to sell the house to a buyer for you, to expedite the process."

Aunt Ginny moaned. "You aren't selling my house are you, Poppy? You promised I could move back in when I start doing better."

"Oh, you have to sell it, Mrs. Frankowski. You will need the equity in the house to pay rent on your room. You don't want to worry about expenses ever again. Let us take the daily concerns of finances off your mind, so you can focus on knitting and television—things people your age like to do."

The memory of Aunt Ginny salsa dancing flashed into my mind, and I almost laughed out loud. I gave Ms. Carson a pained look. "That is very thoughtful of you. Is it standard procedure for the Department of Youth and Family Services to assist with the sale of the house?"

Ms. Carson hesitated. "Well, no. But I have been so concerned for your dear Aunt Ginny that I went above and beyond the call of duty to make sure she is well taken care of. We only have one room left in the facility, and we need to move quickly if we are going to get Mrs. Frankowski in."

My stomach was tied up in knots over what I was about to do, but I pressed on. "I see. Well, in that case I guess selling the house is inevitable."

Aunt Ginny's lip quivered and she sniffed back a tear.

"But I think we want to use a real estate agent of our choosing."

Ms. Carson blanched and her glasses slid down her nose. She pushed them back into place. "You don't want to do that. An agent will take a percentage of equity from the sale for their fee. I already have a buyer lined up for you. You will save thousands of dollars by selling to him directly."

She set a contract on the table in front of me and tried to hand me a pen.

I looked it over. "Who is Jeremy Hereford?"

"That's the person who wants to buy the house." She stabbed the pen at me again.

Aunt Ginny began to bawl.

"I'm not sure I'm comfortable signing this in front of Aunt Ginny. Maybe we should do this later."

Something flashed behind the social worker's eyes. Greed? Anger?

"No! We have to do it now." Ms. Carson tried to regain her composure. "I've already done all the hard work for you; you just need to sign. I can't hold this buyer forever. This deal is only available if you sign right now. Think of Aunt Ginny's welfare."

Aunt Ginny stopped crying and sobered up instantly. "Hold on a jalapeno-hot minute! Jeremy Hereford is a real estate developer specializing in flipping historical houses, isn't he?"

Ms. Carson's jaw dropped and she turned a shade of crimson.

"ISN'T HE?" Aunt Ginny all but roared.

"What? I think you may be confused again, Mrs. Frankowski."

Aunt Ginny held up her smartphone. "No, I'm not. I just googled him. Plus, he has some negative reviews on Zillow for being too aggressive with sellers."

Ms. Carson breathed out a tentative laugh that didn't reach her eyes. "Well, there is nothing wrong with that. A sale is a sale. I think we will all have better peace of mind when Mrs. Frankowski is safely tucked away in Sunset Hills."

I put the contract down and looked Ms. Carson in the eye. "Could I see the case documents you've assembled against Aunt Ginny?"

Ms. Carson's eyes shifted from me to Aunt Ginny and back to me again. "I'm afraid I don't have them with me. They are on file at my office for the competency hearing."

Aunt Ginny cocked her head to the side and scrunched up her nose, giving Ms. Carson a patronizing look. "Are they?"

Ms. Carson narrowed her eyes at Aunt Ginny and spoke through gritted teeth. "I can get them to you later. You need to sign the sales agreement now or you will end up out on the street, old lady!"

"That's enough!" A dark-haired woman in a brown tweed suit came through the kitchen door followed by a uniformed officer.

Ms. Carson lunged for the sales contract, but I was ready for her and snatched it away.

"Director Chamberlain! What are you doing here?" Ms. Carson jumped to her feet and slammed her briefcase shut.

"I've spent the morning with Mrs. Frankowski and her niece, and we've been discussing your visits and concerns."

Ms. Carson began to stammer and wring her hands. "Of course, I've told you all about Mrs. Frankowski in my reports."

The older woman took a step forward. "No, you haven't, Rosalind. You've fed me a load of horse manure and made this delightful woman appear to be deranged."

"B-b-bu . . ."

"Can it, Rosalind." The director's voice was severe. "Ms. McAllister told us about the people looking to buy this property on a 'hot tip,' which made me suspicious enough to look into your buyer, who happens to be your boyfriend, Jeremy Hereford."

Ms. Carson's laugh sounded thin and anxious. "What? He's not my boyfriend."

"The two of you have been taking advantage of the elderly all up and down the East Coast, tricking people into selling their houses and forcing them into nursing homes. It ends here. You're fired from the department and we're pressing charges."

"No. I . . ." Ms. Carson's lip began to quiver.

The officer took a step toward Ms. Carson and removed a pair of shiny handcuffs from his utility belt. "You're under arrest for three counts of fraud and one for attempted fraud."

"There's no use denying it, Rosalind," the director barked. "We've had IT comb through your hard drive and capture your e-mails to Mr. Hereford. Your boyfriend is already in custody, and he rolled over on you. He says you came up with the plan yourself and forced him into it."

"I did not force him! It was Jeremy's idea to target these old wheeze-bags. I just found the houses. I want immunity!"

As the officer handcuffed the woman we'd come to know as the Social Worker from Hell, Aunt Ginny stood to face her.

"Ms. Carson, do you know why it's easy to fool old people?"

Ms. Carson looked down her nose at Aunt Ginny.

"It's because we remember when people were decent and trustworthy. Back in our day we had respect for our elders. People took care of each other and weren't out trying to scam everybody all the time. We aren't used to lowlifes like you, so sometimes we get fooled when a scam artist calls on the phone or comes to the door. But we've lived long enough to know that what goes around comes around. You're getting older by the minute, and *your* day is coming."

A patrol car pulled up in front and the officer led Ms. Carson to it while reciting her rights. The last thing we heard her whimper on the way out was, "That old lady played me."

Epilogue

I put the finishing touches on a dairy-free chocolate birthday cake for Henry. Aunt Ginny didn't have any pastry bags so I used a Ziploc bag with the corner cut off to write "Happy Birthday, Henry" in white icing.

It had been a crazy few days here in Cape May. Georgina's attorney, Jim Donohue, arrived just in time for Amber to drop the charges against me.

The district attorney officially charged Missy Sparks with the murder of Barbara Clark. The syringe she nicked me with the night of the PTA meeting was full of the same poison she'd used to kill Barbie. As it turned out, Missy didn't have Botox treatments. She stole the syringe from the spa after one of her vitamin B shot appointments for energy. Apparently, she just has good genes in the wrinkle department. The sanity department is the real area in question. A psych eval is pending, so it hasn't been determined yet if Missy will be doing her time at Edna Mahan Women's Prison or Bridgeton Mental Health Hospital.

Kristen and Joel had a baby girl, born at Burdette Tomlin Hospital in Cape May Court House. Then they had a baby boy. I guess twins are common when you've had fertility treatments, and the little guy was hiding out in there this whole time.

Billy finally turned up. He wasn't missing after all. I guess seeing Barbie at the reunion made him even more sure that he was in love with his fiancée. So they flew off in his private jet to Anguilla and got married in a remote beach ceremony. They returned to town after their honeymoon and had no idea that anything had even happened.

Robert is doing well in the polls and is favored to win the election in a couple of weeks. He is being called "one to watch" for the presidency in eight to twelve years. The news media is comparing him to Bill Clinton. Boy, if they only knew the half of it.

I'd done a lot of reflecting over the past few weeks and realized something big. I was so afraid of going to prison that I failed to see that I was already there. Not all prisons are made out of iron bars. I had created my own prison in my mind when I chose to live shackled to shame and regret. I'd never lived life to the fullest out of fear. Fear of being too fat. Fear of not being good enough. Fear of being humiliated. I should have put myself out there and reached for the stars. It's my life, no one is going to live it for me. Aunt Ginny once told me, "You will never regret the things you fail, only the things you fail to try."

I've been able to stick to my new Paleo way of eating *most* of the time and I feel so much better. I've also lost ten pounds. I'm working toward eating Paleo all the time, but mostly I'm trying to accept myself the way I am. We all look different and won't fit in a cookie-cutter ideal of beauty and I need to stop trying and make peace with my thighs.

Another thing I have to figure out is my relationship with Tim. Every decision we make closes some doors and opens new ones. I messed up our relationship twenty years

ago when a one-night stand left me pregnant, but it opened
a new door to my wonderful husband, John. Twenty years
later, I'm getting a second chance with Tim. I used to
wonder what my life would have been like if things had
gone differently. Now I have the chance to find out. It's
hard to capture the lightning-in-a-jar of your first love.
The heat is still there, but twenty-five years apart has left
us without a lot in common other than our love for cooking. I just hope we aren't trying to force something that
will never work. Only time will tell.

Aunt Ginny sniffed her way into the kitchen, wearing a
black leotard and puffy black tutu with pink ballet slippers. I gave her a big smile.

"What do you have planned for today?"

She poured herself a cup of coffee. "Well, I'm either
going to start a beginners' ballet class, or I might just
dance for joy around the house a while."

"We have a lot to dance about. The check cleared."

Aunt Ginny did a little two-footed pirouette. More like
a *tap tap tap* in a circle, really. "I bet Georgina had a stroke
when you told her you were staying up here with me."

"I think a part of her is relieved not to have me around
to embarrass her anymore."

Aunt Ginny helped herself to one of the Paleo Orange
Dreamsicle Muffins I made for the coffee shop. "I can't
believe you convinced her to take your money out of trust
and let you have it all now."

"With Georgina, there are always strings attached. She
gave me my money because she likes the idea of turning
your house into a bed and breakfast. Her condition was
that she be allowed to invest some of her own money, so
she'd have a ten percent ownership in the business, but not
the house."

"I called Frank. I'm putting the house in your name and

I won't hear any buts about it. I almost lost this house once to that scheming social worker and her shifty boyfriend. I'm not going to let that happen again. You were so smart to figure out what they were up to."

"You weren't the first senior citizen they had tried to shake down with false claims. There was a lady in Paramus they convinced she couldn't live alone and needed full-time care. She signed her house over to them and they flipped it for a lot of money to an investor who turned it into a Jiffy Lube."

"I will always remember that smug look being wiped off of Rosalind Carson's face when that cop handcuffed her." Aunt Ginny cackled.

I loaded the muffins into a basket and put a lid on the cake carrier. "I'm going to the zoo with Gia and his girlfriend today for Henry's birthday. When I come home, we need to go over our remodel plans for the Butterfly Wings B&B if we're going to try to open next summer."

I kissed Aunt Ginny on the cheek and fed Figaro some salmon crunchies. "Try to behave while I'm gone."

"Are you talking to me or Figaro?"

"Yes."

I walked into the coffee shop and Gia's girlfriend was behind the counter. She barely acknowledged my presence. Henry jumped off the barstool and ran to me. "Poppy, you came!"

"Of course I did. I want to see the kitties with you."

Henry's eyes grew huge through his glasses when he saw the cake. "Is that for me?"

"I made it special for your birthday. No dairy."

Henry threw his arms around my legs and hugged me. "Thank you."

Gia came out of the back wearing blue jeans and a faded Boston T-shirt. My knees started to buckle and I caught myself on one of the leather club chairs.

"Daddy, Poppy made me a special birthday cake!"

Gia gave me a sexy smile. It was probably just a regular smile, but he is so sexy. *Snap out of it, Poppy!*

"She did?"

"We allergy sufferers have to stick together, don't we?" Henry nodded.

Gia ruffled Henry's hair. "He's very serious about chocolate. Good choice."

I looked at Gia's girlfriend, who was putting the new muffins in the bakery case. "I'm sorry, I don't think I ever got your name."

She snapped her gum at me. "Karla."

"Thanks for letting me tag along today, Karla."

"Uh-huh."

Oh, boy. It was going to be an interesting afternoon. Gia was no help. He just stood there watching me with that cryptic smile on his face.

Henry looked up at his father. "Can we go now, Daddy? I want to get there before the kitties get tired."

Gia smiled down at Henry. "Karla, why don't you take Henry out to the truck for me?"

Karla came around the counter and took Henry's hand. My heart flipped with longing for a child of my own like Henry.

When they were out of the room, I asked, "Are you sure your girlfriend is okay with me tagging along? It seems very third-wheel of me."

Gia blinked and breathed out a fraction of a laugh.

I suddenly felt very foolish and small. What an impression I was making.

"Karla doesn't have anything to worry about with me. I mean . . . look at her . . . Not that I *wouldn't* go out with you, of course I would . . . I mean you're *gorgeous* but then so is she so that makes more sense. . . ."

Gia shook his head and took a step in my direction.

I took a half step backward and tried to will myself to shut up.

"Not that I think you were asking me out or anything. It may have seemed like I was flirting with you once or twice but I was just trying to be friendly. As far as you're probably concerned I'm just the muffin lady and you know . . . that's cool."

Gia looked like he was trying to keep from laughing and quickly closed the distance between us. "Poppy."

I tried to breathe. "Umm-hmm?"

He was so near I could feel his breath on my face. He smiled down at me. Then he put his hands on my waist and pulled me close. "Karla is my sister." He stared into my eyes with a deep intensity and I lost all conscious thought.

Then he leaned in and kissed me.

Please turn the page for
seven yummy recipes from
Poppy's kitchen!

PALEO CHICKEN ENCHILADAS

Filling

- 2 pounds cooked, shredded chicken (you can even use a rotisserie chicken or leftovers from another meal if you don't want to make it tonight)
- 1 (14 ounce) can El Paso enchilada sauce
- 1 (6 ounce) can diced green chilies
- 1 orange bell pepper, seeded and diced
- 1 yellow bell pepper, seeded and diced
- 1 poblano pepper, seeded and diced
- 1 jalapeño pepper, seeded and diced (leave out if you don't like it hot)—be very careful with this. Wear gloves if possible and wash everything when you are done. Do not touch your face until you have washed up.
- 1 onion, diced
- 2 cloves of garlic, minced
- 1 teaspoon chili powder
- 1 teaspoon dried cumin
- 1 teaspoon paprika (smoked is my favorite)
- ½ teaspoon sea salt
- ½ teaspoon cayenne pepper (leave out if you don't like it hot)
- ½ teaspoon dried oregano

*Non-Paleo option: You can top or fill your enchiladas with 2 cups of shredded cheese. They wouldn't be Paleo but they would still be gluten-free and I'm not going to judge you.

Wrap

8–12 Paleo Tortillas—recipes to follow

Topping

1 16-ounce jar salsa—I used Frontier green tomatillo but any Paleo-friendly (sugar-free, preservative-free) salsa will do.

Garnish—All are optional but Paleo-acceptable:

• Chopped Cilantro
• Chopped Scallion
• Sliced Avocado
• Guacamole—recipe to follow
• Cashew Cream—recipe to follow

Preheat oven to 350°F (177°C). Spray a 9 x 11 baking dish with coconut spray.

Toss filling ingredients together in a large bowl.

Fill each Paleo Tortilla with the chicken-and-pepper mixture and roll up like burritos. If the ends won't fold over, it's okay for them to stay open-ended like tubes.

Place each roll into your baking dish in a row.

Cover with the salsa. Add your optional cheese if you like and never, never tell the Paleo police.

Cover with foil, place in oven, and bake for about 1 hour. Everything is cooked; you are just making sure it is heated through and bubbly.

Let rest for 10 minutes, then garnish and serve.

PALEO TORTILLA RECIPES

Making tortillas is a lot like making crepes. You need a round-bottomed frying pan, preferably ceramic or non-stick. And Paleo-friendly lubricant. I use PAM coconut spray.

There are a lot of ways to make tortillas. I've included three different recipes so you can pick whichever one appeals to you. You can make these ahead and store between layers of wax or parchment paper. They are good for breakfast burritos, sandwich wraps, and if you make just the coconut flour ones, I think you can turn them into dessert crepes—but that's because I try to make everything into dessert.

Simple Coconut Tortillas

½ cup coconut flour
4 large eggs
1 cup unsweetened almond or cashew milk
Pinch sea salt

Combine all ingredients until smooth. I like to use the smoothie cup attachment of my blender but you can do it however you like. Let the batter sit for a couple of minutes so the coconut flour can absorb the liquids. Then pulse, whip, or stir it again.

Heat your frying pan over medium heat and grease lightly.

Pour or ladle about ¼ cup of batter into your pan. The batter should be thin—you aren't making pancakes. Tilt the pan around to spread the batter to the edges.

If the tortillas are too small in circumference for what you want to use them for, go up to ½ cup of batter per tortilla. Cover with a lid and cook until the top has bubbles, looks a little dry, and the edges are brown and curling inward, 2–3 minutes.

Flip the tortilla over (I like using a fork or tongs for this) and cook the other side about 2 minutes. Store between wax paper or parchment until ready to use.

Paleo Tortillas 2

  3 large eggs
  4 egg whites (⅔ cup)
  ½ cup water
  1 tablespoon melted lard or coconut oil
  1 cup tapioca starch
  ½ cup flax meal (not flax seeds)
  2 tablespoons coconut flour
  ½ teaspoon gluten-free baking powder
  ½ teaspoon sea salt
  coconut oil for frying

Combine all ingredients until smooth. I like to use the smoothie cup attachment of my blender but you can do it however you like. Let the batter sit for a couple of minutes to let the coconut flour absorb the liquids. Then pulse, whip or stir it again. If the batter is too thick, add a couple of tablespoons of water.

Heat your frying pan over medium heat and grease lightly.

Pour or ladle about ¼ cup of batter into your pan. The batter should be thin—you aren't making pancakes. Tilt the pan around to spread the batter to the edges.

If the tortillas are too small in circumference for what you want to use them for, go up to ½ cup of batter per tortilla.

Cover with a lid and cook until the top has bubbles, looks a little dry, and the edges are brown and curling inward— 2-3 minutes.

Flip the tortilla over (I like using a fork or tongs for this) and cook the other side about 2 minutes. Store between wax paper or parchment until ready to use.

Cauliflower Tortillas

    1 small head of cauliflower, should yield 3 cups
        riced and packed
    3 eggs
    ½ teaspoon fine-grain sea salt

Preheat oven to 375°F (190°C). Line two baking sheets with parchment paper and grease them with olive oil.

In a food processor rice the cauliflower until you get a texture finer than rice. (If you don't have a food processor, you can often buy pre-riced cauliflower in the produce department of the grocery store.) Once it's riced measure it and make sure you have 3 cups packed.

Place cauliflower rice in a bowl, cover with plastic wrap, and microwave on high for 2 minutes. Give it a good stir and microwave for another 2 minutes.

Place the cauliflower rice in a tea towel and twist it to squeeze out as much moisture as you can (I usually squeeze out over a cup of liquid). This is very important. The cauliflower rice needs to be dry.

Place drained cauliflower rice back in the bowl, add eggs and salt, and mix until combined.

Spread the mixture onto the lined baking sheets into 8 flattish circles. (At this juncture, I want to point out that if you make these into thick circles, top with a little oregano, and bake them a little longer, you'll have pizza crust—but that's for another day.)

Place in the oven for 10 minutes, then peel them off the parchment paper, flip them, and bake for 6 to 7 more minutes.

You can stop here and store the tortillas in the fridge until you are ready to use them.

Heat a nonstick medium-sized pan over medium heat and place the tortillas into the pan, pressing down slightly, and brown them (1 minute per side).

GUACAMOLE

2 perfectly ripe avocados, scooped out (Avocados should be firm and not squishy or soft—but yield to gently pressure. Not hard as rocks. You can also flick off the nubby stem that is usually still attached. If the indentation is yellowish-green and not dark green or brown, the avocado should be ripe.)

1 lime, juiced
2 shallots or 1 small yellow onion, chopped fine
1 teaspoon sea salt
1 handful cilantro, chopped fine
Optional:
1 jalapeño seeded and chopped fine—be very,
    very careful with this and wear gloves
1 ripe tomato, diced small—I call this optional
    because I don't want it in mine.

You can scoop all ingredients into a bowl and mash with
them fork—or pulse for a second at a time in a food
processor. If you go the food processor route, you don't
have to chop your ingredients as fine from the start, but
you do have to be careful that you don't go too far and
make avocado puree.

CASHEW SOUR CREAM

3 cups cashews, soaked for at least 4 hours
1½ tablespoons lemon juice
1 teaspoon honey
1 teaspoon sea salt
½ cup water

Place the cashews in a bowl, cover with water, and allow
to soak for several hours or overnight. (Alternatively, you
can cover with water, heat to a simmer, turn off the heat,
and allow to soak for at least an hour.)

Drain and rinse the soaked cashews.

Place cashews in a food processor or high-speed blender
with the lemon juice, salt, honey, and about half the liquid.

Pulse to process, scraping the sides down as necessary. Add the remaining liquid and process for several minutes until extremely smooth.

PALEO STRAWBERRY VANILLA MUFFINS

¼ cup sliced almonds, toasted
2 tablespoons coconut sugar
1¾ cups almond flour
1 teaspoon gluten-free baking powder
2 eggs
¼ cup coconut oil
4 tablespoons honey
1 scraped vanilla bean (I used Tahitian) or
　　1 teaspoon pure vanilla extract (If you do use
　　a scraped vanilla bean, be sure to put the husk
　　in a bottle of vodka or rum and make your own
　　vanilla extract.)
1 tablespoon lemon zest
3 tablespoons full-fat, unsweetened coconut milk
¼ teaspoon sea salt
1 cup dried or fresh strawberries

Preheat oven to 350°F (177°C). Line a muffin pan with 12 foil muffin tins or grease with coconut oil.

In a small bowl, toss toasted almonds with coconut sugar. Set aside.

In a large bowl, beat together the coconut oil, honey, lemon zest, vanilla bean paste or extract, and coconut milk. Beat in eggs. Add almond flour, salt, and baking powder and beat until combined. Scrape down the bowl as needed. Fold in the strawberries using a rubber spatula. Generously fill each muffin tin and sprinkle toasted almonds/sugar mixture on top of each muffin.

Bake for 18–20 minutes until golden brown and toothpick comes out clean.

Please turn the page for an exciting sneak peek of
Libby Klein's next
Poppy McAllister mystery

MIDNIGHT SNACKS ARE MURDER

coming soon wherever print and e-books are sold!

Chapter 1

Mischief and Mayhem were running amuck in South Jersey. Mischief, or as I called her, Aunt Ginny was on the warpath flanked by her first in command, Mayhem, also known as my black smoke Persian, Figaro the instigator. Today their battleground was the kitchen and the enemy was knee deep in the hoopla installing pearl gray cabinets and black and silver granite counter tops.

Aunt Ginny barked out orders like Patton leading the allied forces through France. "If any one of you puts so much as a single scratch on my Romba cuckoo clock there will be hell to pay! My first husband Lovell brought that home from Germany in 1945. It's survived three wars, a fire, and Hurricane Sandy. I'll be darned if it's going down because of a slipshod kitchen remodel."

I'd been stranded in Cape May with my eighty-ish great aunt ever since I was lured up here to attend my twenty-fifth high school reunion a few weeks ago, and was voted most likely to kill a cheerleader. I'd never wanted to return to the birthplace of my most painful memories, but I'd come to accept that Cape May had a certain charm. One that I'd call "better than a sharp stick in the eye." I'd been away long enough to forget that Aunt Ginny teetered on the edge of crazy. Now it was my job to look after this rickety old rattletrap . . . and the house. With two redheads under the same roof, and one of them having just bought a wakeboard on xtremesports4seniors.com, I think twenty years in the women's prison would have been easier.

We'd been undergoing a major refurbishment to transform the Queen Anne Victorian into a quaint beachy bed and breakfast so I'd have a way to support Aunt Ginny and she could keep her independence. A new roof had been laid, the porch and swing had been repaired, and the entire outside of the house had been freshly painted in Easter egg shades of butter yellow, baby pink and lavender. A wooden shingle hung in the front yard proclaiming us the Butterfly House B&B punctuated with a giant blue and black butterfly. I'd gotten the local radio station to run a call-in contest giving away passes to our special Fall Fling Event. The free weekend got me some generosity points, and sent me four sets of guinea pigs who were all caller number 9. There was still a long list of projects to be completed before we officially launched our grand opening, not the least of which was to find ways to keep Aunt Ginny and Figaro from scaring off the clientele.

I ran upstairs with my checklist to the guest bedroom we'd named the Swallowtail Suite and inspected the work. "Smitty!" A little man with a perfectly round bald head like a crystal garden globe, and deep-set cow eyes danced into the room.

"What's up boss?"

"Smitty, why is this room painted Island Pool? It's supposed to be Buttercream. Island Pool was for the Adonis Blue Suite. It matches the king size duvet in that room."

Smitty returned a blank expression.

"It's a theme."

Smitty scratched his head.

"We've talked about it at length."

Smitty grunted and pulled a folded checklist out of his paint smeared overalls. He frowned and looked up into my eyes. "I can fix that." Then he gave me a Benny Hill backhanded salute and a "whoop whoop whoop" from the Three Stooges and shimmied backwards out of the room.

I sighed. Itty Bitty Smitty, as everyone called him, was my general contractor. He was highly recommended by Handyman Haven and I now suspected he either had dirt on the owner or they sent him to me in a self survival effort to get him off their referral list. He was the only handyman within my budget who was available on short notice. I was starting to see why.

I heard a crash on the first floor and Figaro slinked up the stairs and sat at my feet. "What did you do?" He licked his paw and gave me an innocent look before wiping it on his ear. I ran down the stairs to the kitchen to see workmen cleaning up a stack of broken stone tiles that were leftover from laying the new kitchen floor.

"No problem ma'am. Julio knocked the slate over while backing up to install the new cooler. Everything is a-o-kay."

The new cooler was a seventy-two-inch triple door, brushed nickel refrigerator and freezer that had cost as much as a small car. I bet you could fit forty-seven turkeys in there. If we ever lost the house we could move into the freezer side and sublet the fridge space to another family. I'd spent a fortune on this bed and breakfast gamble, and Aunt Ginny and I had nothing to fall back on if it failed. My mother-in-law had invested just enough into the venture to keep her strings attached so she could yank on me whenever she wanted. I doubted Georgina would approve of our new apricot kitchen or my splurge purchase of a Blue Star Copper infused range with double ovens. When Georgina makes a big purchase it's a wise investment. When I do it, apparently it's superfluous. Between the bed and breakfast baking, and my daily delivery of gluten free muffins to La Dolce Vita coffee shop, the 1970's avocado green General Electric model had to be replaced. I was afraid it would explode if I ran it for more than two hours at a time.

I reached into a box I'd brought with me yesterday when I'd officially moved out of the home my late husband and I had shared for more than twenty years in Waterford. It was a painful move, and with it, part of my life—the part with John—was really over. But I had promised him I would live and be happy. I had no idea how difficult that promise would be to keep when I made it.

"Come here, baby. Let Mama set you up." I pulled out my prized powder pink Italian espresso machine and lovingly placed it on the new countertop polishing the chrome. If John could see us now. Thinking of him made my heart grip in my chest. Each passing day got a little better, but sometimes it still hurt enough to take my breath away. I missed him terribly.

Smitty appeared beside me. "Are we on target to have the kitchen painted by Thursday?" I asked him. "I have four sets of guests arriving Friday afternoon for a complimentary practice run. Those initial reviews could have a powerful impact on business going forward so I need them to be stellar."

"Absolutely. You can count on me, boss."

There was a crash from the dining room, followed by Aunt Ginny's yell, "Smitty!"

Smitty grunted and said, "I can fix that," then ran out to inspect the damage.

Stress like this was why I had Senor Ramone's Tacos and Tater Tots on speed dial in Virginia. I looked around the kitchen. It was coming together. This time tomorrow I'd be up to my elbows in blueberries and almond meal, coconut flour, maple syrup and Tahitian vanilla beans. I added parchment paper and muffin liners to my growing shopping list for the chef supply warehouse, along with commercial muffin tins, sheet pans and a twelve-shelf baker's cooling rack.

I was just about to take my espresso machine for her inaugural run in her new digs when Smitty tore in on his cell phone.

"We have an emergency."

"This isn't another out of marshmallow fluff kind of emergency like last week, is it?"

"The Blue Star is on backorder."

I could feel the panic rising. "No no no! It can't be, Smitty."

Aunt Ginny entered the kitchen, her *I Love Lucy* dyed hair piled up in a beehive on top of her head, and dressed in what looked like pale blue pajamas with a white dragon print on the sleeve. "What's on backorder?"

Smitty turned to her, "The range."

Aunt Ginny whistled and shook her head. "I can't take anymore. I'm strung up tighter than a new fiddle. I'm going to Karate to relax."

"Please don't crane kick Jimmy Kapps today. You already have two strikes."

"He knew what he was getting into when he signed up for the class."

"He's twelve."

"How else is he gonna learn?"

I had a better chance of teaching a badger to ride a bike than winning an argument with Aunt Ginny. "I'll see you for dinner tonight. Which now that I think about it will have to be salads or takeout since we don't have an oven." I narrowed my eyes at Smitty. "How can I run a bed and breakfast if I can't make breakfast Smitty?"

Smitty covered the mouthpiece to his phone and shrugged. "Cereal?"

"I really don't think we want to make a name for ourselves for being the Captain Crunch Bed and Breakfast."

My cell phone vibrated and I saw a text from Giampaolo, the owner of the espresso bar. I'd been ducking him since he laid that sizzling kiss on me. Of course, that didn't stop me from daydreaming about him.

I had three men in my life. Tim, my high school sweetheart. I'd never really gotten over him. Then there was John, who knocked me up in college. His family came from money and mine came from crazy so naturally a shotgun wedding was in order. And finally, Giampaolo, or Gia for short. The sexy Italian barista befriended me during my captivity when I was maliciously and unfairly under investigation by a vindictive blond police officer. But that's another story. I turned into a pool of melted chocolate whenever Gia was around and I'm pretty sure he could tell.

My head was clogged with murky thoughts of men and moving on, and I had to wade through them to read Gia's text. It said he had something important to discuss with me and could I come over this afternoon to do it in person. Before I could tap out so much as a smiley face, there was another crash by the front door followed by Aunt Ginny crying out in pain.

My heart lurched and I ran to the foyer with a prayer that she was okay. Figaro galloped past me to be the first on the scene. Aunt Ginny's tiny frame lay on the parquet wood floor in a heap. I ran to her side and yelled to anyone listening, "Call an ambulance!"

Connect with Us

Visit us online at
KensingtonBooks.com
to read more from your favorite authors, see books
by series, view reading group guides, and more.

Join us on social media

for sneak peeks, chances to win books and prize packs,
and to share your thoughts with other readers.

facebook.com/kensingtonpublishing
twitter.com/kensingtonbooks

Tell us what you think!

To share your thoughts, submit a review,
or sign up for our eNewsletters, please visit:
KensingtonBooks.com/TellUs.